Deadly Diplomacy

To Val

With best wishes

Jean Harrod

Deadly Diplomacy

JEAN HARROD

A CIP catalogue record for this book is available from the British Library.

ISBN 978-0-9929971-0-6 (Paperback)
ISBN 978-0-9929971-1-3 (epub)
ISBN 978-0-9929971-2-0 (mobi)

Book layout and cover design by Clare Brayshaw
Cover images © Aandre68 | Dreamstime.com
              © Wranger | Dreamstime.com

Prepared and printed by:

York Publishing Services Ltd
64 Hallfield Road
Layerthorpe
York YO31 7ZQ

Tel: 01904 431213

Website: www.yps-publishing.co.uk

For Jeff and May

Acknowledgements

There are many people to thank, especially my sisters Jane and Janet, and my friends for all their support and encouragement.

I am grateful too for the help of my wonderful writer friends, Christine, Fiona, Paul and Margaret, who have been with me every step of the way on this journey.

In Australia, thanks to Paul for his expert advice on all aspects of policing; and to Margaret for her knowledge of Canberra and the Federal Parliament.

And thanks to Lisanne for her insightful editorial knowledge and expertise.

About the Author

Born and educated in the UK, Jean was employed as a British diplomat for many years, working in Embassies and High Commissions in Australia, Brussels, the Caribbean, China, East Berlin, Indonesia, Mauritius, and Switzerland. She has travelled extensively around the world and writes about all the countries she had lived in, or visited.

Set in Australia, 'Deadly Diplomacy' is her debut diplomatic crime novel, and the first of a trilogy featuring diplomat Jess Turner and Australian DI Tom Sangster.

Jean now lives in North Yorkshire. An active contributor to regional theatre, she has written and staged several plays.

www.jeanharrod.com

1

She sat alone on the jetty seat in the dark. The breeze blew across the lapping waves, and rustled through the bushes behind her. She shivered, feeling cold in the night air with his warm arms no longer around her. Had she done the right thing telling him everything? He was the last person she wanted to put in danger. But she had no one else to turn to. No one else she could trust enough to confide in. Of course he'd asked for the diary, as she knew he would, insisting it would be safer with him. And he was probably right. So why had she left it hidden in her hotel room?

Before leaving her there on the jetty, he'd pressed his small voice-recorder into her hand. "You *must* get the conversation on the record. You've got the evidence in the diary. Now get the bastard on tape."

That was easy for him to say. *She* was the one with her head in the noose.

"Trust me." He'd squeezed her hand. "Everything will be fine."

Trust him? That nagging worry started up again. It had been a relief to unburden herself; and he'd been so kind. But, thinking about it now, she realised he hadn't seemed shocked, or even surprised.

Come on, be strong, she told herself as she held her watch up to the jetty light. Almost 8pm. She mustn't be late for her appointment; she had to go through with it. She took a deep breath and tightened her grip around the voice-recorder. Calm and in control, that's how she had to appear. She wouldn't be intimidated any more. But, as she went to get up to go back to the hotel, the moon slid behind a cloud, darkening the night. A muffled sound, like a twig snapping underfoot, came from the bushes behind her. Startled, she twisted round. "Hello?"

Silence.

The bushes rustled again in the breeze. "Who's there?" Her voice caught in her throat.

Still no reply.

Suddenly, the jetty light flickered a couple of times, and went out, plunging her into darkness.

Heart thudding, she sprang up.

Too late.

A shadowy figure came rushing along the jetty in the darkness. A ferocious punch sent her sprawling. Crying out, she raised her hands in the air to fend off the blows. Pain seared through her, as her head was smashed against the ground again and again.

Who? She just couldn't see in the dark.

Kicking and struggling, she broke free and staggered up, only to reel backwards off the jetty into the sea. The cold water shocked her into action. Scrambling to get back to the safety of the beach, she heard a loud splash behind her. An arm grabbed her around the throat. "Let me go," she screamed.

Strong hands grabbed her hair and shoved her face down. Water rushed into her nose and ears.

Fight! Her arms flailed around in panic.

Fight! Her heart was hammering so hard, her chest hurt. She had to breathe, had to...

Water poured into her mouth and lungs.

The hands jerked her head out of the water, and twisted her neck round as the moon burst out of the cloud. "*You?*" she spluttered.

"*Treacherous bitch!*"

Her head was pushed back under the water. She couldn't hold her breath; couldn't struggle; couldn't move; couldn't think.

She tried to scream, but only a gurgling sound came out of her mouth as icy cold water rushed in.

Her arms and legs seemed to be floating away from her.

She could hear rushing water in her ears.

Trust me…

2

G'bye mummy!

Screeching tyres. A cracking sound like thunder.

Jess shuddered as if she could still feel the shock of the explosion blasting through her. She stood with her hands over her eyes, trying to blot out the haunting memory of flames spiralling into the sky. The scorching heat, the smell of acrid smoke, squealing...

Squealing?

She turned and lifted the whistling kettle off the gas. Her hand shook as she poured the boiling water into the mug and watched the fragrant tea leaves fizz and uncurl. She looked up. It was only 5.35am on the kitchen clock; too early even for the central heating. Should she go back to bed? What was the point, she'd been awake for hours. Better to get an early start in the office. Shivering, she walked into the hall, lifted her woollen coat off the rack and slipped it over her dressing-gown. Then she went back for her tea and climbed the stairs.

She averted her eyes as she passed the empty bedrooms. She liked the house. It had come with the job, but it was too big for her to rattle around in on her own. It was meant for a family. She ached for her bubbly three year old, with those big eyes and blonde curls tumbling around her little face.

A floorboard creaked.

Amy? Scarcely able to breathe, Jess stopped and listened. But there was only silence. She walked into her bedroom and closed the door behind her. Sometimes the shadows were too much to bear.

Throwing the curtains open wide to let in the day, she stepped out through the balcony door onto the deck. The first breath of freezing, August, winter air caught in her throat. She clasped the hot mug with both hands, took a sip of tea, and settled into a chair to watch the sun come up behind Canberra's Federal Parliament.

The smell of menthol wafted over from two majestic eucalyptus trees that stood side by side in the centre of the lawn. She was forever raking up long strips of their dry bark and spear-like leaves. The trees were a haven for the sulphur-crested cockatoos, which roosted in town during the winter months. Every morning they would fly low over the neighbourhood, screeching out their early alarm call. Then they would gang up on the parched front lawn to squabble over grubs with colourful galahs and rainbow lorikeets.

She liked to sit on her balcony in the silence of dawn, before the town came alive. It was the time of day she felt closest to Jack and Amy. She could picture little Amy running wild in the bush garden, with its tough native plants that could withstand the scorching summers and sub-zero winters.

If only...

The phone's shrill ring pierced the silence. She put her mug down on the deck and hurried inside to answer. "Hello?"

"Morning, Jess. Sorry to wake you."

"Oh hi, Simon. I was outside watching the dawn."

"*Watching the dawn?*" He laughed. "It's brass monkey

5

weather out there." It didn't matter to Simon how early it was, he was always cheerful. "Good evening at the Thai Embassy last night, wasn't it?"

"Mm. Lovely food too."

There was a pause.

"That new Chinese restaurant has finally opened in Manuka, Jess? Fancy trying it next weekend?"

"You haven't rung me this early to ask *that,* have you?" Of course she knew he hadn't. Simon was the Political and Press Officer in the British High Commission, a title given to embassies located in Commonwealth countries. This week he was also 'out of hours' duty officer; and this was definitely 'out of hours'. "What's up?" she asked.

"Another consular case, I'm afraid."

Her heart sank; she'd been hoping for a clear week in the office to catch up on paperwork. "What's happened now?"

"A British woman's been found dead on the beach of a Queensland resort, called The Palms. It's just north of Brisbane. The police say she's been beaten so badly she's scarcely recognisable."

"*Murdered,* you mean?"

"Looks like it."

Jess reached for her notepad and pencil. "How do we know she's British?"

"She's a regular at the hotel, apparently. They have her passport details on computer."

Jess paused. "Are they sure it's her, Simon? I mean, if the body's in a state?"

"Oh, they were still able to identify her." He hesitated. "Hang on, I've got her passport details somewhere."

Down the phone, Jess could hear him shuffling papers. At dinner last night, she'd noticed his blue eyes looked dull grey with fatigue. Simon worked too hard; and now he'd had another broken night. *She should talk,* she thought, catching sight of her own bleary eyes in the dressing-table mirror. She looked over at the framed photo of Jack and Amy on the bedside cabinet...

"You still there, Jess?" Simon came back on the phone. "Yes."

"Our dead woman's called Ellen Chambers. Her passport says she was born on 9 February 1975, in Hull. I've got the number here for you to trace her."

"Go on," she said, trying to grasp the pen with cold fingers.

"It's 70469898." He read out, slowly. "Issued in London on 20 December 2009."

Jess knew it was important to determine where the victim lived. "Was she a resident of Australia or the UK?"

"There's a London home address on her hotel registration form. But the next of kin in her passport is a Susan Chambers. She has a Brisbane address. The police are on their way round to see her now. I've given them your mobile number and email address to pass on to her, Jess. Hope that's okay?"

"That's fine." Jess checked her watch. "Leave it with me, Simon. It's still Sunday evening in London, but I'll ring the Foreign Office 24-hour response unit and put them in the picture, in case the media start ringing. I'll ask them to pass the victim's passport details to Consular Division when they open up. I doubt we'll need to do a trace with the UK Passport Agency if the next of kin is here in Australia."

"Whatever you say."

Jess paused to think. Could she leave this consular case to the British Consul-General in Brisbane? It *was* his patch. Then she remembered he was in the UK on leave. "I'd better fly up to Brisbane this morning, Simon, and liaise with the police and the next of kin." Her thoughts flashed to the Deputy High Commissioner. "Have you told Nigel?"

"I thought you should know first."

"He'll go ballistic if he hears about it through the media."

"*I* should go to Brisbane really," Simon said. "I *am* the Press Officer. But I have to stay here for the Foreign Secretary's visit. Don't forget he's arriving today."

Forget? Jess rolled her eyes. How could she forget? Nigel had been up to high dough about it for weeks, fretting over the programme and guest lists for meetings and dinners. "Don't worry about the media, Simon, I'll deal with them in Brisbane."

"By yourself?"

"What's *that* supposed to mean? I'm the Consul, for God's sake. Look, you might be responsible for the media, but I'm responsible for the protection of British citizens."

"I just thought you'd have your hands full, that's all. But if you're happy to take the media on too, they're all yours." And he hung up, before she could say anything else.

That was Simon, she thought, as she put the receiver back, a diplomat by profession and nature. Except lately, he seemed to have something to say about everything she did. Who did he think he was? He held no authority over her; they were the same grade. Then she cringed as her mind flashed back to Friday evening on the sofa at his place. Who was she trying to kid? She knew his interest in her was more than just work.

Sighing, she glanced out of the window. The huge sun had formed a yellow disc in the cloudless sky behind the Federal Parliament, sparking another day to life.

But not for Ellen Chambers.

Jess pictured a woman's battered body lying lifeless on the beach, blood-red surf oozing around her. Who was Ellen Chambers, she wondered? And why was she at The Palms last night?

She went over to her briefcase on the chair and pulled out her diary to check her schedule. Flipping to the right page, she saw the date ringed. Of course she hadn't forgotten that 12 years ago today she'd joined the Foreign Office as a young diplomat; it just wasn't something she felt like celebrating. It had been both the best and the worst decision of her life. But she didn't want to dwell on the past any more; she'd already been up half the night. She picked up her mobile and pressed the speed dial for the Vice-Consul, although she didn't expect Sharon to be up so early. A social butterfly, Sharon rarely went to bed before midnight. But she'd always been a live wire, even in the British Embassy in Jakarta, where they'd first met and worked together. Again, Jess pushed all thoughts of Jakarta and the past firmly from her mind, and left details of the murder on Sharon's voicemail.

Going over to the wardrobe, she dragged out her cabin bag to pack the essentials. Now she'd got used to the idea of the trip, Queensland's sub-tropical winter weather had its appeal; and it would be good to get away from freezing Canberra for a few days.

Her mobile rang. She went over to the dressing-table to pick it up, but it went silent before she could answer. Sitting down on the stool, she dipped her make-up brush into a pot of bronzer and swept it over her eyelids and cheekbones. Her mobile rang again and, this time, she answered, quickly. "Hello?"

"Is th-that the British Consul?"

The shaky female voice on the line threw Jess until she realised who it must be. "Yes. Is that Susan Chambers?"

"My s-sister's been murdered in Brisbane."

"I know, I'm so sorry," Jess said, kindly, surprised the next of kin was in touch so soon.

"*Please!*" Susan whispered. "You must help me."

There was a crackle on the line; then it went dead.

Jess stared at her mobile, and waited for Susan to ring back. Nothing. When she tried to return the call, she saw Susan Chambers had withheld her number. Frowning, Jess put her mobile down again and picked up her comb. As she ran it through the wet, blonde hair tumbling on her shoulders, she pulled open the dressing-table drawer and fumbled inside. Her fingers tightened around her silver hair-clasp. Once again she saw Jack's smiling face and soft brown eyes. A familiar sadness settled on her as she put his gift to her lips, and clipped her hair back to let it dry naturally.

Taking a deep breath, she went back over to the wardrobe and stepped into her black skirt and high heels. She looked at the assured woman staring back at her in the mirror. *Jess is a real trooper,* her previous line manager had written in her annual appraisal. *Concise, hard-working and conscientious, she's like a terrier when she gets her teeth into something, she never lets go.* Jess sighed. That was the professional woman she wanted her colleagues to see, but she felt their penetrating stares, and heard their whispers murmured in her wake. How could she be so cool? How could she get on with her life so easily?

The bleep of a voicemail interrupted and she hurried back to her mobile to play the message.

It's Susan again. I must talk to you... but don't phone me back. It's not safe... I'll contact you.

Not safe? Jess frowned. What *was* the girl talking about? She replayed the message, listening carefully to every word. Susan Chambers' voice sounded desperate with grief and shock; and Jess knew how that felt. But, however much she felt for Susan, she knew she couldn't wait any longer for her to call again; she had to get to the office to clear emails and talk to staff before she left for Brisbane.

Slipping her mobile into her jacket pocket, she looked around the room to check she had everything. Her eyes softened as they came to rest on the photo of Jack and Amy on the bedside cabinet. Picking it up, she brushed her fingertips across the glass and tucked it into her cabin bag.

3

His face hardened as he touched the knife in its sheath. His heart was pumping so hard he could hear the sound of his own blood coursing around his body. Fear was primeval, it took total control of the whole body and mind; whereas panic was just a nervous collapse and a waste of energy. But it wasn't fear or panic driving him that morning; he was incapable of feeling either emotion. It was pure exhilaration. The day he'd waited so long for had finally arrived.

He stopped to look up at the sky. Light was beginning to streak in from the west, breaking up the purple blackness of night. He listened. The crickets had ended their night chorus. There were no bats flapping around the trees either, which meant they were back at their daytime roosts at the creek.

Satisfied the hotel forecourt was empty of cars and buses, he slipped up to the front entrance and looked through the window into the lobby. Except for a lone receptionist, it was deserted. He took a step back and scanned the building's white-washed façade and four floors of guestrooms. Was anyone watching? But the rooms were still in darkness; and their doors and windows shut tight. All he could hear was the hum of air conditioners vibrating in window frames.

He took another look over his shoulder and hurried on. For a tall man, he was light on his feet, a way of walking that came naturally. He'd been born robust; it was in his genes. And of course he kept himself supremely fit.

As he skirted around the side of the hotel, his eyes darted everywhere. The fresh morning air cooled his cheeks after the night rain. He sniffed the air, like an animal in its territory, and breathed in the scent of damp earth mingling with fallen eucalyptus leaves from the gum trees. The heady aroma energised him, making him feel alive. This was *his* time of day. Both the early morning and night were perfect for hunting. *That* was in his genes too.

He was just *so* ready.

From his vantage point, he studied the hotel grounds. Not a soul about except for one rookie cop posted down at the crime scene. He shook his head in disbelief. Where were forensics and the top guys? The swirling sound of the sea and the strong smell of brine told him the tide was coming in. He looked up at the sky again. There was still no crescent sun on the horizon, which meant he had a few minutes to take a closer look. Just to make sure.

Sidling into the bushes, he tracked his way under cover down to the jetty. Now, he was real close to the young cop, but the idiot was too busy having a quiet smoke to notice him.

He trained his night vision monocular on the corpse, running the scope over her whole body.

Look at the state of you. Well, you've only got yourself to blame, you know. You shouldn't have told anyone. That was your mistake. And now you know why… the devil was by your side!

His fingers tightened around the knife as he drew it from the sheath. He took a few silent paces forward into the shadows of a palm tree, eyes burning as he watched the young cop throw his cigarette butt on the ground and stamp on it, completely unaware of the threat. The anticipation of the kill washed over him like a wave of excitement, the desire strong in the pit of his stomach. He *so* wanted to draw blood; to feel that joy again; that release. But he knew he wouldn't do it, even though he could. He shrank back into the bushes. It wasn't empathy or guilt that stopped him killing the cop; those emotions were beyond him too. It just wasn't in the plan.

Making his way back up to the hotel, he slipped through the staff entrance at the rear of the building. No one about. He ran up the stairs to the next floor and paused outside the stairwell door to peer through the small window. No one in the corridor. He slipped on his gloves. Knowing he didn't have to worry about CCTV in this hotel, or the police, yet, he pushed through the door and walked along the corridor to the room he wanted. Quickly, he inserted a key card into the lock. It clicked open and he stepped inside. The door swished closed softly behind him.

He looked around. *Now, where is it?*

He headed straight for the open suitcase on the luggage stand and carefully searched inside, confident no one would ever know he'd been there. While he worked, he was aware of every sound outside in the corridor, every creak of a door, every voice, every footfall.

Look at these soft, silk panties and stockings. Nice! You always thought you were somethin' special, didn't you? The truth is you were nothin' but a slut.

He frowned and straightened up as he looked around the room. Walking over to the dressing-table, he pulled open the top drawer and looked inside.

You might as well give it up. You know I'm goin' to find it, there's no one round here capable of stoppin' me. I'm so good, I'm invisible. Well I walked straight in here, didn't I?

Didn't I?

4

Hearing the 8am news start on the radio, Jess pressed down on the accelerator along State Circle and overtook a car caked in the red soil of the Outback. It was an unusual sight in the well-heeled streets of Canberra, or the 'Bush Capital' as it was often called because of its location in the heart of the wilderness. Turning off Commonwealth Avenue, she pulled up outside the steel gates of an ordinary three-storey office block in the Embassy quarter of town. She could see nothing over the high perimeter wall except the Union Jack flapping on the roof, to signal this was British territory. She smiled at the security guard and wound down her window.

"Hi, Sam, how are you this morning?"

"All the better for seeing you, Jess." His beaming face looked red with cold as he looked up at the sky. "It's goin' to be a ripper today." He pressed a silver button set into the wall and the gates rumbled open.

Driving in, the sparkling sun blinded her as it bounced off the British High Commission's glass entrance. She had to pull down the sun visor to be able to see to reverse into her assigned space. On the radio, the newsreader was beginning a piece on the UK's gloomy economic prospects. Jess switched off the engine and listened. It made her think of home, and of her last year in London. She didn't want to remember, but how could she forget trying to forge a new life alone? She'd thrown herself into her job at the Foreign and Commonwealth Office. But thoughts of Jack and Amy consumed every waking moment *and* her nightmares. *I must stop thinking...* She laid her head back on the seat rest and closed her eyes. Every nerve in her body was on edge this morning. And she knew why.

Tomorrow would have been Amy's fifth birthday.

Her mobile rang in her pocket. "Hello?" she answered.

"Where *are* you, Jessi*caah*?"

Nigel's voice grated on her. He'd already left two voice messages saying he wanted to see her urgently, and she was going as fast as she could. "I'm here. I had to pack a bag, and book..."

The phone went dead in her ear as he hung up. She let out an exasperated sigh. Nigel sounded really wound up, as she knew he would be with the Foreign Secretary arriving. If anything went wrong with the visit, he knew it would reflect badly on him. And that's all he cared about. She grabbed her bags and got out of the car. Her foggy breath led the way as she hurried up the path, high heels slipping on the frosty stones. Reaching the side door, she punched the security code into the push button lock and let herself into the building. Dropping her bags on the desk in her ground floor office, she hung her coat on the back of the door, and rummaged in her bag for her diary. Then she ran up the stairs to Nigel's office. But outside his door, hearing his loud voice, she stopped dead.

"*Christ, Tony. I can't believe it!*"

She peered through the crack in the door, and saw Nigel sitting at his huge desk, on the phone. She wondered whether to wait or come back later. She had a lot to do before she left for Brisbane, but he *had* said he wanted to see her urgently. She hovered...

"You did *what?*" Nigel's voice was harsh. "But I gave you that in *confidence*."

That made Jess's ears prick up. As she moved closer to the door to hear better, her hand knocked against the wall and her diary clattered to the floor.

"Who's out there?" Nigel shouted.

"It's only me." Jess picked up her diary and stepped into the doorway where Nigel could see her. "I can come back later if you're busy."

He shook his head, and beckoned her in. "There's someone here," he said into the phone. "Can you call me back in ten minutes?"

"Sorry." Jess walked over to his desk and sat down on the chair opposite as he hung up. "I didn't mean to disturb you."

Nigel's dark-ringed eyes stared back at her.

"Everything all right?" she asked, concerned. He looked like he hadn't slept all night, and his cheeks were drawn.

He nodded curtly, and started scrawling on a document on his desk with his beloved fountain pen, or his "diplomatic weapon" as Jess called it. Nigel would never use a ball-point, it might cheapen his words. He was the archetypal diplomat. Schooled privately, and armed with a BA from Oxford, he'd joined the FCO on the fast track to the top. Now, in his late 40s and with a number of high profile jobs under his belt, he was poised to take on an Ambassadorial post after Canberra, a status he craved. By contrast, Jess's route to the FCO had been via the local comprehensive. She often wondered how Nigel would have coped with life on the estate she grew up on.

"*There!*" Peering over his gold-rimmed specs, he pushed a report across the desk. "I've made one or two amendments."

Jess wasn't surprised to see it was her annual consular report. Nigel always had to put his mark on everything. "Is that what you wanted to see me about?" she asked, looking at her watch.

"No." He stood up, and turned to look out of the window. Tailored by Jermyn Street, Nigel looked every inch the old-school Mandarin. Over six feet tall, and portly after years of diplomatic dinners, he quite literally and metaphorically looked down on everyone. "Simon told me about the Brisbane murder," he said. "I want to know what you're doing about it."

"I'm going to Brisbane... on the ten o'clock flight."

His jaw dropped open. "What about the Foreign Secretary's visit? You're supposed to be escorting him around your Section and introducing him to your staff."

"The Foreign Secretary won't miss me. And Sharon's more than capable of standing in. Anyway, I'm needed in Brisbane. I had a voicemail from the victim's sister, pleading for my help."

Nigel spun round.

Jess nodded. "I haven't been able to talk to her yet. I tried to call her back, but for some reason she withheld her number."

When Nigel frowned, the grooves in his forehead seemed even deeper. "What did she say exactly?"

Jess didn't have to think: Susan's words were imprinted on her brain. "My sister's been murdered... I need your help." She paused. "But there was something else."

Nigel raised a quizzical eyebrow.

"She asked me not to ring back because she said it wasn't *safe*. Those were her exact words. It wasn't *safe*." She paused. "Poor girl sounded desperate."

Nigel turned back to look out of the window. Feet planted astride, he stood like a captain on the bridge of a ship. Except he wasn't in charge; the High Commissioner was. Only he'd been in Perth for the last few days, leading a UK trade delegation to drum up business for British companies.

Hearing footsteps and the rustle of papers, Jess looked round to see Simon coming through the door with a newspaper tucked under his arm. Tall, slim, and fit from jogging around Lake Burley Griffin every day, his tie was askew and his shirt sleeves were rolled up.

"Sorry to keep you waiting." He nodded to them both in greeting, and pushed his square-framed glasses into position on his nose. "I *thought* the name Ellen Chambers sounded familiar." He looked excited as he spread a newspaper over Nigel's desk. "Have a look at this." He pointed to an article. "Our dead woman worked for Western Energy Corporation, as Group Finance Director, no less. She was working on that big gas deal with China."

"*Really?*" Jess turned the *Brisbane Echo* sideways to read the article. This would get the media fired up, she thought. A senior British businesswoman murdered while she was working on a lucrative LNG – liquefied natural gas – deal with the Chinese. In a photo above the article, Ellen Chambers stood between two men. She looked attractive with her long blonde hair and smart suit. Jess looked up. "Do either of you know the two men in this photo with her?"

That prompted Nigel to sit down and look at the newspaper. "That's John Langhurst on her left. He's the Chairman of Western Energy." He looked up. "He's married to Linda Shipperton."

Jess knew Linda was the daughter of Robert Shipperton, a former Australian Prime Minister.

Nigel turned back to the paper. "The other man in the photo is the CEO, Richard Price."

Little beads of sweat glistened on Nigel's forehead as sunlight flooded through the window. A thought popped into Jess's head. "Did you know Ellen Chambers, Nigel?"

He shook his head. "I should telephone the Chairman to offer our condolences." He smoothed his hair with his hand, and turned to Simon. "Is he coming to the High Commissioner's dinner for the Foreign Secretary tomorrow evening?"

Simon nodded.

"Make sure I get seated next to him. I want to have a chat about the gas deal."

Jess smiled. Nigel never missed an opportunity to cosy up to Australia's movers and shakers.

Simon tapped his finger on the newspaper. "It says here the Chinese gas team are in Oz for another round of talks to try to break the deadlock?" He lowered his voice. "I hear they're being *really* difficult."

"Well, this murder's only going to make things worse," Jess added.

"I don't see why it should." Nigel's voice sounded casual. "It'll be some low-life who did it. Ellen Chambers was probably just in the wrong place, at the wrong time."

Jess looked up, quickly. "Why would you assume that?"

"What are *you* suggesting happened?"

Simon cut in. "Well I agree with Jess. This murder's bound to shake things up. That contract's worth *millions*. And it's crucial to both countries."

Nigel stuck his chin out. He didn't like to be contradicted and was about to sound off.

Jess quickly changed the subject. "Did the High Commissioner get back okay from Perth last night?"

With a satisfied smile, Nigel shook his head. "His flight was delayed until this morning. Technical problems." He puffed his chest out. "That means I'll have to go to the airport and meet the Foreign Secretary. I *suppose* I'll have to chair the working lunch in Parliament too."

Jess glanced at Simon, who gave her the ghost of a smile. They both knew Nigel was delighted the High Commissioner hadn't made it back from Perth in time for the Foreign Secretary's arrival.

Nigel's ringing phone interrupted. Snatching up the receiver, he listened and covered it with his hand. "Right, you two, let's get on with it," he said.

Taking their cue, Jess and Simon stood up and headed for the door.

"Oh Jessic*aah*..."

She turned back to Nigel.

"Do everything by the book in Brisbane, okay? The media will be watching. No bleeding heart stuff. We don't want any cock-ups, not with the Foreign Secretary here."

It was the patronising tone Nigel reserved for her that really riled. She gave him a long, cool look, and walked out.

Simon followed her out into the corridor. "He's *such* a prick! Ignore him, Jess."

Furious as she was with Nigel, Jess wasn't going to show it. At the staircase, she turned. "You don't have to worry about me, Simon. I can hold my own in this organisation."

"I know you can, Jess." Simon's eyes softened. "Look, we need to talk... about Friday night."

Feeling the sudden rush of blood to her cheeks, she started to walk down the stairs. "I've got a plane to catch."

"Jess."

"I can't do this now, Simon."

"But..."

"I'll be back in a couple of days," she said, glancing over her shoulder.

"*Fine!*" He threw his hands up in the air and walked off.

Jess went back to her office, slammed the door and leant against it. "You don't have to like your boss, Jess," her Dad used to say when she first started working at the Foreign Office and came home with tales of her snooty London colleagues, "you just have to find a way of working with him."

How right he was! Now, her way of working with Nigel was to give him as wide a berth as possible. And then Simon had to go and mention Friday night as well. He certainly picked his moment.

Pushing all thoughts of Nigel and Simon out of her head, she looked over at the beam of sunshine flooding through the window. It lifted her spirits. Never mind the dreary battleship-grey desk and beige walls, she liked her bright, north facing office. It was her haven of peace and quiet. Going over to her desk, she switched on her computer. Almost 70 emails had come in overnight from the Foreign Office and British embassies all over the world. Everything, from the notification of more biometric changes to the British passport to the latest reports of atrocities in Syria, filled her inbox. She scanned through, deleting, archiving, or forwarding unclassified emails to her laptop to answer later.

Curious about Ellen Chambers and Western Energy, she went onto the internet and found the Company's official website. Clicking onto Our Management Team, a photo of Chairman John Langhurst popped up. Jess studied his thin, sun-tanned face and short grey hair. It was difficult to tell how old he was from a photo, probably in his 60s, she thought. Had she met him before? No, she'd have remembered those striking blue eyes.

A photo of Chief Executive Richard Price came next. Though he was already balding, he looked younger than the Chairman. With his long face and tortoiseshell glasses, he looked like some Dickensian character. She was quite sure she hadn't met him before.

Then she looked for Ellen Chambers, but could only find her name and designation as Group Finance Director on the website. Why no photo? Not to be defeated, she typed Ellen Chambers and Western Energy into Google. A few newspaper articles popped up, referring to Ellen's name and position in Western Energy. But there were no quotes from her, and no articles about her. That was surprising. Wouldn't a woman in Ellen Chambers' position have *some* footprint on the internet?

"Morning, Jess."

She looked up to see Sharon sashaying towards her in a figure-hugging black skirt and satin blouse, a pile of papers in one hand and a mug in the other. As usual, she looked immaculate, with her curly auburn hair styled, and her freckled complexion expertly made up.

"I thought you'd need some coffee before you go." Sharon's red-polished nails gleamed as she handed over the mug.

Jess took it gratefully. "Thanks."

"Simon just told me you're leaving for Brisbane on the ten o'clock flight." Sharon lowered herself into a chair and crossed her legs. "I've asked the driver to bring the car round for you."

Jess nodded. "Can you let the Queensland Police know I'm on my way? I'll head straight to The Palms when I get there."

"Have you spoken to Susan Chambers?" Sharon asked. "Only she's been phoning every ten minutes to speak to you."

"Why didn't you put her through?"

"You were upstairs with big Nige." Sharon rolled her eyes. "Bet he's insufferable with the Foreign Secretary arriving?"

"He's fretting about the programme. Can you cover for me when the Foreign Secretary comes round the office to meet the staff?"

"Of course."

Jess frowned. "You know, Sharon, I'm worried about Susan Chambers. She left two voice messages on my mobile, saying she wanted to speak to me. But she didn't leave a number, and said it wasn't *safe* for me to phone her back. God knows what that's all about."

"Sounds paranoid to me." Sharon looked thoughtful. "I *knew* she was going to be trouble. She refused to talk to me on the phone, and just kept asking for you. Anyway, she seems to have calmed down since I told her you were flying to Brisbane. At least she hasn't phoned again."

"Did you tell her I'd be staying at The Palms?"

Sharon nodded.

"Right, well, I'll just have to find her when I get there." Jess looked at her watch again. "Now, if the media call about the identity of the murder victim, put them on to Simon until I get to Brisbane. If anyone else asks, take the line that the police have notified us that a British woman was found dead at The Palms this morning. Tell them we can't confirm her name yet, but we'll issue a press release as soon as we can. Okay?"

"Okay."

"Anything else I should be worrying about before I go?"

Sharon slid the pile of papers she was nursing onto the desk. "Simon went rushing over to Parliament and forgot these agendas. They're for the working lunch." She glanced over. "Nothing wrong is there, only he seemed... distracted?"

Jess looked away. She didn't really have time to stop at Parliament, but she wanted to smooth things over with

Simon. "I'll drop them in on my way to the airport." She pushed the papers into her leather briefcase.

Sharon stood up and hovered by the door. "I know you won't like me saying this, Jess, and you can tell me to mind my own business if you like. But, well, Simon's a good man, you know. He's intelligent, reliable, kind, and..." She took a deep breath. "Very fond of you. And if anyone deserves a second chance at happiness, it's you."

Jess felt her breath catch in her throat, and for a moment she couldn't speak. But when she did finally look up, Sharon had slipped out. *Oh my God!* Jess slumped back in her chair. Was Simon that transparent? Had others noticed too? She shuddered. She had to put a stop to this right now, and get some distance between them before *everyone* started talking. And this Brisbane trip seemed a good time to begin.

An incoming email distracted her.

Thank God you're coming to Brisbane. I can't talk to the police, it's not safe. Don't phone me, I think they're monitoring my calls. I'll find you at the Palms. SC

Not safe? There it was again. Why would the police want to monitor *Susan's* calls? Sitting there, Jess started to feel uneasy. It wasn't just Susan Chambers' mysterious messages worrying her. Call it instinct, experience or whatever, but something about this consular case didn't feel right. She sighed. Sharon was spot on though, Susan Chambers *was* going to be trouble. But it wasn't paranoia she sensed from Susan; it was more like fear.

5

Detective Inspector Tom Sangster stepped out of the car and looked around. His pulse quickened, and a shot of adrenaline surged through his veins in the anticipation of a new murder case. He was anxious to get to the crime scene. He wanted to see it, feel it. But he wanted to arrive alone. He found those first, solitary observations crucial. He glanced at Sergeant Dalton standing beside him. "I'm going straight to the jetty, Dave. See if you can find the local officer who got here first and send him to meet me down there."

"Sure, Boss." Dalton knew the procedure.

At least we're ahead of the media, Sangster thought, as he skirted around the side of the hotel. That'll give us time to get forensics done and our victim out of here before they start poking about. Round the back, the hotel was laid out in a horseshoe shape that gave the impression of the whole building hugging the small bay. He continued down the path in the direction of the beach and jetty, eyes scanning the grounds as he went. The only guests he could see, or rather hear, were some kids splashing about in the swimming pool.

He stopped on a small incline about 100 metres from the jetty. Reaching into his jacket pocket, he pulled out his pencil and sketchpad. He felt more comfortable observing the scene with them in his hands. He could see the small jetty at the far left of the beach, where two forensic officers in white overalls were working. One stood on board a moored boat, and was dusting its handrail for fingerprints. The other was crouched over the corpse. Sangster scanned the beach. The sand still lay flat and undisturbed. Normally by now guests would have staked out their sunbeds before going into breakfast. But uniform had closed it off.

He strode on towards the jetty. As he approached, he saw two bushy, grey eyebrows peering at him from under a protective hood. They belonged to Sergeant Anderson, or the Swiss watch as he was known back at HQ because of his reliability and precision after a long forensic career. Although he would never say so, Sangster was pleased to see Anderson. The man could be opinionated, but he could do his job, and Sangster valued that above everything.

Anderson looked surprised. "Bit out of your Brisbane patch, aren't you, Tom?"

Sangster nodded. "Dave and I were on our way up the coast to another meeting when the DC rang and told us to get over here quick, before the tide came in and you had to move her." He lifted the cordon tape. "Okay to come through?"

"Yeah. No need to suit up. We're about done."

Sangster ducked under the cordon and steeled himself. Looking down at the corpse, he waited for the familiar shudder of revulsion to pulse through him. He'd reacted that way to the sight of violent death on his first murder case and it had never gone away. If anything, it had become stronger over the years.

The woman was lying face down on the damp sand, with her head twisted to expose a bloodied left cheek. The fingers of her outstretched right arm seemed to point in the direction of the hotel as if she were trying to tell him something. Her black evening dress, stretched tight around her swollen body, had ridden up over her thighs, revealing long, sun-tanned legs that lay buckled in the sand.

The eyebrows rose again. "She must be important if *you're* here, Tom."

Sangster didn't reply. Normally, he would stamp on any sarcasm, but he knew this was Anderson's way of dealing with his own emotions at gruesome crime scenes. And he didn't want to encourage any more conversation; he wanted to think.

But Anderson wasn't going to oblige. "So who is she, then?"

"A senior executive working for Western Energy." Sangster felt the stiffness in his right knee as he crouched down. "That energy and resources company."

Anderson looked unimpressed.

"The PM's Office are interested in her," Sangster said.

That got Anderson's attention. "What's she got to do with them?"

Sangster shrugged. "All I know is they've been on the phone to our Deputy Police Commissioner. That's why I'm here."

Anderson huffed. "You'll have your work cut out with *that lot* breathing down your neck."

Sangster gave him a pointed look. "Which means you will too."

Anderson looked away.

Concentration restored, Sangster's eyes swept over the body. The source of all the blood on her cheek was a deep, circular cut. It looked like something had been stamped or imprinted into the skin.

Anderson noticed his interest. "Unusual wound, isn't it?" He grunted with the effort of squatting down to get a better look. "The killer must've caught her with something sharp as he punched her. He could have been wearing a ring, or holding a key in his hand." He paused and lifted up the victim's matted hair. "Take a look at these contusions on the back of her neck."

Sangster crouched closer.

"I think the killer gripped the back of her neck hard between the thumb and fingers of one hand." Anderson demonstrated on the corpse with his own gloved hand. "And held her head under." He let her hair fall back. "That's how she was killed."

Sangster studied her clothes and the position of her limbs carefully. Then he looked into her open eyes and froze. There was moisture in the corners like tears. Another wave of emotion pulsed through him. This time the hairs on the back of his neck rose too. He waited for the moment to pass before turning back to Anderson. "What was the time of death?"

Anderson brushed the back of his gloved hand across his forehead as if to wipe away non-existent perspiration. "Well, she's been in the water a while, which makes it difficult to be precise before we've done the autopsy."

"Your best guess then? I won't hold you to it."

Anderson's eyebrows knitted together in a single bushy line. "Well... I'd say she's probably been dead about 12 or 13 hours."

"That means she was killed sometime between 7 and 8pm last night?"

Anderson nodded.

Sangster stood up and looked around again. So what was she doing down here last night in the dark? Out for an evening stroll? A bit of solitude? This was a private spot and well away from prying eyes. Was she alone? Or meeting someone perhaps? He turned to Anderson again. "What's your sense of what happened down here?"

Anderson frowned and pointed to the jetty. "We've found fresh blood spatter on the boards, Tom. I reckon she was up there when the killer attacked. There are signs of a struggle. There are no railings, so they must have both gone over the side into the water."

"She put up a fight, then?"

"I'll say."

Sangster studied the jetty. He was still deep in thought when he heard familiar footsteps. Turning back, he saw Sergeant Dalton stop behind the crime cordon. Dalton's plump face looked ashen. Small beads of sweat glistened along his receding hairline and trickled down his forehead. He was looking everywhere but at the corpse... and the blood.

Sangster looked away. He'd told Dave he had to get this problem fixed if he wanted to stay on his murder team. "Did you find the local guy who was first on the scene like I asked?" He didn't hide the irritation in his voice.

Dalton looked over his shoulder. "He's on his way."

All eyes turned to the empty path.

Dalton shuffled his feet and pulled out his notepad. "I got the details from him, Boss."

"Well, go on, then."

Dalton cleared his throat. "He says he arrived here at 5.30 this mornin', after gettin' a call from the hotel receptionist. Apparently, a lad called Danny Burton found the body around five o'clock when he started his shift. Danny does gardenin' and maintenance work." Dalton looked over at the electric lamp on the jetty. "Reception asked him to replace that bulb after a guest nearly fell in last night in the dark. As soon as Danny put it in, well, that's when he saw her." Dalton pointed in the direction of the corpse, but he didn't look down.

Sangster nodded. A sharp pain caught him under the breast bone and he stood still to let it pass. He'd drunk too much coffee on an empty stomach again. He should have eaten breakfast, particularly as he'd skipped dinner last night. But the truth was he'd been too worried about Liz to eat. Where the hell was she? He hadn't heard a word from her since she'd walked out on Saturday. The shock of arriving home and finding her gone rippled through him again. Why did she have to be so dramatic? Their row on Friday night had been nothing out of the ordinary. Of course it had been his fault, as usual. He'd forgotten he was taking her out for dinner; and she'd been all dressed up and waiting for him for hours. So when he'd finally got home from work around midnight, she'd been spoiling for a fight. The trouble was, he'd been tired enough to oblige.

Anderson shuffled impatiently beside him.

"Found anything to suggest a motive?" Sangster asked him.

Anderson pushed back his white hood, revealing a sun-freckled bald spot on the top of his head. "If you're thinking it might be a mugging gone wrong, look at her wrist."

Sangster didn't have to; he'd seen her designer watch. "Have you found her handbag, or shoes?"

Anderson shook his head.

"Mobile?"

"'fraid not."

"Any sign of sexual assault?" Sangster asked.

"Nope. Her underwear has been disturbed, but that could have happened during the struggle or from spending the night in the water."

Sangster looked thoughtful. "Has the killer left anything behind?"

Anderson started peeling off his latex gloves. "We've got some prints from that seat over there." He pointed to the one on the jetty. "But they could belong to anyone. And we've got some hair from the jetty boards, but that looks like the victim's. Of course, there's the blood spatter. That *could* be his, or some of it at least."

"Looks like a pretty frenzied attack to me," Dalton piped up. The colour had returned to his cheeks now and he was finally able to look at the body. "Someone was either real mad or off his head on somethin'."

"So we've noticed, Dave," Sangster said, quietly.

"Right, I'm done." Anderson secured the samples in his bag and closed it. Then he turned to Sangster. "Okay if we take her away now?"

Sangster nodded. "I'll need the autopsy report straightaway because..."

"The PM's office are *interested*." Anderson finished for him.

Sangster gave him a curt nod and walked round onto the jetty to look out to sea. On such a calm morning, it was hard to believe what had happened here. He turned and looked down at the corpse on the sand. He took the top off his pencil and started sketching her in his pad. It didn't take him long to get the details down. He laboured over her eyes. He couldn't forget that look in them. He noticed Anderson pulling a comical face at Dalton, who wisely didn't respond. Sangster knew he was the butt of jokes back at the station, but he didn't care. Once he'd drawn someone, it was like every detail was etched into his brain.

In only a few minutes, he'd finished. He beckoned to Dalton to follow him back to the hotel. Striding along, his mind leapt ahead with everything that had to be done. "Get the team in here, Dave, and lock this place down.

We'll need a list of all the hotel guests last night, *and* staff, *and* any contractors who may have been working here yesterday. Line them up for interview and run checks on them."

"That'll take a while," Dalton puffed. "The hotel was packed out last night with people attending a charity do."

"Which charity?"

"Kids with Cancer."

"Best get started, then." Sangster flashed him a look. "So what else do we know about our victim?"

"According to hotel registration, she's British... aged 39... and a regular guest. Checked in alone. Always came alone." Dalton was breathing hard now from walking and talking. "The next of kin is her sister, Susan Chambers. She lives in Brisbane, and works on the *Brisbane Echo*."

"A journo?" Sangster spun round. "That's *all* we need."

Dalton frowned. "Why?"

"The DC just rang to say the Federal guys in Canberra have a red flag file on our victim."

Dalton raised his eyebrows. "What's she been up to, then?"

"He wouldn't say on the phone. Too sensitive. But she's been on their radar a while."

"*Has* she now?"

"Yes. That's why the DC sent us in over the local guys. So you'd better help Anderson get her out of here before the media arrive."

Dalton nodded and turned back towards the jetty.

Sangster strode on alone. He didn't want to get caught by the media either, at least not until he had more to go on. Western Energy was an influential resources company, which meant this murder was bound to get some heat, especially with that Chinese gas deal going on. It would get a high profile in the UK too because the victim had been British. *That* angle would need careful handling. And that red flag file in Canberra could be nothing but bad news. He had to find out quickly what that was all about, because it had to be the reason the PM's office were interested in her. Still, whatever it was, the Federal guys would want to be involved in the investigation, which meant added pressure.

Hearing the crunch of footsteps, he looked up to see a man blocking his path. Sangster studied him with an artist's precision. The deep creases in the man's weather-beaten face stood out against his smooth, silver-grey hair; and his eyes looked troubled.

Under Sangster's intense stare, the man flinched and scraped the gravel with his toe like a restless animal. "Inspector Sangster?" he asked.

Sangster nodded.

"I'm Jim Middleton. I work here. I served Miss Chambers last night in the bar, before she was murdered." He looked down and brushed some imaginary dirt off his trousers. "I think I may have been the last person to see her alive." He took a step forward, then hesitated.

Sangster could see the man wanted to tell him something. "Let's go and sit down." He pointed at the terrace.

Jim nodded and followed him back to a table. Their chairs made loud scraping noises as they pulled them out and sat down.

"Now what is it?" Sangster tried not to sound impatient.

Jim took a deep breath. "Danny Burton was pesterin' Miss Chambers in the bar last night. That's why she left. That stupid idiot just can't leave women alone. I don't know why the hotel keep him on. He's a bloody liability, if you ask me."

Sangster looked at him. "Danny Burton? He found the body, didn't he?"

Jim nodded. "Miss Chambers was having a quiet drink in the bar before that prick came in and hit on her. She gave him the brush off. Said she already had a date. The idiot had it coming if you ask me. But Danny got mad, and she left." Jim paused. "I'm sure Miss Chambers *was* tellin' the truth when she said she had a date. All the time she was in the bar, she kept lookin' at the door as if she was waitin' for someone."

"Did she leave on her own?"

Jim nodded. "As it happens, I followed her out here to collect up the glasses. I saw her walkin' down the path, towards the jetty." He leant forward. "There was someone behind her on the path. A man, I think."

Sangster looked up, sharply. "Can you give me a description? Height? Build? Clothes even?"

Jim shook his head. "I only wish I could. But it was pretty dark out here."

Sangster sat back in his chair and studied Jim. *Why's he telling me this? To be helpful, or deliberately cast suspicion on Danny?* "Was Danny still in the bar when she left?" he asked.

Jim nodded, reluctantly. "But he left soon after."

There was no doubting the shock in Jim's eyes, though. It was a strong reaction that made Sangster ask him how well he'd known Ellen Chambers.

Jim shrugged. "She was a guest. She stayed here a lot. Always had time for a chat."

Sangster looked at his sketch again. "What was she like?"

Jim shrugged. "Nice. Friendly. Liked a gin and tonic. She always gave me a good tip."

"What did you chat about last night?" he asked.

"Oh, I don't know. This and that. She never talked about anythin' personal, if that's what you're askin'?" Jim paused. "Except I know she had a kid sister in Brisbane. So she must have said."

Sangster nodded. "Stay around the hotel, Jim. We'll want to interview you again. Meanwhile, I want you to think about everyone who came in and out of the bar around that time last night, and every little thing that happened. However insignificant, I want to know about it. Okay?"

"Yes, Sir." Jim got up. "I'll be workin' in the bar today. Just let me know when you want to talk again." He went to leave.

"Oh, Jim?"

"Yes."

"Was there anything about Ellen Chambers that seemed out of character or different last night? What I mean is, did she say or do anything unusual?"

Jim ran his fingers through his cropped hair as he tried to think. "No... No. I don't think so... Not last night anyway."

Sangster looked up. "On another occasion?"

Jim's eyes brightened. "The last time she stayed here, about a month or so ago, I remember she came into the bar one evenin' and asked for a bottle of our best champagne. *Really* expensive stuff. She paid in cash and took it out of the bar, along with two champagne glasses." He smiled. "She looked happy the next mornin' when she returned the glasses. All washed and dried they were. That's the kind of person she was." He shook his head in disbelief. "Christ, if only I'd *known* last night... if only I'd *thought*. I could have *done* somethin'."

Sangster just nodded. He wasn't going to tell Jim not to beat himself up about it. He was still under suspicion, like everyone else.

Shoulders hunched, Jim walked away.

Sangster sat back in the chair and rubbed his gritty eyes. He hadn't slept through the night since Liz had left. He'd tried ringing her mobile, but she wouldn't answer. He'd contacted her family and friends, but they said they didn't know where she was. Not that he believed them. But what could he do?

He stood up, thrust his hands deep into his trouser pockets, and stepped off the back terrace. The gravel on the path crunched under his feet; it was a sound he found somehow reassuring. Then something made him look over at the thick bushes bordering the path that led to the jetty. He went over. Curious, he slipped through them and found himself in dense foliage. Accustoming his eyes to the dark, he noticed a track of beaten earth running through the bushes like a trail. He didn't want to traipse along it before forensics had done their examination, but it looked like it went all the way to the jetty. He glanced back at the terrace where Dalton now stood looking around for him. But the bushes were too thick for him to be seen. So, Sangster thought, just about anybody could have made their way down to the jetty on this track last night and murdered Ellen Chambers.

He stepped out of the bushes and walked over to Dalton. He knew this case wasn't going to be easy, especially with the heat he'd get from Canberra and the media. But he'd have to distance himself from all that, and start in the same place as any other murder investigation. He needed to find out everything he could about Ellen Chambers. In particular why Canberra had a red flag file on her. That was his first priority. Then he would talk to her sister Susan Chambers; and to her work colleagues in Western Energy.

But first, he'd find that Danny Burton.

6

He hated sunlight. It made him feel exposed, as if his true personality was stripped away the moment the sun appeared. Even when young, he used to wait until everyone on the farm was asleep at night, then he would creep out onto the porch and sleep in the cool air, under the stars. That's where he could breathe. And it was the only time he knew any peace.

Squinting in the sharp morning sunlight, he looked over at the house. Set in an exclusive Brisbane suburb and hidden behind a high wall and impressive steel gates, everything about it screamed old money. It was just the kind of place he expected that bastard to live in.

All he could see above the wall were two dormer attic windows jutting out of the sloping roof like sentinels. He picked his binoculars up from the passenger seat and trained them on both windows. But there was no twitching curtain or movement inside.

He looked up and down the street. No one about. Not that he expected to see anyone; rich people didn't walk anywhere. Reversing his jeep to the edge of the property, he cast a professional eye along the southern perimeter wall. Despite the obvious security, he knew there had to be an easy way in. There always was. Then he spotted it. At the back of the garden, the wall petered out into a high hedge. He pulled the peak of his cap down over his eyes and drew his knife from its sheath. He got out of the jeep, unconcerned about any CCTV cameras guarding this posh mansion. The jeep would soon be ditched; and no one would ever know he'd been there. He was truly invisible.

He could feel the blood pumping hard through his veins again, making him feel powerful. Killing was easy if you have the right tools and the expertise.

And he was just *so* ready.

Looking both ways along the street again, he slipped along the side wall until he reached the hedge. He chopped some branches away with his knife and pushed them under the hedge so no-one would see them from the road. Stepping through the small hole into the tropical foliage of the garden, his face hardened when he saw the manicured lawn, the tennis court and swimming pool. *That greedy bastard definitely has it coming!*

A distant crunch of leaves sounded...

He froze. Sensing it even before he heard heavy panting, he tightened his grip on the knife. A black dog lolloped out of the bushes to block his way. He could tell by its black hair it was a cattle dog, and by its rheumy eyes that it was almost blind. As it stood awkward and stiff on arthritic legs, anger rose deep inside him. This old working dog should be roaming free on a farm somewhere, not locked up in a suburban garden. But indignation soon gave way to resignation when a growl rumbled deep in the animal's throat as it curled back its lip. Cattle dogs were well known for being protective of their owners; and there was no way he could allow that.

With lightning speed, he lunged forward, gripped the dog's snout and plunged the knife expertly into its heart. The animal was gone before it even knew what had happened.

Closing his eyes, he felt the joy of the kill well up inside him. He stood shuddering. It had been so long...

A voice? He dropped to the ground. Someone was singing... inside the house. A woman. Respectfully, he laid the old dog behind a bush and covered it with leaves. At least it was out of its misery now.

He made his way towards the house, ducking behind trees and bushes for cover as he went. The singing became louder and louder. He crept up the back steps and along the veranda towards the voice. Reaching an open window, he peered through the slats of the wooden plantation blinds.

Naked, she stood at the kitchen sink with her back to him. Droplets of water trickled down her sun-burnished back from her dip in the pool. His eyes moved hungrily over her body, from the curve of her neck, down to her firm, bronzed buttocks. Mesmerised, he watched her gather her tumbling hair together with both hands, and lean over the sink to squeeze out water. His throat tightened, as the heat spread inside...

"Put some clothes on, Belinda!"

Startled by the voice, he ducked down under the window.

"Sorry, Dad," he heard her say. "Thought you'd gone to work."

"Well I haven't." There was a pause. "Get dressed and I'll drop you at Uni."

"No worries, Dad. I'm studying at home today."

His eyes gleamed at the sweet sound of her voice.

A sudden clanging noise rang out. *The electronic gates!* Staying low, he moved to the front of the house and peered round the wall. He ducked back as a black limousine drove in and tooted its horn. He heard the front door open and close, a car door slam and tyres move off on gravel. Peering round the wall again, he was just in time to see the limousine sweep out of the front gates with that bastard in the back.

Shit! His face twisted as he turned to run back to his jeep to go after him. Then he stopped. He could still feel the intoxicating power of the kill coursing through him, like an awakening.

His hand tightened on the knife as he looked back at the house and thought about the curves of her luscious body.

7

"Are you saying she was murdered while under police *surveillance?*" Sangster stood in the hotel car park, his mobile pressed to his ear.

"*Technical* surveillance, Tom," the Deputy Commissioner replied. "Canberra were monitoring her phone calls and emails. She wasn't being physically watched or followed."

"Still..."

"Yeah." The DC's controlled voice had risen a notch, a sure sign he was stressed. "Two Federal Agents are on their way from Canberra to brief us on the background. They don't want to talk on the phone. Too *sensitive*."

Sangster caught the sarcasm. The DC was in charge of the murder investigation because it had been committed within the State of Queensland's jurisdiction. And with the Queensland Police Commissioner out of the country on a goodwill visit to Indonesia, the DC didn't want Canberra overshadowing in his moment in the spotlight. But Sangster didn't care about protocol, or about putting anyone's nose out of joint, he knew they'd have to work with the Federal Police since they were already investigating the victim. "Sir, I really need to know *why* Canberra had Ellen Chambers under surveillance."

There was a pause. "Corruption allegations."

"*Corruption?* What, connected to that big LNG deal with the Chinese?"

"Yes. We'll have to wait for those Agents to arrive to get the full story."

Wait for them to arrive? Sangster couldn't believe what he was hearing. He needed to know *now*. "If they've been monitoring her communications," he said, sharply, "they can give us a read-out of her phone calls and emails since we haven't found a mobile or laptop in her hotel room."

"You can always ask."

Sangster nodded to himself. "What time are they arriving?"

"Around four o'clock."

"Can't they get here any sooner?"

"Apparently not."

"Right, well I'm going to stay out here for a while." Sangster was in no hurry to get back to Police HQ. He wanted to stay close to the crime scene. "There's a lot to cover. But I'll be back in time for that briefing."

"Make sure you are, Tom." And the DC hung up.

Sangster pocketed his mobile. Grabbing the spiral rings of his sketchpad, he pulled it out and flicked to his drawing of Ellen Chambers. *Corruption, eh?* It was as good a motive for murder as any, he thought, except this killing hadn't looked planned, or in any way professional. If anything, the frenzied attack seemed more opportunistic, an act of madness even. Rage and panic blew up quickly, but they were over with quickly too.

Was this over, he wondered?

The toot of a horn made him turn. He looked at his watch as a taxi pulled in the drive: 10.30am – hotel checkout time.

His team had interviewed all the departing guests and taken their contact details. Now he was scanning their faces as they climbed into the vehicles. Faces had always fascinated him. The guests all looked anxious to get away, particularly the lady with the platinum hair. She'd told him earlier she was here with her daughter and two grandchildren for a break. Now, she couldn't leave fast enough. But the tender smile she gave her grandchildren as she helped them into a taxi struck a chord.

His mother used to smile at him like that. From the age of five, when he first started to draw people, he always gave his mother a smiley face. To his child's eye, she was always happy. How wrong he'd been. Back then, it had never occurred to him to draw his father, because he was never at home. He was always away working, or that's what his parents had told him. It was years later, and only after he'd joined the police, that he found out the truth.

His father had another family.

It happened by chance one evening, when he drove a woman home who'd been mugged in the street. When he pulled up outside her house, she jumped out of his patrol car and ran weeping into the arms of a man on the doorstep.

His Dad!

Instinctively, he'd leant his elbow against the driver's window and hid his face with his hand. Stomach turning, he sat watching their tender embrace through his open fingers. He was torn between marching up to the front door and having it out with his father, or just driving away. In the end, he drove away. But he couldn't let it lie; he had to find out the truth. So he went back the next day and talked to the woman's neighbours, then to employees of the bank they told him she worked for. That's when he discovered his dad had been in a relationship with the woman for over 20 years. He couldn't believe it. How could he not have known? Impossible, yet true. It played on his mind for weeks and months after. He wanted to confront his father, but he could never quite bring himself to do it. Then, as time slipped by, the moment never seemed right.

Months later, he tried to broach the subject with his mother, wondering if she knew and would talk about it. He led in with little clues, but she never took the bait. And he certainly didn't want to be the one to tell her, if she didn't know. Eventually, he decided to leave well alone. Their marriage was their own affair.

But a week before she died, his mother told him about his father's other family, breaking the news he had a step-sister. Sangster had wanted to ask so many questions, but her face just seemed to close down, as though she was either numb or she didn't care. Maybe she didn't care? Or maybe she'd learnt to shut down her emotions to cope with the hurt?

When clearing out the family house after she died, he'd found his early drawings of her in a box on top of her wardrobe. Now that box sat on a shelf in his study. He often looked at those drawings. That's the way he liked to remember his mother, as happy and smiling. But to him, his parents' union was nothing but a passionless deception that had put him off marriage for life. And that's exactly what he'd told Liz on the one occasion she mentioned marriage. Liz didn't say anything at the time. But she must have been thinking about it because after dinner, when they were washing up, she suddenly said: "If you love someone enough, Tom, you don't think twice about marrying them." Now, those words were swirling around in his head. Is that why she left? Did she think he didn't love her because he didn't want to get married? Was that it? Of course he loved her. She knew he loved her. Didn't she?

He ran his fingers through his hair. He knew he wasn't a good communicator. Perhaps it was because he'd grown up as an only child. He liked his own company; it was easier somehow. And he'd always found people a bit of a mystery, even back then. He would study their faces, then draw them. It was his way of trying to work them out, investigate them even. Now, he could read faces like an expert, which he found useful in his job. Any tilt of the head, or twitch of a cheek or lip, or even a long stare, would tell him everything. He could capture the essence of someone's character in a single drawing.

Pursuing that talent, he'd qualified in contemporary fine art and design and began work, taking commissions for illustrations. Then he progressed on to portraits, his true calling. But that work alone wouldn't pay the bills. Forced to cast around, he got some work as a court artist, which sparked his interest in the law and policing. Later, at a school reunion, he met a mate who was so enthusiastic about his career in the police, Sangster thought he'd give it a go too. And, while it hadn't been his first career choice, it had become his vocation. Now, 20 years on, he was surprised at how well he'd done. He wasn't motivated by a desire to get to the top, although he'd take that in his stride when it came his way. To him, every crime was an all-consuming puzzle that burned in his brain like a fever; and he couldn't rest or relax until he'd solved it.

Dalton catapulted through the revolving door, interrupting his thoughts. "I've got Susan Chambers' address," he said, waving a piece of paper. "The guys went round earlier to tell her about her sister. She took the news badly, as you would expect. Then she acted weird; she pushed them out of the house, sayin' she didn't want any help. Now, she's not answerin' the door, or the phone."

Sangster frowned as he closed his car door. "The DC's just told me two Federal Agents are on their way from Canberra. They won't get here until 4pm, so I can carry on here for another couple of hours."

"Good, because we've just made an appointment for you to see the British Consul. He should be here around 2pm."

"Not *more* Canberra folk." Sangster sighed and looked at his watch. "Okay, but I *must* talk to Susan Chambers. Have you tried the *Brisbane Echo* where she works?"

"Yes, but they haven't seen her."

"Find her, Dave," Sangster turned to go back into the hotel, "while I have another word with Danny Burton, the lad who found Ellen Chambers' body."

"What do you make of him, Boss?" Dalton asked, quickly. "Bit of a hoon, if you ask me. *He* says Ellen Chambers gave him the come-on."

Sangster nodded. "He's been hanging about the crime scene all morning, trying to be helpful. Even when he was supposed to be mowing the lawn, he was watching us. Convenient that *he* found the body, wasn't it?"

"Perhaps he knew just where to look?" Dalton warmed to this train of thought. "Perhaps he followed Ellen Chambers down to the jetty and tried it on with some force. She fought back, and things got out of hand."

Sangster looked thoughtful. "The barman said he saw someone walking behind Ellen Chambers on the path down to the jetty just before she was killed. It couldn't have been Danny, he was still in the bar at that point." Sangster pushed the revolving door.

Dalton shuffled through behind him.

"But that doesn't mean Danny didn't go down to the jetty, in the hope of getting some action." Sangster turned to face Dalton. "He did leave the bar soon after her. Even if he didn't kill her, he might have seen something."

"Yeah." Dalton hesitated. "Look, about earlier, Boss. I've booked some counsellin' … to fix my problem. I want to stay on the murder team, more than anythin'." He sighed. "I just wish I could deal with it as easily as you do."

Sangster knew he had a reputation for being tough and remote amongst the guys. They were of the old school of policing; and let off steam with the help of the plentiful, local rum. But did they all think he found it *easy* because he didn't join in? Irritated, he looked at Dalton, but he didn't let fly. He knew Dalton had his work cut out at home: a wife with chronic fatigue and a couple of young kids to look after. But there was no point beating about the bush either; he wouldn't carry passengers on his team. "You've got another couple of months to deal with it, Dave. Then that's it."

Dalton nodded, glumly.

Sangster checked his watch. "It's manic back at HQ. The DC's just rung to say he's cancelled all leave and called everyone in."

Dalton gave a wry smile. "That'll upset Roberts. He'll have to give up his fishin' trip."

"Roberts?"

"DC Roberts. He was here, earlier."

Sangster frowned. "Do I know him?"

"Course you do. He's that bald, exercise nut. You know him, always in the gym. Transferred here from Melbourne about a year ago."

Sangster raised an eyebrow. "What was he doing here?"

"He said he had a few days' leave and was goin' out on a fishin' trip." Dalton frowned. "Except, thinkin' about it now, he wasn't dressed for fishin'. He was wearin' smart black trousers and a shirt."

"Was he now?" Sangster never could leave a loose end. "Better check he *is* on leave, Dave. Discreetly mind. Don't go treading on any toes."

8

Jess winced as the edge of the paper sliced into her thumb and a drop of blood oozed out. Wrapping a tissue around the cut, she glanced out of the window at the sound of the plane's engines revving up. In no time, airport buildings were flashing by as they accelerated along the runway and soared into the blue sky, rising south over Canberra. Sunlight sparkled on Lake Burley Griffin below, its central water spout pulsing jets of water high into the sky. Banking right, the plane swooped over the Federal Parliament's 75 metre high flagpole and completed its circle to head north over the business district and snow-capped Mount Ainslie.

Finally, she was on course for Brisbane.

Her mind turned back to the job. She wished she'd been able to smooth things over with Simon. But when she'd eventually found the private dining room in Parliament, he'd already gone. Of course she'd had a look at the place cards around the table. Simon had lined up exactly the right interlocutors for the Foreign Secretary: the Australian Foreign Minister; the Head of the Department of Foreign Affairs and Trade Paul Robinson; and the Heads of all the Security Agencies, which included ASIO and ASIS – the Australian equivalents of MI5 and MI6. Then, she'd just laid a copy of the agenda at each place setting and left.

"Newspaper, Ma'am?"

Jess smiled and selected a copy of the *Brisbane Echo* from the air hostess's tray. She didn't expect to see anything about the Ellen Chambers murder; her body wouldn't have been found until after the daily papers had been printed.

But a business headline caught her eye.

WESTERN ENERGY ATTRACTS OVERSEAS INVESTORS TO THEIR BRISBANE CONFERENCE

She scanned the article. The Conference was all about broadening the exposure of Australia's metal and mining opportunities to international investors, particularly from the USA and Asia. When she saw it was due to start that morning at the Brisbane Convention Centre, she knew why Ellen Chambers had come to Brisbane.

She turned as someone slipped into the empty seat next to her, "Do you like sneaking up on people?" she asked the Australian Foreign Affairs' China expert.

Derek Marshall's sharp eyes twinkled. "Only on beautiful women."

She had to laugh. Like Simon, Derek loved a joke. The pair of them were friends, sparking off each other and talking sport endlessly.

"Off to Brisbane, then?" Derek pushed his tousled grey hair off his forehead.

"That obvious, is it?"

Derek smiled and fidgeted in his seat. He was a restless soul, brimming with intelligence and energy. Being stuck in a plane seat for a couple of hours would be torture for him. "Is your trip connected to the Ellen Chambers' murder?" he asked. "She *was* British, wasn't she?"

Jess nodded, thinking as a Government expert on China, Derek would know all about the LNG deal, and the murder. "Did you know her?" she asked.

He shrugged. "I'd met her a couple of times at meetings and receptions, but I wouldn't say I *knew* her."

"What was she like?"

"Attractive." Derek gave a rueful smile. "Sharp and capable. And a key member of Western Energy's LNG negotiating team. She had a great rapport with the Chinese." He peered over the seat in front. "They're up the front... the Chinese LNG team... in business class. The Chairman of Western Energy invited them to attend his Company Conference."

Jess tapped the newspaper. "I've just been reading about that. Is that why Ellen Chambers was in Brisbane?"

He nodded.

"So what are *you* doing with the Chinese, Derek? Are you their minder?"

"You could say that."

She smiled. "So what's happening with this LNG deal? I'd heard negotiations had stalled."

He leaned in closer. "There's *big* money involved. Important revenues for the Australian economy. Careers have been staked on it."

Jess got the picture. "And your PM will want to go to the Federal election with this deal sewn up. It'll earn big bucks for him to spend on the country." She paused. "So what's the problem? Why have negotiations stalled?"

"Oh, you know..."

She shook her head.

"The Chinese want *control* of the operation." He lowered his voice. "A 55 per cent stake in the joint venture with Western Energy. They're refusing to sign the binding agreement to accept the LNG until they get it."

"Oh, that's just brinkmanship." Jess knew from experience the Chinese were hard negotiators. They knew exactly what they wanted, and would play a waiting game for as long as it took to get it. They had no deadlines to worry about; and no internal pressure from the Chinese public or media for quick results.

"The trouble is," said Derek. "Our pollies need this deal *before* the Federal election campaign starts in November. They'll want to factor in the revenues it will bring. But they can't give too much control to the Chinese; there's a lot of worry out in the electorate about the Chinese buying up the country and its resources."

"Can the impasse be resolved?"

He shrugged. "Western Energy say they're close to a breakthrough. If their Chairman can pull it off, the PM will be *very* grateful." He hesitated. "That should give John Langhurst's political aspirations a boost."

"He wants to go into politics, does he?"

"So they say."

"He'll be a shoe-in, being married to the daughter of a former Australian Prime Minister." She paused. "Tell me Derek, do the police have any idea who killed Ellen Chambers? Or why?"

He looked wary now. "I was hoping you might tell me. After all, we got that intelligence report from London."

Intelligence report?

"And the information in it did come from *your* Embassy in Beijing," Derek continued. "Of course after they got that report, our Federal Police had no option but to start an investigation. They've had Ellen Chambers under surveillance since she arrived back from China."

"She was under surveillance when she was murdered?" Jess tried to keep the surprise out of her voice.

Derek nodded. "Along with Chen Xiamen, the head of the Chinese delegation." He looked at her, sharply. "Didn't you know? The Head of our SIS briefed your Deputy High Commissioner about it last Friday."

Jess felt herself stiffen. So why hadn't Nigel told her?

"And if the *corruption* rumours *are* true," Derek went on, "it would blow this gas deal out of the water. And if any Australians are involved, the shit will well and truly hit the fan. The real worry is it could have dire consequences for our relationship with the Chinese. So we don't want the Chinese getting wind of the police investigation until we know more... But this Ellen Chambers' murder has *really* rattled everyone." He peered over the seat again. "I'd better get back, or the Chinese will be wondering where I am." But he didn't get up straightaway. Instead, he turned and looked her in the eye. "Be careful, Jess. There are some powerful interests involved in this LNG deal. Things are turning really... murky."

She raised her eyebrows.

"Watch your back in Brisbane!" Then Derek was up and walking back to his seat before she could say anything else.

Jess's brain was in overdrive as she watched him go. Was that a warning? It certainly sounded like one. She frowned. Why hadn't Nigel told her Ellen Chambers was under surveillance for corruption? And why hadn't he shown her that intelligence report from the British Embassy in Beijing? *Of course* she needed to know what was in it. Her stomach turned...

Why hadn't *Simon* told her about it? He must have seen that report. As Political Officer, he saw everything. Didn't he *trust* her? That thought played on her mind all the way to Brisbane. And the more she thought about it, the more annoyed she became. But, by the time the pitch of the jet engines changed and the plane started its descent, she'd become more sanguine. There was obviously a lot going on she didn't know about. What was it Derek had said? *Things are turning really murky.* So murky, it seemed, that her colleagues had sent her off on a consular case in the dark? Well, the first thing she needed to do was find out what those corruption allegations were all about. But she'd have to tread carefully, and rely on her own instincts. Wasn't she used to that?

She folded up the newspaper and slipped it into the front seat pocket. Out of the window, the green gardens and swimming pools of Brisbane's modern, suburban houses came into view. Up ahead, city skyscrapers loomed.

As she started putting her papers away, a sobering thought popped into her head. A day or two ago, Ellen Chambers would have been sitting on a plane, preparing to land. Now she was dead, brutally murdered.

Derek's words rang in her ears. *Watch your back in Brisbane!*

★

On the ground, Jess walked into the cavernous domestic terminal and switched on her mobile to get her messages. Putting the phone to her ear, a loud static noise made her jump, then she heard a faint click on the line. Frowning, she slipped the phone into her jacket pocket and set off for the exit.

As she passed the luggage belt, a group of Chinese men in Western suits caught her eye as they chatted and jostled each other for a spot to haul off their luggage. They had to be the Chinese Delegation. She looked around. Derek Marshall was nowhere to be seen, but striding towards them now was the unmistakable figure of Australian Federal Minister Anthony Harris. Unmistakable, because he stood head and shoulders above any of them, and cut a striking figure in his dark suit, and with his shock of blond hair flopping across his forehead. People stared as if he looked familiar, but they couldn't quite place him.

Harris greeted the Chinese warmly, as if he knew them well. That didn't surprise Jess. He *was* the Minister responsible for the mining sector in Australia. She would expect him to be doing whatever he could to help Western Energy secure the LNG deal, even if the Government were publicly saying they weren't involved in the commercial negotiation.

Jess knew and liked Harris. He was a regular guest at the High Commissioner's lunches and dinners. She often sat next to him, and found him down to earth and easy to talk to. But today she was in a hurry and didn't want to get held up. Seeing Harris get into conversation with one of the Chinese, she turned to leave...

Too late.

Harris caught her eye and beckoned.

She had no option but to go over. Getting closer, she noticed how grey and drawn he looked; his crumpled suit gave her the impression he'd been up all night. By contrast, the Chinese man looked relaxed.

"Hello, Jessica."

"Morning, Minister." She looked at her watch. "Or is it afternoon? Australian time zones always confuse me."

"It's 12 noon," he said, distractedly, before turning sideways to the man standing next to him. "Can I introduce you to Chen Xiamen, Chairman of China's National Energy Corporation?"

Chen? So this was the man under surveillance with Ellen Chambers, she thought, as she held out her hand. "Jessica Turner, British Consul."

At first, Chen reacted like most Chinese by inclining his head and avoiding eye contact. But then he surprised her. Shaking her hand with a firm grip, his eyes bore into hers as if trying to read her thoughts. Jess met his glance coolly. His skin felt soft, and his manicured nails caught her eye, along with the expensive Rolex on his wrist. He was obviously well-heeled. She couldn't tell his age, but looking at the fine wisps of grey hair above his ears, she guessed he must be in his 60s.

Chen gave her a broad smile that didn't quite reach his eyes.

Harris intervened. "Are you here about Ellen Chambers, Jessica?" His breath seemed to catch in his throat.

She nodded. "Terrible, isn't it?"

Chen tried a tragic smile this time, but it seemed contrived. Not only did he seem cold and distant, she got the impression he didn't want her around. And that was fine with her. "Well, you must excuse me," she said to Harris. "I have to go." She turned. "Enjoy your visit, Mr Chen. Goodbye." She started walking towards the exit and had almost got away when she heard Harris call out her name. She stopped to wait for him to catch up.

"Sorry, Jess, but can you tell me what the police are saying... about Ellen Chambers, I mean?" Harris coughed. "Sorry, bit of a sore throat."

Glancing over his shoulder, she could see Chen talking on his mobile. "I'm afraid I don't know anything more than the media have reported," she said to Harris. "You will know the police believe she was murdered?"

Harris nodded. "What time do they think it happened?"

"Between 8pm and midnight last night. But I'm only telling you what I've heard second hand."

He pressed on with his questions. "Do they know who killed her?"

She shook her head. "I hope to find out more when I see the police later."

He dug his hand into his breast pocket and pulled out a business card. "Could you ring me on my mobile when you've spoken to them?"

She looked at him. Why would an Australian Minister ask *her* to report what the police had to say? "Of course." She took the card politely. But as she turned and walked away, she could hear Nigel's words ringing in her ears. "Do everything by the book, Jessic*aah*!" And she was quite sure a personal call from her to an Australian Federal Minister would *not* be in Nigel's book.

★

Stepping outside the terminal into warm Queensland sunshine, Jess held her face skywards, like an exotic flower opening to the sun. *Lovely!* Her mobile rang. She fished it out of her jacket pocket, but it stopped before she could answer. She looked at the caller ID. Blocked. That *had* to be Susan Chambers again, she thought.

Spotting the hire cars lined up in gleaming rows under the sun, she crossed the road to the car park. Next to her name on the electronic board, she read her car was parked in bay 76. Finding her white Holden, she pulled the keys out of the ignition and threw her cabin bag and briefcase into the boot. She got into the driver's seat and put her jacket and handbag on the passenger seat.

Exiting through the ID security gate check, a grey jeep slowed to let her into the traffic. She waved her thanks to the driver, and drove out of the airport. Turning onto the Bruce Highway, she headed north, in the direction of the Sunshine Coast.

At first, small, squat trees and tussock grass lined the freeway. Then ghostly gum trees flashed by. Everything looked green and lush in this sub-tropical climate, unlike the dry, brown earth in Canberra. Soon, city pylons and electricity cables petered out to green fields and grazing horses. She was beginning to enjoy the change of scenery when her mobile started bleeping. She counted three text messages arriving. She pulled her mobile out of her pocket and scrolled to the first message.

Call me immediately with an update, Jessica. Nigel was chivvying her, and she'd only just got off the plane.

The second text was from Sharon. *I've spoken to the Queensland Police. Call me back when you can please.*

The third was from Simon. *I need to talk to you, Jess.*

She felt a prick of anger, or was it hurt? Yes, and I need to talk to you too, she thought. Why the hell didn't you tell me about that intelligence report and the corruption allegations? How can I do my job in the dark?

Forcing herself to settle back in the seat, she tried to concentrate on the road. But her mind kept coming back to Simon. It seemed he was never far from her thoughts these days. Of course what Sharon had said about him was true. He *was* kind, reliable, and clever; and they did get on well. But did *he* realise just how much baggage *she* came with?

She still felt guilty about brushing him off on the stairs earlier. But that episode last week had really unnerved her. It wasn't so much that he put his arm around her while they were sitting on the sofa watching TV, although that *had* been a surprise; nor even that he fleetingly brushed his fingers across her breast and nipple. No, it was more *her* reaction that had shocked her. That delicious tingle in the pit of her stomach, the overwhelming desire to move closer to him and rest her head in the nook of his shoulder. Even now she could feel the warmth of his hand radiating through her arm, through her entire body. She had *so* wanted to lean into him. Instead, she'd excused herself like a nervous teenager, and disappeared into the bathroom.

She cringed just thinking about it.

Eventually, she'd gone back and sat on the sofa as if nothing had happened. Simon had just smiled and said nothing, which was typical of him. But the more she replayed the evening in her mind as she drove along, the more uncertain she became. Had she got it all wrong? Misinterpreted his actions?

Then her whole body seemed to droop. What was she thinking anyway?

Oh, Jack!

She could see him so clearly; his smiling face, soft brown eyes, and sun-bleached hair. He'd been like sunshine to her, the light and warmth in her life. As she drove along, cocooned in a world of her own, her mind drifted to that wonderful morning in South Carolina all those years ago when she woke up to sunshine flooding through her window. Jumping out of bed, she'd left the hotel for an early morning jog and swim, something she only ever seemed to do on holiday. Pulling her cotton joggers over her swimsuit, she set off along the stretch of fine, muddy brown-coloured sand. It hadn't looked that inviting, but the sea had pummelled it flat which made it easier to jog on.

Enjoying the freedom on that sunny morning, she'd run a long way before realising how hot she was. Pulling off her joggers, she started running towards the surf until frantic shouting made her stop. Someone was tearing up the beach, pointing vigorously out to sea.

Oh my God! That single black fin gliding in the waves, just a metre from shore.

She could feel the goose bumps even now. If Jack hadn't stopped her...

Ah, but what a wonderful time she'd had with him on that holiday. As a marine biologist, he knew that shoreline like the back of his hand. And they'd spent long, hot days out on his boat, monitoring and tagging the marine life.

They'd slipped so easily from friends to lovers.

The sound of a car horn jolted her back to the present; and she blinked to get rid of Jack's image. Sighing, she looked up at the sky. The sun had disappeared now, and the clouds hung low and heavy. She glanced in her rear-view mirror and sat bolt upright.

The grey jeep from the airport was still there.

She couldn't see who was driving because the driver's sunshade was down. She took her foot off the accelerator to let the jeep pass, but it slowed too. When she accelerated again, it accelerated.

Her heart started thumping and she gripped the steering wheel tight. Seeing a picnic rest area looming, she swerved in at the last minute and stamped on the brakes. The car tyres skidded to a halt on the soft gravel-like surface, throwing up a cloud of dust all around her. She slouched down in the seat while the jeep sailed past. Her eyes stayed glued to it until its tail-lights had disappeared into the distance.

Feeling ridiculous, she flopped back into her seat, and pushed the gear into park. What was wrong with her today? She was so *jumpy*.

Her mobile rang and she fumbled to answer.

"Hi, Jess. Where are you?"

"*Sharon!*" She could hear the relief in her own voice. "I'm on the road to The Palms. And before you say anything, I *know* Nigel wants me to ring."

"He's tried phoning."

"I've been driving. I'm parked up at a picnic spot at the moment." Should she mention that grey jeep? No, Sharon

61

would think she was as paranoid as Susan Chambers. "Have the police confirmed our murdered woman *is* Western Energy's Ellen Chambers?" she asked, voice business-like.

"Yes, and the media are running the story. Simon's handling the Aussie media, and London the UK lot. I've forwarded his updated press lines to your laptop. He wants you to do media interviews at The Palms once you've had a chance to talk to the police and Susan Chambers."

"Of course."

"The High Commissioner has been trying to call you, Jess. With all the brouhaha about the gas deal, he's worried this consular case will be tricky. He said he would have flown direct to Brisbane from Perth to join you but he has to be back in Canberra for our Beloved Leader's visit."

Jess smiled. The High Commissioner would never refer to the Foreign Secretary as our Beloved Leader; not least, because they'd spent their careers in opposing political parties.

"Anyway," Sharon went on, "he said he'll leave things in your capable hands for the time being. But do call him... any time."

"Right." Jess wouldn't hesitate to do that. Unlike Nigel, the High Commissioner had been a prominent UK politician before getting the Canberra job. He had nothing left to prove.

"Oh, and I've spoken to Inspector Sangster." Sharon made a huffing noise. "He wants to see you as soon as you get there. It sounded more like a summons than a request to me. Anyway, I said you'd meet him in The Palms reception at 2pm. Hope that's okay?"

"That's fine."

Sharon paused. "You know, Jess, he seems a bit of a... difficult character."

Jess gave an exaggerated sigh. "What with the mysterious Susan Chambers and the imperious Inspector Sangster, it looks like I'm going to have to deploy all my diplomatic charm today."

Sharon laughed. "By the way, Simon says to tell you Canberra are sending two Federal Agents to Brisbane to help with the murder investigation."

"Are they now?" That must have something to do with the corruption allegations and that elusive intelligence report, she thought. But there was no point asking Sharon to get a look at it and report back. It would be highly classified. If the circulation hadn't included her, Sharon wouldn't have access to it either. But Jess had another idea. "Sharon, have a look through the electronic telegrams from London and Beijing over the last couple of months and see if there's anything in the archive about Ellen Chambers, or a Chen Xiamen."

"Who's he?"

"The lead Chinese negotiator on the LNG contract with Western Energy."

There was a pause. "What am I looking for, Jess?"

Jess hesitated, she couldn't discuss it with Sharon on an open phone line. "I don't know yet, but I'd like you to do a search."

"Okay." There was a pause. "Is everything all right, Jess, only... well, you sounded a bit strange when you answered?"

That grey jeep flashed into her mind again. "Everything's fine, Sharon."

"Good. Speak to you later then."

"Right." Jess hung up and started the engine again. Fine drops of water began misting the windscreen, and she turned on the wipers to clear it. Pulling out of the parking area, she slipped back into the stream of traffic. As she drove, the rain started to fall harder. She was relieved after a few more miles to see her exit sign. Signalling, she turned off the freeway, then slowed and checked her rear-view mirror to see if anyone had followed her off. No one. Satisfied, she drove through the underpass in the direction of the coast.

Two miles later, she turned left at a sign for The Palms resort and found herself driving along a narrow lane, with high hedges lining both sides. The misty rain had given way to a squall that seemed to have blown in from nowhere, blasting blinding rain onto the windscreen. Turning the wipers on full speed, she rubbed the inside of the windscreen with the back of her hand to clear the mist. The draught from the air conditioner blew into her face and up her skirt, chilling her.

Suddenly, blinding headlights came straight at her through the murk. She slammed her foot on the brake and yanked the steering wheel to the left. Tyres skidding on the wet surface, the car spun round and bumped up onto the grass verge, the under-tray dragging along the ground, until the car slithered to a stop in the hedge.

She sat for a moment, stunned. Pushing the gear into park, she flung open her door. *"Idiot!"* she shouted into the pouring rain.

But the other car had disappeared.

Unbuckling her seatbelt, she got out to inspect the car for damage. She could see scratches etched into the paintwork on the bonnet and left wing by the hedge. She crouched down and checked under the car. Everything *looked* all right.

Soaking wet, she got back into the car and turned on the ignition. Relieved when the engine fired up, she reversed out of the hedge and off the grass verge. If she hadn't reacted so quickly and swerved, that car would have hit her for sure. Was it that grey jeep again?

She pushed the gear into drive and continued down the lane. Nervous now, she kept checking her rear-view mirror. But there were no lights behind.

Finally, through her rain-smeared windscreen, she saw the hotel up ahead. Inching the car through the entry gates, she manoeuvred into a space in the car park and switched off the engine. She sat listening to the rain hammering on the roof. The storm's red and purple sky gave an eerie glow. The wind swirled around, moaning and rocking the car gently, as if something was closing in on her.

She felt so alone.

Closing her eyes, she leant forward and rested her head on the steering wheel. Her head spun as she remembered the wild, scorching flames shooting up into the sky.

G'bye mummy!

9

Jess struggled through the hotel room door with her luggage and threw her handbag onto the bed. The room was great. All white and light, with the turquoise sea filling the window frame like a colourful oil painting. Everything looked so clean and elegant. Spirits lifted, she walked over to the window and gazed out at green lawns lined with magenta and purple bougainvillea. The squall had passed now, and the sea shimmered under the sun's direct gaze.

Her eyes rested on a group of teenagers around the swimming pool. Lined up against the perimeter railings, they were taking it in turns to run across the wooden deck and cannonball into the water. Their infectious laughter made her smile. Everything seemed normal again after the storm and that idiot driving her off the road.

She pulled her mobile out of her pocket, and dialled Nigel's direct line.

"*At last!* You took your time returning my call, Jessic*aah*."

"I was driving. I've just got to The Palms."

"She *is* Western Energy's Ellen Chambers." Nigel's voice boomed in her ear. "I've talked to John Langhurst. He's devastated of course. And he's offered to help, so keep that in mind. And I've talked to Queensland's Deputy Police Commissioner. You'll need to keep in close touch with

Inspector Sangster, he's leading the investigation. Make sure you see him before anyone else."

"I've got an appointment with him at 2pm."

"You'll need to see Susan Chambers this afternoon too. Have the media phoned?"

"Yes."

"Simon's handled them so far. You take over now. Do a press conference later. Make sure they know you've travelled from Canberra to assist the police and next of kin and..."

"Nigel," she intervened. "If you've spoken to John Langhurst, you'll know Ellen Chambers was in Brisbane to attend Western Energy's Conference."

"Yes. John Langhurst's up there too. And CEO Richard Price."

She bristled. So why didn't he tell her that straightaway? Why did she have to drag every piece of information out of him?

"Now keep me informed, Jessic*aah* and..."

"Nigel..." She hesitated, wondering whether to ask him about that intelligence report on an open phone line.

"And don't forget the Foreign Secretary's here... By the book. Right?"

The phone went dead in her ear as he hung up.

Bloody man! She stood staring at the phone, wondering whether to call him back. No, she'd ask Simon instead. She'd get more sense out of him... or would she? Nothing seemed certain any more.

Throwing her mobile on the bed, she shook out her clothes and hung them in the wardrobe. Catching sight of her bedraggled hair and damp skirt in the mirror, she picked up her wash bag and walked into the bathroom to tidy up after the soaking she'd got outside.

Ten minutes later, she stood in front of the dressing-table, touching up her make-up. She turned and looked about. There was something familiar about this hotel room. What was it? Then she spotted the gilt mirror on the wall by the bed. The fern leaf design on its ornate frame was exactly the same as the one in that hotel in Paris, with Jack, on their fifth wedding anniversary. That's when he'd bought her the silver hair clasp. He'd never been one for celebrating birthdays or anniversaries, so that weekend had been a real surprise.

A special weekend, for my special girl, he'd said.

And it *had* turned out to be *very* special. He'd given her the best present of all in Paris... *Amy!*

Jess pulled the photo of Jack and Amy out of her bag and placed it on the bedside cabinet. *Now* she felt better.

Slipping her laptop out of her briefcase, she laid it on the desk by the window, powered it up and connected to the hotel wireless internet. Simon's media lines popped up in her inbox. She skimmed through, and downloaded them onto her memory stick. Logging off, she picked up her bag and mobile and hurried out of the door to get a copy printed in the business centre on the ground floor.

At the end of the corridor, she pressed the button for the lifts and waited. But they seemed stuck on the ground floor. Impatient to get on, she swung through the stairwell door and ran down the stairs, rehearsing the press lines over and over in her head.

Distracted, she pushed through what she thought was the door to the ground floor.

"Stop right there!" A deep voice halted her in her tracks.

She froze.

A man in a grey suit glared at her. "Didn't you see the *sign*?"

Turning, she saw a police Do Not Enter sign by the door. *Oh God!* She'd blundered into a cordoned off corridor. "I'm sorry." She looked back into steely grey eyes, "I thought this was the ground floor."

"Please leave." The man turned his back on her while the other officers looked on.

"Can I just introduce..."

"*Ma'am.*" He spun round. "This is a crime scene. *Please leave.*" He clapped his hands. "Come on guys," he said to a group of policemen who stood staring at her, "back to work."

Watching him disappear into one of the bedrooms, Jess knew instantly it was Ellen Chambers' room. Much as she wanted to talk to the police, Jess knew this wasn't the time. Turning, she went back through the door, and bumped straight into a small Asian woman on the stairs. "Oh, sorry."

"He rude." The woman jerked her head at the door.

Jess looked at the woman. With her neatly-tied long, black hair and blue uniform, she had to be a cleaner.

"I find this." The woman stood, nervous, gripping something with both hands. "In dead woman room."

It looked like a diary to Jess. "You'd better give it to the police."

But the woman pushed the diary at her. "I clean room this morning before I know she dead."

"The police," Jess said, slowly, while pointing at the door. "Give it to the police."

"I take spare blanket out top of wardrobe to change. When I get to laundry I find this inside." The woman shoved the diary into Jess's hands. "I no want trouble." And she darted up the stairs.

"Hey, wait," Jess shouted after her. But the woman had already disappeared through the stairwell door on the next floor. Jess could hardly blame her for running off, after the blast she'd just got from that oaf. She was about to go back through the door and give him the diary when she stopped. Did she really want to give him another chance to be rude to her? Glancing at her watch, she saw it was 1.30pm. In half an hour she had an appointment with Inspector Sangster. She'd give it to him instead.

Mind made up, she tucked the diary in her bag and walked down the stairs to the ground floor.

★

Collecting a copy of the press lines, Jess walked out of the business centre and into the lobby. She could have been in an up-market hotel in any Western city. Grey marble covered the floor and pillars, and a decorative fireplace stood at the far end, with several plump-cushioned sofas and chairs scattered around for guests to sink into. Sitting down at a glass-topped table, she scanned the faces looking for Susan Chambers. Ellen had looked slim and attractive in that newspaper photo, with shoulder-length blonde hair. Would Susan look like her sister?

Behind the wood-panelled desk, a receptionist was checking-in a group of noisy Indonesian tourists. She looked miserable. All the staff did. They kept giving each other nervous glances, and huddling in groups to chat whenever they got the chance. Jess could feel the tension. Hardly surprising since a guest had been viciously murdered in the grounds, and the police were swarming all over.

As she sat observing, goose bumps rose on her arms. She felt a presence, as if someone was watching her. She looked up, but couldn't see anyone particularly interested in her. Uneasy, she pulled out her mobile and dialled Simon. His phone switched to voicemail. "I'm at The Palms, Simon. Call me back please."

She looked around again and rubbed her arms to get rid of the chill. Sitting there idly, she remembered the diary in her bag. She pulled it out and laid it on the table. The cover was made of red leather, with the year in gold lettering. It looked expensive. Opening the front cover, she saw Ellen Chambers' name and contact details written by hand. Jess hesitated. It seemed wrong to delve into Ellen's personal diary, macabre even, given the circumstances. But she was so drawn to it, she couldn't help but flick through the pages.

The first thing she noticed was Ellen's neat and legible handwriting. Every one of her appointments had a precise name, with contact details and meeting venue recorded next to the date and time. Ellen Chambers had been a highly organised woman, she thought. Nothing had been left to memory or chance. Reading on, Jess saw that Ellen had spent alternate months in the UK and Australia since the beginning of the year. And she'd visited Beijing at the end of March and... oh, that was interesting, she'd only just returned from a second trip to Beijing.

Reaching the back page, Jess's eyes stopped on several lines of random letters and numbers written in Ellen's neat handwriting. She studied them but they didn't seem to make any sense. She counted the lines. Six in total; but what did they mean? Were they some kind of code? Or passwords perhaps?

As she sat mulling things over in her logical mind, something seemed out of place. She flicked back through the pages, studying all the entries as she went. Then she saw it. Ellen had entered every appointment in the same precise way, except for regular entries marked TH that had no name or contact details beside them. Who or what was TH, Jess wondered.

"Oh!" A sudden movement made her jump, and she looked up at the heart-shaped face of a young woman who'd slipped into the chair opposite. She wasn't wearing a scrap of make-up and looked almost boyish with spiky blonde hair that stood fashionably on end. The young woman flicked a nervous glance over her shoulder and turned back.

Jess smiled. "Hello. I'm Jessica Turner," she said, holding out her hand. "You must be Susan Chambers."

Feverish, blue eyes stared at Jess. "You *must* help me find my sister's killer."

Jess dropped her hand. "That's a job for the police."

Susan struggled to keep her voice down. "My sister's dead. She's a British citizen. I want to know what *you're* doing about it."

Jess put her hand on Ellen's diary, bracing herself for the rage that might come flying her way like spewing lava from a volcano. Relatives reacted differently to tragic news about their loved ones. Some collapsed with grief, while others vented their fury on someone else. And who better than a Government official? "The Queensland Police are leading the investigation," Jess said, calmly. "We're on Australian territory, so the investigation is their responsibility."

"Why are *you* here, then?"

"To liaise with the police, and check that everything is being done in accordance with Australian law and practice." Jess could hear herself trotting out the official line. "And I wanted to see you, Susan."

Susan glanced over at the door. "You *must* get Scotland Yard over."

The fear in Susan's eyes when she turned back threw Jess for a moment. What was the girl so afraid of? "They *could* help, but only if the Australian police ask them to,"

Jess replied, "for example, if part of their investigation took them to the UK, or involved somebody living in the UK. But, as I explained, it's the responsibility of the Australian police to..."

"*No! They* got her killed."

"The police?"

"Listen... *please.*" Susan leant towards her. "I saw Ellen at the Convention Centre yesterday. I thought I'd surprise her, I hadn't seen her for ages. But when I got there she was *really* upset. She said she was in trouble."

Jess's mind flashed to the corruption allegations. "What kind of trouble?" she asked, warily.

"I don't *know.*" Susan wrung her hands. "Ellen started to tell me. She said something about having some *evidence.* But then she just clammed up. Said she didn't want to put me in danger by telling me." Susan got more agitated. "I said I'd help her; I'd go with her to the police. But that's when she got really upset and blurted out we couldn't trust them."

"The police?"

"*Yes.* Ellen said over and over it wasn't safe to go to the police. She begged me not to either."

"And you've no idea why?" Again, Jess thought of those corruption allegations. Susan clearly didn't know her sister had been under police surveillance when she was murdered. But had Ellen found out? Is that the reason she was afraid of the police?

Susan's eyes flashed. "Oh, I know what you're thinking. But Ellen wasn't crazy or paranoid. She was a professional woman in a high-powered job. If she said it wasn't safe to go to the police, then she believed it."

Jess couldn't argue with that logic.

"The money is the trail." Susan's top lip quivered. "That's the last thing Ellen said to me. *If anything happens to me, Susan, the money is the trail.*" Susan caught her breath. "But I've no idea what she was talking about." She held her hands together on the table to stop them shaking. "I should have stayed with her... insisted she tell me... *done* something."

Seeing the despair on that young face, Jess laid her hand over Susan's to comfort her. But Susan jerked it away. Then her shoulders slumped and her eyes brimmed with tears.

The money is the trail? Jess's mind flashed to that old Washington chestnut – illegal intelligence activities by the Nixon administration. What had Ellen been trying to tell her sister? That there was some kind of cover up going on? How mad was that? Jess glanced at Susan. She only looked about 20; and far too young to remember the Watergate scandal. And Jess wasn't going to plant any wild thoughts into her head. Anyway, her priority now was to get more information about the deceased. "Susan, can you tell me more about your sister?" she asked, gently.

Susan bit her lip to stop it quivering. "She's all the family I have... had. Mum and Dad are dead." A single tear squeezed out of her eye, and she brushed it away angrily.

"Why was Ellen staying in this hotel and not with you?" Jess asked.

"She said it was easier to stay here for business, but..." Susan stopped and stared into Jess's eyes as if she were sizing her up, then she went on: "But I think there was another reason."

"Go on."

"Well, my sister was *very* ambitious. All she ever thought about was work. She loved her job." Susan's face softened as she talked about Ellen. "She is... was... Western Energy's Group Finance Director, you know."

Jess nodded.

"And the Chairman had asked her to come over to work permanently in Australia." She looked up proudly. "He wanted her to be the CEO."

"Really?" Jess remembered the Company website. "Don't they already have one?"

"Yes, Richard Price. But he's a liability." Susan pursed her lips. "He's got a drink problem; knocked someone down while over the limit. There was such a stink. We did a piece about it in the *Echo*. Ellen said the bad publicity was the last straw for the Chairman. He's been wanting to get rid of Richard ever since."

"I see. So did Ellen *want* the CEO's job?"

Susan nodded. "She seemed over the moon about it, at first. And she definitely wanted to move to Oz."

"*At first?*"

Susan shrugged. "Ellen seemed to change recently. She seemed happier, more relaxed somehow." Susan lowered her voice. "I think there was a new man around."

Ah, thought Jess. "Didn't she introduce you to him?"

Susan frowned. "That's the funny thing. I was *sure* she had a new man, but she never talked about him or brought him home." She stared at Jess. "I thought, well, I thought it must be someone she didn't want me, or anyone, to know about – if you get my drift."

Jess nodded.

"But then, if he was married," Susan continued, "Ellen *knew* she could trust me." She slumped down in the chair and stared morosely into the distance.

There was a pause while Jess turned everything over in her mind, wondering what consular assistance she could give Susan. "Do you have any family in Brisbane? Cousins, or anyone else?"

Susan shook her head.

"What about in the UK?"

Susan shook her head again. "I'd like to let Ellen's friends in the UK know what's happened, but I don't have their contact details."

Jess felt the palm of her hand shift on the diary. The address book at the back would surely have them?

Susan caught the movement and looked down. "That's *Ellen's!* I gave it to her last Christmas." Susan's eyes narrowed. "How did *you* get hold of my sister's diary?"

"A hotel cleaner found it in Ellen's room and gave it to me on the stairs," Jess said in a level voice. "I'm going to give it to Inspector Sangster."

"*No!*" Susan grabbed the diary and clutched it to her chest. She looked over her shoulder at the door again, as if she were about to bolt.

"Put the diary down, Susan."

But Susan clung onto it.

Trying to distract her, Jess asked: "Do you live permanently in Brisbane, Susan?"

Susan shook her head. "I've been in Australia a year on a training placement at the *Echo*. Look, are you going to help me find Ellen's killer, or not?"

"I've already explained that's a job for the police."

"*Please!* You *must* help me."

The pain in Susan's eyes unnerved Jess for a moment and she looked away only to see that rude oaf from the first floor heading in their direction. Her heart sank when he stopped at their table. "Susan Chambers?" He looked at them both in turn.

Susan tensed at her name.

"Inspector Tom Sangster, Queensland Police Service." He extended his hand to her. "I'm leading the investigation into your sister's death. I'm truly sorry for your loss."

Susan ignored his hand. "Have you found her murderer yet?" she asked, accusingly.

Only the slightest hesitation suggested he was surprised at Susan's reaction. "I assure you we're working hard on it."

"What exactly *are* you doing?"

He dropped his hand. "Look, can we go somewhere private to talk, Miss Chambers?"

Jess stood up. "You both stay here and talk. I'll wait outside on the terrace."

"*No.*" Susan pointed at Jess. "You can say whatever you want in front of *her.*"

The Inspector extended his hand to Jess. "We've met, I think?"

Jess noticed the pink spots on his cheeks. Was he embarrassed or cross? She shook his hand. "Jessica Turner, British Consul." The surprised look in his eyes gave her some satisfaction. Over his shoulder, she saw another policeman standing at reception, waving an envelope. "Is that for you, Inspector?"

Sangster turned and beckoned his colleague over.

The officer approached and held out his hand to Jess. "DS Dalton," he said.

Dalton's hand felt clammy as Jess shook it. Carrying more weight than he should for his height, he looked like he was suffering for it. But he sounded so sincere when he expressed his condolences that Jess warmed to him.

When he turned to have a private conversation with the Inspector, Jess whispered to Susan. "You have to accept they're responsible for the investigation. Tell them everything you've just told me. It's the only way."

Susan looked devastated. "If you won't help me, I've no one else to turn to."

Her words struck right at Jess's core. "Of course I'm going to help you, Susan, but you must talk to the police first. Now," Jess held her hand out for the diary. "I'll be waiting outside on the terrace for you."

But Susan hugged the diary tighter. "I'll give it to Inspector Sangster."

Jess's ringing mobile distracted her and she checked the caller ID. *The High Commissioner!* "I have to take this call, Susan," she said. "Now don't worry. I'll just be outside. We can talk again when you've finished with the Inspector." And with that, Jess hurried out of the door to the terrace, where the mobile signal was stronger.

10

He drove through the traffic, keeping his eyes glued to the target ahead like the expert he knew he was. Although he couldn't see through the black Mercedes' tinted windows, he knew the target was alone and driving himself. He couldn't believe his luck.

He blinked when the sun came out from behind a cloud, and his foot hesitated over the accelerator. Broad daylight wasn't a good time for what he was about to do. But he couldn't wait for nightfall. He had to stop that bastard before he could do any more damage.

He looked at his watch – 2.15.

Pulling the peak of his cap down over his eyes, he pressed down on the accelerator and moved back into the inside lane to keep a car between him and his prey.

Look at you in your limousine, driving along like you own the world. You should have been happy, you know. You had everything. But it still wasn't enough. Oh no, you wanted more.

As the traffic lights ahead turned red, a woman stepped out in front of him to cross the road. He had to stamp on the brakes to avoid hitting her. The jeep screeched to a stop.

The woman's dark eyes glared at him through the windscreen.

He frowned at the familiar image. Dark, staring eyes. Her... lying dead on the kitchen floor. He could feel the knife... the blood.

Why was he thinking about *her* again now? He *had* to focus. Seeing the cars ahead start moving, he slipped the jeep into drive and started following again. When the black Mercedes turned left and began to slow down, he almost smiled. *Now* he knew exactly where the bastard was going. And he was just in time by the look of it.

The Mercedes pulled up alongside the kerb. He stopped a short distance behind and pushed the gear into park. This was good. Divine justice. He'd do it right outside their front door. He pulled on his gloves, and reached under his jacket to draw his gun. Leaving the engine running, he got out of the driver's seat, walked calmly up to the Mercedes, opened the back passenger door and slid inside.

Before the bastard could even turn around, he pressed the barrel of the gun to the back of his head and ducked down behind the seat.

"*Greed,*" he hissed, as he pulled the trigger. "*That was your mistake!*"

The silent bullet made an exhilarating sound as it thudded into flesh and bone.

He waited for that ecstatic ripple of excitement to shiver right through him... and waited. Nothing.

Angry and frustrated, he looked at the body slumped over the steering wheel and shoved the gun back into its holster. Grabbing the bastard's hair, he pulled him back into the upright position with one hand and drew his knife from its sheath with the other.

You wanted more, you greedy bastard. Well, here it is!

11

Jess leant back in her wrought-iron chair and looked up at the grape vines overhead. Their twisted branches, lying dormant after an August winter pruning, crept into all the crevices of the wooden trellis. She could imagine their green leaves fanning out to provide shade for the tables and chairs on the back terrace in summer.

She turned back to her laptop and forced herself to get on with her report. It had to be on desks when London opened.

Dear Colleagues,

DEATH OF BRITISH CITIZEN, ELLEN CHAMBERS: UPDATE

I have arrived at Queensland's Palms Resort. The police confirm Ellen Chambers, Western Energy's Group Finance Director, was found dead on the Resort beach at around 5am this morning. Inspector Tom Sangster, Queensland Police Service, who is leading the investigation, has announced a full murder enquiry.

Ellen Chambers was resident in the UK and worked at Western Energy's London HQ. She'd been visiting Australia regularly over the past year to take part in the negotiation of a lucrative Liquefied Natural Gas (LNG) deal with the Chinese.

Ellen was in Brisbane to attend her Company Conference when she was killed. The Conference opens today at the Convention Centre and runs until Thursday. The Chairman of Western Energy, John Langhurst, and CEO Richard Price are in town for the Conference too.

A piercing scream rang out.

Jess jumped up, but it was only children splashing each other in the shallows on the beach. Her mobile rang.

"Hi, Jess."

"Simon. You sound breathless."

"I've ducked out of the Parliament lunch to call you back. I haven't got long."

"Right. Well, I've got a bone to pick with you," she said, frostily. "Why didn't you tell me the Australian Federal Police were investigating Ellen Chambers when she was murdered?"

"*What?*"

"You should have *told* me she was under police surveillance, along with Chen Xiamen."

"Hold on..."

But Jess was well into her stride now. "And you should have told me about that intelligence report. I expect that sort of treatment from Nigel, but *not* from you."

"Jess," Simon said, patiently. "I've no idea *what* you're talking about."

That took the wind out of her sails. "Oh, when Derek Marshall said Nigel had been personally briefed about it by the Australians, I assumed you knew too."

"Well, I don't," he huffed. "And what's Derek got to do with it?"

"He was on my plane this morning, accompanying the Chinese LNG delegation to Brisbane. They're attending

Western Energy's Conference, by the way. It opens today. That's why Ellen Chambers was in Queensland."

"I see. So what's this police investigation all about? What have Ellen and Chen done?"

"I'd hoped *you*'d be able to tell *me*." She heard that familiar clicking noise again and hesitated. "I'd better end this call."

"*Wait!* I need to know."

"I think my phone's being tapped. I noticed it immediately I arrived in Brisbane."

"Well, if it's the Australians, they know everything anyway."

That's true, she thought, and she had no other way of communicating with Simon in the field. "Derek said the Australian Federal Police launched an investigation into Chen and Ellen after receiving sensitive intelligence concerning corruption allegations in a classified report from London. I don't know what's going on, but the source of that information was our Embassy in Beijing."

"*Our* Embassy?"

"Yes."

"And you say Nigel was briefed."

"According to Derek."

There was a pause.

"*Now* it's all beginning to make sense." Simon sounded cross. "All through lunch Nigel insisted on asking questions about the LNG deal when it was clear the Australians didn't want to talk about it. In the end, their Foreign Affairs Head Paul Robinson got really shirty and our Foreign Secretary had to intervene to calm things down."

"*Really?*"

"Skilful he was. Passed it off as a joke, saying he didn't want to get into a fist-fight at his first Australian engagement. Put Nigel well and truly back in his box."

"I'd loved to have seen that," Jess said, dryly. "But why would Nigel do that? What's the LNG deal got to do with us?"

"*God knows.* I thought he was having some kind of brainstorm." Simon sighed. "Are you *sure* about this, Jess? I mean, it does sound a bit odd."

Am I sure? She bristled. "I'm *sure* I know what Derek Marshall told me."

There was a pause.

"I have to go," Simon whispered. "The Foreign Secretary's calling me back to the meeting."

"Right."

"I'll be stuck in meetings all afternoon. I'm taking a note for the record, so I can't duck out. Then there's the dinner this evening; I'm taking a record of that too. But I'll find out what's going on and phone you either before or after dinner." He paused. "You sure you're okay, Jess?"

"I'm fine."

"Good. Well take care." And he rang off.

Honestly! Jess hung up and leant back in her chair. Did he think she was *imagining* things? To be fair, she had to agree it didn't make much sense. Why would Nigel keep that intelligence report to himself? And why upset the Australians about the LNG deal in front of the Foreign Secretary? Still, the fact that Simon hadn't known anything about it made her feel better. Then she immediately felt bad about being so offhand with him.

The hotel door creaked open, and she looked round as footsteps came running out.

"Did she come this way?" Sergeant Dalton panted.

Jess looked at him.

"Susan Chambers. Did she come this way?"

"She's in the lobby with Inspector Sangster."

He shook his head. "*She's run off.*" He turned and hurried back into the hotel.

Jess rushed after him. She'd just reached the lobby when she heard Sangster shout: "Get after her, Dave. She's driven off in her car."

Dalton darted across the lobby.

"*Wait*," Jess called out. "I'll come with you."

"*No*." Sangster put a restraining hand on her arm.

She glared at him.

"*Please* stay here," he said. "Susan may come back to see you."

Jess was furious. But not with him, with herself for not staying with Susan. *Oh God!* Her stomach tightened as she looked at the empty table. "Did she give you the diary?"

Sangster stared at her. "What diary?"

"Susan's got her sister's diary. A cleaner found it hidden in Ellen's hotel room this morning, before the room was sealed off."

His steely eyes seemed to pierce right through her.

Jess met his stare. "I bumped into the cleaner on the stairs, just after I'd seen you. She shoved the diary into my hands and ran off. I was planning to give it to you at our meeting. Of course I didn't know then *you* were Inspector Sangster." She paused. "The diary was on that table." She pointed to the one she was sitting at earlier. "Susan grabbed it."

"I *need* that diary for the investigation."

"And you'd have it now if you hadn't scared her off."

They stood staring at each other, until he looked away and pulled out his mobile.

All Jess's instincts were telling her to go after Susan, except she didn't know where she lived. She didn't even have her phone number. Why hadn't she got Susan's contact details straightaway? That was the first thing she'd normally do. Was it the fear on Susan's face that had distracted her? Or that worry about the police?

Realising there was nothing she could do, she left Sangster on the phone and went back out to the terrace. At least Susan had *her* mobile number. She only hoped she'd get in touch again.

Sitting back down, she forced herself to finish her report.

The victim's next of kin is her (British) sister, Susan Chambers. She lives in Brisbane and works as a journalist for the Brisbane Echo. She has no other family in the UK, so London do not need to contact anyone. But Susan's behaviour is worrying. She came to the hotel to see me but took off in her car when the police arrived. She told me her sister Ellen thought she was in some kind of trouble when she was murdered.

Jess stuck to the basic facts because the email wouldn't be encrypted and could be intercepted over an open line. She didn't include anything about the corruption allegations because of the intelligence source. Should she mention Susan's distrust of the police, or about her snatching Ellen's diary? No, better not.

Finishing up, she typed:

There is heavy media interest in this case here. Grateful if London could let me know about any UK press interest and email any articles or links.
Jess Turner
Consul, British High Commission, Canberra.

She was just pressing 'send', when she heard the hotel door creak open again. She jumped up when Inspector Sangster walked out. "Have you found her?"

He shook his head.

She sighed. "The poor girl's mad with grief. Have you got her mobile number?"

"No, but we've got her home address. A couple of guys are on their way round now in case she goes back there."

"What on earth made her run off like that?"

Sangster scratched his head. "I was trying to get her to talk about her sister." He paused. "When I asked her if Ellen had seemed troubled or upset over recent weeks, Susan said she had to go to the rest room. She got up, walked across the lobby, and then darted out the door."

Jess gave him a level stare. "She's frightened of you... oh, I don't mean you personally... just the police."

His eyes narrowed. "Is that what she said?"

Jess nodded, watching him carefully. "She told me Ellen was afraid of the police too."

He frowned.

His reaction puzzled Jess. Surely he knew the Federal Police had Ellen under surveillance? Or did he?

There was an awkward silence while he checked his watch. "I *was* planning to show you the spot where Ellen Chambers died," he said.

"Don't worry, if you have to get back."

"I've got five minutes."

"Well, I *would* appreciate it." Jess knew it was important to get the details correct for the British authorities and for families of victims who relied on her for information when their loved ones died overseas. It was as if she were their last link with them; and she felt the weight of that responsibility. She got up and followed him down the path.

Stopping 40 metres from the jetty, Sangster pulled a notepad out of his pocket and stood staring at the pages. He was concentrating so hard, Jess didn't move either. It hadn't occurred to her when she'd blundered onto the first floor that he was a policeman because he looked more like a businessman, or the hotel manager even, in his smart suit and silk tie. He certainly didn't look like an

Australian cop. And he didn't have the same pronounced Queensland accent as Dalton. That set him apart. Where was he from, she wondered? He was quite a bit taller than her – probably around six foot. And, despite his grey hair, she guessed he must only be in his mid to late 40s.

Jess waited a while, but he continued to stare at his notepad. Impatient, she glanced over to see what was so interesting. Her eyes widened. He was looking at *drawings!*

"I like to sketch victims and crime scenes," he said, as if reading her mind.

I bet they love you down at the station, she thought. But then he didn't seem the type of man who cared much about what others thought of him. She looked at her watch; she didn't have time for this.

*

Sangster shut his notepad and started walking again. He didn't look at the British Consul, but he was conscious of her keeping pace beside him. It had never occurred to him that the Consul would be a woman, although he didn't know why. She looked young, in her mid-30s perhaps? Attractive too. But he wasn't warming to Jessica Turner. He'd caught her disbelieving stare at his sketches. Still, he wouldn't hold that against her; most people reacted in the same way. No, it was more her impassive face and eyes. She was way too cool and aloof. Mind you, he *had* given her a blast for walking into that sealed-off corridor earlier. Maybe she was still put out about that? "Drawing helps me focus on the precise details," he heard himself say. "Once I've drawn something, it stays in my memory." He wondered why he felt the need to explain.

She didn't reply, which irritated him even more.

Reaching the jetty, he jumped down onto the sand and stared at the spot where the body had been found. He felt comfortable being at the crime scene again. "This is where Ellen Chambers was found." He pointed to a flat area. "Lying face down, with her left cheek exposed. Her face was covered with cuts and bruises. She'd been badly beaten." He looked up at the Consul. Did she just shiver? He knew she was listening to his every word because she kept jotting notes in her pad.

"Was it a very violent attack?" she asked.

"Frenzied." He watched for another reaction, but there was none this time.

"So what do you think happened?" she asked.

"Well." He pulled himself back up onto the jetty and stood next to her. "We reckon she was attacked up here. She put up a fight. They both went over the side and struggled in the water. The killer held her face under and drowned her." He nodded, as if reinforcing all the details in his mind and looked at the Consul. Her eyes were unreadable, and he found that somehow unsettling.

"A lad called Danny Burton found her. He works here. Gardening, beach attendant. That sort of thing. Cocky little shit." He glanced back, apologetically. But the Consul wasn't listening to him now, she was staring down at the spot where Ellen Chambers had died. And this time, he definitely saw her shiver. *Not quite the Ice Queen, then.*

Reacting to her mood, he said nothing. He looked all around, breathing in the atmosphere. But when he turned back, the Consul was studying him, which made him feel uncomfortable. "Who might have done something like this?" she asked.

"Difficult to say at the moment."

"What's your gut instinct?"

He wasn't used to being asked that. "Well," he hesitated, "we haven't found a handbag or mobile, so robbery could have been a motive. But she still had her expensive watch on."

"A sex attack, perhaps?"

"No immediate sign of that. But we'll find out for sure at the autopsy."

She nodded. "Can I have a copy of the autopsy report when it's ready?"

She was back to her calm, assured self now. A closed book. "Yes," he replied.

"So, you said the attack was frenzied, Inspector. If we could rule out robbery and sexual assault, what else could we be looking at?"

He didn't want to commit himself. "It's difficult to say at the moment."

But she wasn't satisfied with that. "You said the attack was frenzied. Doesn't that suggest the killer was in a rage?"

"Or high on drugs or alcohol."

"Mm." She didn't look convinced. "Could Ellen Chambers have *known* her killer, do you think?"

"Maybe she had an *appointment* with him?" He was still furious about that diary.

His sarcasm wasn't lost on her. "There were no appointments in her diary for Sunday night, if that's what you're getting at." The Consul settled her cool gaze on him. "There was a lunch on Sunday for the Conference delegates who arrived in Brisbane early. It was at the Riverbank Hotel. But nothing for Sunday night."

Of course she'd have read the diary; he should have thought of that before. "Did you see anything else interesting?"

"Well," she paused. "Ellen Chambers was an organised woman, with neat, legible handwriting."

He waited. The Consul seemed to be focusing on a spot close to his right shoulder as she spoke, as if she were seeing the pages of the diary in front of her.

"And she'd recorded all her appointments so carefully, with the full name and contact details of all her interlocutors and the venue. Except... well, I noticed the initials TH entered on various dates." She frowned. "Just those initials, with no name or contact details. Those appointments only seemed to take place whenever she was in Brisbane."

He noticed the Consul bite her lip. Was she was holding something back? Again he waited.

"I was wondering if they were the initials of a boyfriend or lover," she went on. "If Ellen had wanted to keep his identity and their meetings secret, she wouldn't have included any other details, would she?"

Sangster nodded. He had to hand it to Jessica Turner, she was observant and precise. "Did you spot anything else in the diary?"

"Yes, but I don't know if it's of any relevance." She hesitated. "On the back page, there were six lines of words and numbers all jumbled up. They looked like codes... or computer passwords. Something like that. But I'm afraid I can't remember them." She looked up. "Do you think Ellen Chambers' murder could be linked to her job at Western Energy? Only the LNG contract *is* high profile and lucrative."

"It's possible." He wondered whether to ask her about that British intelligence report. She *had* to know about it, and those corruption allegations *were* his only line of enquiry at the moment. Tired of beating around the bush, he said: "Are you asking me if I think her murder is connected to those corruption allegations?"

She nodded, but volunteered nothing.

Now, he was annoyed he'd brought it up. "I'm waiting to be briefed about that. Two Canberra Federal Agents are on their way as we speak." He knew he sounded blunt, but he didn't like being played. "I'm sure you already know all about *that*."

Her eyes narrowed; it was the first time he'd seen a flash of steel in them. But before she could say anything, his mobile rang.

"Tom?" The DC's voice sounded breathless. "Get back here, quickly. There's been another murder... Anthony Harris, the Federal Minister... he's been shot."

"*Shot?*" For a minute, Sangster couldn't quite take in what he'd heard.

"Yes. We found him dead in his ministerial car outside Police HQ. He was on his way to see me."

"*Jesus!*" He looked at the British Consul, who stood pale-faced, watching him.

"Is it Susan Chambers?" she whispered.

He shook his head. "I'm on my way," he said into his mobile and hung up.

"What's happened?" the Consul asked, urgently.

"It's Anthony Harris. He's been shot dead in Brisbane."

"*Oh my God!*" She clasped her hand to her throat. "I only saw him a few hours ago at the airport. What happened?"

"That's all I know," he said.

There was a pause while they both took in the news.

"Is his murder connected to Ellen Chambers?" she asked, quietly.

"I really don't know. Look I'm sorry, but I *must* go."

"Of course."

He hesitated. "Will you ring me immediately if you hear from Susan?"

"Yes. And will you ring me when you know more about the Minister's murder?"

He nodded and sprinted up the path towards the hotel, his mind racing in every direction. Although he was in a hurry, at the top of the path, he stopped. For some reason, he felt uneasy about leaving the British Consul at the crime scene alone after that shocking news. But when he turned round, she was standing with her back to him, staring out to sea. She looked a solitary figure, lost in her own thoughts. He thought back to her cool gaze and guarded eyes. There was something unsettling about Jessica Turner that he couldn't work out. And that made her interesting.

12

"I assure you we'll be there in 15 minutes." Sangster hung up and sat gripping his mobile.

"Is that the DC stressin' out?"

"Can you blame him?"

"I still can't believe it." Dalton's incredulous voice hung in the air as he weaved in and out of the traffic.

Sangster sat tense next to him in the passenger seat, staring at the road. "Who would have the balls to shoot a Federal Minister in the head, in his car, in broad daylight, and right outside Police HQ? It doesn't make sense."

"Someone who wanted to stop him talking to us," Dalton replied.

"Or someone who wanted to kill under our noses." Sangster shifted awkwardly in his seat.

"Where the hell was his security team?" Dalton railed. "Where was his driver?"

"Harris stood them down, and said he wanted to drive himself. Apparently, he phoned the DC and asked to call at 1pm on a private matter."

Dalton glanced over. "What was that all about?"

"The DC doesn't know. When Harris didn't turn up, he phoned his office. No one there even knew about the appointment. Then the DC spotted a ministerial car parked outside in the street from his office window. His secretary went out, and found Harris dead inside."

Dalton braked hard as a car pulled out in front of him.

Sangster jolted forward. When he sat back, he noticed a familiar jagged light in the corner of his right eye. He reached into his pocket for his migraine medication, then remembered he'd left it on the hall table at home.

"Someone must have *witnessed* the shooting." Dalton was getting more and more worked up. "You can't shoot a Minister in broad daylight without *someone* seeing?"

"Apparently you can, because no one's come forward... yet."

"But there's CCTV right outside."

"They're checking it now."

"Didn't anyone see his body in the car, for Chrissakes?"

"Those official cars have heavily tinted windows. But this is where it gets weird, Dave." Sangster glanced over. "The DC's just said it looks like Harris was *killed* by a single bullet to the back of the head. Then, he was *stabbed* through the heart."

Dalton's jaw dropped. "Someone was *really* pissed off with him."

"I'm no expert, Dave, but I always thought post-mortem stab wounds were sexual in nature."

"Is that what this is all about? Sex? Because t*wo* high profile murders in one day can't be a coincidence."

Sangster nodded. "Except the murders are so different. The Chambers' woman was attacked in the dark and drowned with bare hands; whereas Harris was shot in broad daylight, and stabbed through the heart."

Dalton's mobile rang. He answered while still expertly driving.

It amazed Sangster how someone as methodical and slow as Dalton could have such sharp reflexes behind the wheel.

Dalton looked over again. "No sign of Susan Chambers, Boss. The guys have been to her house, and to the *Brisbane Echo*. What do you want them to do now?"

Sangster rubbed his eyes, but that jagged light was still there. He was worried about Susan Chambers. He felt responsible for her running off, and he needed that diary. "I want someone to stay outside her house, in case she returns. Everyone else should get back to the station. And under no circumstances should anyone issue a general bulletin to pick her up. She's scared enough of us as it is. I don't want the whole Force chasing her." He looked over at Dalton. "And I don't want *anyone* to know she has that diary. Is that clear?"

Dalton understood. "You think she's in danger while she's got it?"

Sangster pursed his lips. "Until we know exactly what we're dealing with, I'm going to put a small team together to look for her discreetly."

When Dalton braked again, this time to stop at a red light, Sangster's notepad flew onto the floor. He picked it up and flicked to his sketch of Ellen Chambers lying dead on the sand. Despite the disfiguration, he reckoned she'd been a beautiful woman, and successful. But the attack had been so angry, as if someone hadn't just wanted to punish her, they'd wanted to destroy her. What had she done to spark that rage? He turned to another sketch. "What do you make of the British Consul, Dave?" he asked, as he studied the image of her he'd created on the page.

Dalton shrugged. "Doesn't look much like a Consul, does she?"

"You never know who's who in those embassies. They give themselves titles no one understands, and get up to all sorts under cover."

"She seemed professional enough. A typically reserved Pom, if you ask me." Dalton paused. "Did you notice she's got the same profile as Ellen Chambers? Same build, height and colouring."

Sangster nodded. Except for different coloured eyes, he thought. The victim's were blue, the Consul's are brown. A streak of lightning flashed across the sky, making him blink. Now, with his eyes closed, he could see that jagged line working its way across both eyes. He waited for the clap of thunder to follow. But it never came; nor did the rain. "Get the guys to pick up Danny Burton, Dave, and bring him down to the station for interview."

"What, now?"

"Yes. Danny says he went home after that spat in the bar with Ellen Chambers. But I don't think he's the type of guy to give up on a woman so easily."

"You think he might have done it?"

Sangster rubbed his eyes again and looked up at the black rain cloud hanging over the city skyscrapers, which only added to his dark mood. "I don't know yet. But I've got a feeling he knows more than he's letting on."

★

Bald head pink with stress, the DC paced around his office, while Sangster stood by the window. The DC had a huge desk, but he never sat at it. It was more of a status symbol than a practical piece of furniture; and Sangster couldn't see the point of that. But he did understand the DC's anxiety. He was coming under intense scrutiny from Canberra and the media. And the strain was showing. But if anyone could handle the pressure, it was him. The DC might have worked his way up from the bottom, just like Sangster, but he was a shrewd operator. He was good at schmoozing and keeping senior officials and politicians sweet, but he wasn't a risk taker or in the least bit independent-minded. And for that, Sangster didn't admire him much.

Nor did Sangster care much for those two Federal agents. They'd been so rattled by the Anthony Harris murder, they'd delayed their briefing for another hour while they got more advice from Canberra. Then, when they did start talking, their briefing boiled down to one simple point: Ellen Chambers was suspected of taking a couple of million dollars in bribes from the Chinese to help get them a more favourable deal in the LNG negotiations. Sangster was unimpressed. Why all the cloak and dagger stuff? Why didn't Canberra just say from the start that Ellen Chambers was double-crossing Western Energy by working for the Chinese?

"What I don't understand, Tom, is why a woman in *her* position would take bribes from the Chinese? She was Western Energy's Group Finance Director for God's sake, and probably earning a fortune. *Stupid woman!*"

"Well, what *I* don't understand is why Canberra didn't just say from the start she was taking bribes from the Chinese." Sangster's eyes narrowed. "And why won't they let us read a copy of that British intelligence report?"

"Too sensitive, they say."

"So we just accept what we're told?"

The DC stopped pacing. "What are you getting at?"

Sangster wasn't sure himself. "It feels all wrong, that's all." He paused. "I want to talk to Chen Xiamen, and the rest of the Chinese."

"You heard what Canberra said, Tom. We can't interview any of them until the PM's adviser and the Chinese Ambassador get here from Canberra, tomorrow morning."

"*Anything* could happen before then. We've already had *two* murders."

"We need to go along with them on this, Tom." The DC gave him a pointed look. "The PM's office have made it crystal clear to me that we can't go blundering in and accuse the Chinese of bribing Ellen Chambers."

"What about murdering her?"

"That's impossible. The Chinese were all present at an official function in Canberra Parliament last night. There's no way any of them could have got a flight up to Brisbane and killed her."

"But they could have arranged it," Sangster said.

The DC stared at him. "I mean it, Tom. Don't step out of line."

"Well I don't like it."

The DC paused. "You're going to like this even less. Canberra say *they're* responsible for investigating the murder of Anthony Harris, because he was a Federal Minister."

"So what do they suggest?" Sangster sounded exasperated. "That we split the two investigations up?"

"Look, don't make this any harder than it is, Tom. There are more Federal Agents on their way. I've opened the major incident room, where we can all work together and pool information. Meanwhile, you carry on with the Ellen Chambers' murder." He stared at him. "If you want to."

"Course I do."

The DC nodded, as if to dismiss him.

But Sangster didn't leave. "I want to put a small team together to look for Susan Chambers, quietly. She's scared of us, and we need to find her before she gets herself into trouble."

The DC shook his head. "We can't afford to make any mistakes. Put out a bulletin to pick her up."

"I'm worried she's got that diary," Sangster persisted. "Susan's an investigative journalist, or at least she's training to be. I think she's going to use that diary to start digging into Ellen's life. And that could put her in a lot of danger." He took a deep breath. "Just give me 24 hours. If we haven't found her by then, we'll do it your way."

"I'm not sure."

"The British Consul will help us find her. Susan seems to trust her. I'm sure she's the one person Susan *will* contact."

The DC looked thoughtful. "The British Deputy High Commissioner Nigel Paxman phoned me earlier. Seems a good bloke... on the ball anyway. He told me his Consul was here." He paused. "All right, Tom. You've got 24 hours."

Sangster nodded. "One more thing, Sir. I want to keep that post-mortem stabbing under wraps for the time being. It's weird, and I don't want to get the media stoked up."

The DC understood. "It'll only spread hysteria."

Sangster went to go.

"By the way, Tom, the Chairman of Western Energy called in to see me earlier. I believe you spoke to him on the phone?"

"Yes. I'd planned to stop at the Convention Centre to see him before I got your call about Anthony Harris."

"Not only is he devastated about Ellen Chambers' murder, he's close to the PM, Tom, so tread carefully. Don't go upsetting him, or anyone else at Western Energy."

Sangster rose and headed for the door.

"There's a lot at stake here, Tom," the DC shouted at his departing back.

13

Surely the media had the story by now? Jess scanned the headlines on her laptop again, but there was still no mention of the Anthony Harris shooting. Puzzled, she sat back in her terrace chair and looked across the lawn. The shadow cast by the hotel roof had lengthened in the late afternoon sun, and the air had started to cool. She looked at her watch: 4.15pm. In another 45 minutes, the journalists were due to arrive for her briefing on Ellen Chambers' murder. That's if any of them turned up. The Anthony Harris shooting would be a much bigger headline now, *if* the press knew about it.

She checked her mobile. She wasn't surprised Inspector Sangster hadn't phoned back with news of the shooting; but she'd expected Simon to ring. They had to know about it in Canberra by now. She dialled Simon's number, expecting to get his voicemail.

"Jess?" he answered. "I'm in the car with the Foreign Secretary and High Commissioner. We're in between calls, on our way to the Department of Foreign Affairs and Trade."

Jess understood he was telling her he couldn't chat. She launched straight in. "Have you heard Anthony Harris has been shot dead in Brisbane?"

His stunned silence answered her question.

"I was with Inspector Sangster at The Palms when he got the call," she said. "I don't know any of the details because he raced off back to Brisbane. I've heard nothing from him since." She paused. "The media *should* have the story by now, but there's still nothing about it on the internet."

"*Good God!*"

Down the line, she could hear the disbelief in his voice as he told the High Commissioner and Foreign Secretary. But he sounded sceptical when he came back on. "Are you sure, Jess? Only we've heard nothing about it."

"I'm *sure* I know what Inspector Sangster told me. Mind you, that was a couple of hours ago."

"We've just finished our meetings at Parliament, and no one mentioned it. The whole place would be buzzing if it were true."

"That's weird. Inspector Sangster got the call while he was with me. I heard it all."

"Right," Simon said, purposefully. "We're just arriving at the Department of Foreign Affairs. We'll find out and let you know."

"Thanks."

"*Please* be careful, Jess."

Jess pocketed her mobile. *Am I sure?* But now she was beginning to doubt the shooting had happened. Had there been some kind of mix-up? *Some* mix-up she thought, as she rolled her head from side to side to relieve tension. She looked at her watch again. She needed to clear her head before talking to those journalists.

In the distance, she could see the afternoon sun shimmering on the silvery sea. It looked so inviting. She pushed her laptop into her briefcase and picked up her bag. The scent of star jasmine wafted in the breeze as she walked down the garden path. Approaching the beach, she saw a man standing on the jetty, staring out to sea.

The man must have felt her presence because he turned. And when he saw her, he seemed to half-freeze, with a spontaneous look of surprise, or was it shock, on his face?

Jess recognised him immediately. It wasn't just because he resembled his photo in the newspaper, or because he was particularly striking. No, he just held himself upright and radiated a kind of charisma. He was the Chairman of Western Energy, all right. "Mr Langhurst?" She stepped forward and held out her hand. "I'm Jessica Turner, British Consul."

Something like relief flitted across his face. "Of course." He shook her hand. "Your Deputy High Commissioner said you were here."

Langhurst had a surprisingly strong handshake. "I'm so sorry about Ellen," she said. "It's just terrible."

"Yes," he whispered. "She's quite... irreplaceable."

The deep sadness in his voice moved Jess and she felt tears prick her eyes. They stood in silence for a while, side by side, looking out to sea, until Langhurst gave a long sigh. "Thank you for coming, Miss Turner."

"Call me Jessica, or Jess if you like."

He nodded. "And I'm John."

Conscious that he was deeply upset, she said: "Would you mind if I ask you about Ellen?"

He gave a sad half-smile. "Of course not. But I don't know what I can tell you, except that she was a delightful colleague and a brilliant financial expert."

"Do you know her sister, Susan?" Jess was hoping he might know where Susan was.

He shook his head. "I knew Ellen had a sister working in Brisbane, but I've never met her."

"She was here earlier. She told me Ellen had hoped to move to Australia soon to work for your Company."

He flinched. "Susan Chambers told you *that*?"

"Sorry, am I talking out of turn?"

He frowned. "It's true I wanted Ellen to take over as CEO." He glanced at Jess. "Did Susan mention that too?"

"Yes."

"Well, I'd be grateful if you'd keep it to yourself. Only our CEO Richard Price is still in the job, and I don't want the press making any more trouble." He ran his fingers through his hair. "I expect you've seen the speculation in the media about Richard moving on?" Of course she hadn't, but he didn't wait for her reply. "All those reports about his run-in with the police over drink-driving. These things always find their way into the papers."

How embarrassing for him and Western Energy, Jess thought.

"Poor Richard's been suffering since his divorce last year," Langhurst explained. "Alcohol ruins so many lives."

Jess understood perfectly. "I expect Ellen told Susan about the move because she was excited at the prospect of moving closer to her sister."

He nodded. "I don't deny I wanted Ellen for the job. She would have been perfect. But while everyone was speculating about Richard being on the move, no one knew Ellen was the front-runner to replace him. Perhaps I need to explain that to Susan? I've been trying to contact her to express my condolences. She works at the *Echo*, but they won't give out her private number. Do you have it?"

Jess shook her head. "She left without giving me her contact details."

"I was hoping to see Inspector Sangster here."

"I'm afraid you've just missed him."

He sighed. "In that case, I'd better get back to the Conference. To be honest, I wanted to cancel the whole thing. But guests have travelled from all over the world to attend. I can't let them down."

As they walked up to the hotel in companionable silence, Jess wondered if he'd heard about the Anthony Harris shooting. But as he never mentioned it, she didn't either.

Reaching the back terrace, he stopped. "It was good to meet you, Jessica."

"Good to meet you too, John."

Under his intense gaze, she had the feeling she was being assessed. She must have come out favourably because he pulled out a business card and gave it to her. "If there's anything I can do, give me a ring on my mobile. Any time."

She smiled. "And here's mine." She gave him a card, then asked. "Do you mind if I ask one question that's been bothering me?"

"Of course not."

"Why was Ellen such a key person on your LNG negotiating team when she was resident in London? Don't you have anyone in Australia who could do the job?"

He shook his head. "No one like her. Ellen was fluent in Mandarin, you see. She'd worked in China for years before joining Western Energy. She knew the Chinese well. They liked her. Trusted her." He gave a sad smile. "I was the one who lured her away from her job in China. And I never regretted it. Not for a moment... until now."

A polite cough interrupted and they turned to see the young receptionist standing by the door.

"Excuse me, Miss Turner, there are some journalists waiting for you in the lobby."

Jess looked at her watch: 5pm on the dot. She turned back to Langhurst. "Sorry, but I have to go."

He put a light hand on her shoulder. "I'm sure I'll see you again soon, Jessica," he said, before walking off in the direction of the car park.

Alone now, Jess wondered if she had time to check the headlines on her laptop to see if the Anthony Harris shooting was public knowledge yet. But she didn't want to antagonise the journalists by being late. She took a deep breath and went into the hotel.

★

"Well, let me ask you this, then. Does the British Government *think* Ellen Chambers' murder is connected to the gas deal?"

Jess looked back at that annoying journalist by the door. He was persistent, she'd give him that. How many different ways could he ask the same question? "I'm afraid I can only repeat what I've already told you," she said with a note of finality. "All we know at the moment is that Ellen Chambers was found dead on the beach here at five o'clock this morning."

"But is the British Government investigating the *possibility* of a connection?"

"The Australian police are responsible for investigating Ellen Chambers' death. The gas deal is a commercial transaction between Australia and China." She tried to keep her tone even. "The British Government are not involved in that project."

He wouldn't give up so easily. "Did *you* know Ellen Chambers?"

She shook her head. "No. I'd never met her."

"Did any of your *colleagues* in the British High Commission know her?"

She gave him a cool look, wondering what he was getting at. "She was a senior executive in a prominent company, so some of my colleagues may have met her."

He brushed his straggly brown hair from his eyes, and continued to stare. "Had she ever been *employed* by the British Government?"

A hush settled around the room as the other journalists sensed he was onto something. So did Jess. *Employed by the British Government?* What did he know that she didn't? John Langhurst said Ellen had worked in China for several years before joining Western Energy but Jess couldn't speculate about that now. "All I know is that Ellen Chambers was an employee of Western Energy when she died. I don't know what she did before that."

"Where's her sister, Susan Chambers?" he asked. "Been spirited away by your lot, has she?" He looked around the room for effect. "Only, none of us have seen her."

Jess's eyes narrowed. "I've seen Susan today." She wanted to quash any speculation that the other Chambers girl was lying murdered in a ditch somewhere. "As a press *colleague* of yours, I'm sure you'll want to give her privacy to come to terms with her sister's death."

"Murder," he retorted.

By now, Jess had had enough. She'd answered all their questions and had nothing more to say. The worrying thing was they clearly knew nothing about the Anthony Harris shooting, but at least she hadn't had to field any questions about that.

A noise over by the terrace doors caught everyone's attention. A couple stumbled in, and stood staring like rabbits in headlights. With all eyes on them, they mumbled their apologies and backed out.

When Jess turned back, the annoying journalist had disappeared. She cast her eyes around the room, but there was no sign of him. Taking advantage of the interruption, she checked her watch. Half an hour of questions was enough. "Right, if that's all," she said before anyone else could say anything. "We'll finish now."

Saying a quick farewell, she picked up her bags and walked out. Crossing the lobby, she swung through the glass door onto the terrace. She glanced at the bar. She could do with a drink, but she didn't want to go inside, in case the journalists followed her. All she craved was some peace and quiet. Feeling the late afternoon air cooling her burning cheeks, she started walking and found herself being drawn to the jetty again. As she stood in the same spot as earlier with John Langhurst, she went over their conversation in her head. He'd certainly thought a lot of Ellen Chambers. So much so, he'd seemed... well, devastated by her death. Yes, that's the word she'd use. Devastated. Would a boss be that cut up about a colleague, she wondered? Or were they more than colleagues?

She sat down on the seat and looked out to sea. The sun was already hanging low in the sky on its daily descent. In the shallows, a lone pelican stood on a semi-submerged rock, his long bill snapping at fish in the water and coming up empty every time. Seabirds wheeled and circled over the surf, ready to gobble up any small fish the ebbing tide exposed.

A faint rustling in the bushes behind made her look over her shoulder, but there was no one there. A shrill noise made her jump; she answered her mobile.

"Sorry to disturb you again, Jessica."

She recognised Langhurst's voice immediately. "It's all right, John, you're not disturbing me."

"How did it go with the journalists?" he asked.

"Oh, you know what they're like."

"Indeed I do." He sounded sympathetic. "I'm ringing to ask for your Deputy High Commissioner's number. I seem to have mislaid it."

"Of course," she said, rattling the number off the top of her head.

"Thanks." He paused. "Have you heard any more from the police? Only they're not telling me much."

"I'm afraid not."

"I see." He paused, and said quietly: "You know, I still can't believe she's gone."

"I know." Jess was warming to John Langhurst. "I'm at the jetty now. It's so beautiful."

"Ellen loved it."

"Did she stay here a lot?"

"Yes."

"On Company business?"

"Mostly, yes."

Jess's brain slipped back into work mode. "I believe she visited China twice this year too. Indeed, she only came back from the second trip last week."

There was a pause. "You're very well informed, Jessica,' he said, without a trace of sarcasm. "I hope the police are as switched on."

"Well, it's not hard. Ellen scheduled her life down to the last minute. She was so well organised."

He sighed, deeply. "Yes. That's one of the things that made her so good at her job." Then he asked: "How long do you plan to stay at The Palms, Jessica?"

"Just for tonight." She wouldn't stay a minute longer than she had to. She didn't like the atmosphere one bit. "I'll move into town in the morning and work out of the British Consulate-General."

"In that case, can we meet up at the Convention Centre tomorrow? I'd like to help Susan and the family. But first, perhaps you and I could talk through the logistics of arranging the funeral, and getting Ellen back to the UK."

"Of course."

"What time will you be leaving The Palms?"

"After breakfast."

"Excellent. What time should I expect you?"

"Would 12.30 suit, John? Only I have some meetings at the Consulate first."

"Perfect. The Conference will break for lunch around then, so that suits me fine. Until tomorrow," he said. "Goodbye, Jessica."

"Goodbye." Jess hung up, feeling sorry for him, especially having to carry on with the Conference as if nothing had happened.

She turned and scanned the beach. Most people had left for the day. A lone jogger ran along the edge of the sea, leaving a trail of footprints in the damp sand. Every so often he jumped over any debris, or beached jellyfish, lying in his path.

Her gaze stopped on a woman with two small girls. The children were playing happily together, building sandcastles then jumping on them and starting over. When their mother began packing up, the youngest child started crying. She kept wriggling and running away as her mother tried to dress her. "No Mummy. No." The woman caught her, holding her tight while she tried again. "I wanna play," screamed the child, in full-blown temper tantrum now. The woman picked her up and tucked her under her arm. Looking embarrassed, she started walking off the beach while the older child skipped along behind, unperturbed.

"I wanna stay Mummy." The child sobbed, tears streaming down her face. "*Stay!*" She kicked and thrashed.

Jess closed her eyes, thinking back to their last holiday together, in Bali, when Amy was two. She could see Jack wading into the sea, with Amy on his shoulders, talking to her all the time. She could hear Amy giggling as he dipped her gently into the water. Amy too could turn on those temper tantrums in a flash when it came to going home.

Jess ran her hands through her hair and rubbed her cheeks. What she wouldn't give to feel Amy's little arms around her neck, and her soft kiss. Just one last time, to tell her she loved her. To tell them *both* she loved them. A tear slipped down her cheek.

Later, as the breeze blew in off the water and ruffled her hair, she stirred and looked down at her watch. She'd been sitting there so long the sun had sunk below the horizon, leaving behind a mottled indigo and orange sky in its wake.

Then darkness came sweeping in from nowhere.

Whipped up by the strengthening wind, the waves banged the moored boats against the jetty, making their railings and fittings rattle and tinkle.

Goose bumps rose on Jess's arms and legs as she looked around in the twilight. She was all alone.

She stared at the water, murky now in the gloom.

Then soft moaning sounded around her. Human moaning? Or was it just the wind howling across the bay?

A chill tingled up her spine. She was thinking of Ellen Chambers fighting for her life. In the dark water, she imagined Ellen's white face twisted in terror, her blonde hair fanning out in the waves, her mouth wide open, screaming in panic as she sank below the water.

Jess's heart was thumping so hard now, she couldn't breathe. She had to get away from this place. But she couldn't seem to move.

Behind her the bushes rustled again, then an eerie silence hung in the air. The moaning started up again, all around her, getting into her head, under her skin. What the hell was it?

As the breeze tugged at her hair and clothes, she got a creeping sense that someone else was there. Her throat tightened. Springing up, she grabbed her briefcase and bag and ran down the jetty, past the bushes, and onto the path leading back to the hotel.

Breathless, she stopped half way up and looked over her shoulder to see if anyone was following. A sudden breeze whipped through a nearby palm tree, making its spiky leaves rattle. She jumped as a branch brushed her cheek, and fled up to the back terrace, into the safety of the hotel.

14

Sitting in the gloom in his office, Sangster wondered how Dalton was getting on in the interview room downstairs with Danny Burton. He looked at his watch. He'd give him another ten minutes or so. Then he'd go down.

The only light in the office came from a metal lamp that shone a dull beam and cast shadows on the bare walls. There was nothing on the desk except for a mug of pencils of every shape and size, a cup of cold coffee, and two buff-coloured files. They were unsolved murder cases. Two young women, both killed by the same man after a violent sex attack. It was that strange bruise on Ellen Chambers' cheek that had got him checking the files. But there was nothing like that in here. And the Chambers' woman didn't fit the victim profile: she was older.

His stomach growled, but he didn't feel like eating because his head was still hammering. Rubbing his temples, he pulled a packet of paracetamol out of the drawer and swallowed two tablets with a swig of cold coffee.

He got up and went over to a small table in the corner of the room, where he'd laid out his sketches. He could feel the tension in his neck and rolled his head from side to side to release it. He was glad to be away from the incident room. The DC was on a short fuse at the best of times, but all this crap with Canberra was sending his temper and blood pressure spiralling.

Sangster picked up his sketch of Ellen Chambers lying dead on the sand and studied it. Why was she staying at The Palms when her colleagues were in town at the Riverbank Hotel? And why did she always stay there? Did she just prefer her own company? Or was she meeting her lover there, as the British Consul suspected?

The blinds rattling in the breeze distracted him. He laid the sketch down, and went over to close the window. Looking out into the darkness, his long, pale face and hollow eyes reflected back in the glass. He ran his fingers through his spiky, grey hair. He was really worried about Liz now. Why hadn't she returned his calls?

Heavy footsteps sounded in the corridor outside and Dalton came in, breathing hard from climbing the stairs.

"How's it going with Danny?" Sangster asked.

Dalton pulled a face. "What a jerk!"

"Anything at all?"

"Nah." Dalton flopped down on a chair. "He's insistin' he didn't kill Ellen Chambers. But, like you said, he's pleased with himself about somethin'."

Sangster looked thoughtful. "She was a bit of a ghost, our girl, wasn't she? I mean, hotel records show she spent a lot of time at The Palms, but no one knows anything about her. No one *knows* what she did. No one *saw* her with anyone."

Dalton nodded. "Doesn't add up, does it?"

Sangster shook his head. "Someone knows something."

"One thing I did find out, Boss. There was a reception and aboriginal show on at 6.30pm last night at the Convention Centre for the Western Energy Conference delegates. It was a big bash before the Conference started proper this mornin'. Ellen Chambers was supposed to attend that reception. She told her colleagues she would be there, but she never showed."

"Didn't anyone *miss* her?"

"Nah. The place was crowded. People just helped themselves to food, and moved around. Attendance wasn't obligatory, so half the delegates didn't bother to turn up. It's goin' to be a bugger workin' out who was there and who wasn't."

Sangster saw the fatigue in Dalton's eyes.

"Oh, and I had a word with a mate who's workin' with DC Roberts. He *is* on leave." Dalton paused. "He's a quiet sort of bloke, according to the guys. Goes for the occasional drink but keeps himself to himself."

Sangster looked thoughtful. "Did you say he transferred up here from Melbourne a year or so ago?"

Dalton nodded.

"Ask him to come in, Dave. I want to have a quiet word."

"I would if I could, Boss, but he's not answerin' his phone. Must've gone out on that fishin' trip after all."

Sangster frowned. "What do we know about Roberts' past record in the police?"

"Nothin'! Want me to do some diggin'?"

"Yes, but keep it discreet." Sangster went over to the table and stared at his sketches again. He picked up the one of the British Consul this time. He didn't know what to make of Jessica Turner, but she was the link with Susan Chambers and that diary. Susan might not trust him, but she trusted the Consul.

As if reading his mind, Dalton asked: "Any news about the Chambers girl?"

Sangster shook his head.

"She's gettin' herself into a whole heap of trouble."

*

Sangster walked into the interview room, sat down and stared across the table at Danny Burton. Bronzed, and with a well-honed physique and sun-bleached hair, Danny looked like all the other young men who spent their lives surfing and hanging out at the beach. But there was a cockiness about him. He didn't flinch under Sangster's stare either. Sangster pulled his sketch pad out of his pocket. "So where were you between 8pm and midnight last night, Danny?"

"I already told your sidekick." Danny pointed at Dalton, who'd slipped into the chair beside Sangster.

"So tell *me*." Sangster's eyes never left Danny's.

Danny gave a smug smile. "I got off duty around seven last night. Then I went into the hotel bar for a beer. No crime in that, is there?"

Sangster didn't say anything. He could see Danny was composed and enjoying the attention. Wanting to shatter that composure, Sangster looked around the stark interview room, then up at a patch of mould growing on the ceiling. "Now, why would you do that, Danny?" He sounded bored. "Why would you buy a beer in an expensive hotel bar when you can get it cheaper in the pub down the road?"

"I couldn't wait. I was thirsty."

Sangster opened his sketchpad on his lap just below the table and took a pencil from his breast pocket. He stared at Danny again and started drawing his broad face, and the straggly blond hair flopping over his forehead and the collar of his T-shirt. That gleam in his eyes. What was it? Arrogance? Amusement? Did Danny know something?

Danny shifted in his seat and tried to look at Sangster's notepad.

"Do you know what I think?" Sangster said, continuing to draw Danny's eyes, knowing he couldn't see anything from his side of the table. "I think you went into the bar because you saw Ellen Chambers go in." He looked up. "That's what happened, isn't it?"

Danny shrugged. "If you say so."

"If I said you'd murdered her, would you agree?"

Danny laughed with contempt.

Sangster laughed too. "What *were* you thinking, Danny? A woman like that? She was way out of your league." When he saw Danny's face harden, he knew he'd hit a nerve. "We know she gave you the brush off."

Danny's cheeks reddened.

"Is that why you killed her?"

Danny crossed his arms. "I didn't kill her."

Sangster leant forward. "Is that why you killed her, Danny, because she turned you down?"

"*I* didn't kill her." Danny coiled his fists on the table.

Sangster studied Danny's bulky frame and the tiger tattoo at the top of his muscular left arm. A woman wouldn't stand a chance against him. "So, I hear you like to lash out at the ladies, Danny?" Sangster goaded. "You've done it before, haven't you?"

Danny sat rigid, eyes burning.

"You beat your girlfriend up last year, put her in the hospital."

The muscles in Danny's neck tightened.

"I bet Ellen Chambers didn't want you hanging around, Danny." Sangster laughed again. "The beach bum."

"*She* was nothin' special."

Sangster didn't move. "So, how'd you do it, Danny? Did you follow her down to the jetty? Easy, was it, once you'd got her alone?"

Danny's face twisted. "*I* didn't do it."

"You used those fists on her last night, Danny, didn't you?" Sangster leant forward. "You thought you'd teach her a lesson. But she fought back, didn't she?"

"*I* didn't do it."

"Did you mean to kill her, Danny? Or did you just want to teach her a lesson? Was that it? You wanted to teach her that no one makes a tosser out of Danny Burton."

"It wasn't *me!*"

Sangster's eyes pierced Danny's. "Who was it, then?"

Danny slumped back in his chair.

"You did follow her down to the jetty, didn't you, Danny? And you did see her with someone."

There was a pause.

"Didn't you, Danny?"

Danny stuck his chin out. "What if I did?"

This was Dalton's cue to intervene. "So why lie to me about that, Danny? Why didn't you tell me you saw her with someone?"

"You wouldn't have believed me."

"Who did you see, Danny?" Sangster asked.

"It was too dark to see. The jetty light was out."

"So what did you see?"

Danny smirked. "I saw them kissin' and cuddlin'. Then they started arguin'. Suddenly, she jumped up and looked straight at me. So I legged it."

"Then what?"

Danny shrugged. "I went home." He looked at Sangster. "That stuck-up bitch had it comin'."

Sangster forced himself to keep his voice level. "Tell me about this man, Danny. Height? Colour of hair?"

"I told you, it was too dark to see. And he was sittin' on the seat, facin' out to sea." Danny made a show of thinking hard. "He must have been smokin' because I saw a match light up."

"If you don't tell me who you saw, Danny, I'm going to charge *you* with her murder."

"I keep tellin' you," Danny whined. "It was too dark to see."

Sangster slapped the palms of his hands down on the table, making Danny flinch. "I've had enough of this."

"Can I go now?" Danny asked.

Ignoring him, Sangster got up and walked out.

Dalton followed him into the corridor. "What do you think, Boss?"

Sangster ran his fingers through his hair. Did Danny follow Ellen down to the jetty and kill her because she rejected him? He shook his head. "I don't think he did it, Dave. But I think he knows who *was* down at the jetty with Ellen Chambers."

"Right, we'll keep the pillock in the cells until he tells us."

Sangster shook his head. "He's not going to tell us anything. But the question is why? Does he know the man she was with? Is he keeping quiet out of some kind of loyalty?"

"Or is someone buying his silence?"

Sangster nodded. "Look, have we got Danny's prints and DNA?"

"Yep."

"Then let him go, but have him followed. If Danny *knows* who was with Ellen Chambers on the jetty last night, he won't let it rest." He paused. "And he might just be stupid enough to lead us to whoever it was."

15

He scowled and patted the gun under his jacket. He should
have left town as soon as he'd dealt with that bastard. But
things had got complicated. Now, he had that meddlin'
idiot to silence too. What's more, he still hadn't got that
diary. He hadn't found it in that bitch's room or amongst
her possessions. Someone had taken it. And he had a good
idea who.

Outside the hotel entrance, it was deserted. Antennae
tuned, he stood listening for any sound. Apart from the
bats flapping in the trees and the background hum of
crickets, it was all quiet. Looking up, he could see lights on
in many of the rooms, and flickering shadows on curtains,
as guests watched TV or got ready for bed.

He heard the concierge say goodnight to the bubbly
receptionist. He recognised her voice the moment she
replied. Earlier, she'd been only too willing to chat and tell
him everything that had gone on since last night's murder.
She even said she felt safe on duty on her own all night
because the hotel manager had hired two security guards
to patrol the grounds. "And lightning never strikes twice,"
she said, patting his arm. He'd seen those two overweight
idiots plodding around the grounds. Even with this full
moon lighting up the night like a security light, they

weren't capable of catching school kids throwing stones, let alone a supreme pro like him.

He watched the receptionist through the glass as she checked for messages in the pigeon-holes behind the desk. Reaching for the top, her dress rose up over her thighs. Reluctantly, he turned away. He had work to do.

For a moment, he stood drinking in the night, feeling the energy zipping around his taut body.

Sneaking around the side of the hotel, he sidled into the bushes. Staying under cover, he made his way down the track, alongside the garden path for about 100 metres. Then he stopped and took out his night vision monocular. He put it to his eye and trained it on the back of the hotel building. He could see every brick, every railing, every movement through the single scope. He ran the monocular along the second floor, counting all the room numbers until he stopped at the one he wanted. There was a light on inside, although the curtains were closed.

Then he saw her, sitting outside on the balcony. She was wearing a flimsy nightdress, with a wrap over her shoulders. There was an unusual stillness about her, like a creature not wanting to be seen in the dark. She wasn't asleep though, her eyes were open. He turned the scope to full magnification. Through the material, it picked out her rounded breasts, and smooth nipples. He could almost reach out and touch them. Then he moved the scope down her body, and in between her long legs. His face twisted. Maybe he was going to enjoy this delay after all.

*

In the darkness, Jess sat on her balcony looking out to sea. She'd been on the go since dawn, but she was too keyed up to sleep. The full moon hung low in the black sky like a huge, luminous china plate, and wispy clouds floated across it in the breeze. It looked so beautiful. In the distance, she could hear waves crashing onto the beach, and the incessant buzz of crickets.

Come on Simon! She'd been waiting for him to call for hours. The dinner wasn't still going on, surely? Perhaps he'd gone back to the office to send a report of the talks to London? Simon was *always* working. She smiled as she pictured his head bent over the computer, deep in concentration, bashing away at the keys.

Picking up her glass of wine from the small table, she took a sip of the Hunter Valley Semillon. The Aussies could certainly make wine, she thought, as the cold liquid slipped down to her stomach. She shivered and pulled the shawl tighter around her shoulders. Should she go to bed and get some rest? But what was the point? She wouldn't be able to sleep with things milling around in her head. And she wanted to talk to Simon. She was counting on him to make sense of everything.

Her mind flashed back to Susan. She could see the girl now, brushing away a tear as she talked about her sister. Perhaps she could persuade her to go back to the UK for a couple of weeks? At least she'd be safe there. Except she had to find her first. Where to start looking? She didn't have her address or telephone number, but she knew she worked for the *Echo*. So that's where she would start in the morning.

Hearing a familiar bleep, she picked up her mobile and opened the text.

Sorry. Dinner still going on. I'm going back to office after. Don't wait up. I'll call first thing in the morning. Simon.

Jess flopped back in the chair, disappointed. It had been a weird day and she really wanted to talk to Simon. Until now, she hadn't realised just how much they *did* talk every day. They were always going out after work for a drink or a meal, or ringing one another.

She closed her eyes and listened to the rhythmic waves lapping onto the beach.

Her mobile rang in her hand. "Hello?"

"Jess, it's me."

"*Susan!* Where are you?"

"At a friend's house."

"*Thank God!*" Jess grabbed her notebook and pen. "Give me the address and telephone number."

"Not over the phone. They might be listening in."

Jess frowned. "Well, can I meet you somewhere? Or you could come back here and stay the night if you prefer."

"The diary's safe, if that's what you're worried about."

Jess stiffened. "I'm more worried about you, Susan. Look, it doesn't matter about the time. I've got a hired car. I can come over now and we can take the diary to the police together."

"*No. I* need the diary tonight."

"What for?"

There was a silence.

"Susan?"

"Ellen was pregnant," Susan said, flatly.

"*Pregnant?*" That shattered the picture of a career-oriented Ellen Chambers that Jess had built up in her mind.

"Yes." Susan was trying to hold back the tears. "I've been going through Ellen's diary. I've made a list of names and contact details for every appointment she had over the last three months. I've been phoning every one of them."

"You're *interfering* with the investigation."

Susan ignored her. "One of them was a gynaecologist here in Brisbane. I rang him, pretending to be Ellen. That's how I found out she was pregnant."

So the killer had taken two lives, Jess thought, not just one. "What else have you found out?" she asked.

"Nothing yet."

"So why do you need to keep the diary, Susan?"

Silence.

"Look, we must take that diary to the police now."

"No. I have to check out *everything* in the diary. It's the only way I can help Ellen." Susan's voice was pleading now. "Look, can we meet up in the morning, *please?*"

All Jess's instincts were telling her they shouldn't wait. She tried again. "We need to do it now, Susan. We'll go to the police together. I won't leave you this time. I promise." She took a deep breath. "And then I wondered if you'd like to go home to the UK for a while. You could spend some time with friends or relatives until..."

"*What about Ellen?*"

"There's nothing you can do for her now, Susan."

"Yes there is. I can find her killer." Susan's voice wasn't hysterical any more; she sounded calm and purposeful. And that worried Jess even more.

"Well, if you don't want to go to the UK, come back to Canberra and stay with me. That way you'll still be in Australia. I'll be keeping in touch with the police and authorities, so you'll be kept right up to date with the investigation."

Susan let out a little sob.

"It's all right, Susan," Jess said. "It'll be all right."

Susan was struggling to speak. "I have to stay here, Jess. Please understand. I have to do this... for Ellen."

Jess sighed. She didn't like it, but she understood.

Susan went on. "I was just ringing to let you know I'm okay. I don't want you to worry about me."

"*You don't want me to worry about you?*"

"Jess." There was a pause. "You're the only person I can trust now. *Please will you help me?*"

There it was again, that cry for help that so touched Jess. "All right, Susan," she said, wearily, "but the police won't like it."

"Thanks, Jess. I really mean that."

"So where shall we meet in the morning?"

"I'll phone first thing and let you know."

Jess bit her tongue; there was no point saying anything else. "Right."

"See you tomorrow morning." And with that, Susan hung up.

Jess snapped her phone shut and looked up at the night sky. She was deeply worried about Susan. But there was nothing more she could do or say to get through to her. Still, at least the poor girl had phoned.

Hearing the signature music for the late TV news bulletin, she stood up and went back into her room. A picture of Anthony Harris filled the screen. *At last!* She rushed over to turn up the sound, and sat down on the edge of the bed to listen.

Anthony Harris was found in his official car outside Queensland Police HQ at 4pm this afternoon suffering from a gunshot wound to the head. He was rushed to hospital but pronounced dead on arrival. The police are appealing for anyone who may have seen the Minister or his car in the area this afternoon to come forward urgently.

This murder comes quickly on the heels of that of Ellen Chambers, a senior executive in Western Energy, whose body was found on the beach at The Palms Resort early this morning.

Although Anthony Harris was the Minister responsible for energy and resources and had close links to Western Energy, police say it is too early to speculate about whether the two murders are linked.

Tony Harris, as he was known to his close family and friends, was well respected by his electorate who praised him as a loyal, and hard-working local MP...

The newsreader continued with an obituary of the Minister's life while Jess lay back on the bed, mind reeling. Shot in the head? Why? What did it mean?

Oh my God! She sat up. Did he just call the Minister *Tony* Harris? She stared at the TV, as the thought percolated through her brain. Was *he* the TH in Ellen Chambers' diary? Was *he* having an affair with her? Was *he* the father of her unborn child? He *was* a high profile Federal Minister *and* married. Could that be the link between the two murders?

She grabbed her mobile to phone Sangster and went out onto the balcony where the signal was stronger.

16

Sangster couldn't stop his hand shaking as he put the key in the lock of his front door. I'm just tired, he told himself, as he turned it and pushed the door open. When he was greeted with only darkness and silence, his chin drooped onto his chest.

As he walked in and flicked on the master switch in the hallway, the lights blinded him. He threw his keys onto the hall table, and went straight into his study, where he switched on the TV to get the cricket. The Ashes series stood all square, with the decider in progress at Lord's. That was one good thing about the time difference, he could watch the cricket live from London. That would fill the silence for a while.

When he walked into the bedroom and saw Liz's side of the wardrobe still empty, he pushed his own clothes along the rail angrily to fill the space. He pulled his notepad out of his pocket and threw it on the bed. Hanging up his suit and tie in the wardrobe, he pulled on his joggers and T-shirt and walked barefoot out onto the balcony.

The cold from the tiles seeped through his feet, cooling him down after one of the strangest days he'd ever had as a policeman. *Two* high profile murders: a senior British executive, and then a Federal Minister. He still couldn't believe it. No one could. Of course all the relevant procedures had kicked in, but that didn't mean they weren't all still reeling from the shock, especially Canberra.

He took a deep breath of night air. From up there, he could see the twinkling city lights all over Brisbane. Somehow, it made him feel less lonely.

He pictured Liz sitting in the cane chair, with her legs tucked under her and a glass of wine in hand. They would often sit in the cool evening air, chatting about their day. Being with her had felt so right; he'd bought this spanking new apartment for her six years ago, with his life savings.

She said she loved it. But obviously not enough to stay.

"Where are you, Liz?" he whispered into the night.

*

Jess dialled Inspector Sangster's mobile, without even looking at the time.

"Liz?" he answered.

That threw her. "Er... this is Jessica Turner, the British Consul."

"Evening Ma'am." He sounded so disappointed, she couldn't help but wonder who Liz was.

"Sorry to ring so late, Inspector, but I wanted to let you know Susan Chambers is fine. She just called."

"Oh, good." The relief in his voice was palpable. "Where is she?"

"Staying with a friend."

"Give me the address and I'll send someone round."

"She wouldn't tell me on the phone. She thinks her phone's being tapped. But she wants to meet me first thing in the morning. I'll get the diary off her then."

He sighed, with exasperation.

"Let's not be too hard on her, Inspector. She's shocked and frightened."

"She's obstructing my murder investigation," he said, gruffly. "So where are you going to meet? At the hotel?"

"She's going to ring me first thing to say when and where."

"More bloody nonsense. Well, ring me in the morning as soon as you hear from her."

That sounded like an order, but Jess let it go. She was more preoccupied with what Susan had told her and whether to relay it to him. "Susan said her sister was pregnant when she was murdered." Jess knew she wasn't betraying Susan's confidence because the autopsy would reveal that.

He took a sharp breath.

"Yes. It was a surprise to me too," she went on. "Susan told me earlier she had the impression Ellen had a new man in her life."

"Who?"

"Ellen never mentioned him, which made Susan think he was married." Jess hesitated. "The thing is, I was just listening to the late news, to an obituary on Anthony Harris actually. And, well..." She hesitated, wondering what he would make of her theory. "The newsreader said he was known as *Tony* Harris to his family and close friends. So now I'm wondering if *he* was the TH in Ellen Chambers' diary. You remember I told you about those initials this afternoon?"

Silence.

"Well, it would make sense, wouldn't it?" she continued. "I mean, he *was* married, with a high profile job. If news of an affair, not to mention a pregnancy, got out, it could have ruined his career *and* his marriage."

"Mm."

"I may be wrong about this, Inspector. On the other hand, it *could* be a link between the two murders." She paused. "Mind you, it doesn't explain who would want them both dead." She paused. "Why did it take so long for the media to get news of the shooting?"

"Politics," he replied, without explaining. "But there is something about his murder that hasn't been released to the media." He stopped.

Jess waited.

"The cause of death was a single bullet to the back of the head, which killed him instantly. Then the killer stabbed him in the heart."

"*Oh my God!* Why would anyone do that?"

"We don't know yet," he said. "But we're keeping that information strictly under wraps. We don't want to start any public panic about a psycho on the loose. I'm sure you understand what I'm saying."

"Of course." She was pleased he'd confided in her.

"Is there anything else you can tell me?" he asked.

Jess couldn't decide whether she detected a note of sarcasm in his voice or not. Should she tell him about the conflict between the Chairman of Western Energy and his CEO, or that Ellen was being groomed to take over from Richard Price? That could be a motive for murder. No, she thought, not yet. John Langhurst had told her that in confidence. The Inspector would have to find that out for himself when he interviewed him.

Sangster repeated. "So, is there anything else you can tell me?"

"No."

He sighed. "So, where are you now?"

"On my hotel balcony, looking at the moon."

"It's a ripper, isn't it?"

Surprised by his reaction, she asked: "Do you live in town, Inspector, or at the coast?"

"In town. I have a great view over Brisbane from my top-floor apartment."

"You'll be able to keep an eye on everyone from up there then, won't you?"

He gave a small laugh. "With this full moon, there'll be a king tide at the coast tonight. The river levels will rise too."

"You live in a beautiful part of the world, Inspector."

"Call me, Tom. Inspector makes me sound old."

"And you can call me Jessica, or Jess if you like. Ma'am makes me sound like The Queen."

He laughed. It was a deep, throaty laugh that made Jess smile. So, despite that deadpan exterior, he had a sense of humour.

But he was quickly back to business. "I'm sure I don't have to tell you that Susan Chambers is jeopardising the investigation by holding onto that diary. She doesn't understand what trouble she's in. I could charge her for withholding evidence."

Jess sighed. He was back to his usual gruff self now and she'd had enough of that for one day. "Yes, well, I'll let you go now, Tom. No doubt we'll talk again tomorrow."

"No doubt," he replied, and hung up.

★

Sangster threw his mobile onto the bed. He needed that damn diary. It might well hold the clue to Ellen's killer or the motive for her murder. Mind you, he was glad the British Consul had phoned to tell him the Chambers girl was okay; and glad too that they were working together. He'd known all along she'd be the link between Susan Chambers and the diary.

Glancing at the bed as he picked up his notepad, he went out and slammed the door behind him. He'd sleep in his study again tonight.

Grabbing a beer from the fridge, he flopped down on the sofa-bed to watch the cricket. As he swigged from the bottle and flicked through his notepad, his mind began to sift through the day's events. He stopped at his sketch of Ellen Chambers' corpse lying on the sand. It had all started with *her* murder. He picked up his large pad, and lay back down on the sofa to start a bigger version.

Pregnant, eh? Is that what this is all about? An affair she was having with the Federal Minister? Is that why they were both dead?

The cricket droned on in the background, and he glanced towards the screen from time to time to catch a particular shot, or a replay.

Liz hated his sketches of murder victims. "It's like living with ghosts," she said. Not only did she refuse to go into his study, she insisted on keeping the door shut all the time. "Keep them in there, Tom, we don't want them intruding in our lives."

And he had *tried*. Very hard. But they *did* intrude. And he couldn't seem to stop them. And that's why deep down he knew Liz wasn't coming back this time. His head drooped and he pushed the heel of his hand into his eye. After a while, he picked up a soft charcoal pencil, and carried on with his drawing. Ellen Chambers' face told the horror of her final moments. He laboured over that cracking bruise on her cheek, heightening the shadow it created. No one had a bad word to say about Ellen Chambers, he thought. Professional, clever, reliable, considerate – those were the words that kept cropping up when her colleagues spoke about her. That was the *professional* woman, but no one seemed to know anything about her private life. And the one person who did know, her sister Susan, had gone into hiding. So who was Ellen Chambers, he wondered? Eighteen hours into the investigation, he still knew nothing about her. Something wasn't right. He just didn't know what.

He went back to her eyes. Now, what were they trying to tell him?

★

Jess relaxed back in her chair, glad she'd phoned Sangster. He seemed easier to talk to tonight, relaxed even. And judging by the relief in his voice, he'd been worrying about Susan too. What on earth did the girl expect to find in that diary? Closing her eyes, she could see Susan's frightened face. She would try really hard to persuade her to go back to the UK for a couple of weeks, where she'd be safe.

Jess yawned. She ought to go to bed since Simon wasn't going to phone tonight. She hoped he wasn't going to work through the night; he needed to rest. She could hear waves crashing onto the beach now. The pounding seemed to shudder through the entire building. She looked up at the full moon. There'll be a king tide tonight, that's what Sangster had said.

A soft buzzing sounded in her ear, and she flapped away a mosquito. As she sat in the silence, goose bumps suddenly rose on her arms. There it was again, the feeling that she wasn't alone. That presence. Her eyes flashed open and she strained to listen. A soft rustling sounded from the bushes by the path. She peered over the railings into the darkness and caught a glimpse of a shadow in the moonlight.

★

So why do you need to keep the diary, Susan? Those words, spoken out loud in the silence of night, were rattling around his head.

He couldn't believe his luck. *Now* he knew for sure who had that diary. And he wasn't about to let those bitches go anywhere near the police.

He looked back up to the second floor balcony. Excitement surged through him as he thought of those breasts, and the wave of pleasure on her face as she sipped the wine. Did she think she was safe on that balcony? He could climb up there in seconds. His face twisted. She was making this so easy.

He put the monocular in his pocket, and looked at his watch. It was time! Drawing his gun, he took a couple of steps forward.

The damp mist shrouded the trees and bushes, giving them an ethereal light under the moon. He listened. The only sound came from the sails and rigging of the moored boats at the jetty tinkling in the breeze.

The crunch of dead leaves underfoot made him hesitate. The footsteps were meant to be stealthy, but they echoed through the dead of night. He sniffed the air, as he stalked through the bushes. *I'm so close, I can smell you.*

Every nerve in his body tensed as he closed in. *You meddlin' fool.* He aimed the gun. *Stupidity – that was your mistake!*

A faint gasp was all he heard as the silent bullet slammed into the target. His prey slumped to the ground. Breathing heavily, he drew out his knife and thrust it into the heart. That exquisite joy started in the depths of his soul, pulsing through him in waves of pleasure.

When it was over, he pulled out the knife and looked all around. There was no-one about.

He took out his mobile and dialled a number. "It's done," he said and hung up.

17

Out of the window, Jess watched the pale yellow sun gathering strength as it rose and burnt off the early morning sea mist. Unlocking the balcony door, she walked outside. Everything looked postcard perfect. What a night. She'd been so tense, she'd only had a few hours' sleep. Still, she was used to surviving on that. In the distance, she noticed several police officers at the jetty. There seemed to be a lot of activity down there again. More investigations?

Scanning the beach and gardens, she saw the young man who'd been pruning roses yesterday. Now he was fishing leaves and debris from the swimming pool with a long pole and net. He glanced up and locked eyes with her. Uncomfortable, she pulled her robe around her and walked back into her room. She flinched when she saw the time. London had woken her at 6am to touch base on the Ellen Chambers' case before closing for the day. The time difference was annoying. It was impossible to hold a coherent conversation when jolted from sleep.

She walked over to the door and poked her head out into the corridor. No newspaper. She wondered whether to call Simon. As Press Officer, he had all the newspapers delivered to his house every morning. *And* he got up at the crack of sparrows. Her mobile rang and she ran over to the desk to answer.

"This is your seven o'clock alarm call," said Simon. "Sorry I didn't phone last night, Jess, but the dinner went on late. Then I went back to the High Commission. I didn't finish until one o'clock this morning."

"You could have phoned, I was still awake."

"Listen, Jess." He lowered his voice. "I didn't get the chance to ask Nigel why he hadn't told us about that intelligence report; he was stuck to the Foreign Secretary's side like glue. Then he rushed off after dinner." He paused. "Like he was avoiding me."

"Avoiding you?"

"That's why I went back to the High Commission to look for that report." He stopped.

"And?"

"It wasn't recorded in the top secret Registry log. And it wasn't locked up in the strong room either." He hesitated. "We shouldn't really be talking about this on an open phone line." But he went on anyway. "I found it eventually, in Nigel's cupboard, in his office."

"Christ, Simon, if he finds out..."

"I know where his PA hides the combination. She's got a terrible memory and has to keep it written down." Simon gave a nervous chuckle. "The report was tucked at the bottom of his in-tray... it was from GCHQ."

That was the UK Security Services' listening station. "Go on," she urged.

"They'd picked up chatter in China saying Ellen Chambers was taking bribes from Chen Xiamen. Then our Embassy in Beijing did some digging."

"So Ellen Chambers *was* working for the Chinese?"

"Apparently, they were paying her to help them get a controlling percentage of the joint venture."

"Really?"

"According to the report, the negotiations were going well and the Chinese seemed happy enough with a 25 per cent share of the joint venture. Suddenly, about a month ago, they started demanding a controlling share, almost as if they knew they could get it."

Jess's brain whirled. "With Ellen Chambers on the inside, you mean?"

"So it seems."

"But would she have the power to sway the negotiation that much on her own, Simon?"

"I don't know. I suppose having someone on the inside would make the Chinese believe they could get a better deal."

"But why would she do it? It doesn't make sense. She had a job she loved, according to her sister. And a fat corporate salary. Why jeopardise everything for *more* money?" She plopped down on the edge of the bed. "Poor Susan's going to be devastated."

"You're not going to tell her?"

"Of course not." Then she sat bolt upright. "So why did Nigel keep this report to himself?"

"*Exactly!*"

The silence seemed to crackle down the line.

"Have you told the High Commissioner, Simon?"

"I haven't had a chance. He only got back from Perth in time for the dinner last night, and he was cranky enough as it was. I've just left a message on his voicemail asking for a meeting first thing this morning. Mind you, I don't want to tell him about that intelligence report and drop Nigel in it, at least not without talking to Nigel first. And I don't particularly want to own up to breaking into Nigel's combination cupboard either."

"I'm bloody furious Nigel kept that report from me."

Jess paused. "Do you think he'd read it? Maybe he just shoved it under his papers and forgot it?"

"*You're* defending *him?*"

"He did seem distracted yesterday."

"Well, it's possible, I suppose. But Nigel never makes mistakes."

"Mm." Jess went quiet. "At least you've all heard about Anthony Harris's murder now. So what's the latest?"

"It's had everyone flapping around in Canberra, I can tell you. The High Commissioner tried to phone Mrs Harris to offer condolences, but she's in Singapore on business."

Jess looked at her watch, she had to get on. "Simon, I haven't got much time, but I need to tell you a few things before you go."

"Fire away."

She explained to him how she'd come to have Ellen's diary and how Susan had run off with it. "I feel terrible," she confessed. "The police need the diary for their investigation."

"It doesn't sound like you could have stopped her, Jess."

She knew he was trying to make her feel better, but it didn't work. "Then Susan rang me last night. She's still got the diary. She said she wanted to see me this morning. I'm waiting for her to call now."

"It's important to get that diary to the police, Jess."

"That's exactly what I plan to do when I see her this morning. But that's not all, Simon. Susan thought Ellen was having an affair. She never met the man, but she thinks that's why Ellen always stayed at The Palms. She met him here privately and," Jess hesitated, "the thing is I got a look at that diary before Susan grabbed it. And I noticed Ellen met someone with the initials TH regularly when she was in Brisbane. I think those initials might have stood for Tony Harris. The Minister's family and friends call him Tony. I think Ellen might have been having an affair with him. And that's the link between their two murders."

"*Christ, Jess!* That's a lot of supposition."

She carried on. "If Ellen Chambers was under surveillance for corruption, could Anthony Harris have been in involved in that too?"

"You're getting fanciful now, Jess."

"You think?" Annoyed at his tone, she changed the subject. "Yes, well did I tell you the Chinese delegation came up from Canberra on the same plane as me yesterday morning? Anthony Harris met them at the airport, before he was murdered. He introduced me to Chen Xiamen. Now there's a cold fish."

"I suppose Harris had the job of schmoozing the Chinese in his Brisbane electorate."

"So, what do we know about this Chen Xiamen?" she asked. "Who is he in the Chinese pecking order?"

"He's the Chairman of the China National Energy Corporation," said Simon, "and known for being really ambitious. The word is he's in line for a position in the Standing Committee of the Politburo in Beijing. Though rumour has it he's got something of a chequered past."

"What's he done?"

"I don't know. But his current role seems to be a make or break one for him."

"So, getting a great result out of this LNG contract would be crucial for him," she said. "A last ditch effort to get the top political job he's always wanted. I guess he'd be willing to pay bribes. Do whatever it takes?"

"Maybe." Simon sounded cautious. "Anyway, I thought I'd try and find out more. So I sent an email to London and our Embassy in Beijing urgently requesting information on the *source* of the corruption allegations against Ellen and

Chen in that intelligence report. That seems to me what's missing in all this. Who is behind these allegations?"

"Good point. Can you let me know as soon as you hear from them, Simon?"

"Of course. By the way, I've flicked through all the newspapers this morning. The press were coming from the angle that Ellen's murder was probably a mugging, or a sex attack gone wrong. Of course now they're focused on finding a connection with Anthony Harris's murder. Let's hope forensics can release some hard facts soon, before the media start making it up. Oh, and you've been quoted extensively, Jess. So there's no chance of any anonymity, your picture's in every paper."

"Is it?" Conscious of the time, she switched her phone to speaker and started getting ready. "I met the Chairman of Western Energy here yesterday."

"How'd he seem?"

"*Really* cut up about Ellen Chambers. I'm going to meet him at the Convention Centre later. In fact, I'm going into town to work out of the Consulate-General now. There's no point in staying here, I've done what I can. I'll get a room in the Riverbank Hotel, where the Western Energy lot are staying. It'll be easier." She pulled her navy blue linen trouser suit and her white blouse out of the wardrobe.

"Did Langhurst say if he was still flying to Canberra for the High Commissioner's dinner this evening?"

"He didn't mention it." Jess sat down on the dressing-table stool and brushed her hair. "I feel so sorry for Susan Chambers, Simon. She told me her sister was frightened of the police before she was murdered. And now Susan refuses to talk to them. She's so young."

"Don't let your feelings cloud your judgment, Jess."

"Of course I won't," she snapped. "I told you, I plan to get that diary to the police before lunch. By then, I'm hoping they'll have the initial autopsy results on Ellen Chambers. Oh, and I'm going to dodge the media for a few hours, if that's okay?"

"Sure, we'll be fine until they start fretting about their lunchtime bulletins."

She picked up her lipstick. "By the way, when I talked to the journalists yesterday afternoon, one of them was a complete pain. He kept on and on about whether any of us *knew* Ellen Chambers, and whether she'd worked for the British Government."

"What was he getting at?"

"You tell me."

Simon paused. "Who was he?"

"He never told me his name. Or the media outlet he worked for. He bombarded me with questions, and slipped out. But I got the distinct impression he knew something about Ellen Chambers that I didn't." She hesitated. "Then I had a wander down to the jetty. What a chilling experience *that* was."

There was a pause. "Look, I've got to attend HC's dinner this evening. But I could fly up to Brisbane tomorrow afternoon to give you a hand, if the High Commissioner agrees."

"No need. I'm fine."

"Jess..."

"I tell you I'm fine."

"All right. Let's talk again later... By the way, great job on the media, Jess. Thanks." And he hung up.

She snapped her mobile shut. Why did he have to sound so surprised about that?

★

The lift doors slid open. Scanning her mobile for messages, Jess frowned as she hurried across the lobby. She'd left two messages for Nigel, and he still hadn't rung back. She'd expected him to be too busy yesterday with the Foreign Secretary's visit to keep phoning her. But she was surprised he hadn't called at all. That wasn't like him.

She became aware of an animated buzz of voices and looked around. So many guests seemed to be checking out. Her ears pricked up at a distant wailing noise. Was that a siren? A police siren?

Threading her way across the lobby through guests and suitcases, she searched all the faces, looking for Susan. Would she suddenly appear like yesterday?

Her eyes stopped on a familiar figure at reception.

Was that Chen Xiamen? He had his back to her, but she recognised that dapper suit and the way he puffed himself up to look taller. She looked around for the rest of the Chinese, but Chen seemed to be alone. Should she go over? But when he turned and she saw his face, she instinctively slipped behind a marble pillar out of sight. Gone was the relaxed mask of yesterday. His lips were pursed tight with temper as he marched towards the main entrance and out of the door. She hurried over to the window and was just in time to see him jump into a taxi and drive off. What was all that about?

She lingered in the lobby for another few minutes in case Susan Chambers showed up. When she didn't, Jess walked over to the dining room to get some breakfast. At the entrance, she picked up a local newspaper from the stack on the counter and waited to be seated. The tables, covered in white linen cloths, stretched the length of the room in neat rows all the way to the terrace doors. But hardly any of them had been laid. There were only two waitresses on duty, and they both looked flustered. Her mobile rang and she answered.

"Morning, Jessica."

Langhurst's friendly voice made her smile. "Ah, good morning, John."

"I just wanted to check you're still coming to the Convention Centre at 12.30?"

"Yes, I'll be there."

"Good. Where are you now?"

"At the hotel, grabbing a quick breakfast before I check out."

There was a pause. "I feel useless waiting for news," he said. "Are you sure there's nothing I can do to help?"

"Not as far as I know." Then she remembered what Simon said. "Are you still planning to attend the High Commissioner's dinner in Canberra this evening?"

"Yes." Langhurst's voice was businesslike now. "I'm going to duck out of the Conference later and get the four o'clock flight to Canberra. I'll be on the first plane back in the morning, so I won't miss much."

"Excellent. I'm sure the High Commissioner will be delighted to see you."

"Right, well if there's nothing I can do, I'll see you at 12.30, Jessica."

"You will," she replied, brightly, and hung up, just as one of the waitresses came over.

"Sorry to keep you waiting, Ma'am." The words seemed to stutter out of the woman's mouth. "We're, well, we're all behind... we just can't believe it."

There was something about the woman's shocked face that made Jess ask: "Can't believe what?"

"Haven't you heard?" The woman leaned closer. "There was another murder at the jetty last night."

Jess felt her stomach turn. *Please don't let it be Susan.*

"Danny Burton," the waitress went on. "He was shot, just like that Minister yesterday afternoon." Seeing Jess's blank expression, she whispered: "Danny was a gardener here. He's the one who found Miss Chambers' body yesterday morning. Who's going to be next? That's what we're all wondering. We're terrified to go out of the hotel."

Jess didn't know what to say or do. Should she go down to the jetty? Phone Inspector Sangster? Was he down there already?

"Follow me," the waitress said.

Numb, Jess followed her to a small table and sat down.

The waitress poured her a cup of coffee, and disappeared.

Jess got up again and walked over to the doors at the far end of the dining room. Stepping out onto the terrace, she could see the jetty. Should she go down? She could see uniformed officers milling around and the crime scene cordon up again. Thinking she'd only get in the way, she went back to her seat and pulled out her mobile to call Sangster. Was he already down there? If so, he wouldn't want to be disturbed. She took a sip of coffee, but it tasted bitter in her mouth. She started flicking through the newspaper again, but she couldn't concentrate.

"Morning, Jess."

She jumped up when she saw it was Sangster. "I've just heard about Danny Burton."

He pulled out a chair and sat down. "He was shot last night. A single bullet to the back of the head, and a knife to the heart."

"Just like Anthony Harris?" She shuddered. "Why would anyone kill Danny Burton? Did *he* murder Ellen Chambers?"

Sangster shook his head. "But I think he knew who *did*. And that's why he was killed."

"Do you have any idea who?"

"No."

She sat back in her chair and studied Sangster's face. There were deep lines etched around his eyes and mouth that she hadn't noticed yesterday. *Three* murders and the police didn't seem to have a clue. Then she remembered the shadowy figure on the path last night. "What time was Danny killed?"

"Around midnight. Why?"

She sat forward. "After I phoned you, I saw someone on the garden path, about half way down to the jetty."

His eyes narrowed.

"It sounds ridiculous, but I had this feeling that someone was watching me while I was sitting on my balcony. So, I went inside."

"What time was that?"

"11.30. I remember the time because the late TV news had just started."

"Did you get a look at whoever it was?"

She shook her head. "I heard a rustling in the bushes and saw a shadow on the path. But it was too dark to see." She paused. "Where was Danny's body found?"

"In exactly the same spot as Ellen Chambers'."

"The *same* place?"

His eyes flashed. "This man's confident. Real confident. He shot Anthony Harris in broad daylight outside the police station under our noses. Now, he's taunting us by putting Danny's body in the same place as Ellen Chambers'. He thinks we're all idiots." His mobile vibrated for the second time since he'd sat down. He glanced at the caller ID but didn't answer. "I have to go."

She nodded.

But he didn't move. "Have you heard from Susan?"

"Not yet. I hope to God she's all right." Jess could hardly hear his reply for the racket behind. Turning, she saw the two little girls from the beach yesterday sitting at the table behind with their mother. They were banging their spoons on their cereal bowls for a game.

"Didn't she say she'd ring first thing?" he repeated.

Jess nodded and he looked away, to hide his annoyance.

For some reason, Jess's logical mind turned to another loose end that had been bothering her. "Tom, did the Federal Police question Ellen Chambers about taking bribes from the Chinese? Is that how she found out they were on to her?"

He looked up. "What makes you think she knew?"

"Why else would she have been afraid of you all?"

He frowned. "As far as I'm aware, she was under technical surveillance. That means they were monitoring her phone calls and emails, but not following her. So I don't see how she could have known."

Jess frowned. "Well if the Federal Police didn't tell her, could someone else have told her? Someone on the inside?"

He caught her drift. "Anthony Harris, you mean?"

She nodded. "He *was* the Federal Minister responsible for energy resources and mining. So he would have been close to the deal and players in every way." She paused. "If he'd been having an affair with her, surely he'd have told her the police were onto her? Maybe he even challenged her about what she was doing? Maybe that's why he was killed too."

He nodded. "It's possible."

She couldn't help but ask the next question. "So *was* Harris the father of her unborn child?"

Sangster shifted on his chair. "I'm expecting the lab results any time."

Jess sighed with frustration. "So what does Mrs Harris have to say? Did she know her husband was having an affair?"

He stiffened. "She's in Singapore, on business. She's travelling back today."

Jess suddenly felt a familiar weariness seep through her. "It's so tragic for the family."

He nodded and looked at his mobile. "I have to go," he said again. Still he didn't move.

"So what has Chen Xiamen said?" Jess asked. "And the rest of the Chinese?"

Sangster's eyes turned steely. "We have to wait for the Chinese Ambassador and the PM's China expert to get here from Canberra before we can interview them."

That's when Jess understood the depth of his anger and frustration. He was trying to carry out an investigation in the dark, and she knew how that felt. "I didn't know the Chinese were staying here," she said.

Sangster looked at her. "They're not; they're at the Riverbank in town."

"Well I've just seen Chen leave here."

He frowned. "Did he say where he was going?"

Jess remembered Chen's face. "He looked furious about something, so I didn't speak to him. I just saw him talking to the receptionist. Then he went out and got into a taxi."

Sangster's mobile vibrated again, but he just looked at her.

It was her turn to feel uncomfortable now and she took a sip of coffee.

"I'm sorry for being bad tempered yesterday, Jess" he said.

Surprised, she put down her cup. "Oh that's all right."

"No, it's not. I was rude... I've no excuse. It's... well, it's just this job sometimes."

Jess nodded and leant back in her chair. She knew an olive branch when she saw one. "And I'm sorry about the diary, Tom."

The bleep of an incoming text message sounded, and he picked up his mobile.

Hearing a shriek of laughter, Jess turned and saw one of the little girls jump down from her chair. The other followed suit and they chased each other up and down until the little one careered into Jess's table, spilling coffee, and knocking Sangster's notepad onto the floor. Jess glanced down as the pages fluttered open. Such amazing sketches.

Sangster banged his phone down on the table and stared at the two children. "Listen, you two. Sit back up at that table and do what your mum tells you."

The two children scampered back into their chairs and sat with their heads bowed.

"You were saying, Jess?" He leant down and picked up his pad.

Jess smiled at the girls, then at him. "I said I was sorry about the diary, Tom."

Sangster studied the Consul. She looked her usual cool self this morning. Only the dark circles under her eyes suggested she was feeling the heat too. His vibrating phone distracted him and he checked the caller ID. This time he picked it up. "Have you got those autopsy results, Anderson?"

He couldn't hear the reply over the racket from the two kids, who were now wailing. He got up and walked out into the lobby to take the call. "Right, go on," he said.

"We've rushed through the Ellen Chambers' autopsy first, Tom. The cause of death *was* drowning."

"Right."

"And that cracker of a bruise on her left cheek, well, he broke her cheekbone with that punch and probably knocked her to the ground; she's got three cracked ribs on her right side. The index and middle finger of her right hand are broken too. She fought hard."

"A-ha."

"And she's got a hairline skull fracture and bruises consistent with her head being banged repeatedly on the ground. Oh, and you remember that marking in the centre of the bruise on her cheek. I think it may have been made by a ring, with a small stone in the middle. From the angle of impact, I'd say he was right-handed."

"Was she pregnant?" Sangster asked, quickly.

"Yes. You were right about that – 16 weeks."

"Is Anthony Harris the father?"

"We've just finished him and sent his DNA to the lab." Anderson sighed. "As soon as I know, you'll know."

"It's real important."

"We've been working right through the night." Anderson's tone was almost accusatory when he asked: "Is Evans still at the jetty with corpse number three?"

"Yep. Same MO as Harris. A bullet to the back of the head. Clean and clinical. Then a stab wound through the heart."

"This psycho likes to get his rocks off on the job, doesn't he? Bit of a joker too, positioning the body in the same place as our first victim. He's taunting you, Tom."

Sangster stiffened. "He's confident, I'll give you that. That's why I need those autopsy results."

"We're going as fast as we can."

"Good, because I don't think he's finished yet."

"Well you'd better catch him quick, mate. Our overtime budget can't stand any more of this." And Anderson hung up.

★

Jess watched Sangster go into the lobby to take his call. She hoped he wouldn't be long; she wanted to get off to Brisbane. She took another sip of coffee. Putting the cup down on the saucer, her eyes were drawn to his notepad that lay next to it. She glanced over at the door. No sign of him. Leaning over, she turned the notepad round and flicked through the pages.

What she saw made her gasp; page after page of drawings, with such fine detail bringing scenes to life. He's the real deal, she thought. Fascinated, she stopped at one of Ellen Chambers lying dead on the flat sand. Her eyes were so lifelike, and yet so dead.

"So, what do you see?"

She looked up at Sangster, as if seeing him for the first time. It was hard to believe there was such an artistic soul behind that gruff exterior. "Sorry, I was curious. These are *really* good."

He picked up the notepad.

"There's something about the way you've drawn her eyes," Jess went on.

He looked at her.

"She's clearly dead, yet you've captured a sort of light in them." She paused. "Oh I think I see what you mean. You think she *recognised* her killer? Is that what that light signifies?"

He looked stunned that she understood. "Do you deal with many bodies in your job, Jess?"

"Some." She looked away. "You know, immediately after death, I think it's possible to see pain or fear or shock on people's faces and in their eyes." She felt a little embarrassed. "I don't know, maybe it's just the shock of realising they're on the point of death. But it's there sometimes."

He studied her until she felt uncomfortable again. "I must go. I'm checking out now, and moving to the Riverbank, where the Western Energy delegation are staying. I'll be able to work out of the British Consulate-General."

He nodded. "That seems sensible." He went to leave. "Let's touch base later."

"I've got appointments all morning. But I could come to the police station around 2pm, if that suits, Tom?"

"That's fine." He hesitated. "You know, you're the only link with Susan and that diary now, Jess. She's in danger while she still has it. So..."

"So I'll ring you as soon as I hear from her, Tom."

He nodded and walked away.

18

Back in her room, Jess's head was teeming with questions. She went over to the window and looked towards the jetty. The police were still down there, with the beach cordoned off again. But she couldn't see Tom anywhere. Was he right, had Danny witnessed Ellen's murder? Is that why he was killed in exactly the same place?

Conscious she was running late, she looked at her watch and went over to her cabin bag that lay open on the rack next to the wardrobe. Pushing her wash bag inside, she turned to the bedside cabinet for the photo of Jack and Amy.

She froze.

Her frantic eyes darted around the room until she spotted the photo lying on the bed. What was it doing there? She stood still. The bed was still unmade, so the cleaners hadn't been in. As she looked around, the hairs rose on the back of her neck. The bottom drawer of the dressing-table was open.

Someone had been in her room.

She ran over to her cabin bag and searched it. Nothing missing. Grabbing her briefcase, she looked inside. Her laptop, memory stick and camera were all still there. Again, nothing missing.

But someone had been in her room. She was sure of it.

She picked up the phone. Should she call hotel security? But how long would it take for them to come up and investigate? Would they insist on calling the police? Would she have to wait for them too? She checked her watch again. Not only was she really late; she couldn't wait to get away from this place.

She put the receiver back. With nothing taken, she decided to get off to Brisbane and tell Tom later when she saw him. Packing up the rest of her things at lightning speed, she was careful to slip the photo of Jack and Amy into her briefcase where it would be safe.

Pulling her cabin bag to the door, she stopped and looked around to check she hadn't left anything. She shivered. The atmosphere in the room had changed. With the morning sun on the other side of the building, it looked dark and uninviting. Tainted even. And nothing like the bright, elegant room she'd walked into yesterday. Stepping into the corridor, she slammed the door behind her, thankful she didn't have to spend another night at The Palms.

19

"Ready for today's consular problem?" Sharon asked, in her usual upbeat way.

Jess braced herself, unsure of how much more she could cope with.

"A yacht went down around midnight off the coast of New South Wales, not far from Sydney. There were three people on board; one of them a British girl, travelling around Australia on a gap year."

"Any survivors?"

"An Australian lad managed to cling to wreckage until a passing vessel rescued him. There was a terrible storm at the time, really rough seas. There's little chance of the other two being found alive."

Jess slumped back in the chair. Another young Briton lost while on the adventure of a lifetime. Another family plunged into unimaginable grief. She knew parents found it hard to let their kids go travelling on gap years. And with good reason. Most came back safe and sound, but there was always one that didn't. "We'll need to find out who the girl was and notify her family, Sharon."

"Our Sydney Consul-General's got it covered. I just wanted to let you know, in case you heard it on the news."

"Okay, thanks. Let's talk again later."

Jess hung up and looked out of the window of the Brisbane Consulate-General. From her bird's eye view on the fifteenth floor of the city centre office block, she gazed right over Brisbane River. The water looked benign, like a swathe of crystals bobbing and sparkling in the sunlight, as boats tacked their way along in the breeze. But that was deceptive; the rivers and seas around Australia could be treacherous.

She placed her laptop on the absent Consul-General's desk and looked around. She liked his office. The outer wall was floor to ceiling glass, which meant the room was flooded with light. A small conference table and chairs filled the space at the far end; and a beige sofa with two armchairs stood in the middle of the room. Only the Sydney Consul-General had a better office, she thought, overlooking the spectacular Sydney harbour and Opera House.

She coughed and rubbed her throat. What with the early morning phone calls, coffee with Inspector Sangster, half an hour spent briefing the Brisbane staff, and more calls to Canberra, she felt all talked out.

And it was only 10.30.

But Susan Chambers still hadn't rung. Her anxiety grew as she looked out of the window, across to the skyscrapers this time. She was out there in the city somewhere.

Come on Susan. Ring!

Opening her briefcase, she reached inside for her diary to plan the rest of her day. But it wasn't there. She checked the desk. Not there either. Where was it? She could remember checking dates in it while she was on the phone to London earlier. After that, she put it in her briefcase before going down to breakfast.

Her stomach flipped...

Had it been in her briefcase *after* breakfast when she thought someone had been in her room? She remembered seeing her laptop and camera when she checked, but not her diary. But why would anyone want *her* diary?

Then a dawning realisation crept over her...

What if they hadn't realised it was *her* diary? What if they'd thought it was Ellen Chambers'?

She went to call Inspector Sangster and hesitated. Was she *sure* someone had taken her diary? She didn't want to start any unnecessary panic. The familiar bleep of an incoming text sounded and she opened it straightaway.

meet you café aqua, queen street at 1100. come on your own. don't tell police. SC

Susan! Jess looked up at the wall clock. She only had 15 minutes to get to Café Aqua. *Don't tell the police.* Honestly that girl was testing her patience to the limit.

On my way! she texted back.

Reaching for her bag and briefcase, she sped out of the office. She thought she'd leave her car in the office underground car park, and walk to Queen Street. It was close enough.

Taking the lift to the ground floor, she strode across the marble lobby towards the entrance. She was going to be very firm with Susan this time. No more messing about. She *had* to get Ellen's diary to the police. Squinting as she walked outside into blinding sunshine, she stopped and rummaged in her handbag for her sunglasses. Out the corner of her eye, she glimpsed a shadow on the pavement just over her right shoulder. She put on her sunglasses and looked around. Nobody there.

Hurrying along, she couldn't stop thinking about earlier in her hotel room; the bottom drawer of the dressing-table open, the photo of Jack and Amy lying on the bed. Had the intruder been after Ellen Chambers' diary all along? The entry door hadn't been forced, so whoever it was must have used a key card.

How easy was that?

She could feel goose bumps shivering around her body, despite the warm sunshine. Had Ellen Chambers' killer been in her hotel room? What if she'd come back at the time? It didn't bear thinking about. Inspector Sangster's words rattled around her head. *Susan's in danger while she still has that diary.*

She looked down at her watch, and caught another flash of movement.

That shadow again?

A feeling of dread swept through her. When she stopped and turned sideways to look in a dress shop, a figure behind darted into a shop doorway.

Someone was following her.

She started walking faster. Lengthening the shoulder strap of her bag, she slipped it over her head to rest across her body and clutched her briefcase to her chest with both hands. I haven't got the diary, she wanted to shout.

But Susan has! That thought made her slow down. If she went straight to Café Aqua, she would lead whoever it was straight to Susan, and to Ellen's diary.

Her mind was spinning when she stopped at the next pedestrian crossing to wait for the traffic lights to change to red. More people came up behind her. Someone jostled her, and she felt a tug on her briefcase. Instinctively, she clung on. Turning to face her assailant, her high heel got caught in a crack in the paving. Her ankle buckled. She felt herself losing balance.

She could see the bus coming.

"Watch out," a woman shouted.

She toppled over into the road.

Screeching tyres was all she heard as the wheels of the bus just missed her head. Stunned, she lay for a minute, listening to the low hum of traffic, and loud voices all around. Everything seemed dreamlike. She struggled up and sat on the kerb. Many hands were helping her now, everyone anxious to find out if she was all right. She looked at their faces. Who had tried to steal her briefcase?

Still clutching it with one hand, she brushed her trousers down with the other and pushed her hair from her face. Amazingly, apart from grazing her hand as she tried to cushion her fall, she was unhurt. "I'm fine," she said to her helpers.

An old woman kept asking if she wanted to go to hospital. "No need." Jess felt embarrassed now. "No damage done."

It took a while to satisfy everyone she was okay, but eventually the crowd dispersed. When she stood up, her legs felt wobbly. Nervous, she looked around and hurried across the road. The sound of her high heels tapping on the pavement as she walked somehow reassured her that she was okay. But she couldn't stop replaying the incident in her mind. Someone had tried to snatch her briefcase; she was sure about that. Did they push her into the road, or did she fall?

Turning right into Brisbane Street, she walked along until she reached a department store. Quickly, she slipped through the front door and hurried through cosmetics to women's clothing at the back. There, she ducked behind a tall rack of scarves and peered out to see if anyone had followed her inside. She could hear herself panting, and tried to catch her breath quietly.

Seeing a shop assistant eye her suspiciously, she grabbed a scarf off the rack and wrapped it around her neck as if trying it on. When the woman had gone, she threw it back on the rack.

Her eyes locked onto a figure, dressed in dark clothes, standing near the escalator with his back to her.

Her stomach turned.

Then he seemed to disappear into thin air. Frantic, she looked around and ducked behind the scarf rack again, holding her breath. There were no footsteps or rustling of clothes, but she could feel a menacing presence all around her. She *had* to get away.

She looked over at the store's back entrance. It was so close. Taking a deep breath, she darted towards the door and zipped outside. She sprinted along the street, running too fast to look behind to see if he was following. Turning the corner, she ducked into the first café she came across.

As she burst through the door and stood breathing heavily from running, everyone turned to look at her. She nodded and sat down at a table facing the door to recover her composure. She pulled out her mobile and called Sharon, who answered straightaway. Relieved to hear Sharon's voice, she told her what had just happened.

There was a shocked silence. "Are you all right, Jess?"

No, I'm not all right, she thought. I'm definitely not all right. How could I be? Someone tried to steal my briefcase and push me under a bus. She took a deep breath. "I'm fine, Sharon."

"Did you get a good look at him?"

"Just a back view. He was dressed all in black."

"How do you know he was following you?"

"I don't." Jess struggled to think straight. "But I'm sure he was. He wants Ellen Chambers' diary. He thinks I have it."

"Ellen Chambers' diary? What does he want that for?"

"I don't know, Sharon. Maybe the killer left his business card in it." Jess didn't mean to sound sarcastic. "Look, I have to go."

"We're having a meeting in half an hour with the High Commissioner," Sharon intervened. "Simon wants to send reinforcements to help you. Do you want me to tell them what just happened?"

Jess paused to think. This was going to send everyone into a spin, and the last thing she wanted to do was to divert attention away from the murder investigations. "Explain about the hotel intruder and my missing diary," she said. "But don't make too much of a drama of what just happened."

"But, Jess..."

"I *must* go. I have to find Susan. I'll phone again later." And she rang off before Sharon could say anything else.

She *had* to get to Café Aqua.

Rising, she picked up her briefcase and bag and headed to the back of the café. In the ladies, she took off her jacket, folded it up and stuffed it into her briefcase. She pulled her white blouse out of her waistband and let it hang loose over her hips. Finding her sliver clasp in her bag, she pulled her hair back with both hands and clipped it into a bun. Then she popped out her contact lenses, put on her brown, square framed glasses and looked in the mirror. Would he still recognise her? She hoped not.

She checked her watch: 11.15. She was really late now. *Wait for me Susan!* Striding along in the direction of Café Aqua, she tried not to look over her shoulder, while her damp palms kept slipping around the handle of her briefcase. She couldn't stop thinking about Ellen Chambers' diary.

She *had* to find Susan.

★

Café Aqua was heaving when she got there, the noise bouncing off the bare, white walls and tiled floor. Jess stood in the doorway taking in the heady aroma of roasted coffee beans. Two waitresses buzzed about taking orders, and clearing tables while the espresso machine drummed and hissed in the background as the barista worked up a fever to deal with the rush. Nothing could come between Australians and their mid-morning coffee.

She spotted Susan sitting on her own at a table in the far corner. Relieved, she walked over. As she went, she eyed a group of men sitting on chrome stools at the long bar that stretched the length of one wall to the back of the café. But they weren't interested in her; they were glued to the game of footy playing on the flat-screen TV suspended from the wall above the bar. Their animated cheers and groans added to the general hubbub.

Jess's gaze was drawn to Susan, who sat with her head down over a sheet of paper on the table in front of her. "Hello," she said.

Susan jumped and looked up. "I thought you weren't coming." Her voice sounded accusing.

Jess felt her anger flare, as the wheels of that bus flashed through her mind. "Where have you *been* all night, Susan, I've been worried sick." She wanted to pull Susan to her feet and frog march her to the nearest police station. But her anger subsided when she looked into Susan's puffy, red eyes. Lashing out wouldn't help if she wanted to gain her trust.

Jess pulled a chair round and sat down in a position where she could talk and keep an eye on the door. "The police have been out all night looking for you, Susan. You *know* Inspector Sangster needs that diary."

"I've been at my boyfriend's place," Susan replied.

Boyfriend? That surprised Jess. "Well, at least you haven't been on your own. So that's something."

"He's out of the country, on assignment for the *Echo*. But don't worry," Susan went on, "I've phoned him. He's flying home from East Timor today."

"Maybe *he'll* be able to talk some sense into you."

Susan bristled. "When were you going to tell me about Anthony Harris and Danny Burton?"

Jess heard the controlled fury in Susan's voice and hesitated.

"I had to *hear* about the murders on the *news*."

Jess looked her in the eye. "How could anyone tell you about them, Susan? You won't give us your contact details."

Susan was unperturbed. "What did they have to do with my sister's murder?"

Jess held up a hand to stop Susan's questions. Should she tell her what she knew? If she wasn't straight with her, she would never gain her confidence. "Look, all I know is that Danny's body was found in the same place as Ellen's early this morning. One theory they're working on is that Danny was killed because he witnessed your sister's murder."

Susan's eyes flashed. "What makes the police think he saw Ellen's murder?"

"I'm told he was pestering your sister in the bar last night. She gave him the brush off. Said she was waiting for someone."

"Who?" Susan sat forward.

"I don't know." Jess replied. "Anyway, the police think Danny may have followed Ellen down to the jetty."

Susan slumped back in her chair and eyed Jess. "How do you know all this?"

"Tom Sangster just told me. He was at the hotel."

"Oh, Tom now, is it?" Susan raised an eyebrow. "He's got you eating out of his hand already."

Jess ignored the jibe; they didn't have time for this.

But, as the waitress passed by, Susan ordered two coffees.

"We don't have time for coffee," Jess said. "I need to get you and the diary to the police now." She stood up. "Come on."

But Susan didn't move, she was studying the sheet of paper on the table. "There were no appointments in Ellen's diary for Sunday night," she said. "She attended a lunch for the Conference delegates earlier, but there was nothing in her diary for Sunday night."

"I know." Jess looked down at the paper. "What's that?"

"A list of all the names and contact details for every appointment in Ellen's diary over the last six months. I'm checking them out." Susan looked up. "I told you last night I was doing it. That's how I found out Ellen was pregnant, by phoning her gynaecologist."

Jess sat down again. "And I said you were interfering with the police investigation."

But Susan wasn't listening; she was on a track of her own. The emotional young woman of yesterday had gone. In her place, was a determined journalist, with a tenacious look in her eye. And that was much more worrying.

"Her appointments seem to check out," Susan went on. "So the initials TH in her diary are all we've got left to work on." She glanced up. "I think Ellen was meeting her lover at The Palms on Sunday night. That's why she didn't have anything in her diary." Her voice rose. "It was Anthony Harris, wasn't it? That's the connection between their murders. They were lovers."

Jess said nothing.

"That's why Ellen stayed at The Palms when she was in Brisbane, and not with me. She met him there, didn't she?" Susan's voice was getting louder and louder. "Go on, tell me. You *know* don't you? It was Tony bloody Harris."

The door opened. Jess tensed as a man in a dark suit walked in. She looked back at Susan. "Come on. We can talk on the way to the police station."

But Susan wasn't listening; she was pulling something out of her tote bag. "I found this in Ellen's diary." She laid a tiny, square object on the table.

Jess picked it up. "It's a camera memory card." Her eyes narrowed. "I didn't see it in the diary."

"It was tucked in the cover, at the back." Susan reached into her bag again. "A store in town printed these out for me this morning." She laid three photos next to each other on the table. "According to the date on the camera card, Ellen took them during her visit to China last week."

Jess studied the photos. All three were of crowds milling around the same buildings. They were definitely taken in China, because some of the older people were wearing the dark blue Mao jackets of the old regime. Jess peered closer. "Those blue roofs look familiar... I think I went there when I visited Beijing a couple of years ago." She paused. "It's the Temple of Heaven, I'm sure of it."

"What's that?" Susan asked.

"A tourist attraction in Beijing. I think it was an imperial sacrificial altar for Taoist monks at one time."

Susan frowned. "Not very good photos are they? The buildings are out of focus."

Jess nodded. The focus *was* on the crowds, yet individual faces were too small to make out. Her head was whirling, as she tried to link everything together. Curious, she turned to Susan. "What started your sister's interest in China when she was younger?"

Susan shrugged. "I don't really know. Ellen went to Leeds Uni to study accounting, but after a couple of months, she switched to Chinese studies. That was a bit out of the blue, but we didn't think much about it at the time. She spent the final year of her degree in Shanghai, as an exchange student at Fudan University."

"Then what did she do?"

"She went *back* to Uni to qualify as an accountant." Susan frowned. "I thought *that* was odd, but Ellen was always interested in finance. After that, she worked in the Beijing Office of a multinational company for about five years before being head-hunted by Western Energy." She stared at Jess. "Why do you ask?"

"If she spent all those years living and working in Beijing, wouldn't she already have photos of the Temple of Heaven?"

Susan's eyes flashed. "What are you thinking?"

Jess was thinking how everything kept coming back to Ellen Chambers' connection with China. *Follow the money trail.* That's what Ellen had told her sister to do if anything happened to her? Was Ellen talking about the money from bribes she was supposed to be taking? Or something else?

As if reading her thoughts, Susan said: "That LNG deal's worth billions. Could her murder be connected to that? Maybe there was a problem with the negotiation or contract? Maybe Ellen found out something? Maybe she upset the other members of the consortium. Maybe... oh, I don't know." She shook her head in frustration.

Jess glanced over at the door again.

Susan eyed her, suspiciously. "Have you called the police?"

"No."

"Then why do you keep looking at the door?"

Jess hesitated. She wasn't going to lie to Susan. "It's just that, well..." She tried to sound calm but her throat was tight. "Someone searched my hotel room this morning while I was at breakfast."

Susan's jaw dropped.

"I didn't think anything was missing at the time, but now I can't find my diary." She looked at Susan. "I think they were after your sister's diary and took mine by mistake."

Susan blanched.

Jess's heart skipped a beat. "Where's Ellen's diary?"

"In a safe place," Susan whispered.

"*Safe?* What do you mean *safe?* For God's sake, Susan. I'm sitting here now, but someone's been following me all morning. They've already searched my hotel room and stolen *my* diary."

Susan's eyes widened.

"Now, no more nonsense. Where's that diary? You said you'd bring it!"

"*Christ! The diary!*" Susan jumped up and dashed to the door.

"*Wait!*" Jess shouted after her.

But Susan wasn't stopping for anyone.

Jess pulled her purse out of her bag and threw a 20 dollar note on the table for the coffees.

She picked up the camera card and shoved it into her jacket pocket. Rushing to the door, she got there just in time to see Susan speeding off in her car.

20

Sangster ran up the stairs to the conference room on the second floor of the Convention Centre. He had an appointment to see the Chairman and CEO of Western Energy at 10.30. He had a number of questions to ask them, and he wanted to do that face to face, to see their reactions.

And he wanted to talk to the Chinese.

Finding the room, he peered through the glass window and saw the Conference still in session. In the centre, the table was set up in a large rectangle, where delegates sat behind their company's name and logo. Further back were several rows of chairs for observers and clerical support staff. He slipped through the door, and sat on a chair in the back row nearest the door.

At the far end of the room, a tall, balding man was giving a presentation, with the aid of graphs and statistics beamed onto the wall behind him. His voice was small and thin, and his tortoiseshell glasses made him look like a benign professor. But Sangster noticed his set jaw and eyes that darted everywhere. His name plaque said he was the CEO of Western Energy, Richard Price. Next to him sat the Chairman, John Langhurst, with his head bowed. It was impossible to tell if he was listening or not.

Sangster scanned the faces of the delegates he could see. They were all nationalities: Western, Asian and African. Some were listening, some looked bored, and others were reading or scribbling on papers on the table in front of them. No one looked familiar.

He spotted the Chinese delegation sitting together on a row of seats set aside for observers. Sangster counted them. Only five, when there should be six. Next to them sat a man in a grey suit, with grey hair flopping over his forehead. He kept looking up and fidgeting around in his chair, before returning to work on the iPad on his lap. He *had* to be their Department of Foreign Affairs minder.

Sangster went over. "Derek Marshall?" he asked, as he sat down next to him.

The man's eyes were alert. "Yes."

"Inspector Tom Sangster, Queensland Police." He held out his hand, and spoke quietly. "I'm investigating the murders of Ellen Chambers and Anthony Harris."

Derek shook his hand. "What can I do for you, Inspector?"

"You can tell me where Chen Xiamen is," he said, tightly.

Derek shifted on his seat. "He has a long-standing engagement with the local Chinese community." He paused, then added: "I checked with the PM's office that it was okay for him to go."

"So what was he doing at The Palms this morning?"

"The Palms Resort?"

Sangster nodded. "The British Consul saw him there."

Derek looked uneasy. "I don't know."

"Can you phone and check he's where he should be now?"

"Certainly." Derek Marshall jumped up and left the room.

When Sangster looked up again, both John Langhurst and Richard Price were staring at him. He held up his wrist and tapped his watch.

★

Sangster ushered John Langhurst into a small office in the Conference Centre allocated for police interviews. A wooden desk and chair stood by the window, with a small sofa and two matching chairs positioned close by. Sangster looked at the grey blinds and grey carpet. Everything about the place was so grey, which only added to his mood. "Please take a seat." He gestured to the sofa, and sat down on one of the chairs opposite the Chairman.

Feeling stifled in the airless room, Sangster loosened the knot in his tie and picked up Langhurst's file to refresh his memory. Chairman of Western Energy for nine years, Langhurst had spent most of his career working in banks and top-flight Australian companies. The man was obviously well connected, although he hadn't always been. He'd started life as the son of a miner from Newcastle, New South Wales. That was some journey, Sangster thought. Had he achieved all that through merit? Or by marrying the daughter of a former PM? Still, by all accounts, he was welcome to Linda Shipperton. A hard-headed cow was one of the kinder things he'd heard her called.

He glanced up at Langhurst, who looked wiry and strong, as if he kept himself fit. Judging by his tanned face, he'd been out in the sun a lot recently, which tied in with what he'd said about having been on holiday with his family. Langhurst had an air of authority about him too. But that didn't bother Sangster. As far as he was concerned, *he* was in charge in here. "Let's recap what you told me on the phone, Sir." Sangster pulled out his notepad. "On Sunday night you attended the Conference reception here at the Convention Centre, but you only stayed a short time?"

The Chairman clasped his hands on his lap. "I only went for half an hour to greet the guests and make sure everything was running smoothly. Then I went back to my hotel suite to catch up on paperwork. I'd been away a week."

"And you didn't leave your suite again for the rest of the night?"

"That's right."

"And you're sure you didn't see Miss Chambers at all at the reception on Sunday evening?"

The Chairman shrugged. "The last time I saw Ellen was at the lunch we hosted at the Riverbank Hotel on Sunday for Conference delegates who'd arrived early in Brisbane."

"What time did Miss Chambers leave the lunch?"

"About 2.30pm with the rest of us. She said she was going back to The Palms for a few hours before the evening reception."

"Weren't you worried when she didn't turn up in the evening?"

"Not really." The Chairman sighed. "I thought she was either running late, or giving it a miss. I wouldn't have blamed her. I only went to show my face."

From his slightly elevated position on the chair, Sangster studied Langhurst, who looked calm but had troubled eyes. Sangster pulled out his small sketchpad and pencil from his jacket pocket. "Did Richard Price attend the reception?" he asked.

"Yes. Richard was there."

"What time did he leave?"

Langhurst looked puzzled. "He was still there when I left, I *think*, but... well, I can't be sure. It was a bun fight in there." He flared his nostrils, prompting Sangster to capture that gesture of disapproval on paper. He wouldn't have described John Langhurst as a handsome man, but there was something compelling about him. Did women find him attractive, he wondered? Did Ellen Chambers fall for him and have an affair? "So, tell me, Sir," he asked, "how well did you get on with the deceased?"

"Very well, Inspector. We had a good working relationship. She was a great colleague. Very smart."

"Did you see her outside of work?"

The Chairman hesitated. "She occasionally accompanied me to official functions and meetings."

"Did you ever see her socially?"

Langhurst gave him a strange look and shook his head.

"So, Miss Chambers was in Australia to work on the gas deal with China? And she'd been coming over from the UK every other month?"

"That's right."

"Did she ever go to China too?"

"The negotiation *is* with the Chinese."

Sangster ignored the barb. The Chairman didn't suffer fools gladly. Nor did he. He waited for a proper answer. This was *his* show.

Finally, Langhurst said: "We only came back from China the week before she died."

"You went to China with her?"

"Yes, along with Richard Price. We went for another round of talks with the Chinese."

"Did the three of you get on well while you were there?" Sangster asked.

Langhurst gave him a curious look. "Of course."

"There were no disagreements?"

"None at all."

"Did anything out of the ordinary happen in China? Anything to upset Miss Chambers, I mean?"

Langhurst looked thoughtful. "Nothing I can think of."

Sangster nodded. "Did Ellen get on well with Richard Price?"

"Yes."

"Any rivalry? Or disagreements?"

The Chairman looked irritated now. "Ellen got on with everyone."

Sangster crossed his legs. "Are you saying she never had *any* disagreement with *anyone* in the Company?"

The Chairman's nostrils flared again. "That's exactly what I'm saying."

Sangster shifted in his chair. This man was too composed. He toyed with the idea of challenging him about the corruption allegations against Ellen Chambers to break through that infuriating exterior. But he'd been warned off that line of questioning by the DC until they'd got clearance from Canberra. So he tried an indirect approach. "Are there any particular *problems* with the LNG deal? Or with the Chinese negotiators?"

The Chairman stretched out his legs. "There's a lot at stake, Inspector, so you can appreciate how delicate the negotiations are. It's an important export deal for Western Energy, and for Australia."

"Too important to fail?"

Langhurst raised an eyebrow. "It won't fail."

He's confident too, Sangster thought. Far too confident. "How well do you know Chen Xiamen?" he asked, keen to establish how close the two men were.

Langhurst shrugged. "I talk to him across the negotiating table."

"You've had no private meetings with him or met him socially?"

"No." Langhurst smiled. "You clearly haven't been involved with the Chinese, Inspector. There is no personal contact. Everything is done at official level."

Sangster ignored that. "What would you say he was like?"

Langhurst gave him a pointed look. "What are you getting at?"

Sangster was feeling annoyed now. *Don't upset anyone, Tom.* The DC's warning was ringing in his ears. *Langhurst is a friend of the PM.* "It's a straightforward question, Sir," he said sharply. "What are your impressions of the man? Is he someone you can do business with?"

Langhurst sat forward. "Chen is intelligent, shrewd and speaks good English. Obviously he's a man I can do business with."

That's when Sangster knew he was wasting his time. Langhurst was too at ease. Too smug. He wouldn't open up about negotiating tactics or personal relationships with the Chinese, any more than he would discuss the corruption allegations against Ellen Chambers, if he knew about them. In fact, Langhurst looked so assured, he gave the impression of being untouchable. That made Sangster wonder just how much the Australian Government were pulling the strings on the LNG deal behind the scenes. Of course publicly they kept saying it was a commercial matter and they weren't involved in the negotiations. But was that true? Had Anthony Harris been the kingmaker in this deal? Had something gone wrong? Had he been involved in corruption alongside Ellen Chambers? If they'd been having an affair, were they sharing the proceeds of crime too? Is that what this was all about?

Sangster stared at Langhurst. "Did Anthony Harris attend your reception on Sunday evening?" he asked.

"No, Inspector. He was invited, of course, as a politeness, but I didn't expect him to come." Langhurst shook his head. "His murder is *such* a tragedy. He was a brilliant politician and a well-respected MP. It's just so sad this had to happen." He paused. "And that poor young man last night, murdered in the same place as Ellen."

"Did you know Danny Burton?" Sangster asked.

"I heard about his murder on the news this morning." Langhurst leaned in closer. "What's going on, Inspector? I have a duty to protect the rest of my staff. If you think anyone else is at risk, you *need* to tell me."

Sangster stiffened. "We're investigating every possibility at the moment, Sir. But I assure you, you'll be the first to know if we think anyone else is in danger." He sat back to collect his thoughts.

Taking that as a sign he'd finished, the Chairman looked at his watch and went to stand up. "Well, if that's all." But Sangster remained seated. "Just a few more questions, if you don't mind."

"Of course." The Chairman's only sign of irritation was another quick glance at his watch.

"Did you know Ellen was pregnant when she was murdered?" Sangster asked, quietly.

An involuntary shudder shook the Chairman. Clearly taken aback, he pushed his chair back and stood up to look out of the window. "No," he said, thrusting his hands into his pockets. "I didn't know that."

"Did you know she had a boyfriend?" Sangster asked, satisfied he'd *finally* got to Langhurst. "Or who the father of her baby might be?"

Langhurst turned back. "No, Inspector. Why would I?"

Sangster nodded. "Did Ellen Chambers know your wife, Sir?"

The Chairman was clearly rattled now. "What does my wife have to do with this?"

Sangster shrugged. "I'm simply trying to establish if Ellen and your wife knew each other."

Langhurst stared at him. "They knew each other, Inspector, but not well."

Sangster nodded and closed his notepad. "Well, I think that's all for the time being, Sir." He picked up his file and walked out.

Well, that was some reaction, Sangster thought as he walked in the direction of the staircase to look for Dalton. Langhurst hadn't known Ellen Chambers was pregnant, that's for sure. And he hadn't liked that question about how well she'd known his wife either.

He looked down at his sketch of the Chairman. He could still see those flaring nostrils and clasped hands. All that display of confidence and ease must take a lot of self-control, he thought.

★

Later, back in the stuffy interview room, Sangster scrolled through his mobile inbox for messages. Still nothing from Jess. Why hadn't she called? She ought to have heard from Susan by now. He would call her as soon as he'd finished with Richard Price.

He opened the file Dalton had given him on the CEO. It made interesting reading. In contrast to the Chairman's background, Richard Price had been born into a landowning family in the State of Victoria. Given the best education money could buy in both Australia and the US, he had moved smoothly up the ladder of success. But things had not gone so well in his private life. His wife divorced him last year; and his credit rating had been downgraded in the last six months.

Feeling someone's presence, Sangster looked up.

Price stood in the doorway, watching him.

"Come in, Mr Price." Sangster pointed to the sofa. "Take a seat."

Price looked at the sofa as he walked over, ignored it and sat down on the chair near Sangster. He crossed his long legs, with a fixed half-smile on his lips.

Sangster tapped his foot on the carpet, and pulled his chair round to face Price. He put great stock on first impressions; and this man had not made a good start. He picked up his notepad and pencil. "So, Mr Price, can you tell me when you last saw Miss Chambers?"

Ignoring the question, Price launched in: "I've heard there's been another murder?"

Sangster looked at him. "Did you know Danny Burton?"

"Why should I? I've never stayed at The Palms. He worked there, didn't he?" Price didn't wait for an answer. "Why was he killed, that's what I want to know? Did he have something to do with Ellen's murder? Or Harris's? Or both?"

Sangster tried to remain patient. "We're investigating that now."

"Well, any murder is shocking. But a second, and a third..." Price looked at him and shook his head. "*Very* unfortunate for you, Inspector."

"Even more unfortunate for the victims," Sangster retorted. "Now, let's get back to your colleague, Ellen Chambers. When did you last see her?"

Price still had that half-smile on his lips. "At the Conference lunch on Sunday."

"And how did she seem?"

"Her normal self," Price said, calmly. "But we only chatted for a couple of minutes. We were busy looking after our guests."

"Before that, when was the last time you saw her?"

"On Friday morning, at the office in Melbourne."

"How did she seem?"

Price shrugged. "Fine, I'd say."

Sangster shook off his irritation. Tilting his sketchpad so Price couldn't see what he was doing, he started scratching away in his notepad: those huge glasses, thin face and lips. "Did you get on well with her?" he asked.

"Well enough," Price replied.

"How well?"

"As well as anyone."

Sangster paused. He didn't like his questions being batted back with a glib remark. We'll see about that, he thought. "Did you often travel with her, Mr Price?"

"What are you getting at, Inspector?"

Sangster tapped his foot on the carpet again. Why did these men find answering a few questions so difficult? What were they hiding? "I'm simply asking if you often travelled with her."

"Yes, on business." Price shifted in his chair for the first time. "You probably already know the Chairman, Ellen and I were in China last week."

Sangster nodded. "What kind of a relationship would you say you had with Miss Chambers?"

"As good as anyone else."

"Even though she was in competition for your job?"

That half-smile faded from Price's face.

Sangster launched in, quickly. "How well do you get on with your Chairman, Mr Price?"

Price looked away for the first time. "He's not an easy man to get on with, as others will tell you."

"But Miss Chambers got on with him?"

Price nodded. "John listened to her."

Sangster detected a slight bitterness in his voice. "Did you see her outside the office? Socially, I mean?" he asked.

Price hesitated. "No."

"Sure about that, Mr Price?"

"Yes."

"Did you know she had a boyfriend?"

Price shook his head, with no obvious surprise on his face.

Sangster watched Price's reaction to the next question very carefully. "Did you know she was pregnant?"

But Price just shook his head.

That casual reaction perplexed Sangster; it was nothing like the Chairman's. Had Price already known about the pregnancy? Sangster pressed on. "Did the Chairman know Ellen well outside the office?"

Price nodded. "He liked having her around."

"What did his wife think about that?"

Price snorted. "Have you met Linda Shipperton?"

Sangster ignored that. "So he was... closer to Ellen than any of you?"

Price gave a rueful smile. "He talked to her a lot about the business, about future plans and projects. So, yes, I suppose you could say he *was* closer to her."

Sangster was getting more irritated with this man. "Are you married, Mr Price?"

"Divorced."

"Recent, was it?"

Price looked at him. "A year ago."

"Do you have a girlfriend?"

"No one special. But I don't see what this has to do with Ellen's death."

Sangster glanced up. "Messy for everyone, divorces, especially carving up the assets."

Price's expression changed in a flash. The shutters came down.

Sangster leant forward. "Do you have financial... problems, Mr Price?"

Price crossed his arms. "I don't see what this has to do with your enquiry." He leant forward to emphasise the point.

A strong whiff of alcoholic breath hit Sangster. "Answer the question please."

Price hesitated. "In the divorce settlement, my wife got our two properties. I kept our financial investments. But, with the crash, I've had some, er, difficulties."

"How has that affected your personal credit rating?"

Price's face flushed.

Sangster didn't want to kick a man when he was down, but he had to know the truth. "How much debt would you say you're in, Mr Price?"

"I still don't see what..."

"*Please*, Mr Price."

Price sank back in his chair. "A lot."

"You can't afford to lose your job then?"

"Are you asking me, or telling me?"

Again, Sangster ignored that. "And the Chairman was grooming Ellen to take over from you?"

Price stuck his chin out. "I didn't kill her because they were after my job, if *that's* what you're implying."

Sangster looked at the indignant face glaring at him and stood up. "Right, well, that'll be all for the time being." Nodding at Richard Price, he walked out and headed straight downstairs to the lobby to look for Dalton. He was glad to be out of that stuffy room and away from Richard Price. He didn't like the man, who clearly had personal problems. But would he turn to murder to solve them? Still, the fact that he hadn't reacted to news of Ellen's pregnancy was surprising. But when you're watching stock markets collapse...

He stopped on the stairs when he saw the Chinese delegates and Derek Marshall, pacing around in the lobby below.

When Derek spotted Sangster, he ran up the stairs to him. "Chen Xiamen didn't turn up to his appointment with the Chinese community. No one's seen him since breakfast. And he's not answering his mobile." He ran his fingers through his mop of hair. "I've no idea where he is."

Sangster stared at Derek's mortified face, hardly able to control his temper. "I want to talk to the Chinese delegates."

Derek hesitated. "My instructions are that no one should talk to them until the Chinese Ambassador and the PM's Adviser get here."

"*Three* people have been murdered." Sangster's voice was icy. "Do you want blood on your hands too?"

Derek looked at his watch. "The PM's Adviser should be landing any minute, on the 12 o'clock flight from Canberra."

Sangster's eyes never left Derek's. "Can you interpret for me?"

Derek stood for a moment, obviously weighing up all the consequences. "Okay," he said, looking around. "But let's go somewhere private."

21

As the taxi sped through the Brisbane streets, huge drops of rain splashed onto the windscreen. Dodging a bus, it turned onto George Street and drew up behind a line of traffic waiting to get through the lights.

Jess sat in the back. The motion of the windscreen wipers seemed to clunk back and forth in time with her heartbeat. She shivered as the air conditioning chilled her damp skin, and turned to look out of the back window again. Was he still following? Or had he gone after Susan? The knot in Jess's stomach tightened. She hadn't handled Susan very well in the café. She should never have let her get away like that.

Her mobile rang.

"Jess?" Sharon's voiced sounded tense. "Are you okay?"

"I'm fine."

"I've been worried about you."

"And I'm worried about Susan Chambers. She's run off again with that diary."

"I *knew* she was going to be trouble."

"And you were right. Listen, Sharon, I'm running late." Jess pushed her hair out of her eyes and looked at her watch. "I'm in a taxi on my way to the Convention Centre to see John Langhurst." She paused. "What did the High Commissioner say when you told him what happened to me?"

"He was so shocked, he phoned the Federal Police Commissioner immediately to ask him to guarantee your safety."

"Oh God."

"You're not going to like this either." Sharon hesitated. "He's sent Nigel to help you."

Jess's stomach fell. That's exactly what she'd been dreading. Of course as second in command, Nigel would have to represent the High Commissioner in an emergency, but she'd been hoping he'd be too busy to come.

"Nigel tried to get out of it," said Sharon. "Had a real strop. Insisted he was needed for the Foreign Secretary's visit. Simon jumped in and volunteered to go instead. But the High Commissioner wouldn't hear of it. Simon has organised the whole visit so he has to stay. I tried too, Jess. But the High Commissioner wanted me to hold the fort while you're away."

Jess looked up; the traffic lights were *still* red. "Thanks, Sharon, but the High Commissioner is right. Look, I can't talk now; I need to phone the police to tell them about Susan."

"Simon said he'll have his phone on silent throughout this afternoon's programme, so text him regularly to let him know you're okay."

"Right."

"And I'll be in my office, staying by the phone for the rest of the day. Call me any time."

"I will." As Jess hung up, she was conscious of movement alongside her. She turned sideways. A taxi travelling in the opposite direction stopped beside her to let another car into the stream of traffic. She glanced into the back...

Chen Xiamen?

She leant closer to the window and peered out. Yes, it was definitely Chen, talking into his mobile.

Jess didn't move for fear of catching his eye. As his taxi moved off, she turned and watched out of the back window until it disappeared. Where was he going now, she wondered?

Jolting when her taxi finally pulled away, her thoughts flashed angrily back to Susan. How could she run off like that? The stupid girl had no intention of handing over the diary. Not only was she interfering with her sister's murder investigation and withholding evidence, precious police resources were being spent looking for her. Of course grief was making her reckless, but even so... Jess knew she had no choice now but to leave Susan to the police.

She dialled Inspector Sangster and heard his voicemail click in. "Tom, it's Jess Turner. I've just met Susan Chambers at Café Aqua, Queen Street. She didn't bring the diary, I'm afraid. And she disappeared again without saying where she was going." She hesitated. "She told me she'd spent the night at her boyfriend's place. I don't know his name, but I believe he works for the *Echo* too. So I hope that helps you find her. Of course, if she contacts me again, I'll ring you immediately." She paused. "Oh, and I've just seen Chen Xiamen in a taxi in town. He seemed to be heading away from the Convention Centre, so perhaps you've already seen him there." She hung up, feeling bad about handing Susan over to the police, but she couldn't do anything else now.

Suddenly the taxi driver slammed on his brakes. Her head jerked up to see a man dart out in the front of them. She grabbed the door handle, ready to jump out. But the man just dodged the traffic and ran across the road.

She sat back in the seat, trying to calm herself down as her taxi accelerated away and turned onto Victoria Bridge. As they crossed over Brisbane River, she looked down at the water and closed her eyes. She shuddered, imagining again Ellen's white face framed by floating hair, and her mouth open in a scream, as she sank beneath the waves.

When the taxi finally reached the south bank and drew up outside the Convention Centre, Jess couldn't wait to get out. She paid the driver and looked up at the three-storey building, with its huge glass entrance. She ran up the bank of steps to the front door, splashing through little puddles of water as she went. At the top, she stopped to brush the rain off her jacket and stamp the water out of her shoes. Standing there, something made her turn.

Below, she could see Inspector Sangster leaning against his police car bonnet, talking on his mobile. He had, of course, already seen her. He slipped his mobile into his pocket and ran up the steps to her. "I got your message," he said, not in the least breathless. "What time did you see Chen?"

"About ten minutes ago, on my way here."

He nodded. "I've no option now but to put out a full-scale search for Susan. We need to find her, for her own safety."

Jess nodded. "I'm sorry, Tom. She's distraught, unpredictable. I can't tell you how worried I am about her... and that diary." She stopped and glanced at him again.

"What's wrong?" he asked, instinctively.

She cut to the chase. "I believe someone stole my diary from my hotel room this morning, thinking it was Ellen's.

His eyes narrowed.

She nodded. "When I got back from breakfast, I noticed signs that someone had been in my room: a drawer slightly open, a photo moved. The bed was unmade so I knew the cleaners hadn't been in. I checked around, but I didn't notice anything missing at the time. Now I realise my diary's gone." She paused for breath. "And when I was on my way to meet Susan, someone followed me and tried to snatch my briefcase." She tried to make her voice sound calm. "He must have thought I had the diary in it."

"Who was it?" he asked, quickly.

"I didn't see. I was just aware of this presence following me, a shadow reflecting on the pavement, a dark figure darting into shop doorways. And then, when I was standing in a crowd of people waiting to cross the road, I felt this tug on my briefcase." She stopped. Did someone try to push her under a bus? She wasn't sure of anything now. "I stumbled into the road as I hung onto it." She hesitated. "I might have been pushed."

"*Pushed?*" He looked shocked.

"Don't worry, I'm fine."

"You said 'he'. What do you remember about him?"

Jess thought hard. "I didn't see anyone in the street, just a dark figure. I ducked into the department store in Queen Street to shake him off. Then I saw the back of a man, dressed all in black, standing by the escalator. One moment he was there, the next he'd gone. I'm sure it was him. I can't tell you why though." She paused. "He was tall."

His face looked grave. "Right, well, we've had a call from Canberra. Your High Commissioner wants you to have a police escort for the rest of the day."

She looked at him. "I was being followed because someone thought *I* had Ellen's diary. But, *Susan* has it."

"Don't worry, we'll find her," he said. "But I must have one of my officers stay with you."

She shook her head. "Look, I don't need anyone for the time being. I'm here to meet John Langhurst. I won't be going anywhere else. Then, I'm coming over to the police station at 2pm as planned. Let's take it from there."

He looked sceptical. "You'll stay in this building?"

"Yes."

"In that case, I'll have a car collect you at 1.45pm and bring you to the station."

She nodded. "After that, I'll only be going to the Consulate-General to do some work. Then I'll check into the Riverbank for the night. Oh, and my boss, Nigel Paxman, will be arriving from Canberra in the next couple of hours, so I won't be alone."

He gave a resigned shrug. "All right, but if Susan rings, you'll let me know?"

She nodded. "By the way." She reached into her jacket pocket. "Susan found this camera card tucked in the back cover of Ellen's diary."

He took it, eagerly. "Have you seen the photos?"

"Yes, Susan had them printed in town. But don't get too excited. There are only three. They seem to be tourist snaps taken during Ellen's recent trip to China."

He looked disappointed. Turning, he ran down the steps to his car.

Jess watched him go, feeling alone again once his car drove off. She sighed and walked into the Convention Centre. But almost immediately, she spotted John Langhurst standing at the top of the stairs, watching the door with great interest. When he saw her, his face opened into a smile and he waved. Descending the stairs, he looked dignified yet natural. He may be the boss, she thought, but there's no Nigel puff-up about him.

He walked over. "Lovely to see you again, Jessica." He sounded subdued. "I hope you've got time for some lunch."

"Can we eat in here?"

He looked dubious. "We'd be better off in the fish restaurant around the corner."

She hesitated. Eating a big meal was the last thing she felt like doing; and she'd told Tom she'd stay put. "I'd be happy with something light in here, a coffee even."

"Come on Jessica, you've got to eat."

She had to admit she hadn't eaten a thing at breakfast with everything that was going on. And the Chairman was trying to make an effort. "All right," she said, not wanting to be rude. "That's kind of you."

"Good." He smiled at her. "That's settled then. We'll walk if the rain has stopped and get some fresh air. It'll do us good."

★

Sangster stood in the mortuary studying Danny Burton's X-rays. His skeletal structure looked entirely normal, except for the bullet lodged in the cranium. Sangster turned to Anderson who was at the autopsy table ready to start the post-mortem. "Can you get that bullet out first?"

"Patience, Tom." Anderson was in deep concentration.

"Ballistics want to check it has the same firearm fingerprint as the one you got out of Anthony Harris." He paused. "That bullet came from a Glock 17, fitted with a silencer."

Anderson nodded. "Which means the barrel of the gun that fired it will be slightly longer than usual, with a thread at the tip." He glanced over to check Sangster was listening. "The telltale sign was the damage done to the shape of the bullet as it collided with the silencer's segments at the mouth of the barrel on exit."

Sangster nodded with grudging respect. Was there anything this man didn't know?

"Using a silencer," Anderson went on, "would explain why no one heard gunshots at either crime scene. But it doesn't explain how the killer got close enough to shoot them both in the head without them knowing anything about it."

"How do you know they didn't?"

Anderson looked down at the cadaver. "Because I can't find a single defence wound on either of them."

Sangster stared down at Danny Burton, now still and silent in death. He remembered Danny's clenched fists in the interview room yesterday. He'd been such a life force, with his well-muscled body and tiger tattoo. But now his fiery eyes were closed; he looked young and peaceful lying on the table.

Anderson was bending over the corpse with a magnifier, taking a closer look at the knife wound to the heart. "There aren't any serration marks," he said. "This was a single stab to the heart, to the aorta to be precise. A very clean job by the look of it." He looked up. "Normally bleeding from the aorta would be fast, like a kind of high-pressure hose. But there's no sign of that here. Because this young man was already dead when the knife went in."

Sangster nodded. "What can you tell me about the wound?"

Anderson looked again with his magnifier. "It's a clean cut, made with a very sharp blade, probably high quality steel though we'll test for that." He stood up and stretched out his back.

It was only then that Sangster noticed the dark circles under Anderson's eyes. He'd been working through the night again, and it showed. "Any idea what kind of knife was used?" he asked.

"Well it wasn't your regular kitchen knife." Anderson measured the depth of the wound to Danny's heart. Then he was silent for a while. "I've seen this kind of cut made during pig butchery."

"*Pig* butchery?"

Anderson stared at the wound again. "You know, Tom, It could be one of those bushcraft knives used for camping and hunting." He glanced up. "Maybe your man's a hunter?"

Sangster stared at him. *A hunter?* Of course, that would make perfect sense. That's how he got up so close and personal. But it didn't explain why he would shoot his victims, then stab them in the heart. "Right," Sangster said. "I don't think I need to see any more of this. You've confirmed the cause of death, but let me know straightaway if you find anything else. And get that bullet to ballistics."

Anderson didn't reply. He was bent over the table again, lost in his work.

Peeling off his gloves and gown, Sangster threw them in the bins provided and walked out into the corridor. He took a deep breath to get rid of the smell of death from his nostrils and looked around for his Sergeant.

Dalton was pacing around by the exit. There was no way he could observe an autopsy. Seeing Sangster, he waved some papers. "The Federal Police have given us the call log from Ellen Chambers' mobile phone. We've been checking her calls over the last few weeks."

"And?" Sangster tapped his foot on the ground.

Dalton shivered. "Can we get out of the icehouse, Boss?"

Sangster nodded, and they walked up the stairs together and out of the building.

Looking more comfortable in the fresh air, Dalton went on: "The calls are mostly to her colleagues and work contacts. She rang the personal mobiles of the Chairman and CEO of Western Energy a lot."

"As you would expect."

Dalton nodded, eyes gleaming. "*And* she called Anthony Harris several times."

Sangster broke into a smile. "Are you saying she had *personal* access to him?"

Dalton nodded. "And there's something else interesting. She called the British Embassy switchboard in Beijing three times over that period. Once before she left for China; once while she was there; and again when she got back. Don't know who she spoke to though."

Sangster's eyes narrowed. "What about Chen Xiamen? Did she call him?"

Dalton's face fell. "No. Not on her mobile anyway."

Sangster frowned; that didn't make sense. "Right, let's get back to the Convention Centre. I want to talk to Western Energy's Chairman and CEO again. And I want to ask the Consul about Ellen Chambers' calls to the British Embassy in Beijing.

★

"How's your fish?" Langhurst clasped his sun-tanned hands together on the edge of the table.

"Good, thank you," Jess replied. And it was. She loved barramundi, a local freshwater fish. Although she'd eaten most of hers, he'd hardly touched his. He seemed more interested in her, and gave the impression of listening intently to everything she said. That's quite a skill, she thought, making people feel interesting. Then she chided herself for being so cynical. The truth is they got on well, finding a wide range of political and economic issues to talk about. She found him interesting and well-informed. She hoped he found her the same. So, when he asked her about her education and career in the Foreign Office, she found herself telling him, which was unusual because she never talked about herself. But when he strayed into personal territory by asking about her family, she clammed up.

He got the message and sat back in his chair for a breather.

So did Jess. While there was a lull in the conversation, she looked around. Like most Australian restaurants, the furniture and décor were simple and practical. A huge glass tank full of live lobsters filled the front window to entice customers. But the advert wasn't working today because only two other tables were occupied. The rain earlier must have put people off.

Langhurst looked wistful. "Ellen loved fish," he said. "It was one of the things she liked most about Australia."

"Me too."

"You're like her you know, Jess."

"In that I speak with an English accent?"

"Ellen was well-informed like you." He paused. "You even look like her, you know. That's why I got such a shock when I saw you standing at The Palms yesterday afternoon." He swallowed. "I thought it was her."

Jess sat silent for a while. She didn't want to ask him about Ellen, but she couldn't help herself. "When did you last see her, John?"

"At lunch on Sunday at the Riverbank. I remember telling her I'd ordered lobster and prawns for the reception that night, especially for her."

"Reception?"

He nodded. "We had an opening reception for the Conference. Of course, Ellen never showed up. If only she had..." He made an effort to rally himself. "It was a bit of a scrum in there. You know, crowds of people milling around, drinking and eating. I didn't stay long. I can't stand those parties."

"Me neither," she said, with feeling. He seemed happy to talk about Ellen; and Jess *was* curious. "How did Ellen seem to you?" she asked.

He shrugged. "Her normal self. After lunch, she said she was going back to The Palms for a few hours and that she'd see me later..." His voice trailed away again and they fell silent.

Jess concentrated on eating another mouthful of fish. There were so many questions she wanted to ask, but she didn't want to appear to be interrogating him. Feeling his eyes studying her, she glanced out of the window.

A sudden movement outside made her jump.

Langhurst followed her gaze. "Is something wrong?"

She shook her head. "I just thought I saw someone, that's all."

"Who?" He stared out of the window and looked back at her.

She hesitated, wondering whether to confide in him. It would sound ridiculous, but he did seem concerned. "I think someone's following me."

"Following you?" He twisted round and went to get up. She grabbed his arm. *"Please. It's nothing."*

He stared at her. "Why would anyone follow you?"

She hesitated, wondering whether to tell him about Ellen's diary. "It's probably just a journalist looking for a story." She tried to sound dismissive. "I'm a bit jumpy after all these murders, that's all." Then she deliberately changed the subject. "Tell me, John. Did you go with Ellen on her last trip to China?"

He looked out of the window again, then turned back. "Yes. The three of us always went for every round of talks. Richard Price, Ellen and me. We only got back last week."

"Did Ellen and Richard Price get on well?" she asked, thinking back to what Susan Chambers had said about the Chairman wanting Ellen to take over as CEO.

But Langhurst was unfazed. "Ellen got on well with everyone, especially the Chinese. She knew them and their customs. And she spoke excellent Mandarin." He sighed. "It's an important deal."

Conscious she was grilling him, Jess turned her attention back to her food. She felt guilty about how much she was enjoying lunch, but John Langhurst *was* good company. So intelligent and charming. Had he and Ellen been more than just colleagues, she wondered? Could he have been Ellen's lover and the father of her unborn child? It was obvious he'd cared a lot about her. Jess studied his fine, chiselled features. She could see why Ellen might have been attracted to him. And he would have wanted to keep an affair quiet, a married man in his position. Yes, he ticked all the boxes as Ellen's potential lover, except he didn't have the initials TH. Only Tony Harris fitted that scenario. "Is your wife in Brisbane, John?" she asked.

He shook his head. "We spent last week on holiday with our two boys at the Great Barrier Reef. They flew home to Melbourne on Saturday and I came to Brisbane." He looked at her. "Why do you ask?"

"Well, I know *we* haven't met before," she bluffed, "but I've got a feeling I've met your wife."

"Really? When?"

"I'm not sure. Probably at some reception," she replied, all the while thinking that he and Ellen would have had the time and the space to meet up in Brisbane over the weekend, *if* they'd been romantically involved. She hesitated before asking her next question. "Did you know Ellen was pregnant?"

He looked away. "Not until Inspector Sangster just told me."

There was something like despair on his face when he looked at her again. She knew she ought to stop questioning him, but she couldn't. "Do you know who the father could be?" she asked.

He shook his head. "Tell me, Jessica, how did *you* know Ellen was pregnant?"

"Susan Chambers told me."

"Ellen told her sister?"

Jess hesitated. "Not exactly, but Ellen *had* seen a gynaecologist here."

"Susan *knew* that?"

Jess closed down now, she'd already said too much. Turning her gaze away, she became aware of someone watching them.

A tall man hovered in the doorway, his dark eyes gleaming behind tortoiseshell specs. He walked over and bent down to talk to the Chairman. "We've been trying to contact you, John." His voice sounded accusing. "Your mobile's switched off."

Langhurst turned to Jess. "Can I introduce you to Richard Price, our CEO?"

Jess looked up at the same slim, hollow-cheeked face that she'd seen in the photo in the *Echo* yesterday. "Hello," she said, holding out her hand.

Price shook it without even looking at her. "Inspector Sangster wants you *both* to return to the Convention Centre immediately," he said in a self-important tone.

Does he now? Jess was both irked and relieved that Sangster seemed to know exactly where she was.

22

Sangster paced about on the steps of the Convention Centre. Where the hell was she? She'd refused an escort, on the grounds she'd be staying inside until 1.45. Now, she'd gone off for lunch with John Langhurst.

He rubbed his temples, wishing he could get rid of his migraine. Even now he could feel hammering behind his eyes. *Maybe your man's a hunter?* Anderson's words were rattling around his head. He could see Anthony Harris sitting at the wheel of his car outside Police HQ, and the killer slipping into the back seat and shooting him in the head before he could even turn around. But *why* kill Harris? To stop him seeing the Police Commissioner? Was he about to confess to having an affair with Ellen Chambers? But he wouldn't need to see the Police Commissioner about *that*, would he? No, there had to be more to it.

And Danny's killing was even more puzzling. Cocky and fit, Danny would have been ready to fight off anyone. In the dead of night down at the jetty, every sound, every movement would have been magnified in the silence. Yet the killer managed to creep up on him and shoot him in the back of the head without so much as a scuffle?

Sangster felt an icy chill in his spine. This killer was damn good. So good, he had to be a professional. But who would bring in a killer like that? Obviously someone who wasn't afraid of anyone in the police.

He was still dwelling on that when he caught sight of blonde hair shining in the sunlight. Relief flooded through him when he saw the British Consul walking alongside John Langhurst in the distance. They looked in deep conversation and totally at ease with each other, which surprised him. A sullen-looking Richard Price lagged a few paces behind.

Jess looked up, and waved when she spotted him.

All three of them increased their pace.

"Sorry, Tom," she said, breathless from running up the steps when she reached him. "We just stepped out for a bite to eat."

"Let's go inside," he said, curtly. "I need to talk to you all again."

*

The three of them sat in the interview room while Sangster stood by the window. Jess knew he was annoyed. It was her fault; she shouldn't have left the building without telling him.

Eyes glinting, he fixed on the Chairman: "I need to have another word with you, Sir." He turned. "And with you too, Mr Price."

"Of course." The Chairman looked at his watch. "I'm supposed to be leaving for Canberra on the four o'clock flight for a dinner with the British High Commissioner this evening." He looked at Jess. "I'd better cancel."

Price chipped in. "And I'm speaking at the Conference shortly, Inspector. So I don't have much time."

Sangster rounded on Price. "We're investigating the murder of your colleague, *Sir,*" he snarled. "I'm *sure* you'll want to give us all the time we need."

Cheeks flushed, Price sank back into the chair.

At that moment, Jess could understand why the Chairman wanted to get rid of *him*. She turned to Langhurst. "Shall I phone the High Commissioner to let him know you can't make dinner?"

The Chairman looked at Inspector Sangster for guidance.

"You don't have to alter your plans." Sangster gave him a pointed look. "When are you coming back?"

"On the first flight in the morning. But..." Langhurst stopped and looked at Jess. "Maybe I should stay here?"

She shrugged. "Not if Inspector Sangster thinks it's okay for you to go."

Langhurst nodded.

Sangster turned to Jess. "I'd like to talk to you first, if I may. Of course, as a diplomat with immunity, you don't have to comply."

"Let's do it now." She stood up. "That's if you don't mind waiting, John."

"Of course not." Langhurst stood up, politely. "You stay here and talk. Richard and I will wait in our conference office along the corridor."

"I'll come along as soon as I've finished with the Consul," Sangster said to him.

Langhurst turned to Jess. "I can drop you back at the Consulate-General on my way to the airport."

"We'll take her back," Sangster cut in, quickly.

"Fine." The Chairman put a comforting hand on Jess's shoulder. "I'll see you soon," he said, softly. Then he left the room, with Richard Price.

Once they'd gone, Sangster said formally: "Ma'am, for your own safety, you should have stayed in the building."

She took the rebuke. "I know. I'm sorry, Tom."

He nodded. "Have you heard from Susan Chambers again?"

"I'm afraid not."

He fixed her with one of his intense stares. "In that case, you need to tell me everything she said to you about her sister. *Everything* please. I know you've had several conversations with her."

Jess sighed. Susan had told her things in confidence, but this was a murder investigation.

She went over to the window and looked out at the city and river. She could see Susan's distraught white face... "I've already told you about Ellen's diary," she said, "and about the initials TH inside and the codes at the back... And I've given you the camera card Susan found in it." Jess turned round. "Have those photos turned up anything?"

"They're being examined in the lab as we speak."

She looked away, trying to remember exactly what Susan said to her at The Palms. "Susan told me John Langhurst and Richard Price don't get on. The Chairman wanted Ellen to move permanently to Australia to take over as CEO." Jess added, "I don't think Richard Price knows that."

He nodded.

She shrugged. "Or maybe he does? Anyway, it seems Richard has become a heavy drinker since his divorce, to such an extent he's become a liability for the Company. Susan said something about doing an article on him in the *Echo* after he got involved in some traffic accident while over the limit." She turned to face Sangster. "Mind you, I don't know what truth there is in any of that. There's always so much backbiting in any organisation. It's like an emotional cauldron as people plot their way up the career ladder. Human nature can be so ugly."

"You're telling me," he said, stiffly. "Did Susan say anything else?"

She hesitated. *The money is the trail.* Those words popped into her head again. "Well there is one thing that's been bugging me."

His eyes never left hers.

"Apparently, the day before she was murdered, Ellen said to Susan – and I quote – *the money is the trail*. If anything happens to me, Susan, *the money is the trail* – unquote. I don't know if she was talking about the bribes she was supposed to be taking from the Chinese, or something else."

Sangster didn't move a muscle. "Bribes she was *supposed* to be taking from the Chinese. Are you suggesting she wasn't?"

Jess sighed. "I don't know what I'm suggesting, Tom. I just know that it doesn't make sense."

"Did you know Ellen Chambers phoned the British Embassy in Beijing three times in the last couple of weeks?"

She looked at him in surprise. "No."

"The log of her mobile phone calls confirms that."

"That's news to me, Tom." She paused. "But I'll see what I can find out."

He gave a satisfied nod. "Is that everything Susan said?"

"As far as I can remember."

"Good." He stood up. "Would you mind waiting while I have another chat with the other two? Then we can go to HQ."

"Okay." Jess stood up and picked up her bag and briefcase. "I'll wait for you downstairs in the café, if that's all right."

He nodded. "Don't leave the building. *Please*."

She walked along to the end of the corridor and took the escalator down to the mezzanine café. It was the lull between lunch and tea, and there were few people around. She went over to the bar and ordered a brandy, which didn't even raise an eyebrow from the barman. Taking it over to a table by the window, she sat down and pulled out her mobile. She really wanted to talk to Simon. She pressed his number on her speed dial, but got his voicemail again. She groaned and typed up a text message for him.

Call me when you can. Jess.

Then she tried Nigel, but his mobile switched to voicemail too. She looked at her watch. Where was he? He should have landed by now. She sent him a text message, saying that she was in the Convention Centre with Inspector Sangster and John Langhurst, if he wanted to join them.

She picked up the glass and took a swig of brandy. The fiery liquid flowed through her like balm.

She looked up.

Richard Price stood staring down at her. "Cold?" He seemed amused by her discomfort. "Or scared?"

She put the glass down and sat back in her chair where she could see him face to face. She couldn't fathom out Richard Price. He gave off an aura of cold detachment. Or was it arrogance? "Would you like a drink?" she asked, to be polite.

He pulled a face. "Some of us have *work* to do."

Why did he have to be so provocative?

He sat down opposite her, which suggested he wanted to talk. But he didn't say anything.

So she asked: "How well did you know Ellen Chambers?"

He shrugged. "She was a work colleague."

"I understand you travelled together to China for negotiations. You must have got to know each other quite well on those trips."

"What are you now?" he asked. "Sangster's sidekick?"

She shrugged and looked out of the window. If he didn't want to talk, that was fine with her.

"We worked together, that's all." He said after a while, "I wasn't the father of her baby, if that's what you're getting at."

Jess stared at him. "You *knew* she was pregnant?"

He shrugged.

"Did she tell you?"

He gave a little smile.

Now he was being smug. But why? She studied him. Being provocative came easily to Richard Price, but could he take a bit of needle too? "The Chairman seems very upset," she said. "But then I hear he had an *excellent* working relationship with Ellen. Special even."

Price shifted in his chair. "What *else* have you heard?" His voice was loaded with sarcasm.

She looked at him. "That Ellen was set to go right to the top of the Company."

A look of pure anger flitted across his face.

That hit a raw nerve. He definitely knew the Chairman had been grooming Ellen to take over his job.

Price stared. "What exactly *are* you doing in Brisbane, Miss Turner?"

"I'm here to liaise with the police about Ellen's murder; and to help the next of kin." She looked at him. "Do you know her sister, Susan Chambers?"

His eyes narrowed. "The British Government just can't keep its nose out of this gas deal, can it?"

Jess stared back. What was he getting at? "I told you, Ellen was a British citizen. I'm here about her murder."

"You don't expect me to believe *that,* do you?"

The venom in his voice was unmistakable, but Jess wasn't fazed. "Did you come down here to pick a fight?" she asked, voice cool. "Or do you want to talk to me about something?"

He fidgeted on the chair. "When you saw Susan Chambers yesterday, what did she tell you about her sister and Western Energy?"

Ah, so he wants information, she thought. She looked him in the eyes. "Susan was so upset, she hardly spoke."

"*Oh, come on!*"

"You asked me a question and I've answered you," Jess said, firmly.

Without saying another word, he got up and walked off.

And with that, her already low opinion of Richard Price sank further. But why would Ellen Chambers tell *him* she was pregnant? Unless it was *his* child? She shuddered. Surely not?

Her phone beeped with an incoming text message.

Still in meetings with Foreign Sec. Will phone asap. Simon

Sighing, Jess picked up her brandy and drained the glass. She needed to get back to the Consulate-General to do some work. She gathered up her bag and briefcase. She'd get a taxi if Inspector Sangster wasn't ready to go.

Climbing the stairs, she headed in the direction of the interview room to look for him. But there were so many doors leading off the corridor, she became confused. When she heard voices, she walked towards them until she found herself standing outside a door that was ajar. Peering through the crack, she saw the Chairman standing behind a mahogany desk, glaring at Richard Price who sat opposite him.

"You *should* know everything that goes on, Richard." The Chairman wagged his finger. "Why didn't you stop her?"

"*I* couldn't stop Ellen doing anything," Price replied.

"What happened in Melbourne on Friday, before you all came up here?"

"I already told you. We had a working meeting to go through the gas deal again. Everything seemed fine, so I..."

"For God's sake, Richard. You're supposed to be *running* the show. We *can't* let anything go wrong now."

Jess felt uncomfortable eavesdropping, but she didn't move.

"Are you insinuating I don't *care*?" Price sounded incredulous.

"Of course not.*"*

"What are you saying, then? That *I'm* responsible for her death?"

The Chairman sighed with impatience. "All I'm saying, Richard, is that Company interests should come first for you. And if they don't, well..."

Price snorted. "That's rich coming from you. Why don't you ease off and give *me* some space to complete the deal? I am the bloody CEO, you know. You're too close to..."

"*To what*?" Langhurst exploded. "I *should* be able to expect loyalty and support from my CEO."

"That's *bollocks!*"

"For Christ's sake, Richard, this deal's huge. We should be watching each other's backs, not tearing each other apart."

Price stared at him.

"Look, we might not agree on much," Langhurst's voice was more reasonable now. "But we need to present a united front, at least for the sake of the Company."

It was at that point Price glanced over at the door as if sensing someone outside.

Jess backed away, straight into Inspector Sangster.

"Well now," Sangster whispered in her ear. "Susan was right about those two. They don't get on, do they?"

23

Jess sat silent beside Sangster in the back of the police car, while Dalton drove through the traffic. Drinking that brandy had been a mistake: her head was throbbing.

Out of the window, the sun sparkled on the river in the sunshine. The umbrellas had disappeared and everyone was out and about again. She looked at her watch – 3.25pm. She checked for messages on her mobile and frowned. Nothing from Nigel. He couldn't *still* be in the air, could he?

Hearing a familiar scratching noise, she glanced over to see Sangster sketching in his pad again. She didn't want to appear to be watching him because that would be intrusive. But out of the corner of her eye, she could see Richard Price's long face and owlish glasses filling an entire page. He looked more like a cartoon character from a satirical magazine than a CEO of a prominent company.

Sangster flicked over the page.

There was no mistaking the next sketch was of John Langhurst. Sangster had captured the intensity of the Chairman's striking eyes. But why had he drawn a huge pair of clasped hands underneath his head and shoulders? The size of them on the page looked grotesque. What was that all about? But she wasn't going to ask.

When a mobile rang, they all jumped. But it was Sangster's.

"*Liz!*" He answered, sounding relieved. "Where are you?" He threw his pad down on the seat and turned sideways for privacy. The pages fluttered over...

Jess flinched as she saw herself on the page. *Oh my God!* Curious, she studied the sketch. Every detail of her face was meticulously drawn, except... there was something weird about her eyes. He'd drawn the shape of them, but left them blank. She gasped, inwardly. Is that how he sees me? An empty soul, with dead eyes? Had she withdrawn that much? Winded, all she wanted to do was get out of the car, and away from him. Instead, she was forced to sit and listen to his conversation.

"No, Liz. Don't go. We need to talk..." He twisted in his seat, as the car drew up at the steps of Police HQ.

Jess opened the door and got out quickly, just as her mobile rang.

"Jessic*aah, where are you?*"

"Hello, Nigel."

"I'm *waiting* for you at the Consulate-General!"

Moving away from the car, she kept her voice light. "Didn't you get my text message? I sent one a while ago saying I was in the Convention Centre with John Langhurst and Richard Price. Now, I'm at Police HQ if you want to join us."

"I don't."

"Okay, I should be back within the hour."

"Right." And he hung up.

It was clear Nigel was furious at having been sent to Brisbane, which meant he was going to be even more difficult than usual.

She turned to see Sangster still in the car. But Dalton had got out and was leaning on the bonnet. He didn't want to listen to that conversation either.

Sangster wound down the window and called out.

"Dave, take the Consul up to my office. I'll only be a minute." And he ducked his head back in the car to continue his call in private.

Dalton glanced over at Jess. "Relationship break–up," he said.

Jess nodded but said nothing as she followed Dalton through the main entrance, up two flights of stairs and along a corridor until they came to a door with a brass plate that read Inspector Sangster.

Dalton showed her inside. "Take a seat. Tom won't be long."

Although he stood behind Sangster's desk, Jess noticed Dalton didn't sit in his chair. "Don't mind Tom," he said. "He comes over a bit fierce, but he's good at his job." He gave her a small smile. "If anyone can find Ellen Chambers' killer, he can." He started pacing around again as if anxious to get away.

Jess sat down. "Don't worry about me, I can wait on my own."

"Are you sure?"

She nodded.

He gave her a grateful look. "See you later," he said and disappeared out of the door.

With Dalton gone, Jess looked around. There was nothing on Sangster's desk except for a tray of papers, a lamp, and a mug of pencils. Then she noticed a corner table covered with sketches. A rubbish bin stood nearby with discarded bits of scrunched up paper on the floor around it. Unable to contain her curiosity, she went over to the table and sifted through the drawings one by one, trying not to get them out of order. Was there another one of herself?

A chilling image halted her search.

Here was a larger sketch of Ellen Chambers lying dead.

In this one, her eyes were open wide with fear; her hair fanned out in the waves and her mouth was open as if screaming.

Exactly the same face she imagined she'd seen in the water at the jetty last night!

She jumped as the door squeaked open and Sangster walked in. "Sorry." She put the sketch down, guiltily. "But your drawings are brilliant."

For a brief moment he looked desolate. "My partner hated my sketches of murder victims. She said it was like living with ghosts."

"They are *very* realistic." Jess grimaced. "Not the kind of drawings most artists do of their clients, are they?"

The Venetian blinds rattled in the breeze. He walked over, closed the window and sat down at his desk. Pulling a packet of paracetamol out of his pocket, he popped two pills out of the card, poured a glass of water from the bottle on the windowsill and swallowed them down whole. He looked over and offered Jess the pills, as if he knew she had a headache.

"Thanks." She walked over while he poured another glass of water and handed it to her. Taking a pill, she looked at his pale face and worn-out eyes. For the first time she noticed a hairline scar on his forehead.

"Here's a copy of the autopsy report on Ellen Chambers." He handed it to her. "Nothing we don't already know. She was 16 weeks pregnant, by the way"

Jess took it, gratefully. "Is that what this is all about, do you think? An illicit affair that ended up with her being pregnant?"

"Possibly." Sangster rolled his shoulders to loosen them, and looked at her. "What do you make of Richard Price?" he asked.

She didn't have to think hard. "He's a piece of work. *And* he was about to lose his job to Ellen." She hesitated. "He had a motive for killing her."

Sangster nodded. "What about the Chairman?"

She chose her words carefully. "I think he was very fond of Ellen. I can see it in his manner whenever he talks about her."

"Do you think they were lovers?" he asked, bluntly.

Jess looked thoughtful. "I don't know, but I can see why she might have been attracted to him. He's intelligent and attentive... *and* wealthy."

"Always helps, doesn't it?"

She smiled. "But *how* do these three murders fit together, Tom? Because they do, don't they?"

He got up, and went over to his drawings. Shuffling through them, he picked one up and showed it to her. "This is Danny Burton. Did you see him, or talk to him at The Palms?"

Jess studied the sketch. There was no mistaking it was of a young man she'd seen around the hotel. "I saw him working in the gardens, but I never spoke to him." She looked up. "What was he doing at the jetty at that time of night? He couldn't have been working."

"Waiting for someone, I think."

She sat forward. "Who?"

"When we questioned Danny earlier, he admitted seeing Ellen sitting on the jetty seat with a man on Sunday night. He claimed it was too dark to see who it was." Sangster glanced over at her. "But I think he knew exactly who it was."

"So why wouldn't he say?"

"Probably thought he could profit from it."

"*Profit?*" She paused. "Do you mean *blackmail?*"

Sangster nodded. "I think that's why he was killed.

Danny Burton was playing a dangerous game... just like Susan Chambers."

"Don't say that; she's just a girl."

"But she's not a *child*," he pointed out.

She shook her head. "What about Chen? Have you caught up with him?"

"*No!*" Sangster's mood changed at the mention of Chen, his eyes turning steely. That was Jess's cue to depart. She picked up her bag and briefcase. "Well, I won't take up any more of your time, Tom. You're busy, and I've done what I came up to Brisbane to do."

His mouth dropped open. "You're not going back to Canberra? What about Susan Chambers? You're the only person she trusts. You have to stay until we find her and that diary."

"I was *about* to say I'm staying another couple of nights in Brisbane because of Susan. She's my only concern now, in terms of my job that is. It's crazy. I've been burgled, had my diary stolen, been followed around town. I feel like I'm caught up in a movie without a script."

He gave her a sympathetic nod.

"But what really puzzles me," she said, "is how *different* the Anthony Harris and Danny Burton murders were to Ellen's. I mean, *she* was killed in a frenzied attack and drowned, whereas *they* were killed with weapons, in a cold, clinical way." She gave him a searching look. "Were all three murders committed by the same man, Tom?"

"*Good* question." He ran his hand through his spiky hair.

"What's your gut instinct?"

He walked over to the window and pulled up a slat of the blinds to look out. Before he could say anything his mobile rang. He checked the caller ID and answered immediately. "What've you got, Anderson?"

The news was obviously something he wanted to hear because his face brightened as he listened to the caller. He hung up and gave Jess a grudging smile. "DNA tests on the foetus confirm Anthony Harris *was* the father of Ellen Chambers' baby. You were right about their affair."

"*Now* we're getting somewhere," she said. "So *Harris* must have been the TH in her diary."

He nodded. "What were you saying before the call, Jess?"

She paused to think. "I was asking if you thought the same man committed all three murders."

He looked thoughtful. "The same MO was used for the murders of Anthony Harris and Danny Burton. A shot to the back of the head, followed by a stab wound to the heart." He picked up a piece of paper and flicked the edge. "Ballistics confirm the bullets found in both men were fired by the same gun. That has to be the work of the same man, particularly as we didn't release any details about the post-mortem stab wounds after the Harris murder." He paused. "But the Ellen Chambers' murder?" He shook his head. "I don't think he did that."

"So what are you saying?" Her voice was incredulous. "There are *two* killers?"

"You asked for my gut instinct."

She sat back. "You just said the same gun was used to kill Harris and Burton."

He nodded. "A Glock 17 pistol."

"So who would typically use that type of weapon?"

"We would."

"*The police?*"

He nodded, gravely.

★

Later, Sangster closed the door of the incident room and ran down the stairs two at a time. Just look where all this tiptoeing around the Chinese had got them. Chen Xiamen, a major player in this chaos had been allowed the space to vanish. Is that what the Government planned all along? Allow Chen to disappear so they wouldn't have to confront him about the bribes he'd been paying? So they wouldn't have to confront the Chinese Government and jeopardise the deal? So they could blame it all on Ellen Chambers and continue with the negotiation as if nothing had happened?

He walked into his office and slammed the door, furious he'd allowed himself to be warned off talking to Chen. He went over to the window and stared out into the twilight. Traffic was building up in the street as staff cars queued to get out of the car park. He ran his fingers through his hair, feeling strangely disconnected. How long had he been in Brisbane now? Six years was it? He'd only transferred here because that's what Liz had wanted. Perhaps he should go back to Sydney? Perhaps he should leave the police? Make a clean break of it. Do something else. Go somewhere else. Abroad maybe? There was nothing to keep him here now.

He sat down at his desk to think. He didn't like coincidences. They happened, of course. But a distinct pattern had emerged from these murders. Ellen Chambers had been murdered in a fit of rage. So what had sparked that rage? Was it the affair and pregnancy? Or the bribery and corruption? Or both? Had she been waiting for her killer on the jetty on Sunday night? All these questions kept rattling around in his head.

You think she recognised her killer? The Consul's words at the hotel this morning had lodged in his brain. *Is that what the light in her eyes signifies?*

Yes, he thought, Ellen Chambers' murder *was* personal, but Anthony Harris's and Danny Burton's weren't. No, they were more like professional executions.

The door squeaked open and Dalton peered round. "Okay to come in?" He walked in and sat down without waiting for a reply. "No sign of DC Roberts," he said, clutching a file to his chest. "The guys went round to his house, but it was all locked up. They talked to the neighbours, but they haven't seen him for a while. Didn't even know he was a policeman."

Sangster raised an eyebrow.

"So I talked to the guys in his team," Dalton went on. "But they don't know much about him either. He never gives out anythin' personal. Prefers his own company and they leave him alone." Dalton looked uneasy. "So I pulled his personnel file," he said, handing it to Sangster. "I'd better put it back before anyone sees it's missin'."

Sangster looked surprised; he didn't know Dalton had it in him. He went to open the file, but Dalton rattled off its contents by memory.

"Roberts joined the police in Perth in 1996," he said. "In 2004, he transferred to Melbourne; and last year, he transferred up here. But this is where it gets interesting; for about 18 months before he came up here, Roberts left the Melbourne police to work for some security company."

"Which company?" Sangster asked, sharply.

"I don't know. I expected to find a letter of reference from them on the file. But there isn't one."

Sangster frowned. "Find out, Dave."

"Will do." Dalton scratched his head. "His file contains some... complaints about him from the public. He tends to go in a bit hard on occasion. Mind you, there are no actual charges against him."

"Didn't he present good credentials from the other police services before we agreed to take him on?"

"Yeah, but that's how it works, isn't it? They give good references to anyone they want to move on." Dalton hesitated. "There's been one complaint about him recently... from a prossie working in the Valley. Said he'd been rough with her."

"As a policeman or a client?" The Valley was the entertainment and red light area.

Dalton's eyes gleamed. "Client."

"*For Chrissakes!* What did Roberts have to say about it?"

"Said he'd never been with the woman; and she was tryin' to make trouble for him because he'd pulled her in for illegal street work. Anyway, she dropped the complaint."

Sangster's eyes turned hard. "Find him, Dave. And get that prostitute in here. I want to know exactly what happened. And I want to know exactly where Roberts had sex with her."

"*If* he did."

Sangster ignored that. "And pull his official mobile phone records, and his home phone. I want to know *everyone* he's been talking to for the last couple of months."

"Should I get permission?"

"Just do it, okay?" Sangster stood up. "You got that, Dave. Find the security company Roberts worked for in Melbourne; find that prostitute; and pull his mobile phone and landline records." He picked up the ballistics report. "Here," he said, handing it to Dalton. "From the bullets found in Harris and Burton, the weapon used was a Glock 17. The gun has been modified with a silencer-capable barrel, which explains why no one heard anything.

Dalton looked hopeful. "The modification *should* make the weapon easier to trace."

"*If* it was carried out by a registered gunsmith. The team are checking. They've circulated the information to other State police services in case the modification was carried out in their jurisdictions." Sangster paused. "Of course, if it was done by a non-registered gunsmith, it's going to be harder." Sangster walked to the door. "I'm going to Roberts' house now... I want to take a *personal* look at him."

Dalton didn't ask any more questions; he was preparing himself for the blast he knew would follow his next bombshell. "One more thing, Boss."

Sangster turned round.

"Anthony Harris's wife phoned from Changi Airport just before boarding a flight home. She's frantic because her daughter hasn't been answerin' her mobile or their home phone all night."

Sangster stared at him. "Hasn't anyone *spoken* to Harris's daughter since he was murdered?"

Dalton shook his head. "The guys called round to his home, but no one answered the door. They tried the girl's Uni, but no one's seen her. They thought she'd gone to Singapore with her mother. So we assumed that's where she was too."

Sangster could barely speak. "You *assumed?*"

★

Roberts' house was clean. Too clean. Sangster stood in the living room, looking around. The smell of bleach permeated his nostrils. Even the carpet beneath his feet still showed the parallel tracks of recent vacuuming. Apart from the basic furniture, the place had been cleaned out. There were no personal effects anywhere. No books, no ornaments, no clothes, no photos. Nothing. Roberts had wiped the place clean and removed all traces of himself.

Sangster walked over to the window and looked out at the neat suburban garden. Even the lawn had been recently mown and the hedges clipped. He could see the neighbours peering over the fence, wondering what was going on. He turned away and walked to the bathroom.

"Nothing," the forensic officer said as Sangster entered. "It's all been scrubbed spotless. There's not a single hair in the shower or sink; and nothing in the medicine cabinet."

"He knew we were coming." Sangster went into the bedroom. The mattress was left exposed, with no sheets or bedcover to examine.

The forensic officer followed. "We've been through all the cupboards and drawers. There's no rubbish in any bin inside or outside the house. Must've bundled everything into a rubbish bag and taken it with him." He glanced at the bare walls. "It's as if he were never here."

Sangster opened the wardrobe and a couple of drawers to check for himself. All empty.

While the forensic officer went to check the kitchen again, Sangster remained in the bedroom. As the forensic officer opened the back door, a wind blew through the house and a chill descended. Sangster imagined Roberts standing in the doorway, laughing at him. Was he nearby, watching them now? Was he getting a kick out of this? In the silence, Sangster looked around and tried to conjure up Roberts' face. He considered himself to be an expert on faces, but he could hardly remember what Roberts looked like. He'd seen him, of course, around HQ. But Roberts had never worked on his team or been involved in any of his cases. He was one of those nondescript quiet men who, from Sangster's professional experience, often turned out to be the most dangerous.

Sangster had no evidence. None whatsoever. But something about Roberts tripped all his alarm bells.

24

All the way from Police HQ, he was careful to keep a car between himself and the taxi.

It wasn't hard to follow because he knew where the meddling bitch in the back was going. But now they were stuck in traffic, he could feel himself getting wound up. He was sick and tired of all this running around; he should have left this stinking city before dawn. And he would have if it hadn't been for *her*. But he had to get that diary. That was the deal.

He pulled his cap down over his eyes and peered through the windscreen. He could see her looking out of the back window. She didn't know who he was, but she could feel him in pursuit, like a deer fleeing the hunter. Last night, watching her on the balcony, he'd sensed she was going to be trouble. And what a runaround she'd given him all day. But the thrill of the chase was secondary to the thrill of the kill. The urge to slip out of the car and grab her now was strong. But he had to be patient. She was leading him to the diary. Once he had it, he could do whatever he liked. He held her life in the palm of his hand. *He* would decide when and how she died. And no one would ever know it was him. The police were running around like idiots. No clue. And that was the third thrill: being invisible. Truly invisible.

Rolling his head from side to side to ease his neck, he closed his side window to keep the noxious city fumes out of his nose. He couldn't wait to get away and breathe real air again. He could almost see the wide blue sky, and silver grass waving in the breeze through the saplings; and, at the end of the day, that huge, orange sun, setting behind stark, rocky gullies.

The bush was calling him home.

Suddenly her face flashed into his mind. He rubbed his eyes, but she was still there. Her dark, lifeless eyes stared up at him as she lay on the kitchen floor, with the desert rose he'd picked on his way home from school still in her hand. His heart started pounding. He'd been thinking about her more and more these days.

He could still feel the knife in his hand.

*

Jess couldn't breathe in the airless taxi. She couldn't think either; the driver had the radio on so loud. She opened the window to let in some air, and checked her mobile. *Still* nothing from Susan. The girl had no idea what she was getting herself into. Jess thought back to her first meeting with Susan. Was it only yesterday afternoon? Her stomach turned. If only she'd given Ellen's diary to Inspector Sangster straightaway.

She rubbed her temples, wishing the traffic would move. What on earth was going on up ahead? Nervous, she twisted round again to look out of the back window. That woman driving the blue Holden behind was still there. Behind her, the driver of a white truck had his peaked cap right down over his eyes.

Her mobile vibrated in her hand and she opened the text message from Simon.

HC hadn't seen that report. Nigel said he hadn't read it due to pressure of work. Huh! Nothing more from Beijing yet. Really worried. Will phone later.

Simon x

A kiss at the end of the message. She smiled. A kiss? That was the first time he'd ever done that...

Then she heard the news bulletin on the radio.

Within the last hour, there has been another development in the Palms Resort triple murder investigation. Queensland police confirm that Federal Government Minister Anthony Harris and resort gardener Danny Burton both suffered stab wounds to the heart, after being shot dead. These two murders followed on from the killing of senior Western Energy Executive Ellen Chambers, whose body was found at the Palms Resort on Monday morning. She'd been attacked and drowned.

Detective Inspector Sangster, who is leading the investigation, moved quickly to scotch rumours that a serial killer was operating in the Brisbane area. He said that details of the post-mortem stabbings had not been released to the public earlier for operational reasons. He also stressed that the general public should not be unduly alarmed: police believe the three murders were targeted. However, he urged everyone to remain vigilant. "Whoever carried out these murders is very dangerous, and should not be approached," he said. "If anyone has any information, they should call the police immediately."

Poor Tom, Jess thought. He'd be furious news of the stabbings had got out. The last thing he needed was a media frenzy about a serial killer.

"*Bastard!* The taxi driver shouted suddenly.

Jess jumped and looked up at two angry eyes watching her in the driver's mirror.

"They should shoot him when they catch him," he carried on. "Poor Tony didn't deserve that. He's one of the good guys."

"Tony?" she asked. "Oh, you mean Anthony Harris?"

"He was a great bloke. I don't know what's happening to this bloody country. Things like that don't happen here."

Jess just nodded.

"The world's gone mad. First that English woman is murdered, then Tony, then some gardener. What the bloody hell's goin' on, that's what we all want to know. Here, in Brizzie, of all places. There's probably a roadblock up ahead, lookin' for the nutter. I bet that's why we're not movin'."

Jess thought that highly unlikely but she understood his strength of feeling. Then she realised the taxi driver had called the Minister Tony. "Did you know Anthony Harris?" she asked.

The driver nodded. "Known him for years. He lives near us. His daughter and mine are on the same course at Brisbane Uni. That poor kid! She'll be devastated about her dad. It's a bloody tragedy for the family *and* for the rest of us." Tirade over, he slumped back in his seat and stared morosely out of the window.

Jess did the same until her eyes focused on a café window...

That dark, wavy hair was unmistakable.

Frowning, she wound down the window to get a better look.

It *was* Nigel, sitting at a window table, engrossed in conversation with... Chen Xiamen. *Oh my God!* She shrank back into the taxi so they wouldn't see her. What were they doing? How did they know each other? She tried to think, but she couldn't come up with a rational explanation.

She reached for her mobile to call Sangster to tell him where Chen was. But what if Nigel's meeting with Chen was above board? What if the British Government didn't *want* the Australians to know about the meeting? What if Chen was passing information to the British Government? She needed to check with Simon and the High Commissioner.

First she called Simon and got his voicemail. "Call me back urgently, Simon, *Please*." Frustration levels mounting, she called the High Commissioner and got his voicemail too. They were both still in meetings.

"*Come on! Get a bloody move on!*" The taxi driver shouting at the traffic only added to her jitters. She looked over at Nigel and Chen, then over her shoulder. Something was wrong. Very wrong. All she knew was she couldn't stay in this taxi a minute longer. "I'll walk the rest of the way," she said to the driver. "It'll be quicker."

"Are you sure?" he asked, with obvious relief.

"Absolutely." She pulled out her purse. "The Consulate-General's just up the road." She handed him the fare. "You can do a U-turn and get out of this traffic."

"Thanks, doll," he said, as he took the money and rammed the gear shift into drive. "Take care now. Mind you don't run into that nutter."

Clutching her bag and briefcase, she jumped out of the taxi, and rushed across the pavement, and through the iron gate into the city Botanic Gardens where no car could follow. There, she dodged behind a tree and waited to see if anyone followed her in. Heart pounding in her ears, she waited. No one.

She looked around. The railings bordered the main road all the way to the Consulate-General, which wasn't far. Would she be safer walking down the street where there were cars and people, or inside the garden railings?

Instinct made her decide to stay inside the gardens. She couldn't forget the wheels of that bus this morning. Taking a deep breath, she started walking along the path in the direction of the Consulate-General. She could hear traffic noise behind the railings to her left; but to her right flowed Brisbane River. She looked over her shoulder. No one.

Relieved to be in the fresh air, she slowed down, but her mind was still buzzing. How did Nigel know Chen Xiamen? The LNG deal had nothing to do with the British Government or the British High Commission. What's more, how did Nigel know how to contact Chen? Even the Queensland Police couldn't find him. Nigel's sickly face yesterday sprang into her mind, his obsession with the LNG deal at the talks, the way he suppressed that intelligence report. What did it all *mean*?

Come on, Simon, ring!

Coming across a weeping fig tree, with extending branches providing a canopy of shade, she sat down on the seat underneath and looked out across Brisbane River. In the silence, she could feel her taut nerves jangling. A soft breeze from the water blew in her face. She sat very still, letting the peace wash over her until her body began to slow down. Soon, for the first time that day, she started to feel disconnected from all the madness around her. She felt safe sitting there, where no one knew where she was. But that peace wasn't going to last.

Her mobile rang in her hand. "Simon?" she answered.

"It's me, Jessica."

"Oh hello, John." She was relieved to hear Langhurst's voice.

"You sound upset," he said. "Are you all right?"

"I'm fine. How are you?"

"Oh, you know." He sounded weary. "Still shell-shocked. And I was, well, I was worried about you."

She was touched. "Oh, don't worry about me," she heard herself say.

"I don't want anything to happen to you, Jessica. Really, I don't."

Hearing a soft rustling, she jerked her head round. No one there.

She looked across the river. The sun had gone down now and twilight was gathering pace. "It's Susan *I'm* worried about," she said. "She's got Ellen's diary; and the police need it for their investigation."

There was a pause.

"Are you still with the police?" he asked.

"No, I'm on my way back to the Consulate-General to do some work."

"They *are* looking after you though, aren't they?"

Then she did what she always did when someone showed her any kindness or concern, she changed the subject: "Did you get to Canberra okay? she asked.

"Meetings. Meetings. All I ever seem to do is attend meetings." He paused. "Jess, have you ever thought of leaving the Foreign Office? Working somewhere else... in business perhaps? I mean, don't you want to settle down in one place? Make a good life somewhere. Travelling all the time must take its toll."

She felt her breath catch in her throat. He could never guess the pain his words evoked. Her job had cost her everything she held most dear.

"We could do with someone like you on our team," he went on, unaware. "Why don't you come and work for Western Energy?"

Was he offering her a job?

He went on, quickly: "It would be a good position, with a good salary. In fact, I'd like you to work with me, I really would."

She was speechless.

"Look, you don't have to give me an answer now. Think about it. But don't take too long."

"I'm really flattered but..."

"*Think* about it," he insisted. "Promise me you'll do that."

"Of course."

"Good. You're just like Ellen," he said. "Smart. Unassuming. Never miss a trick."

Jess was so surprised, she didn't know what to say.

"Now, I'd better go and get ready," he said.

"You've got the High Commissioner's dinner tonight, haven't you?"

"Duty calls." He sounded weary again. "I'll ring you tomorrow if I may, Jess."

"Of course. I'll look forward to hearing from you."

"See you soon," he said and hung up.

She sat staring at her phone. Amongst all the madness, she hadn't expected to be offered a job. Now, replaying the conversation in her head, she realised he hadn't been specific about what *kind* of job. She didn't know much about the energy and resources sector, although she could always learn. Derek Marshall had said Langhurst wanted to go into politics. Now that was more her thing. Working for an Australian politician could be interesting, exciting even. And she did love Australia, so staying here would be great. No point getting carried away, she told herself, but it *was* flattering to be offered a job like that. Made her feel good about herself. Was that how he'd head-hunted Ellen Chambers in China, she wondered?

She closed her eyes and put her head back on the seat. She could hear the hum of traffic in the background and the soft rustling of leaves in the breeze. It was calming sitting there after such a bizarre day. In fact, it had been so frantic she hadn't had much time to think about this special day.

"Happy birthday, darling," she whispered, as her thoughts drifted back to Amy's third birthday party in Jakarta, the last one they'd all spent together. She remembered the cake she'd baked. In her usual rush, she'd forgotten to add the baking powder and the cake had come out of the oven as flat as a pancake. Jack had ridden to the rescue and covered it with loads of marzipan and icing. And Amy and her little friends had stuffed it down like nectar.

Oh Jack!

Hearing that soft rustling again, she opened her eyes. At first, she thought the tree was full of birds. That is, until the squeaking started.

Goose bumps rose on her arms. *Bats!*

Overhead, they hung from every branch of the tree, like ripe fruit. Wide awake, their eyes were watching her as they prepared to fly across the river for their night-time feed on native fig trees.

Flesh crawling, she leapt up and fled down the path.

25

Back in the Consulate-General, Jess sat rigid behind the desk in the early evening gloom. Nigel and Chen? Her head whirled. Nigel couldn't be involved in corruption, could he? No, that didn't make sense. She frowned. Of course Nigel would have known Anthony Harris. She remembered the little beads of sweat on Nigel's forehead when they talked about Ellen Chambers' murder yesterday morning. Was he telling the truth when he said he hadn't known her? But even if he *had,* that still wouldn't explain how he knew Chen Xiamen, and well enough to meet him in a back street café in Brisbane of all places.

She *had to* talk to Simon.

She phoned him again and got his voicemail. She phoned the High Commissioner's mobile, and got his voicemail too. *This was ridiculous!* She was just about to ring Sharon when she heard the Consulate front door slam.

A chill shivered up her spine. It *had* to be Nigel. The staff had all gone home, and he was the only one with a key to let himself in.

As she waited in the semi-darkness, listening to every sound outside, her heart quickened.

Nigel appeared in the doorway, face ashen. His normally combed-back wavy hair hung limp over his forehead.

"Hello, Nigel," she said, quietly.

He walked over to the Consul-General's desk, as if he expected her to vacate it for him.

She didn't move.

He stared at her, then sat down on the sofa. "You'd better tell me everything that's happened since *you* arrived in Brisbane yesterday."

The accusation in his voice, as if she were personally responsible for the madness, riled her. *He* was the one with some explaining to do. She fought to keep calm. Maybe there was a rational explanation for him meeting Chen? She had to give him the chance to tell her.

Taking a deep breath, she recounted everything that had happened since she landed in Brisbane in as factual a way as she could manage. She didn't hold back about being followed from the airport, or about her room being searched, or about almost ending up under the wheels of a bus. But she did leave one thing out: seeing *him* with Chen in that café. She would wait. If he told her about it, she would know the meeting was above board and she could trust him again. "And that's about it," she said, watching his reaction.

Eyes guarded, he said nothing.

She could feel a gnawing anger inside, which surprised her. She hadn't felt any emotion like it for a long time. But there it was bubbling away, like a seething volcano. "Have you anything to tell me, Nigel?" She heard the edge to her voice.

"Why should I? I've been in Canberra all the time?" He shook his head. "What a nightmare! First Ellen Chambers, then Tony Harris, and now this Danny Burton."

She looked out of the window to hide the turmoil inside; he wasn't going to tell her *anything*. Should she confront him? Then her stomach flipped.

Did he just call Anthony Harris *Tony*?

The penny dropped. *Of course!* That's who he'd been talking to on the phone yesterday morning when she'd stood outside his office. *Christ, Tony... I can't believe it.* What was it he'd said after? Something about handing over something *in confidence*.

Oh my God! She put her elbows on the desk and gave him a piercing look. "Tell me what's going on, Nigel?"

His eyes bore into hers. "What are you talking about?"

She struggled to keep her voice under control. "I should have known the Federal Police had Ellen Chambers and Chen Xiamen under investigation for corruption before I set off from Canberra. And why didn't you tell me about that intelligence report from our Embassy in Beijing?"

He took off his glasses and started rubbing the lenses.

"Had you seen it?" she asked.

Still nothing.

"Nigel?"

"I don't have to answer to you," he said, icily.

"You let me come up here to deal with a consular case and deliberately withheld the background. I have a right to know why."

"I hadn't read that report before you left. I wasn't aware of its significance." His voice was controlled, but he didn't look at her.

Did he think she was completely stupid? "I think you *had* read it, Nigel. And you were well aware of its significance. *For God's sake! Three people have been murdered!*"

He looked startled by her anger. "What do *you* know?" he sneered.

"*Tell* me, then!"

But he just looked away, which infuriated her even more.

"So what did Anthony Harris have to say before he was murdered?" she asked.

His eyes narrowed.

"That is who you were talking to on the phone when I came into your office yesterday morning, wasn't it?" She paused. "Christ, Tony, you said. Then you mentioned you'd given him something in confidence. What was it, Nigel? What did you give the Federal Minister in confidence?"

"Were you *eavesdropping?*"

She ignored the accusation; she had him cornered and he knew it. "So what had Harris done, Nigel?" She paused. "He knew about the murder of Ellen Chambers by then, didn't he? After all, he *was* her lover and the father of her unborn child."

"*Unborn child?*" Nigel looked shocked.

"Ellen was 16 weeks pregnant when she was murdered. Did Anthony Harris have something to do with her murder, Nigel? Is that why he phoned you?"

Nigel glared at her, furious at being challenged.

But Jess was on a roll. "And what about Chen Xiamen, the man suspected of paying bribes to Ellen Chambers? I've just seen you both having a cosy chat in a back street café. The police can't seem to find him. So how did you?"

"You're *imagining* things now."

"And you're *lying*." She knew she had him on the back foot. "Don't bother denying it. I just saw you with your heads together."

His face turned hard as he stood up. *"How dare you!"*

The gloves were truly off now. She pushed the chair back and stood up to face him. "You know exactly what's going on, Nigel; and you're somehow involved." She lifted her chin. "You like to think we're all fools, but we're not."

"*You bitch!*" He towered over her, fists clenched.

Time seemed frozen as they glared at each other.

Then he turned and stormed out.

As he slammed the door behind him, Jess staggered back onto the chair, heart hammering. *What the hell just happened?* One minute he was quiet and upset, the next he turned on her like a raging bull. She was shaking as she replayed every word of the row in her head. But now she was convinced she was right; Nigel was definitely involved.

She flicked on the metal desk lamp, which shone its bright beam over the desk. Outside, the last of the winter light had almost faded. The lights in a nearby office block were blazing. She could see people still working inside, which meant they could probably see her. Had they witnessed that argument? Feeling vulnerable, she got up and snapped the blinds shut. She went over to the door and poked her head out. Everything was in darkness.

Her ringing mobile shattered the silence.

"Jess."

"Simon." She could hear the relief in her voice. "I'm so glad to hear from you."

"What's wrong?"

"It's Nigel! We just had a blazing row, and he's stormed out of the Consulate-General. God knows where he's gone."

"*A row*? What about?"

"I accused him of lying. He got mad and..."

"*Christ, Jess!* What did you do that for?"

"Because he *is* lying, Simon. I don't care what he told you and the High Commissioner, he deliberately kept hold of that intelligence report and deliberately didn't tell us about the police investigation into Chen and Ellen Chambers. And on my way back to the Consulate-General from Police HQ, I saw him in a café with Chen. When I mentioned it, he accused me of imagining it."

"Could you have been mistaken?"

"*No way!* He's lying, Simon."

"This is going to send the High Commissioner into the stratosphere." Simon's voice was tense. "He just had a strop at the Federal Police Commissioner; he thinks he's not being kept in the loop. He pointed out in no uncertain terms that Ellen Chambers was a British citizen and demanded to be given all the information. Now, I've had to ring up the heads of Foreign Affairs and Trade and all the Security Agencies to get them here for dinner an hour earlier than the other guests, for a drink in his study."

And Jess knew what that meant; HC was going to give them all a grilling. She'd witnessed that before, the High Commissioner sitting at his desk in his dinner suit, gold cufflinks glittering in the lamplight. He'd be rolling a fat cigar between the finger and thumb of his right hand like a weapon. If the assembled group didn't tell him what he wanted to know, he'd light up and suck on it until a cloud of smoke filled the room. Everyone would be loosening their collars and ties to breathe. But he wouldn't let anyone out until he'd got what he wanted.

"Our security technician has been over to sweep his study for bugs," said Simon. "HC insists he wants a full and frank discussion."

"Any more news from our Embassy in Beijing, Simon? Do we know the *source* of the corruption allegations?"

"Not yet." Simon sighed with frustration. "They have to get clearance from London to transmit sensitive information."

Jess understood the intelligence implication.

"HC has asked for the e-gram to be delivered to his residence immediately it arrives." Simon paused. "That's where I am now. He came home early to work in his study before dinner. I've just been helping Lady Patricia with the table placement. Not that she needs my help."

Jess could picture the High Commissioner's wife slotting a place card into a silver holder at each setting on the dining table. The sinking late-afternoon sun would be bathing the surrounding hills and garden in the orange glow of sunset, and beaming through the dining room window onto the crystal glasses and glittering silver cutlery.

She looked around the Consul-General's shadowy office in the lamplight and felt a pang of loneliness. She wondered, as she had so often, what stroke of fate had led her to join the Foreign Office, and end up living alone in far flung places. That offer of a job at Western Energy was becoming more attractive by the minute.

"Still there, Jess?"

"Yes."

"I'll go and tell HC about Nigel and Chen," Simon said. "Or do you want to talk to him?"

"You tell him," she said. "I'm finding it hard to keep my temper at the moment."

There was a pause. "What are you going to do now?" he asked.

"Work on here for a couple of hours, where I can stay by the phone. I need to talk to London. Then, I'll check-in the Riverbank for the night – it's not far from here."

"Right. I'll talk to the High Commissioner and ring you back. It may take a while. Just don't leave the Consulate-General until you hear from me."

"Okay. But if Nigel rings, don't let him talk you round, Simon. He's *involved*." She paused. "And that makes him dangerous."

"*Jess,*" Simon said, crossly. "I can't let you handle this on your own."

"You have to see out the Foreign Secretary's visit."

"*Sod* the Foreign Secretary... I'm coming up to Brisbane tonight."

"No, Simon. Someone has to carry on with business."

"*For God's sake, Jess!*"

"Simon," she said, voice firm. "I'm not going to do anything stupid. I'll wait here. You ring me back and tell me what the High Commissioner wants me to do."

"Are you sure?"

"Yes," she said, with a confidence she no longer felt.

★

Jess tried to settle at the computer, but she couldn't concentrate. Nigel's angry face kept flashing before her eyes. She'd seen his true colours tonight, and it was an ugly sight. Too agitated to work, she closed her laptop screen and raised a slat of the blinds to peer out. Only one or two lights still burned in the nearby office block; most people seemed to have left for the night.

She stood up to go and make herself a cup of tea. Flicking on the lights in the main office, she glanced through the bullet-proof glass window at reception, and stopped dead.

The front door to the Consulate-General stood wide open.

Nervous, she looked around. Was she alone? She stood watching and listening, but there was only silence. She glanced up at the CCTV monitor, beaming pictures from the camera outside the front door in the corridor. All quiet. Nigel must have stormed out and left the front door open.

She went over to the front door and peered out. Everything seemed eerily quiet now everyone had gone home. Suddenly, the lift motor cranked up from the bowels of the building. She heard it climb higher and higher. Was that Nigel coming back? She slammed the front door shut, turned the key in the lock, and hurried back to watch the CCTV monitor.

But it wasn't Nigel. It was Tom Sangster, who stepped out of the lift and rang the front door bell.

She unlocked the door and let him in.

"You alone?" He stepped inside.

She nodded.

"Any word from Susan?" he asked, quickly.

"Sorry, Tom."

"Damn! Where is that girl?"

His face was pale with fatigue and worry. He was obviously under immense strain.

"I came to talk to your Deputy High Commissioner," he said, wearily.

"I'm afraid he left a while ago."

Sangster's eyes narrowed. "Where's he gone?"

Jess hesitated. "I don't know."

He stared at her. "Everything all right?"

How could she tell him she'd just had a blazing row with Nigel? What an impression that would make. "Fine."

"Sure?"

She nodded.

"Only I've been ringing his mobile," Sangster said, "but he's not answering."

"He left here a bit... distracted."

"Distracted?"

"Oh, just internal issues," she said.

It wasn't so much the query in his eyes, as a softness she hadn't seen in them before that threw her. "It's nothing," she mumbled.

He was standing close to her now, almost touching. She was so aware of him beside her that her hand was shaking as she tried to lock the front door again.

He took the key from her hand gently and locked it for her.

"Thanks," she said, avoiding his eyes. She turned and walked back into the main office, while he followed. All the while, her mind was sifting through everything that had happened since she'd last seen him. Should she tell him about seeing Chen and Nigel in that café? Perhaps he already knew? Is that why he wanted to talk to Nigel? She stopped and turned. Looking into that exhausted face, she knew at that moment that she trusted him a damn sight more than she did Nigel. "I saw Chen Xiamen about an hour ago," she said, quietly.

He looked startled. "Why didn't you call me?"

There was a pause.

"He was in a café round the corner with my boss, Nigel Paxman."

"*What?*" Sangster's face hardened. "How did *he* know how to contact Chen?"

She put up a hand to stop his questions. "I don't know, Tom. It seems I'm being kept in the dark."

"You and me both," he said, angrily.

She understood his frustration perfectly.

"I have to go," he said. "What are your movements for the rest of the evening, Jess?"

"I'm going to work here for another couple of hours. Then I'll check into the Riverbank for the night."

"I still expect Susan to contact you." His voice was low, but urgent. "You're still our best hope of finding her and keeping her safe. And we must get that diary from her. You understand that, don't you?"

She nodded. "I'll call if she gets in touch."

He gave a long sigh. "Right, well, I'm going to send an officer over to accompany you here for the rest of the evening. He'll escort you to the hotel too."

She could feel herself tensing. "Are you saying I'm in danger?"

"All I'm saying is this isn't over yet." He fixed her with one of his penetrating stares. "But please ring me immediately if you hear from your Deputy High Commissioner. Better still, tell him I want him to come down to the station?"

"I know he's involved in all this," she said, softly. "Can you tell me what he's done?"

He held her gaze for a moment, then looked away.

"I see." Her voice was cool now. She'd been kept in the dark by Nigel. Now *he* was doing it too.

"Jess..." Sangster touched her arm.

That touch both surprised and somehow reassured her.

"Look, you know Ellen Chambers was under investigation for corruption," he said.

She nodded.

"Well, there were two other people in Australia under investigation with her." He lowered his voice as if there were ears everywhere. "Anthony Harris... and your Deputy High Commissioner."

"*Nigel?*"

He nodded, gravely.

Jess stood rooted to the spot. *Nigel and Anthony Harris under investigation?* She was so shocked she couldn't think straight.

His ringing mobile interrupted. "Sangster," he answered.

Watching him on the phone, Jess saw his face turn from weariness to shock.

"Where did the murder take place?" he asked, calmly, almost as if he were expecting it.

Another murder? Oh God, Jess thought, please don't let it be Susan.

"I'm on my way." He hung up and looked at her.

Her stomach was turning somersaults. "Is it Susan?"

He shook his head. "It is a young woman, but not Susan."

"Who, then?"

"I'll ring you as soon as we've confirmed her identity."

"If you can't confirm her identity, how do you know it's not Susan?" Jess could hear the panic in her voice.

"I promise you, it's *not* Susan," he said, gently, as he stepped outside the front door. "Now lock this after me and don't open it for anyone other than my police officer."

26

Jess locked the front door and threw the bolts. She should have been feeling shocked and upset at the news of another murder. But she just felt numb. It was as if Ellen Chambers' murder had released some contagion that was spreading out of control; and no one could stop it.

Desperate to find out who the latest murder victim was, she went back into the Consul-General's office and switched on the TV. Tom said it was a young woman. How could he be so sure it wasn't Susan? When the weather report came up, she knew she'd missed the news. Rushing over to the desk, she powered up her laptop to scan the media.

"Brizzie serial killer on the rampage," screamed the headlines. *"Psycho loose on the streets."*

Oh God! Jess read on. There was nothing about the latest murder, but they all had the full story on Anthony Harris and Danny Burton now. The bullet in the back of the head, and a stab to the heart, had them fascinated. *Poor Tom!* That's just what he *didn't* want. The pressure on him must be unbearable. She paused. Thinking back to that moment with him and the key earlier threw her into confusion.

She could hear a phone ringing persistently in the main office, but she wasn't going to answer it. Anyone she needed to talk to had her mobile number. She *had* to get through some work. Clicking onto her inbox, the endless chain of emails popped up. She switched her mobile to silent to get through them quickly. But her mind kept coming back to that argument with Nigel. There was no way they could ever work together again. She'd have to request a move, a cross-posting to another country, which would be a shame because she didn't want to leave Australia. But if she took that job with Western Energy, she wouldn't have to.

What was she thinking? Nigel was under *surveillance* for being involved in corruption?

If it were true, diplomat or not, they'd throw the book at him.

Unable to concentrate, she headed out to the kitchen to make a cup of tea. It was so quiet, she could hear the soles of her shoes swishing on the carpet. In the kitchen, she filled the electric kettle with water and switched it on. Putting a teabag in a mug, she heard a strange noise. She listened. It sounded like tapping. Tiptoeing out of the kitchen, she looked around the main office. She could hear the TV still on low in the Consul-General's office.

The tapping started again.

It was coming from the front door.

She crept into the reception area and looked at the CCTV monitor. No one outside. She went up to the front door and put her ear against it.

The handle rattled... someone was trying to get in.

"*Open the bloody door!*" a familiar voice shouted.

"*Susan!*" Jess threw back the bolts.

"*Hurry up, Jess! Someone's coming up in the lift.*"

Fumbling for the key, Jess unlocked the door.

Susan barged in, and slammed the door behind her.

Jess scowled at Susan. "You frightened me to death."

"You frightened me too. I've been ringing for ages." Susan was breathless from running. "I thought something awful had happened to you."

Jess went back to the CCTV monitor and waited. But the lift didn't stop on their floor. She glared at Susan and hurried back into the CG's office to activate her mobile's ring tone.

Susan followed her, and flopped down on the sofa to catch her breath.

"How did you know I was here?" Jess asked.

"I phoned your side-kick Sharon in Canberra," Susan replied. "Snooty cow."

"Where the hell have you *been* all day, Susan? I've been worried sick. You just ran out of that café. The police are looking for you."

Susan huffed. "I've been completing my research on Ellen's appointments in her diary." She pulled out the list from her tote bag, and spread the pages on the coffee table. "It took *time*, Jess. I've been combing through it *all day*."

"*For God's sake!*" Jess shook her head in exasperation. "So what have you found?"

Susan slumped back. "Nothing."

"Then give me that diary!"

Susan looked away.

"Where *is* it?"

Susan didn't respond

"Where *is* it?"

Susan stared at her. "All that crap about a serial killer is rubbish. And you know it. It's a diversion; a smokescreen. And a pretty sick one too," she said, crossly. "Why won't you tell me what's going on?"

"Because I don't know."

"My sister's dead. I deserve to know. *Please, Jess!* You can trust me."

"*Trust* you?" Jess stared back. "After the way you've behaved?"

Susan looked sheepish. "I've only been a journalist for a couple of years. But I *know* if something smells or not. This doesn't just smell, it *stinks*."

She's right, Jess thought. As she looked into those intelligent, pleading eyes, she wondered how much she would have to tell Susan to make her give up that diary. Tom needed it, and *someone* had to save Susan from herself. But Susan was too smart to be fed snippets of information. That would only make her more determined to dig deeper until she got to the truth. She'd be more likely to gain Susan's confidence if she told her the truth, and made her understand the danger she was in and how important it was to get that diary to the police. The trouble was, how would Susan react to news of her sister's involvement? She was grief-stricken enough as it was.

"You *can* trust me," Susan said, as if she understood the turmoil going on inside Jess. "And I *mean* that."

Jess's instincts were telling her she had no option but to trust Susan. "Okay. But only if you promise to keep the details to yourself; and to not publish the story, or get anyone to publish it for you. Is that a deal?"

"Absolutely."

Jess sighed, deeply. "All I know is that the Federal Police are investigating allegations of corruption connected to Western Energy's gas deal with China." Jess paused. "The deal *your* sister was working on."

"*Corruption?* What sort of corruption?"

"The authorities suspect the Chinese of paying bribes to someone in the Australian consortium to help them get a controlling percentage of the joint venture."

"You mean, someone in Western Energy was *working* for the Chinese? What, like a mole?"

"That's one way of putting it," Jess replied. "Your sister visited China recently, didn't she? It's in her diary."

"That's nothing unusual," Susan said. "Ellen went a lot." Her eyes widened. "*Are you saying the authorities were investigating my sister?*"

Jess nodded.

"*What?*"

"I'm just telling you what I know."

Susan looked shell-shocked. "Ellen wouldn't do anything like that," she whispered. "Believe me, even as a kid, she couldn't tell lies or take anything that wasn't hers." She frowned. "How did they find out?"

"Listening to phone calls."

"Phone tapping?"

Jess nodded. "Now will you tell me where the diary is?"

"I've got it hidden, in a safe place."

Jess slapped her palms on the desk in frustration. "I want to see those numbers and letters on the inside back cover."

Susan pulled out her notepad. "I copied them down in here." She turned to the right page and walked over to Jess to show it to her. "Why? What are you thinking?"

"Well, I was wondering if they could be passwords for internet banking. The first line would be a username, wouldn't it?" Then Jess pointed to the letters *tci* at the end of the first line. "You see those letters. I think they might stand for the Turks and Caicos Islands. It's a British Overseas Territory in the Caribbean, an offshore tax haven."

Susan's mind leapt ahead. "Are you saying my sister stashed Chinese bribes in an offshore tax haven?"

Jess didn't answer. "The second line of letters and numbers would be a password; and the third memorable information to get into the account."

"But there are *six* lines."

"I think there must be *two* accounts."

"*Two accounts?*"

"Yes."

Susan slumped back on the sofa. "Is that why Ellen was murdered?" Her voice was barely a whisper. "Because they thought she was taking bribes from the Chinese, and stashing the money offshore? Did the Government have her killed for that?"

Jess stared at her. "Why would they do that?"

"To shut her up?"

"It would have been easier to charge her with fraud."

"Not if the Government wanted to hush it up. They wouldn't want to upset the Chinese and jeopardise their precious LNG deal."

"No, Susan," Jess said, gently. "If that were the case, Western Energy would have just sacked Ellen and whisked her out of the country, with the Australian Government's blessing." She looked at Susan's slumped body. "No, there has to be more to it than that."

Susan bit her lip to stop it trembling. "Well I don't believe for one minute Ellen was taking bribes. You wouldn't either, if you'd known her." Her voice faded, then she collected her thoughts. "What about Anthony Harris, then? Was he involved in the corruption too? Is that why he was murdered? Maybe the Government had him killed too? You people will hush anything up. You don't care who gets caught in the crossfire."

"*You people?*" Jess stared at her. "You've been watching too many movies."

"So what's the link between their two murders, then?"

Jess came straight out with it. "You were right. Anthony Harris was having a secret affair with your sister. DNA tests on the foetus confirm he was the father of her baby."

Susan's face turned from shock to pain. Tears sprang into her eyes. "He's just the kind of man Ellen would go for," she said, quietly. "Older. Distinguished. *And* he lives in Brisbane because his electorate is here. *And* he's married with a wife and kids, so he'd have to keep their affair quiet because of his job and public profile."

Jess nodded. "*And* someone wanted them both dead."

"I know one thing, Jess. My sister wouldn't get involved in corruption unless, well, someone *forced* her. Or... unless she was trying to *protect* someone." She jumped up. "That's it. I bet she was trying to protect that Anthony Harris." She started pacing about. "How *could* he have had an affair with my sister when he's married with kids?"

"Calm down, Susan."

"*I am calm!*" Susan kept pacing around.

"Let's just think this through," said Jess, fighting to keep a handle on her temper. "In his official ministerial capacity, I'm sure Harris would have been kept informed about the LNG negotiations with the Chinese. So he's *bound* to have been told about the Federal Police investigation into Chen Xiamen and your sister. The question is: did *he* tip Ellen off about the investigation? If he'd loved her, he'd have wanted to protect her, surely?"

"*Of course!*" Susan stopped abruptly. "That's why Ellen was so upset and scared of the police when I saw her on Saturday. By then, she *knew* they were investigating her for corruption... because Anthony Harris had *told* her?"

Yes, that sounded plausible. "Tell you what, Susan," Jess said, getting up. "Get onto the internet, on my laptop. Look for banks in the Turks and Caicos Islands. See if you can access any online accounts with the codes and passwords you copied from Ellen's diary."

Susan rushed over to the laptop on the desk, as Jess started walking to the door. "Hey, where are you going?" Susan asked, suddenly plaintive.

"To make some calls."

★

In the kitchen, Jess stood in the dark, reluctant to put on the light. Had Anthony Harris tipped off Ellen that she was under investigation for corruption? She looked at her mobile. *Come on, Simon!* There was so much she needed to know, but she resisted the urge to phone him again. He'd phone as soon as he had instructions from the High Commissioner about what they should do next.

The sound of a car backfiring in the street made her jump. The noise seemed to ricochet up the building's concrete walls. It spurred her into action. The first thing she had to do was phone Tom Sangster and let him know Susan was safe. She tried his mobile, but it was engaged. "Tom, it's Jess," she said, leaving a message. "Susan Chambers is at the Consulate-General with me. She's fine. She's still got Ellen's diary, although not with her. I'm trying to persuade her to give it up. When your police officer arrives, I'm taking her to the Riverbank with me for the night. I won't let her out of my sight again."

She had to get that diary and Susan safely into police custody.

She walked out of the kitchen determined to do just that. But when she went into the Consul-General's office, she found Susan slumped across the desk. "*Susan?*"

When Susan raised her head, there were tears rolling down her cheeks. "I've found Ellen's offshore bank account, in the Turks and Caicos Islands, Jess. You were right about those numbers and letters." A strangled sob came from her. "Why'd she do it? She didn't *need* the money."

Jess frowned. "You found that account quickly."

Susan nodded, morosely. "It was in the Turks Bank. Two sums paid in over the last six months. Both for a million dollars."

"Who paid the money into the account?" Jess asked, quickly. That seemed to her to be the key in all this. If they discovered who paid the money into the account, they'd find out who was behind all this.

Susan shrugged. "There were only numbers next to the transaction."

"How *very* convenient!"

Susan's eyes narrowed. "What do you mean by that?"

Jess sat down on the sofa, heavily, trying to think. "It doesn't add up, does it? You see, I happen to know that the British authorities monitor all funds transmitted through our Overseas Territories, for money laundering and terrorist financing. Large sums like a a million dollars would attract attention. Two transfers would really make them sit up."

"So?"

"So, your sister was a smart lady. She wouldn't transfer such large amounts and attract the authorities' attention, unless *she* didn't open the account."

Susan's eyes lit up.

Jess nodded. "What if someone else set it up in Ellen's name, *without* her knowledge. Then transferred those two large amounts into it *deliberately* to get the British authorities' attention?"

"You think she was *framed?*" Susan jumped up, triumphantly. "I knew it. I *knew* Ellen wouldn't do anything like that." Then she stopped. "So why would Ellen write those bank account details in her diary? How would she know about it?"

Jess shrugged. "Maybe she found out about it, and realised she was being framed. Maybe she found out *who* was framing her and *that's* why she was killed."

Tears gone, Susan's eyes burnt like coals. "I *have* to find out the truth, Jess. I *owe* it to Ellen."

Susan's desperation to clear her sister's name and somehow redeem her, was more than Jess could bear. "Come on," she said, kindly. "Let's think. Now, what about those other three lines of numbers in the back of the diary? Did you try them? Is there a second bank account?"

"No," Susan replied, "at least not that I could find in the Turks Bank. But it definitely looks like another account." Susan started hitting the keys to find the search engine. "Where else can I look?"

Jess shook her head. "We're going to need expert help to find the second account. The first one in Ellen's name was set up to be easily found. But I don't think the second one was." She paused to think. "That must be the reason someone wants Ellen's diary so badly. They want to stop the police discovering those codes and numbers and stop them finding the money in that *second* account. Because if they do find that account, they will find out who is *really* behind all this corruption and murder."

Susan looked at her with something like admiration in her eyes.

"Look, I'm going to report this to my colleagues in Canberra now," Jess said, looking at her watch. "Then we'll go over to the Riverbank for the night." She looked at Susan's red eyes and haggard face. "It's getting late. You need something to eat and some rest."

"I'm all right."

"You're not. You're coming to the hotel with me now and that's final. I'm not letting you out of my sight until we've given that diary to the police."

This time there was no argument from Susan. "Okay, Jess. We'll do it your way... for now."

"Right, well, would you go and make us both a cup of tea in the kitchen while I phone my colleagues?"

Susan stared at her without moving.

"Please, I would like some privacy," Jess said, firmly.

Susan turned and went out of the room.

Jess switched off the TV and picked up the phone to call Simon again. She didn't care if he was in the drinks, she had to speak to him. When his mobile switched to voicemail, she hung up and tried again. She checked her watch. Perhaps they were in dinner now? If so, it would only just have started, no doubt with the High Commissioner's welcoming speech to guests. She could just picture him tapping a spoon on his wine glass to get everyone's attention. He'd be telling them what an honour it was to welcome the Foreign Secretary to his Residence and to Australia.

Simon's voicemail clicked in again. *Pick up, Simon! Pick up!*

As she hung up and dialled again, she couldn't help but wonder who John Langhurst was sitting next to at the table. He'd been such good company at lunch...

"Jess," Simon whispered. "Hang on."

Down the phone, she heard a door creak open and close.

"I've just left the dining room," Simon said as he came back on. "Are you, okay?"

"I'm fine."

"Sorry not to have phoned sooner, it's all kicked off here. HC's been talking to the Australian agency heads in his study. Paul Robinson was late arriving from Foreign Affairs, but he's just told the High Commissioner that when the police had Ellen Chambers under surveillance, they discovered she was having an affair with Harris."

"Ah. So the police *did* know about the affair," she whispered. "Inspector Sangster told me forensics confirmed Harris was the father of her unborn child." She paused.

"Tell me, Simon, do the police actually *know* who killed Ellen Chambers or Anthony Harris and Danny Burton?"

"If they do, they're not saying."

There was a hushed silence down the phone.

Simon sounded tense. "As soon as they found out about the affair, the Federal Police started digging quietly into Harris's background and his finances to see if he was involved in the corruption scandal too. But they haven't traced any funds to him, or found evidence of his involvement."

She paused to think. "Did Anthony Harris *know* the police and Australian Government had discovered his affair with Ellen Chambers? I mean, did anyone talk to him about it?"

"I don't know."

"So we *still* didn't know whether Harris tipped Ellen off about the investigation?"

"No." Simon went on. "We know that she had a bank account in the Turks and Caicos Islands. The Financial Crimes Unit in our Overseas Territory uncovered it. They trace..."

"I *know*. They trace funds moving in and out of the Territory. And I know about the bank account, with 2 million dollars in it. That's why I'm ringing you now. We've found that account. Susan logged onto it from my laptop."

"Susan?"

"Yes, she's here in the Consulate-General with me. Anyway, she logged onto Ellen's account with the passwords Ellen wrote in her diary. But you know, Simon..." Jess hesitated. "It all seems a bit too... convenient." She took a breath. "I'm wondering if the authorities were *meant* to find Ellen's bank account. After all, we found it easily enough. And there were two separate transactions of 1 million dollars each."

Simon understood her meaning. "What are you saying? That she was set up."

"That's exactly what I'm saying. Look, Simon, have you received that e-gram from Beijing yet?"

"I'm told it's on its way."

Jess groaned in frustration. "You know that journalist at The Palms who kept asking me lots of questions about Ellen Chambers, like who she'd worked for before Western Energy?"

"Yes."

"Do you think he might have *known* something about her?" She paused. "Like, well, could Ellen have been working for Australian Intelligence? Could that be what he was getting at?"

"That's exactly what HC just asked the Head of Australian Foreign Affairs," Simon replied. "Paul Robinson said HC should ask his *British* colleagues that question."

"Ah!" said Jess, as if everything was falling into place. "It would make sense if Ellen had been working for MI6. I mean, she kept such a low public profile; you'd have hardly known she was a senior executive. And no one knew anything about her or who her friends were. Or what she did in her spare time."

"HC kept saying Ellen wasn't senior enough to sway the negotiations on her own."

"Mm." Jess paused, when she heard another voice in the background at Simon's end.

"The High Commissioner's here, Jess. I'll put him on." She waited.

"Jess?" HC's deep voice came down the phone. "Are you all right?"

"Yes, Sir, I'm fine. Susan Chambers is too. She's here at the Consulate-General with me."

"Good." He sounded relieved. "I'm sorry you've got caught up in all this. Now listen, there's no time to explain. Go to Police HQ *now*. Take Susan with you, and stay there until I get to Brisbane. I'll be leaving within the hour on a private plane." He paused for breath. "Now, when you get to Police HQ, don't say anything to anyone. Just wait there for me. And if you see Nigel," HC's voice sounded icy. "Tell him to wait there for me too."

"Have the Australians admitted they had Nigel under surveillance, along with Anthony Harris and Ellen Chambers?"

"Yes," he replied, angrily. "And Simon says *you* saw Nigel with Chen."

"I did."

"Bloody idiot!" he hissed. "Look, when you get to Police HQ, just stay there, Jess," he repeated. "Don't leave with anyone. And that includes Nigel. Is that understood?"

"Absolutely."

"Good. I'll put Simon back on."

Jess waited for Simon, mind whirling.

"The old man's livid," Simon said when he came back on. "I can't believe Nigel could be so stupid."

"Me neither." She paused. "Does that mean you'll be coming up to Brisbane with the High Commissioner, Simon?"

"No." He sounded more upset than cross. "HC's insisting I stay here to look after the Foreign Secretary. I've tried to persuade him otherwise, but he won't hear of it." He paused. "I feel I'm letting you down."

"Of course you're not," she said, quickly, to cover her disappointment.

He sighed.

Susan put her head round the door and tapped her watch.

Jess nodded at her. "Sorry, Simon, I have to go. Susan's here."

"Jess," he said, softly. "Are we still on for that new Chinese restaurant in Manuka on Friday?"

She smiled. "Definitely."

27

Sangster spotted two sets of blue lights pulsing in the early evening darkness outside a smart-looking suburban villa. He drove his car up onto the nature strip outside and parked alongside other emergency vehicles. He sat looking up at the house, which was hidden behind a high brick wall and electric gates. All the lights were blazing full on, advertising that something untoward had happened inside. Looking up and down the street, he could see lights burning in several of the other swanky homes, and noses peering out from behind blinds and curtains to see what was going on.

"Evenin', Sir," a young constable called out as Sangster approached the gate. "They're waitin' for you round the back." He shook his head. "It's not a pretty sight."

Grim faced, Sangster walked along the drive and skirted round the side of the house on the grass. He kept off the wooden veranda encircling the sides and back of the building in case of compromising evidence. He heard the sound of retching as he turned the corner and spotted a young female officer doubled over and clutching her jacket to prevent soiling it as she threw up on the grass.

He could already smell the corpse, and hear the flies.

Dalton was standing outside the back door, his face sickly in the yellow glow of the terrace lamp. "You been inside?" Sangster asked.

Dalton shook his head.

"Is it Belinda Harris?"

Dalton nodded.

Sangster sighed. "What happened?"

"I sent a couple of officers round to talk to her about her father's murder, like you asked." He pointed at the young woman being sick. "They couldn't get any reply from the front door, so they came round here." He pointed to the back door. "That was locked too. But when they looked through the kitchen window, well, that's when they saw her... lying on the floor in..." – he breathed in deeply to keep his voice even – "all that blood."

Sangster glanced at the beads of sweat running down Dalton's face. "Wait out here, Dave," he said. "Better still, go and ring HQ and find out if there have been any developments."

Nodding with relief, Dalton walked off to make some calls.

Steeling himself, Sangster pulled on some shoe covers and gloves and stepped inside the kitchen.

The grey, bushy eyebrows rose as he entered.

"Evening, Anderson." Sangster's voice was flat and unemotional.

Anderson just nodded, as if the sight had knocked all the usual banter out of him.

When Sangster studied the blood sprayed around the kitchen, and seeping across the white, limestone floor, he saw its normal glossy red colour had deepened and dried. He didn't need Anderson to tell him the corpse had been here some time.

"Arterial wound." Anderson's voice was businesslike. "The knife punctured the aorta, causing the blood to spurt out." He paused. "There was no silent bullet in the head this time. He stuck the knife straight into the poor kid's heart!"

Sangster's eyes focused on the young woman. She was lying naked on the floor, on her back. With all the blood drained out of her, her face and skin had turned white.

"He killed her here in the kitchen," said Anderson. "Then he covered the body with a sheet." He pointed to a blood-soaked sheet he'd already bagged. "And look at that."

Sangster followed Anderson's gaze. There was a single rose in her left hand.

"He must have put that there too," said Anderson.

Sangster frowned. There'd been nothing like that at the Harris and Burton shootings. Yet this girl had been killed with a knife to the heart, so it had to be the same man. But why cover her with a sheet? To protect her dignity because she was naked? And why put a flower in her hand? Was this some kind of sick romantic gesture?

"I don't think she was sexually assaulted," Anderson said as if reading his thoughts, "but we'll confirm that in the lab." He glanced up. "I think this girl was naked when that psycho arrived. There's a pool outside. I reckon he caught her after her morning swim."

Sangster nodded. "She's been here a while."

"Since yesterday, I'd say. I can't give you an actual time yet, but I reckon more than 36 hours."

"If you're right, that means she was killed yesterday morning... *before* her father, Anthony Harris."

Anderson nodded.

Sangster's eyes had been glued to the corpse, but now he raised them to take in the detail of the kitchen. Expensive black granite worktops, wooden units and stainless steel appliances, everything he would expect in a house like this. His eyes stopped on the plates and mugs drying on the rack.

"Two of everything," Anderson chipped in. "She didn't eat breakfast alone."

Had she eaten breakfast with her killer, Sangster wondered. Or with her father perhaps? He looked at Anderson. "Perhaps the killer came here looking for Anthony Harris yesterday morning? Maybe he missed him, but got his daughter instead? But why kill her?" He paused. "Had she rumbled him? Or does he just *enjoy* killing." He nodded to himself. Perhaps that's it. This nutter's genie's been let out of the bottle. Maybe he's suppressed his desire to kill for so long, he can't stop now he's started. He's enjoying it too much.

"I tell you Tom, in all my years I've never seen anything like this." Anderson's voice was hoarse. This bastard's a psycho and *real* dangerous." He jerked his head towards the door. "He got the dog out the back too, probably to keep it quiet. Knifed it in the heart, then covered it with leaves." He nodded. "This man's a hunter all right."

Except now he's turned to hunting humans, Sangster thought. It made sense. And it would explain how he'd got up so close to Harris and Burton to shoot them without them having a chance to defend themselves. He turned to Anderson. "Has he left anything behind?"

Anderson nodded. "See those footprints in the blood? They'll be his." He frowned. "He's bloody confident now. Must reckon no one's ever going to catch him."

Sangster bristled. "Or he wants us to know it's him. Maybe he's proud of what he's done. He wouldn't be the first killer to want notoriety."

Standing there looking at the young life snuffed out so violently, Sangster felt a weariness creep all over him. He nodded to Anderson and walked back outside. A waft of fresh air hit him in the face, blowing the stench from his nose, and the fatigue from his brain.

"Okay, Boss?" Dalton looked at him with concern.

Sangster nodded and pulled off the gloves and shoe covers.

"They've got a trace in Melbourne on the gun," Dalton said, quickly. "A registered gunsmith down there remembers modifying one about 18 months ago."

"Have they got a name and address?"

"Yep. They turned out to be false, but they've got a description of the man who took the gun in." Dalton stared with a mixture of excitement and alarm on his face. "Tall, muscular, physically fit, balding..."

"Roberts!" Sangster stared at him, his worst fears realised. A policeman was the monster responsible for these barbaric murders.

Dalton frowned. "Doesn't make sense though. Roberts would know we'd trace the gun back to him."

"It makes perfect sense, Dave. He wants us to know it's him. For some reason, he thinks he's untouchable." Sangster gritted his teeth. "Get an All Points Bulletin out on him, Dave, airports too. Pick him up before he goes to ground, if he hasn't already." He paused. "Did you find out who he'd worked for in Melbourne before coming up here?"

"Not yet."

"And what about his mobile phone records? I want to know everyone the bastard's been talking to."

"They're working on it, Boss."

"Go back to HQ and supervise the work yourself, Dave. We need to find that connection between him, Ellen Chambers, Anthony Harris and Danny Burton. And we don't have much time. I reckon the only thing keeping him in town now is that diary." He looked at Dalton. "At least he hasn't got that, or Susan Chambers. She's at the British Consulate-General. I've just had a message from the British Consul."

Dalton's face broke into a smile.

Sangster nodded. "I'm going to pick them up on my way back to HQ. Susan's still got that diary. We have to protect them from that maniac.

28

"Don't worry," Jess said, wishing she felt as confident as she sounded. She peered at the CCTV monitor. It all looked quiet outside the Consulate-General front door. She glanced over at Susan's exhausted face. The poor girl hadn't eaten or slept since she'd heard about her sister's murder. Jess needed to do something about that.

"Now, we're going to take the lift to the basement car park, Susan." She tried to sound reassuring. "We'll get my car, and drive straight to the Riverbank Hotel. It's not far away, but we may need the car later. We can check into a room, get cleaned up and have something to eat. Then we'll decide what to do. Okay?"

"Okay," Susan repeated.

Jess squeezed her hand. The High Commissioner had told her to take Susan to Police HQ and stay there until he arrived. But Susan wouldn't hear of it. She refused point blank. But she had agreed to go to the Riverbank. So that was a first step. "Now whatever happens, Susan, we must stay together." She unlocked the front door, and peered out. Where was that police officer Tom was supposed to be sending over? They'd been waiting for over an hour. More likely, they were too stretched to spare anyone. She pulled out her mobile and dialled Sangster to check, but she got the engaged tone. "Tom," she said, leaving a message. "Just to let you know your police officer never showed up. Anyway, I'm taking Susan to the Riverbank now. I know you're busy so I'll talk to you later." She turned to Susan. "Come on," she said and stepped outside the front door.

Susan followed.

"Press for the lift while I lock up."

Susan did as she was told. But there was no sound of the lift cranking up.

"Press again." Jess tried to sound calm, as she walked over to the stairwell door and peered through the glass window at the top. All quiet.

Susan stabbed the lift button again and again with her finger until they heard the motor start. They stood listening while the lift came up to their floor. Jess could feel her heart hammering. She was holding her breath as the lift stopped on their floor and the doors slid open.

"It's empty." Susan breathed.

In a flash, they were inside and pressing for the basement garage. The doors closed. They watched the button of each floor light up as they descended. Jess's finger hovered over the lobby button. Should they stop and check for that police officer? No, better not.

The lift shuddered to a halt in the basement garage. Keeping her finger on the 'open lift' button, Jess peered out. Dimly lit, with concrete walls and floors, it looked more like a bunker. She scanned the empty garage... the shadowy pillars.

"Where's your car?" Susan whispered.

"Not far from the exit. It's the white Holden." Jess pulled the car keys out of her pocket. "Come on." She strode out of the lift then stopped. Her heels clicking on the concrete floor sounded like machine gun fire in the enclosed space. Rising onto her tiptoes, she scurried over to her car and pressed the zapper to open the doors.

Nothing happened.

She pressed again. "It won't open."

Suddenly the sound of the lift motor firing up was magnified in the silence.

"*Quick!*" Susan hissed. "*Someone's coming.*"

Hands shaking, Jess rammed the ignition key into the door lock. To her relief, it clicked open. She slipped inside and opened the passenger door.

"*Go!*" Susan shouted as she jumped in.

Jess fired up the ignition, and reversed out of the parking bay, tyres squealing on the smooth surface. She accelerated towards the exit, then slammed her foot on the brakes. The security grill was down.

Susan had seen it and was out of the car in a flash. She pressed the button to open it and jumped back in the car.

They sat watching the grill inch its way up.

"*Come on!*" Susan twisted in her seat to look over her shoulder.

Jess caught a flash of movement in her rear-view mirror. She inched the car closer to the grill. It hadn't risen enough to get under. She squirmed in her seat as she looked in her driver mirror at a shadowy figure coming up from behind.

Her palms felt damp as she gripped the wheel. "Hold on, Susan." She took her foot off the brake, and stamped on the accelerator. "*Duck!*" she shouted as she drove the car straight at the rising grill.

There was a loud scraping noise across the roof as the car shot under the metal shutter and out into the night.

★

Jess drove, grim-faced, with one eye on the road and the other in the rear-view mirror. All she could see were dazzling headlights in front and behind. She was conscious of Susan twisting round in her seat to look out of the back window.

"*Slow down, Jess.* The Riverbank is just up on the right."

Spotting the hotel, Jess brought the car to a stop and manoeuvered into a parking space in the middle of a row of cars. She immediately switched off the engine and lights. "Have we lost him?"

Susan looked in her passenger mirror, then over her shoulder again. "I think so. I can't see anyone stopping."

"Did you get a look at him?"

"No. Did you?"

"No." All Jess had seen was a dark shadow running up behind the car. But it was him. She was sure of that. It wasn't only the dark clothes, it was the way he moved, so quick and agile. She glanced across at the hotel entrance. A doorman stood in the doorway, while a porter loitered on the steps ready to pounce on any guest with a suitcase. Should she leave the car parked on the street, or drive into the hotel's underground car park? In the silence, she could hear the blood pounding in her ears. She checked both wing mirrors. No one on the pavement, and no headlights in her rear-view mirror.

Relaxing her grip on the steering wheel, she looked up at the sky. There was no moon now. The cloud cover made the night even darker, and a mist was rolling in from the river. Or was it mist? She wrinkled her nose. Was that smoke she could smell? She glanced over at the hotel again. Her eyes latched onto a familiar figure coming out. "That's Richard Price!" Wiping the condensation from the window with the back of her hand to see better, she watched him stop under a street lamp to light up a cigarette. "There's no mistaking those specs."

Susan leant across her to get a better look.

Over the road, Price paced about, puffing on his cigarette. He was looking up and down the street as if waiting for someone. "Did Ellen ever mention him?" Jess asked.

"Ellen never talked about any of her work colleagues."

"So what have *you* found out about him?" Jess asked, dryly. "He must be on your list."

Susan gave her the ghost of a smile. "He was divorced from his wife recently. And his credit rating has been downgraded. Strange for someone in his position, I thought. So I did some digging. His wife got their two properties after the divorce. He kept the financial investments, but he's lost most of it to the financial crash."

Jess had to hand it to Susan, she was going to be a great investigative journalist one day.

"Which means," Susan continued, "he couldn't afford to lose his job to my sister. Perhaps *he's* been the one taking bribes from the Chinese?"

Price looked at his watch again and threw his cigarette butt onto the ground. As if on impulse, he stepped into the road and hailed down a passing taxi. Jumping inside, the taxi moved off.

"Quick," said Susan. "Follow him."

Jess was about to switch on the engine, but stopped. "No, it's too dangerous. Let's stick to the plan." She pulled out her mobile.

"Who are you phoning?"

"Tom Sangster. To tell him where we are."

Susan glared at her.

"He's the only one who can help us now. As I said, the

High Commissioner wants us to go to Police HQ and wait for him there. He's coming up to Brisbane tonight."

"And as I said, I'd rather wait in the hotel until he gets here. It'd be safer."

"*Safer?*" All Jess's emotions were bubbling up again. Anger seemed to be pouring out of her. "We'd be safer without that bloody diary. If we'd given it to the police yesterday afternoon, we wouldn't be sitting here now."

"If *I'd* given it to him, you mean?"

"I didn't say that."

"It's what you meant though."

Jess pursed her lips.

Susan stared at her. "And Anthony Harris and Danny Burton might still be alive... Go on. Say it."

And someone else is dead too, Jess thought, wishing she knew who the latest victim was. "It's time to hand over that diary, Susan. It's not worth your life, or mine." Jess's head was throbbing as, in the distance, she became aware of sirens.

"Okay, Jess." Susan's voice sounded weary. "We'll do it your way. Let's go and get the diary."

"Where is it?"

"At my house."

"All this time?"

"It's well hidden."

"Right." Jess picked up her mobile from her lap. "I'm calling Tom Sangster first."

Susan put her hand on her arm. "Let's get the diary first. We can call him from my house."

"It's too dangerous to go alone, Susan."

The wailing sirens were getting louder and louder now. Suddenly, a fire engine flashed by the end of the street. "I *thought* I could smell smoke." Jess sat forward. "Where's the fire?"

The hotel porter ran out onto the road to get a better look as another two fire engines flashed by. Jess wound down the driver's window and stuck her head out. The smell of smoke hung thick in the air. "The fire's close!"

But Susan was already out of the car and running over to the porter. He started talking to her and pointing excitedly.

Jess waited, frustrated, in two minds: the safety of the hotel or go and get that diary?

Susan ran back and jumped into the car. "There's a fire at my paper, the *Echo*... You don't think it's because of me, do you?" She put her head in her hands as reality struck home. "Does someone think I left the diary there?" Distraught, she turned to Jess. "Tell me it's not possible."

Jess reached over and squeezed her hand. "We don't know what's happening."

Two haunted eyes looked over at her. "This is all my fault."

Jess said nothing.

Then, as if she'd flipped a switch, Susan said. "Quick, swap seats. We have to go past the *Echo* to get to my house. It'll be quicker with me driving. I know the way."

★

Jess sat rigid in the passenger seat, gripping the armrest with one hand, and her mobile with the other. *Oh my God,"* she whispered, as Susan pulled the car up alongside the kerb some distance from the fire and stared in horror at the scene. The gagging smoke filled the atmosphere, making them cough.

Down the street, Jess could see the road blocked by fire engines, their lights flashing in the darkness. A lone police officer stood in front waving his arms and hands, trying to turn traffic and people away.

Her chest tightened as she watched huge plumes of black smoke billow out of the windows of the lower floors.

Suddenly a loud explosion blasted from within the building, blowing out windows and shattering glass. She could hear shouting and screaming, as the fire gathered momentum, shooting flames into the sky. Ash, smoke and debris from the explosion fell onto the car and all around them. She could hear squealing tyres as nearby traffic ground to a halt.

Squealing tyres…

Jess froze. She closed her eyes, and saw little Amy waving through the car window. *G'bye mummy!*

The sound of crashing metal. *Boom…* the crack of the explosion, like thunder reverberating around. She could *feel* the heat of the flames, spiralling up from the street into the sky, *smell* the thick, acrid smoke that stung her eyes and clogged her throat. She couldn't breathe.

"*Amy! Jack!*" she cried out. "*Oh no!*" Her heart was racing, her body trembling as once again she saw her beautiful daughter and husband being ripped apart by the explosion and burnt to ashes in the heat and flames as they sat trapped in the car. Obliterated…

"Jess?"

She couldn't answer Susan.

"Jess, what's wrong?"

She stared blindly ahead.

"*Jess?*"

She could hear the rising panic in Susan's voice and dragged her hands up over her eyes. "The fire and explosion," she whispered, fighting to control her emotions. "The fire and explosion – in Jakarta – my husband and daughter."

"*Jess?*"

"I can't get the sight out of my head... I see it every day... a nightmare. That day... the accident... over and over." Her rasping breath filled the silence. "I'm standing in the hallway... I can hear tyres... I-I hear crashing metal... a loud explosion... I can *feel* the heat of the flames... *smell* the choking smoke. I can't breathe... I can't move... I can't get to Jack and Amy... I'll never get to them..."

Susan stared at her, eyes wide.

Gasping for air, Jess went on: "A petrol tanker smashed into Jack's car as he turned out of the driveway, and burst into flames." Jess struggled to find the words. "My little girl, I see her face every single day. She was *so* full of life." Her voice was barely a whisper. "And it was all *my* fault."

There, it was, out in the open, finally.

There was a shocked silence.

"*Your* fault?"

Jess nodded.

"I don't understand. You said it was an accident?"

Jess shook her head. "I can't talk about it."

Susan sank back in the seat. "I-I don't know what to say."

"There's nothing *to* say. They're gone. And I have to live with that." Jess took a deep breath. "And with what I did."

"What *you* did?"

Jess nodded. And then she knew that of all people, Susan was the one who would understand the grief... the guilt. "You see, I *always* took Amy to nursery on my way to work. Every morning without fail, except..."

Susan looked at her.

"Except *that* morning." Jess felt the nausea rising in her stomach. "I was running late. The house was a tip. I couldn't find my computer memory stick for my presentation. I blew up at Jack for not keeping the house tidy, for not helping me more." She looked at Susan with stricken eyes.

"What happened, Jess? Tell me."

"I upset Jack; made him angry. He grabbed Amy. He said he'd take her to nursery to give me time to get ready." Her voice had lowered to a whisper now. "He stormed out and slammed the front door." Jess jolted as if she could still hear that door slamming. "I went over to the door, and poked my head out to say goodbye. And that's all I ever see. My little Amy waving through the back window of his car, shouting *G'bye mummy!* as Jack drives off. Then I hear the sickening screech of tyres; the explosion; the fire. *Oh God!*" Jess leant forward and put her head on the dashboard.

They sat together in silence, each with their own pain. Then Jess took a deep breath of air that burnt her lungs. "I'm sorry, Susan. I shouldn't have burdened you with all that."

"If... if I'd given the police Ellen's diary yesterday," Susan stuttered, "none of this would have happened." She turned to Jess, eyes pleading. "I'm sorry."

"I know." Jess reached over and took her hand. "Now let's get that diary and take it to the police before anyone else gets hurt."

29

The moon shone bright in the sky, making the billowing smoke appear translucent as it drifted high into the air. Sangster got out of the car and looked up. It gave Brisbane a weird, other worldly feel that he'd never experienced before. He felt the hairs stand up on the back of his neck. A lunatic was wreaking havoc across the city, and no one knew what he was going to do next. *It's like being in a thriller movie, without any script.* Jess's words hit home. He coughed as the acrid smell permeated his eyes and nose, competing with the lingering stench of death. For the first time since becoming a detective, he felt powerless and apprehensive. A feeling that scared him.

"Evenin', Sir." The young porter's eyes shone with excitement. "That's the *Brisbane Echo* building goin' up in smoke!"

"Keep an eye on my car," Sangster said, tersely. "I'll be five minutes."

"Yes, Sir."

Sangster walked up the steps, through the revolving door and into the Riverbank Hotel. He'd been both relieved and annoyed to get Jess's voicemail. Relieved that Susan Chambers had turned up and they were going to the hotel for the night; and annoyed that his police officer hadn't shown up. Where the hell was he? Belinda

Harris's corpse sprang horribly to mind. He couldn't take any more chances; he'd personally take the Consul and Susan Chambers back to HQ.

He went up to the reception desk. "Detective Inspector Sangster," he said. "I believe the British Consul, Miss Turner, and Miss Chambers have checked in?"

The receptionist nodded. "I'll have a look, Sir."

Everyone seemed to be in a state of high excitement. Staff kept rushing out of the front entrance to have a look at the fire in the sky and chat to porters. Then they'd come back in to relay the latest to anyone who would listen. He tapped his foot on the floor and stared at the receptionist who was studying the computer.

Feeling his impatient gaze on her, she looked up. "I'm sorry, Sir, Miss Turner hasn't checked in yet."

He frowned. "Are you sure?"

"Yes, Sir."

He felt his stomach turn. He pressed a speed dial number on his mobile quickly as he marched out of the front entrance.

Dalton answered immediately. "Boss?"

"They're not at the Riverbank." Sangster could hear the tension in his own voice.

"Where are they, then?"

"How the hell do I know?" he snapped.

There was a pause. "I think I've found the connection, Boss." Dalton sounded strangely subdued.

The young porter sidled up to Sangster again. "Lookin' for someone, Sir?"

"Hang on, Dave," Sangster said into the phone, and turned to the porter. "Have you seen two women stop by here within the last half hour? One is in her mid to late 30s, slim, with shoulder-length blonde hair and wearing a trouser suit. The other is in her early 20s, slim too, with short, spiky blonde hair, probably wearing jeans and trainers."

The porter's eyes flashed. "Couldn't miss those two lookers, could I?" He pointed across the road. "They drew up over there in a white car... a Holden it was."

"How long ago?"

"Oh, about 15 minutes. The young one got out and came over to ask what all the smoke and fire engines were about." He stopped. "Went sheet white when I told her the *Echo* building was goin' up in smoke. Ran back to the car and they drove off."

Sangster put his mobile to his ear. "Dave, the hotel porter saw the Consul and Susan here 15 minutes ago. He told them about the fire at the *Echo* and they drove off again. That's where they've gone... to the fire." He paused. "You said you've found the connection?"

"Yeah." Dalton hesitated. "You know Roberts worked for a security consultancy in Melbourne in between leaving the Melbourne Police and joining up here?" He stopped.

Sangster tapped his foot. "Yes."

"Well, we've found the company," Dalton said, quickly. "It advises companies and high profile people on their personal security, and on the physical security of their premises and homes, that kind of thing."

"Ah." Sangster realised its significance. "Did Roberts do some consultancy work for Western Energy?"

"That's what I reckon. And he's still in touch with them. His mobile phone records show he phoned their Melbourne HQ switchboard recently."

"That's it, Dave," Sangster fired back, excited. "That's the link."

"Yep. Our guys in Melbourne have gone round to the Company, to check with the boss."

"If Roberts has done work for Western Energy, he would have known Ellen Chambers, John Langhurst, and Richard Price... all of them. Maybe even Chen Xiamen."

"Yep," said Dalton again.

"Right. Ring me immediately you hear back from the Melbourne guys," said Sangster. "If Roberts hasn't already done a runner, he'll still be looking for that diary. I'm going to the *Echo* to look for the British Consul and Susan Chambers." He paused. "You stay at HQ, Dave. I want you to call in every colleague who's been working with Roberts recently. I don't care what they're doing. Get them in. They might not realise it, but one of them knows something useful about Roberts, like a girlfriend, or where he hangs out when he's not at home."

"What about the DC?" Dalton asked. "I didn't check with him."

"I'll ring him from the car and report all this," said Sangster. "And keep trying the Consul's mobile. If you get her, tell her to drive Susan straight to Police HQ. Tell her exactly what happened to Belinda Harris. And *don't* leave out any details."

For *Chrissakes,* he thought as he hung up, when is that woman going to be frightened enough to stay put?

30

While Susan sped along, weaving her way through the traffic as though she was on a racing circuit, Jess was strangely calm in the passenger seat. She kept checking the mirror on the passenger sun visor, and twisting round to look out of the back window, but it was impossible to tell if anyone was following in the dark.

She noticed that the pedestrian-clogged streets and city office blocks had given way to wide suburban streets with houses and empty pavements. "Are we nearly there?" she asked.

"Yep..."

"*Watch out!*

Susan drove through a red traffic light, just missing a lorry coming in the opposite direction. The driver latched onto the horn.

Susan eased her foot off the accelerator, and swung right so sharply Jess hit her head on the side window. "Don't look round." Susan sounded panicky. "But that black Merc has been behind for a while."

Jess checked her vanity mirror and kept her eyes glued to the Merc while Susan sped on. Up ahead, the traffic lights turned from green to amber. Susan made no attempt to slow down.

As they approached, the lights turned red.

"*Stop!*" Jess shouted.

Susan stamped on the brakes, bringing the car to a sudden halt.

Tensing, Jess watched the Merc draw alongside them and held her breath as the driver opened his window. Loud music thumped out. He grinned at her as he flicked out his cigar ash and closed the window. Suddenly, she jerked back in her seat as Susan hit the accelerator and sped off again.

At the next T-junction, Susan drew up behind a queue of traffic turning right while the Merc sailed on ahead. Racing down a maze of local streets and over traffic humps that almost pitched Jess out of her seat, Susan did an emergency stop outside a house.

As Jess lurched forward, her seatbelt activated and her mobile flew out of her hand.

Susan scrunched the gear, and reversed the car into the driveway.

Pinned to the seat, Jess struggled out of her seatbelt and groped on the floor to pick up her mobile. She looked over at Susan. "There's no chance anyone would have been able to keep up with you."

"Come on." Susan jumped out of the car.

Jess picked up her bag and scrambled out after her. The house was in total darkness. But as they approached the front door, she noticed it was slightly ajar.

Susan hesitated. "I'm sure I closed it this morning."

"*Wait!*"

But Susan rushed inside and switched on the light.

Cautious, Jess turned and looked both ways along the street. Everything was quiet in the late evening. Lights were off in most houses, leaving only a few security lights to glow in the dark. The moon was out again now, casting shadows through the trees onto the pavement.

She turned back to the front door. "Susan?" she called out, as she stepped over the threshold. But when she walked into the sitting room, she stood rooted to the spot in shock. It looked like a tornado had ripped through. She couldn't see an inch of carpet for all the ornaments and books littered around. The cabinet drawers lay upside down on top of their scattered contents. The TV sat on its side, with its screen smashed. Even the sofa seat cushions had been slashed open and their insides pulled out.

This was no discreet search like the one in her hotel room. Whoever did this had gone berserk or wanted to terrify.

Susan had sunk to her knees among the debris.

"Come on." Jess put a ripped seat cushion back on a chair and pulled Susan to her feet. "Sit here while I check the front door."

Susan did as she was told.

Jess went back into the hallway. The front door lock had been forced open and was broken. She peered outside. Everything looked quiet in the garden and street in the dark. A light breeze blew up and tugged at her hair. She shivered, pushed the door to and slipped the security chain in place.

Back in the sitting room, she went straight over to the curtains and pulled them closed in case he was still out there. "Don't worry." She put her arm around Susan. "Everything will be okay." But her words sounded hollow.

Suddenly Susan jumped to her feet and ran upstairs.

Following her, Jess watched from the doorway while Susan knelt down at the cupboard under the bathroom sink and pulled out a wash bag. Unzipping it, Susan tipped Ellen's diary out onto the floor. "He didn't get it," she said, sitting back on her heels. "What on earth did my sister get mixed up in?" She looked up with such a pained expression that Jess felt tears prick her eyes. "You'll help me, won't you, Jess?"

All Jess's protective instincts welled up. "You know I will, Susan. Now you have a good look round and see if anything's missing while I go and phone Inspector Sangster."

There was no protest from Susan this time.

Jess walked down the stairs to the front door. Despite the security chain, it didn't look very secure. She dragged the hall table across the floor and pushed it lengthwise against the door, like a barricade.

In the kitchen, she picked her way through the smashed china on the floor and rattled the handle of the back door to check it was locked. She reached into her trouser pocket for her mobile and dialled Tom Sangster.

"Jess." The relief in his voice was palpable. "Where *are* you?"

"At Susan's house... It's a mess... the whole place has been turned upside down... We came to get the diary."

There was a sharp intake of breath. "Did he get it?"

"No. Susan had it hidden, in a wash bag in the cabinet under the bathroom sink." She didn't wait for him to say anything. "Listen, Tom, I need to tell you this quickly, in case anything... happens. I think someone wants this diary because of those codes in it. Remember I told you there was a jumble of letters and numbers on the back page?"

"Yes."

"The first three lines are passwords and memorable data for a bank account in Ellen Chambers' name in the Turks Bank. It's in the Turks and Caicos Islands, a British Overseas Territory in the Caribbean, an offshore tax haven. There's two million dollars stashed in that account."

"So she *was* taking bribes."

"Well...." Jess hesitated. "According to my colleague in the British High Commission, the British Government discovered this bank account a couple of weeks ago."

"*A couple of weeks ago?*"

"Yes. The Financial Crimes Unit in the Territory uncovered two transactions of a million dollars going into that account. They routinely monitor funds going in and out of the Territory for criminal activities like money-laundering."

"Are you telling me the Australian Feds knew about this?" There was no mistaking the anger in his voice.

"Yes. I believe that information was contained in the intelligence report that London sent your Government." She paused. "And that's what prompted the Federal Police to investigate Ellen and Chen Xiamen in the first place."

"*I see.*"

"But the thing is," she hesitated. "It's all a bit too... easy. The British authorities spotted the two transactions immediately. And Susan found the account online and accessed it with the codes in Ellen's diary in a matter of minutes." She paused. "I think the account was *meant* to be discovered. You see, I think Ellen found out she was being framed, and wrote those codes in her diary as evidence." She paused again. "I also think there's a second bank account that we haven't found. That's what the other three lines of words and figures in the back of her diary must represent. That's why someone wants it so badly. Because if we find that account, I think we'll discover who murdered Ellen Chambers and who's behind all this."

"Right," Sangster said. "Lock yourselves in. I'm coming to get you."

"That maniac smashed the front door lock when he broke in. I've slipped the security chain in place and

pushed the hall table against the door to barricade us in."
She hesitated. "Who was the fourth murder victim, Tom?"

He paused. "Belinda Harris, the Minister's daughter."

"*Oh dear God!*"

"I think the killer went to the house looking for Anthony Harris and found his daughter instead. She was stabbed in the heart, no bullet in the head this time. Can you *see* how dangerous this man is, Jess? It's like a switch inside him has been activated. He likes to kill. I think he's an expert stalker and hunter. He's enjoying the thrill of the chase and the kill too much to stop now."

"Who *is* he, Tom?"

Sangster paused. "One of ours gone bad... DC Roberts. He transferred to the Brisbane Force from Melbourne last year."

Jess was in shock. "But why? Did he know Ellen? What's he doing this for?" She paused to breathe. "You said there were two killers, Tom? Who else is involved?"

"Look, talking is wasting time. Wait there, Jess. I'm on my way." And he hung up.

A policeman? Jess couldn't believe it. No wonder Ellen was so afraid. She stared out of the window into the back garden. Goose bumps shivered down her back and arms. No sign of any movement. *He's an expert stalker and hunter. He's enjoying the thrill of the chase and the kill too much to stop now.* She snapped the blinds shut. She didn't feel safe in this house.

She went upstairs and found Susan sitting on the edge of her bed, staring at a photo in a frame.

It looked to Jess like someone had punched the glass with their fist and smashed it. "Is that Ellen?" she asked.

Susan nodded. "It was taken here last December." An angry tear burned down her cheek. "Why did he have to go and break it?"

Jess tried to comfort her. "She was glamorous, your sister. Lovely long blonde hair."

"Yes." Susan rubbed a hand over her short hair. "I missed out on all the good genes."

"Nonsense, you look just like her."

"I can't believe she's not here any more."

"I know." Jess looked around. The intruder had tipped all the clothes out of the wardrobe and drawers, onto the floor. "Tom Sangster's on his way to pick us up," she said, as she tiptoed her way through the debris strewn across the floor to close the curtains. A movement outside caught her eye. She could see a car pulling up a few doors away. She rushed over to switch off the light.

"What's wrong, Jess?"

"Tom can't have got here that quickly."

Susan went over to the window. "It's a white car."

"The police use white, unmarked cars, don't they?" Jess watched a man get out of the car. She screwed up her eyes as he stepped under a street light... those dark clothes... that peeked cap pulled down over his eyes. Her heart started thumping. She watched him put his hand inside his jacket. A flash of metal glinted under the light. She grabbed Susan's arm. "Is there a back way out of here?"

"Yes, through the alley."

"*Let's go!* Put that diary back in its hiding place in the bathroom cabinet. If he gets us, he won't get that too."

Susan rushed into the bathroom.

Waiting for Susan at the top of the stairs, Jess heard the front gate squeak open. "Quick, Susan." She ran down the stairs and into the kitchen, with Susan right behind her.

She could hear footsteps crunching along the front path.

Susan was fumbling with the bottom bolt of the back door. "It's stuck."

Jess pushed her aside and wriggled the bolt with all her strength. It slid back with a thump, catching her finger in the metal casing. A drop of blood oozed out. "Come on." Jess opened the back door, and ran down the path, misty rain blowing in her face. She could hear him ramming the front door against the hall table, trying to force it open.

At the back gate, Susan gasped and turned back.

Jess grabbed her arm. "What are you *doing?*"

"The gate's locked. The key's inside."

"Forget it, we'll climb over." Jess grabbed the top of the wooden fence and pulled herself up. Scrambling up onto the top of the fence, her legs straddled either side. "*Come on, Susan.*"

Susan shinned up the fence with ease, swung her legs over and lowered herself into the alley.

Jess jumped down, falling awkwardly in her high heels.

Susan helped her to her feet, and started running.

Jess tried to follow, but her heels kept sinking in the mud. Wrenching one shoe off, then the other, she ran barefoot down the alley with a shoe in each hand. Reaching the end, she followed Susan into the street. The soft rain had turned harder, and was beating down on the pavement in front of her.

"Head for the church," Susan shouted over her shoulder.

Jess looked back, thinking she saw a flash of movement.

"Hurry *up,* Jess." Susan darted over the road and headed into the field.

Jess followed. Her eyes had adjusted to the dark now, but she hadn't a clue where she was. The ground was soft and heavy going in the field. She could feel wet mud oozing through her toes, as she kept looking over her shoulder. Heart hammering with exertion, she gasped for breath. Finally, she squeezed through a thick hedge and found herself in a church graveyard. Collapsing on the ground behind a tall gravestone next to Susan, she doubled over to get her breath back.

"Have we lost him?" Susan asked.

Jess was still curled up, breathing hard. "I think so."

"We need to get out of the rain."

Jess nodded. Pulling herself to her feet, she rushed over to the heavy church door. It creaked as she turned the handle and pushed it open. She beckoned Susan to follow her inside. Closing the door behind them, the cool, damp air wrapped around her. It was a relief to get out of the rain. Already accustomed to the dark, her eyes were drawn to the only source of light, at the altar. Walking towards it, she saw a large clay pot filled with pebbles. On the top, several tea lights had been lit. Behind it, stood a large board, covered with prayer notes.

In the gloomy, flickering light, she looked down at her mud-caked feet. She was still gripping one shoe in her right hand. Where was the other one? She reached into her trouser pocket for her mobile, but it wasn't there. She turned to Susan. "Give me your mobile."

Susan gasped. "It's on charge at home."

Jess felt her stomach sink.

She looked around the church to get her bearings. They'd entered through the main door at the side and were now at the front altar. Rows of wooden pews lined the nave all the way to the back, where there was a narrow staircase leading to an upper gallery. Next to that was another exit door. She walked towards the back of the church.

Susan followed, her trainers making a squelching sound on the stone floor as she went.

Reaching the back door, Jess tried the handle. It was open. She looked out. The rain was still falling like stair rods. She closed the door and flopped down in the pew beside it.

Susan sat down next to her.

Both of them were so shell-shocked, neither spoke. Jess looked down at her muddy clothes and feet. She could feel her soaked hair plastered flat against her head. But she felt comforted somehow in the church. The scent of lilies from the two altar vases filled the air. She breathed in. The quiet peace began to calm her raging mind. Then, she froze...

She heard the sound of a car drawing up. A door slammed. Light footsteps crunched on the gravel path.

A wind seemed to blow up from nowhere and whistle through the old timbers. All the tea lights near the altar went out. They were in total darkness. Heart banging in her chest, as the front door handle rattled, Jess grabbed Susan's arm. "*Quick! Let's go!*"

Pushing Susan out of the back door, she heard something whistle past her and thud into the wooden door. She whipped the long, silver key out of the lock, went out and slammed the door behind her. Fumbling to lock the door from the outside, she heard footsteps pounding towards them on the stone floor inside. With shaking hands, she turned the key in the lock and threw it in the bushes.

"Run," she shouted at Susan.

31

Sangster pulled up outside the suburban house and switched off the engine and lights. He knew he was at the right address because he could see Jess's white Holden parked in the driveway. Winding down the window to scan the street, he winced at the reek of fire drifting over from the city. This was all too quiet.

The house was in darkness except for a light on in a downstairs room. His eyes swept across the façade and windows, looking for any sign of life inside.

The front door was wide open.

He pulled his gun out of its holster. Back-up was on its way, but he couldn't afford to wait. Jess and Susan might be hurt inside. Every nerve alive, he got out of the car and crept up the path. His eyes darted around. He couldn't afford a mistake. Roberts was a formidable killer.

A sudden gust of wind rattled through the palm trees, making him spin round.

No one.

Reaching the front door, he listened for any movement.

Belinda Harris's body flashed into his head.

He steeled himself for what he might find inside as he slipped silently through the open door into the hallway. Dead silence.

Gun poised, he moved into the sitting room where the light was on. Picking his way through the debris on the floor, he went into the kitchen. A handbag lay on the draining board. *Was that Jess's?*

He noticed the open back door into the garden. Was anyone out there? He had to leave it.

Moving back into the hallway, he climbed the stairs step by step in the darkness. The top stair creaked, making his heart pound. He braced himself, but there was no sound or movement. Quickly, he checked the bathroom and back bedroom. When he went into the front bedroom and looked around, he let his arm drop.

There was no one in the house.

His sheer relief at not finding any more bodies left him drained, and he stood to take a couple of deep breaths to compose himself. Then he ran down the stairs and out front to his car. Opening the boot, he grabbed his police torch and raced back into the house, straight through the kitchen, and out to the back gate. He lifted the latch but it was locked. He hauled himself to the top of the fence and saw an alley running between two rows of houses. Shining his torch onto the ground, the beam picked out some fresh footprints in the soft earth. As he lowered himself down into the alley, his shoes sunk in the wet mud. He stood and looked around. Twisting his wrist to change the flood beam to a focused spot beam, he walked along the alley. Something caught his eye. A high-heeled shoe. *That was definitely Jess's.* He felt elated: they'd escaped this way.

He sprinted to the end of the alley, emerging out onto another road. There were no houses in this road, just the pavement he was standing on, and a field opposite. He looked all around. No sign of anyone. With no clue as to where the women had gone, he had no option but to retrace his steps along the alley. He climbed back over the fence and ran back into the house.

Pounding up the stairs into the bathroom, he knelt down at the bathroom cabinet under the sink and pulled out a wash bag. Unzipping it, he turned it upside down. Ellen Chambers' diary fell onto the floor.

Hearing police sirens, he shoved the diary back into the wash bag and ran with it downstairs and out of the front door. He could see the blue lights of a patrol car flashing in the darkness. As it approached, he ran up to the driver's window. "Have you seen Roberts?" he shouted to the driver.

"No."

"The two women have escaped over the back fence. Drive around the area and look for them."

The policeman nodded and drove off.

Sangster pulled out his mobile and called Dalton. "Roberts got here before me."

Dalton gave a sharp intake of breath.

"It's all right. It looks like the women got away. I found the Consul's shoe in the back alley." He paused. "Get forensics out here straightaway, Dave. I want evidence to prove Roberts was in this house."

"Right."

"And I want the whole area scoured for the two women. They're on foot, so they can't have got far."

"Right."

There was a pause.

"I've got the diary, Dave. It was right where Jess said Susan had hidden it."

"That's something I suppose."

"Listen carefully, Dave. I want you to write these letters and numbers down." Sangster turned to the back page of the diary, and read the codes out loud to Dalton, explaining what Jess had said about the two bank accounts. "The Government know about the account in Ellen Chambers' name in the British Overseas Territory of the Turks and Caicos Islands. That account is easy to find. It was meant to be. But I'm sure you'll need the technical experts to find the second account hidden in those letters and numbers. When they do, and discover who that account belongs to, we'll find out who's behind all this."

"Right, Boss. I'm onto it."

"And Dave." Sangster paused. "I want you to go straight to the DC and tell him what's happened. But I don't want anyone else to know we have that diary. If Roberts finds out, he'll have no reason to keep the women alive if he's holding them. Do you understand?"

"Yes, Boss," said Dalton. "And we've had a response from that Melbourne security consultancy Roberts worked for. They say Roberts spent two months working on a project at Western Energy. He advised all their top officials and families on their personal security at work and in their homes."

"He's had access to their families and houses?" Sangster was incredulous.

"Yep. He also spent a month in the Western Energy's HQ, trainin' staff on security awareness."

"So he knows them all?"

"Yep." Dalton hesitated. "But what I don't get, Boss, is *why* he's done so little to conceal his identity. That proves he's not the full dollar, if you ask me."

"Oh no, Dave. He's not stupid. Quite the reverse. As I said before, he *wants* us to know it's him. He's pleased with himself. He'll never stop killing now he's started. He's enjoying it too much, and he thinks he's got us beat. Well the bastard had better think again."

32

The pavement glowed white in the moonlight as Jess ran. Only the sound of her ragged breathing cut into the silence of the night. With lungs ready to burst, she stopped and bent over to catch her breath. No time to linger. Looking up, there was no sign of Susan. Younger and fitter, she was well ahead. *Run, Susan, run!*

Jess glanced over her shoulder and caught a flicker of movement. Tom's words echoed in her head.

You see how dangerous this man is…

She looked about in panic. All around, houses stood on large suburban blocks, spaced some distance away from each other. What should she do? Scream? Bang on doors?

Something brushed against her face. She cried out.

He's an expert tracker and hunter…

Stumbling sideways, she dropped down behind a garden hedge out of sight. She felt dizzy with exhaustion and fear. She turned and looked up at the sprawling brick house. It was set well back from the road, with a long driveway. An electric lamp lit up the swimming pool area. Inside, everything was in darkness. There was no one at home.

He's enjoying the thrill of the chase…

She gasped as a soft breeze rustled through the hedge, making it sway. It wasn't cold, but she could hear her teeth chattering. Clamping her jaw tight, she crouched down.

A twig snapped close by.

She thought she heard a faint exhalation of breath.

He likes to kill...

She fell back, flapping her arms in terror to ward off the gun she imagined pointed at the back of her head, tensing for a knife piercing her heart.

A footstep swished through the grass.

She jumped to her feet and ran for her life. On and on she fled, half running, half limping until she saw a bright light ahead. A neon sign. A petrol station.

She ran up to the forecourt. There were no cars. Seeing a light in the office, she ran over and pulled the door handle. It was locked. She pressed her face against the window and saw a jacket on the back of a chair. "*Help!*" she shouted, banging her fists on the window. "*Open the door!*"

Suddenly, a face reflected in the window from behind. Eyes widening in panic, she went to run.

Too late.

She saw a raised arm. She felt a crack to the back of her head. Searing pain engulfed her as she slipped to the ground.

★

She felt she was floating in that twilight zone: half asleep, half awake. Her head was pounding so hard, her eyes seemed to throb in rhythm. She forced her eyes open, but there was only darkness. She could hear the low rumble of an engine and feel herself being shaken about. She tried to sit up, but her head hit something. Putting out her hand, she jumped when she touched something warm.

The pain in her head was excruciating... the smell of petrol... the nausea. Mercifully, she floated away again into deep sleep.

33

Sangster's knuckles were white on the steering wheel as he completed a full circle of the area. This was pointless. He'd have to leave the search to the patrol cars and get back to HQ. Driving to the end of Susan's road, he stopped and looked across the field. Seeing the prominent tower and pointed gable of a church on the other side of the field, his foot hesitated on the accelerator. Just a quick check before heading back.

Driving around the field's deserted perimeter road, he pulled up outside the church and lowered the window to get a good look. The brick and concrete building stood in total darkness.

His stomach lurched: the door was open!

He grabbed his torch and drew his gun. He walked through the cast-iron gate, and stepped onto the path. After one crunching footstep on gravel he jumped onto the grass, making his way silently to the church door as he dodged the gravestones. The rain had stopped now and the air was humid. He could feel the water from the grass seep through his shoes. Outside the open door he listened for any movement inside. Nothing. He stepped over the threshold and paused to accustom his eyes to the dark. Not a sound.

He switched on his torch and followed the beam around the church. It picked out muddy footprints on the stone floor. Following them, it led him to the back of the church, right up to the back door. He tried the handle, but it was locked. Flashing the beam around the area and along the back pew, he saw pools of water on the seat. Had Jess and Susan got soaked in the rain and sat there? He returned to the door and tried the handle again. Definitely locked. The beam of the flashlight reflected something shiny. That's when he noticed the bullet lodged in the wood. Suddenly his mobile rang, echoing in the church. He jumped, eyes constantly scanning, as he answered.

It was Dalton. "Good news, Boss. We found that prossie who complained about Roberts being rough."

Sangster kept his eyes watchful as he listened.

"She admitted Roberts picked her up for working the streets," Dalton went on, "but she says he let her go with the promise of sex."

"Did he now?" Sangster said, tersely.

"When he was ready, he picked her up in his jeep and took her to a motel in the Valley. Same place on two occasions, she says."

"What's the name of the motel?" Sangster barked.

"The Golden Burra." Dalton went on. "But here's the strange thing, Boss. She says the first time she went to the motel, Roberts was weird but okay. He made her strip and lie on the floor. He put a flower in her hand and sat next to her for an hour, but he didn't want to have sex. So when he called and picked her up the second time, she wasn't worried. But she should have been, this time things got nasty."

"What happened?"

"He made her strip naked and lie on the floor again, but this time he got out a knife. He kept running the blade all over her body. She got scared and tried to make a run for it. He held her down and cut her left breast until the blood ran. That was enough for him to… satisfy himself."

"She's lucky to be alive."

"Shall I send someone to check out the motel?" Dalton asked. "Maybe he's livin' there?"

"It would be a good place to hide out. No one asks any questions."

"Yep," said Dalton. "The woman said she saw a suitcase and some clothes in there. It didn't look like he'd rented it for the night."

"Right. I'm on my way to the motel, Dave. Meet me there. But before you leave HQ, get forensics over to St Mary's Church. It's on the other side of the field, close to the Susan Chambers' house."

"Is that where you are?"

"Yes. There's a bullet lodged in the back door." He could feel his stomach turning. "There are signs the women have been here, but there's no sign of them now."

Dalton's voice faltered. "Do you think he's got them?"

Sangster struggled to catch his breath. "If he has, he's taken them somewhere else now." He hurried over to the main door. "I'm going straight to the Valley, Dave. Radio those motel details to me in the car."

"Right, Boss. See you there."

Sangster ran down the gravel path to the car. If ever your cool head and sharp brain worked for you, Jess, let it work for you now.

34

Kneeling in front of the grate, he watched the papers curl and burn as he put a match to them. Lively sparks shot in the air warming his hands and face. He'd always loved the glow and crackle of flames, especially around a campfire in the deep stillness of night, with only the sounds of crickets and nightjars, and the sigh of the hot wind rustling dry leaves, to keep him company. Even as a boy he was happiest in the bush. He liked being out there, all alone. Just him and the wilderness, where no one could mess with his head or hurt him.

But that was then. Things were different now. He'd be going home a man; a rich man at that. He'd buy the farm. Be his own boss. Kowtow to no one.

Little pieces of blackened paper floated up as he stuck a poker into the charred remains and swirled them around to make sure they were completely burnt.

He still felt pumped up from the sight of the *Echo* building going up in flames. What a blaze! It was those two bitches' fault. He thought they were in there with that diary. Still, he'd got them now, and they'd soon tell him where they'd hidden it. He'd make them sorry they ever led him on that chase.

He stopped poking the embers as another thought took hold in his brain. Imagine setting fire to the *whole* stinking city and watching it burn to nothing but dust and ashes, back to the bush it once was.

He forced himself to focus on the job in hand. He had to get the diary *and* the money before he could leave.

He was just *so* ready.

He pulled out his police ID and looked at it one last time. He tossed it in the grate. Watching it go up in flames too, total exhilaration coursed through him. He wouldn't miss DC Roberts, that's for sure. Part of him wished he could stick around to see those idiots' faces when they found out, *if* they ever found out.

The invisible man, me!

He stood up and went over to his open suitcase on the single bed. Next to it lay his gun and knife. He looked around the dingy motel room, with its small bed and vinyl furniture. He wouldn't miss the saggy mattress, that's for sure. Still, he'd felt comfortable here with no one asking any questions, and regular action from the girls on the street outside.

He picked up a grainy photo of a woman, holding the hand of a small boy. He stared at it for a while, and placed it carefully inside the suitcase.

Yes, it *was* time. He felt almost elated at the thought of going home after all these years.

But when his mobile rang, his mood changed in a flash. Only one person had this number. He answered and listened. Then he said: "I *told* you I'd get the diary, didn't I? And that's exactly what I'm doing. But I want the money first." He wasn't stupid, he knew the bastard would do him over if he could. "No. *You* bring the money here. You know where I am." His voice was hard. "And make sure you come alone." He punched the end call button and threw the mobile on the bed.

"*Controlling bastard!*" he spat, as he picked up the gun and stroked the barrel.

"Now that's *your* mistake!"

★

Hunched over the steering wheel, Sangster peered at the Golden Burra Motel through the car windscreen. Light evening rain misted the glass, distorting his view. He switched on the wipers to clear it, but they just made it worse. He wound down the window and looked out.

The motel was a single-level block of accommodation, with a palm tree on either side of the driveway entrance. The rooms were set out in the shape of a horseshoe, with individual parking spaces marked out in front of each one.

"Golden Burra" was advertised on a painted board on top of what looked like an office or reception at the entrance. Next to it a neon vacancy sign was lit up. He could see lights flickering on the office blinds. Someone was in there, watching TV.

He wrinkled his nose as if smelling something putrid. This was just the kind of dive Roberts would frequent. Maybe he'd been renting a room here all the time? It would be cheap enough. And it would explain why he was never at home. How long had Roberts been in the police? Eighteen years? He shuddered to think what he'd got away with during that time.

Come on, Dave! He drummed his fingers on the steering wheel as he waited. But Belinda Harris's blood-soaked body flashed into his mind again … the flies. His stomach turned just remembering the smell in that kitchen. *Poor kid!* He looked over at the motel again. What was he going to find in there? Jess and Susan? Alive or dead? He drew out his gun. He couldn't afford to wait any longer.

As he went to get out of the car, headlights flickered in his rear-view mirror. He hesitated and sank down in the seat to watch. A saloon car drew up parallel with him, then turned right into the motel and parked outside a room with a light on inside. Sangster sat up as the car door swung open and a figure got out. The single, dim lamp over that room door picked out the man's hair, his physique and clothes. He rapped on the door, then turned round...

"*A-ha!*" Sangster whispered to himself as he saw *that* face. "So that's who's behind all this."

The room door opened slowly. Sangster strained to see who was inside, but he knew it *had* to be Roberts.

★

When Jess came round again, she was lying flat on her back. The burning acid in her stomach felt ready to explode. She gulped, desperate for some fresh air, but she could hardly breathe. She still had the smell of smoke in her nostrils. Opening her eyes, she could see nothing but darkness at first. But, as they began to focus, she became aware of a soft glow. Lifting her head, she saw the moon shining through a slit of a window near the ceiling.

Squinting, she looked about and found she was on a narrow bed. But it was the feeling of motion, a gentle rocking up and down and side to side, that made her struggle into a sitting position.

As a wave of nausea washed over her, she realised she was on a boat.

Except for the sound of creaking as the boat rocked in the water, there was nothing but silence. And no sense of forward motion, or engine noise. But an occasional shudder through the timbers suggested the boat was docked, and bumping against its mooring. Were they on the river, or the sea, she wondered?

Aware of pins and needles creeping into her toes, she rubbed her feet and drew her knees up to rest her groggy head on them. Flashes of memory started coming back... she was running down the street... the petrol station... the face... the raised arm. *Oh my God!*

How did she get on this boat? She could remember a rumbling engine, being shut in, and being shaken around. Had she been in the boot of a car?

She heard a groan.

Swinging her legs over the side of the bed, she went to stand up, but her feet flailed around in mid-air. That's when she realised she was on a bunk bed, on the top. She lay back on her side, and peered down at the bottom bunk.

"*Susan!*" Her stomach turned. She'd been clinging to the hope that Susan had got away. Had she been in the boot of the car too?

Seeing a ladder, she shuffled towards it and put a foot gingerly on the top rung. Turning and slithering down, she dropped to her knees and shook Susan. But Susan didn't move. She felt for a pulse at Susan's throat. The beat seemed regular, but she was out cold.

Jess flopped down on the edge of the bed and rubbed her temples to ease the dizziness. Now, with her senses attuned, she could hear the low hum of traffic in the distance, and an occasional horn. But it didn't sound like a car horn; it was more like a foghorn from a boat.

They had to be on Brisbane River, close to the city.

Another wave of nausea rose inside as pain shot through her head. She clapped her hand over her mouth, but couldn't hold back the inevitable. Retching, she turned and heaved up the contents of her stomach onto the floor. With a shiver of relief, she sat back down on Susan's bed to recover.

Now she could see they were in a small cabin, with only the bunk beds and wood-panelled walls. Disorientated, she saw a light switch. But she didn't flick it on. If anyone was outside, she didn't want to let them know they were awake. Then she saw a handle and pulled it. A small door opened; it was a locker. Then she saw what had to be the handle of the cabin door. She pulled it, gently. Nothing. She didn't dare rattle it for fear of making too much noise. She tried again, but it was definitely locked.

Fighting to keep calm, she climbed back up the ladder and stood on the top bunk to look out of the slit-like window. Like a ship's porthole, there was no way of opening it. And it was too dark outside to see anything but the moon and stars in the night sky. She flopped back down on the bed. So many thoughts crowded her mind. Why hadn't he killed them? A quick bullet to the back of the head would have been easy. Why bring them here?

There was only one answer. He wanted the diary, and he thought they still had it.

And that gave them a chance.

She climbed back down the ladder. "Wake up, Susan!" she whispered, as she shook her. "Wake up!"

Susan groaned. "Jess?"

"Yes. Come on," Jess whispered. "Sit up." She dragged Susan up into the sitting position and pulled her legs down over the side of the bed. "Put your head between your knees."

"My head's killing me," Susan moaned.

"*Shush!* Keep your voice down. He may be outside."

"Where are we?" Susan whispered.

"Locked in the cabin of some kind of boat."

Susan grabbed her arm. "I can't breathe."

"Are you hurt?"

"I hate being shut in."

"It's all right," Jess soothed. "Try to focus on getting out of here."

"Are you serious?"

"Yes. By rights, we should be dead now. The only reason we're not is because he thinks we still have your sister's diary."

Susan flinched. "It's still at my house."

Jess shook her head. "Tom Sangster will have it now. I told him you'd hidden it in the bathroom cupboard. Remember? We put it back there when that maniac came for us."

Susan's face twisted in horror. "We're dead if he finds out we haven't got the diary."

"He won't find out," Jess said with a confidence she didn't feel. "And while he still thinks we have it, we have a fighting chance."

"You reckon?" Susan sounded sceptical, but she rallied a little and looked around. "Where do you think we are?"

"Can you hear traffic?"

Susan nodded. "We must be on the river."

"I can hear a foghorn in the distance. Do you think it's the ferry?"

"Maybe," Susan replied. "But they stop running at 10pm, and it must be the early hours of the morning by now." She sat silent for a while. "Can you feel that bumping?"

Jess nodded. "I think we're docked close to the city."

"I'm trying to think where we could be." Susan paused. "There's a big dockside marina, and several floating docks in the area. Brisbane River is tidal, so many docks aren't the permanent kind."

Jess nodded, remembering Tom's words last night. *A full moon? That means there'll be a king tide tonight.* Would he find them, she wondered? She knew he'd be looking. And that gave her hope.

With a clearer head and eyes now accustomed to the dark, she looked around. Then she started searching the locker. Feeling her way, she found clothes, towels and some canned food and bottles.

"*Listen!*" Susan hissed.

Jess stumbled as the boat listed sideways. Someone had jumped on deck. Then she heard heavy footsteps and a sloshing sound. What was that smell?

Thinking fast, she pulled one of the bottles out of the locker. "Stand back, Susan." Grasping the neck with one hand, she smashed the bottle against the ladder. Glass and liquid shattered and splashed to the floor. A strong smell of wine pervaded the cabin.

Jess touched the sharp, jagged bottle neck she was holding with the fingers of her other hand. She had a weapon.

"*Quick!*" said Susan as footsteps got closer. "*He's coming!*"

Jess's heart lurched.

35

Jess lay coiled like a spring on the top bunk, her heart pounding with fear. She heard a key click in the lock. As the door opened slowly, light flooded into the cabin from outside. Opening her eyes a fraction, she saw a dark silhouette in the doorway. A gun gleamed. Her hand tightened around the neck of the broken bottle, wedged under her leg.

He stepped inside and peered at them, as they lay pretending to still be out cold. Then he sniffed the air as if he could smell the wine, and turned to the locker.

Jess seized her chance. Sitting up, she put one foot on the edge of the bed, and sprang onto his back.

He staggered forward in surprise, hitting his head on the locker. With one arm around his neck, she yanked his head back and rammed the jagged glass into his throat.

With a wounded howl, he slammed an elbow into her ribs.

She fell winded onto the floor, dropping the broken bottle.

Susan jumped out of the bottom bunk, picked it up and plunged it into his stomach.

Time froze.

A shot rang out, and Susan slumped to the ground.

He stood over Susan, gun aimed at her head.

"*No!*" Jess dived at his feet.

As he toppled backwards onto the floor, his gun clattered to the ground and slid under the bunk beds. He rolled onto his side to reach for it.

Jess kicked him in his wounded throat to stop him.

He flinched with pain, and turned back to her.

"*Bastard!*" she taunted, knowing she had to divert him away from Susan.

His murderous eyes locked onto Jess.

Idiot! She sneered.

His lip curled.

Jess scrambled to her feet. Rushing through the door, she found herself in a small galley. She grabbed the handle of a frying pan.

As he appeared in the doorway, she swung it with all her strength, hitting him in the face.

He went down again with a thud.

She ran towards some steps, climbed them on all fours and pushed open a door. A soft rush of air blew in her face as she stumbled outside and frantically looked around.

They were on a large sailing yacht.

She couldn't see much in the darkness. The only artificial light came from a oil lamp positioned close to the wheel. She ran to the side safety rail. The yacht was moored at the far end of a floating dock, with a long walkway leading to the bank. "*Help!*" she shouted into the darkness. "*Over here! Help!*"

But her voice drifted away on the breeze.

She went to climb over the safety rail onto the dock, but her foot slipped on the wet deck. She went down with a thump.

Lying on the deck, she felt a searing pain through her right ankle. But what was that overpowering smell? She touched the deck and sniffed her fingers. Petrol? She gasped. Was he planning to set light to the yacht? And with her and Susan inside?

The door crashed open.

She scrambled to her feet, and went for the safety rail again.

"*Stop!*" he shouted, "Or I *will* shoot."

She froze, then turned. It was the first time she'd seen his face properly. Long and thin, with drawn cheeks, his eyes were ice cold and distant. She could make out the dark bloodstain on his neck and shirt collar where she had plunged the glass into his throat. At that moment her mind became clear. She had to try and talk to him, to stop him killing them. It was their only chance. "You're injured, DC Roberts," she said, calmly. "You need help."

He clutched his stomach where Susan had stabbed him with the glass. "Where's that diary?"

Despite his injuries, he stood completely still. How badly hurt was he? Were his wounds just superficial? "I don't know anything about a diary," she said, "but I know you need help. Let me drive you to hospital and get those wounds treated."

His glacial expression chilled her. "*You're* in no position to help me."

She looked over the railing at the dark, murky water. She might be able to jump over and swim away. But what about Susan? She turned back, she had to try to keep him talking. "You must realise you've been set up?" she continued.

His eyes narrowed.

"Look Roberts, your police colleagues *know* you killed Danny Burton, and Anthony Harris and his daughter."

His voice was hard and uncompromising. "I'm *not* Roberts."

"There's no point denying it. They're looking for you."

"I *tell* you I'm *not* Roberts."

Not Roberts? Who the hell was he then? But she let it go. "You didn't kill Ellen Chambers, did you?" she said, reasonably. "You didn't start this nightmare, but there's no trail back to the person who did, to the person you're protecting. He'll get away with this because *you're* the only person linked to all these murders. Don't you *see* that?"

She saw the rage in his soulless eyes as her words hit home. He tightened his finger on the trigger...

"*Stop!*" A familiar voice boomed out. "Give *me* the gun."

It was John Langhurst!

Jess's legs buckled with relief and she sank to her knees.

He vaulted over the safety rail, onto the deck. "I said give *me* the gun!"

The yacht wobbled. The next movement was so quick, so unexpected, it took Jess by surprise. There was a scuffle. The gun fired. She heard a gasp as Roberts toppled over the side and splashed into the water.

Grabbing the railing, she looked over.

Roberts' eyes locked onto hers.

Trance-like, she watched those murderous eyes sink beneath the dark water. He made no sound, not even a splash or a ripple as he disappeared. She stared at the spot, expecting him to burst to the surface again... and waited.

"He's dead." Langhurst's voice broke her stupor. "He can't survive in there with that bullet in his chest." He put his arm around Jess and helped her to her feet. "Come on, let's get out of here."

At that moment, a strong gust of wind blew, parting the clouds. A shaft of moonlight beamed down, lighting up the deck and Langhurst's feverish eyes. The realisation hit Jess like a thunderbolt. "*Oh My God!*" She staggered sideways. "*It was you!*"

Langhurst stared at her, then sighed. "I had no choice, Jessica. Ellen was going to betray me." His face twisted in pain. "After all these years. I *made* her. I *trusted* her."

Jess couldn't speak or move.

"She was *mine* until *he* came along... Anthony bloody Harris." Langhurst stared into the night, as if seeing another time. "At first, I thought she'd tire of him and the affair would be over. But then Harris started talking about leaving his wife." He gasped as if wounded to the core. "Ellen was going to leave *me*. After all I'd done for her."

"But... your wife?"

He paused, as if searching for the words to explain. "I provide Linda with money and status to keep her in the style she's used to. In return, she helps with my career. That's all."

Now Jess understood. "And with her connections, she'll help with your political career too?"

Langhurst's eyes never left Jess's. "If you know about that, you'll understand why I can't leave Linda. Not yet anyway. But I always loved Ellen. Then *Harris* came along to ruin everything." He sounded bewildered. "I didn't *intend* to kill Ellen, Jessica. You *must* believe me. We had an appointment for eight o'clock on Sunday night. I just wanted to talk to her, to put things right. I arrived early and saw her leave the bar. I followed her down to the jetty."

His face hardened. "But Anthony Harris was there waiting for her, so I hid in the bushes." He took a deep breath as if it was hard to speak. "Ellen got angry when Harris said he still hadn't told his wife about their relationship. That's my girl, I thought, give him what for and the affair will be over. But then she started ranting about how she couldn't rely on *any* man. I couldn't believe it when she told Harris *I'd* taken bribes from the Chinese and framed *her* to take the blame."

"You *framed* the woman you say you loved?"

"Only when I knew she was going to leave me for Harris," he said, indignantly. "When I was tipped off that the Federal authorities suspected someone in Western Energy of taking bribes from the Chinese, I knew then how I'd get even with Ellen for her betrayal."

"*You* set up an offshore bank account in her name, *knowing* the British authorities monitor large transfers into their Overseas Territories. And Chen, your partner in this I suppose, transferred the money via a traceless holding company. That's what happened, isn't it?"

Langhurst smiled. "Clever girl, Jessica."

"How did you expect to get away with it?" she asked, quietly. "You framed Ellen for taking bribes, but the authorities know Chen was involved. He'll be arrested."

"Oh don't be so naïve. Why would the Australian Government arrest Chen? That's a sure way of scuppering the deal; and that's the last thing they want. No, they won't challenge the Chinese. Never. This will always remain a secret."

Jess shivered at his words. "So simple and effective... until everything started to unravel."

"Yes," he said, wearily. "When Ellen told Harris on Sunday night that she was meeting me later, he gave her his voice-recorder to get me to confess secretly on tape. They planned to take it to the police together the following morning." Agitated, Langhurst started pacing. "It was like something snapped inside me; something uncontrollable. Ellen was going to the police to destroy my whole life. After everything I'd done for her. How *could* she?"

"So you killed her; and hired DC Roberts to kill Anthony Harris."

Langhurst huffed with contempt. "And what a psycho *Roberts* turned out to be. I thought he was an oddball when he came to review our Company security. He made it clear then he was for hire." He paused. "Still, what a smokescreen all that serial killer nonsense was. *Bloody fool!* All he had to do was get the diary from Ellen's hotel room, and silence Anthony Harris." He took a deep breath. "Then that idiot Danny Burton tried to blackmail me. Turned out he'd been spying on us all at the jetty on Sunday night." He stopped pacing and stared at Jess. "Danny signed his own death warrant... but you don't have to."

She felt an icy chill in her heart.

"The first time I saw you at The Palms, Jessica, I thought Ellen had come back to me. You're so like her, you can replace her."

Jess stared in disbelief. Was he completely mad?

"I know all about your husband and child," he said. "You've come through it all, Jessica. You're strong and focused. And working for me, you'll have everything money and power can give you. Look, let's go and get that diary," he said, reasonably. "We'll destroy it. Then everything will be down to Roberts." He searched her face. "Now he's dead, there *is* no other evidence to connect me to any of this."

Except for me, she thought; he'll kill me, and Susan, if I don't go along with him. She didn't think twice. "All right," she said, calmly. "We'll go and get the diary together. And, well, I'm sure I would find working for you interesting."

He smiled, broadly. "And lucrative."

"And lucrative." She did her best to smile back. "But we must help Susan. Quick," she said, moving towards the door, "she's been shot, but I think she's still alive."

"*No.*" He stood in front of her. "*Susan* has to be collateral damage, my dear. She'll tell the police I killed her sister."

Jess could scarcely breathe. "How can she?" she asked, quickly. "Only you and I know that."

"As soon as she sees me, she'll know. I'm supposed to be in Canberra, don't forget."

"*Please*, John. She's just a young girl."

He picked up the oil lamp and took off the glass cover. "Here!" he said, pushing it towards her. "Set fire to the yacht. Destroy all the evidence."

Jess recoiled. "But Susan," she whispered.

"Do it, Jessica," he said, angrily. "Destroy all the evidence *and* Susan. *Prove* you're with me now."

"I *am* with you, John," she said, desperately. "But we don't have to kill Susan. I'll talk to her; I'll get her onside."

"*Do it!*" he barked.

Frantic, she looked from him to the safety rail. Could she push him over? It was so close.

"Don't even *think* it," he shouted as he held the naked flame of the oil lamp up high. A whoosh of flames ran up the petrol-soaked sail cloth.

Jess jumped back in shock.

"It's your *own* fault." Langhurst's voice was hard now. "When you told me how Ellen recorded everything so neatly in her schedule, I *knew* you had the diary. I tried to get it back without hurting you. I made sure you were at breakfast before Roberts searched your room. Remember? I rang you?"

Her heart quickened as his hand tightened around the gun. She looked up at the flames spreading across the sails, lighting up the sky. "*Why*, John? *Why* take bribes from the Chinese? You don't need their money, surely?"

"Oh, but I do, Jessica. For my election campaign. You see, once I'm elected to the seat of Flinders, I'll soon become party leader. Then, in time, Prime Minister."

"*You? Prime Minister?*"

A loud crack sounded. The rigging and a flaming sail came crashing to the ground, igniting the deck.

Jess jumped away from the scorching flames, and rushed to the door to get Susan.

But Langhurst blocked her way.

"*Susan!*" she screamed.

Suddenly, in the smoke and confusion, a figure jumped onto the deck. "*Drop the gun, Langhurst!*"

Tom! Jess stumbled as the yacht rocked about. An arm grabbed her round the throat from behind; the barrel of a gun dug into her temple.

"Don't move," Langhurst shouted at Sangster, "or I'll kill her."

Sangster stood still. "Let her go, John. There's been enough killing. You can't get away."

"Throw the gun on the floor, Inspector, and kick it away."

"*No, Tom!*" Jess choked as smoke enveloped them. "He'll kill you."

"I'll kill her if you don't." Langhurst gripped her throat tighter to shut her up, and dragged her back from the flames creeping along the burning deck.

Still Sangster didn't move. "We have the diary, Langhurst. We know you framed Ellen."

Langhurst's whole body tensed. "You know nothing."

"You're wrong." Sangster shook his head. "We have your bank account, with 20 million dollars the Chinese paid *you* to get them the deal they wanted. And we have a photo of you and Chen at the Temple of Heaven in Beijing. You told me you had no *personal* contact with the Chinese? Everything is done at *official* level, you said. But Ellen caught you both red-handed on camera meeting secretly amongst the crowds."

Sangster's words hung in the flaming heat and smoke.

Jess heard a desperate gasp in her ear. Langhurst moved the gun from her temple and pointed it at Sangster. His finger tightened on the trigger.

She pushed his arm upwards.

Unbalanced, Langhurst released his grip on her throat.

She spun round and shoved him hard.

Sangster fired.

The bullet slammed into Langhurst's forehead. As he fell backwards, his own gun fired.

Excruciating pain seared through Jess. Stumbling sideways, she grabbed the safety rail before toppling over the side. Hanging on grimly, her head spun as she felt her legs sinking into the cold water.

Hands grabbed her. "Hold on, Jess," Sangster shouted.

"*Susan?*" she whispered, as she started shivering violently. "*Amy.*" She couldn't breathe.

"Hold on, Jess. I've got you."

Uncontrollable shuddering racked her body. She heard more voices; saw more faces. What was going on? Something pressed against her face.

Exhausted, she sank back, succumbing to the darkness.

36

Jess struggled to move. Her limbs felt heavy. When she opened her eyes, everything looked a blur through the mist. She could see pale winter light, casting the room in dark shadows. She could make out metal equipment, and the dull gleam of wooden floors.

She could hear women's voices around her. She blinked and tried to focus. She couldn't think. Her throat hurt and her mouth felt dry. Then she started to see the room more clearly. She looked down at the starched white sheets. She was lying propped up in a bed, a hospital bed.

Hearing rhythmic breathing, she looked across and smiled. His pale face looked peaceful in the glowing light of the bed lamp as he dozed in the chair next to her. He was so close, she took his hand. "I *knew* you'd come," she whispered.

Simon jumped and gave her a huge smile. "Thank God you're all right." He leant towards her and pushed a stray tendril of hair back from her face with tenderness. "You've been shot in the chest. I thought..." He couldn't finish the sentence.

Then it all came flooding back to her and she struggled to sit up. "*Susan?*"

"Don't move," Simon said, trying gently to keep her still. "Susan was shot in the stomach by Roberts. She's recovering in intensive care, but she'll be all right."

"And Tom? Is he all right? He saved us, didn't he? On the yacht."

Simon nodded. "He's fine. He's down the corridor, with the High Commissioner. We've all been waiting for you to come round."

"The High Commissioner's here?"

"Yes. He's on the phone to London, trying to get clearance to waive Nigel's diplomatic immunity."

Jess frowned. "Waive his immunity?"

"The Federal Police want Nigel to help them with their investigation."

"Why?" She tried to sit up again. "What's he done?"

"Apart from almost getting you killed, you mean?" Simon unclenched his fist, then shook his head. "We'll talk later; you're still too weak."

"No," she urged. "*Please* Simon. I have to know."

"All right." He sighed. "Well, it seems Nigel and Anthony Harris go back a long way. They've been friends since their student days at Oxford."

"*Really?*"

"Yes. Nigel tipped Harris off about that intelligence report. He *knew* the British and Australian authorities were onto the gas deal corruption. *And* he knew the police had found out about Ellen Chambers' affair with Harris. But the Australian authorities didn't *tell* Harris they knew about the affair, because they wanted to find out if he was involved in corruption too."

"I see," Jess said, wearily.

Simon nodded. "The Head of Australian SIS personally briefed Nigel about it, and specifically asked him not to divulge the information to anyone except the High Commissioner."

"Are you saying Anthony Harris knew *nothing* until Nigel told him?"

"Exactly."

"And Nigel actually *gave* Harris a copy of that intelligence report?"

"Yes."

"Oh my God!" Jess started coughing.

Simon jumped up and held a glass of water to her lips. She took a sip and swallowed.

"You need to rest now," he said.

"No! Please keep going, Simon. I *am* okay."

He sighed again. "Remember that phone call Nigel took when we were in his office on Monday morning?"

"That was Harris, wasn't it?"

Simon nodded. "He'd just heard about Ellen's murder. He was devastated of course. He told Nigel he'd been with Ellen on the jetty at The Palms *before* she was murdered. He'd gone to confront her about the corruption allegations; and that's when she told him the whole sorry story. Harris believed Ellen when she said she wasn't taking bribes, and that she'd been set up. And he *swore* she'd been alive when he left her, and that he'd had nothing to do with her murder."

Jess felt shocked to the core. "Nigel knew all that, and said nothing. Not even to the High Commissioner?"

Simon nodded. "And he let you go off on what we thought was a routine consular case without any kind of warning. So you see *Nigel* was the catalyst that started off this nightmare. If he hadn't tipped off Harris and given him a copy of that intelligence report, none of the events of the last few days would have happened."

Jess flopped back onto the pillow. "Nigel must be devastated now he realises what he's done."

"That's an understatement." Simon brightened. "Of course, he won't be resuming his position as Deputy High Commissioner. He'll be returning to London within the next 24 hours. He'll face disciplinary action, if not criminal charges."

Jess closed her eyes, remembering that row with Nigel in the Consul-General's Office; his clenched fists; that look of hatred. Of course by then, he understood the trail of death and destruction he'd started. And that he'd ruined his own career.

"And John Langhurst?" she asked.

"Dead."

"And that maniac Roberts?"

Simon hesitated. "They're still searching the river for his body."

She gasped. "You don't think…"

"No, the police are sure he's dead. It was high tide last night. They think his body must have been swept down the river, and out into Moreton Bay."

She shivered, remembering those cold eyes that were beyond human reach. Would she ever forget them? Then something came back to her. "You know, Simon, when we were on the yacht, he said he *wasn't* Roberts."

Simon raised an eyebrow. "Who was he, then?"

"I've no idea. But he was so adamant he wasn't Roberts, I somehow *believed* him. Can you mention it to Tom please? It's worrying me."

Simon nodded.

"And Chen?" she asked. "Where's he?"

"Skipped the country."

"*Impossible!*"

"You'd think! Bloody convenient for everyone, if you ask me."

This will always remain a secret. She shivered, remembering Langhurst's words on the yacht. Had the Australians deliberately let Chen go to protect the deal?

"It was just as we thought," Simon went on. "The Chinese were perfectly happy with 25 per cent of the joint venture until Langhurst told Chen he could get him a bigger share. Wouldn't that have that gone down well in Beijing? A notch in Chen's belt to get him the top political job he wanted."

"So John Langhurst put Chen up to pitching for a controlling stake of the joint venture?"

Simon nodded. "Knowing it was an impossible ask for the Australian side.

It was a bluff of course. Chen was always going to settle for 45 per cent."

"And Langhurst would get the credit from the Australian Government for breaking the deadlock and delivering the deal. *Plus* 20 million dollars for his own political campaign." Jess could only believe it because it was true. She sank back into the pillows, finally able to relax. "Susan will be so happy her sister was innocent. She's the only one who believed in Ellen." She sighed. "If only Anthony Harris had told the police everything as soon as Ellen was murdered."

Simon's mobile rang. "That'll be Sharon again. She's been phoning every ten minutes to find out if you're awake. I've been trying to stop her jumping on the first plane north."

Jess smiled. "Give me the phone. I'll talk to her."

"No you won't," he said, firmly. "You'll rest now. And when you're well enough, you're coming home with me. I'll take care of you."

"But..."

"You're coming home with me and that's final!"

She smiled at him. "I'm really happy you came, Simon."

"Me too." He leant over and kissed her gently on the lips.

37

Brisbane, one month later.

Jess felt a tingling in her spine. Pulling her black jacket tight around her, she slipped off her shoes and wriggled her cold toes to get the feeling back in them. She glanced at Susan, sitting pale and distraught next to her. Then she looked over her shoulder at Tom Sangster, who sat alone at the back of the church.

His eyes lit up when he saw her.

She smiled and turned back.

The vicar's sombre voice echoed around the cavernous nave. The heavy scent of lilies wafted in the air. Lovely, she thought, but too much associated with death for her liking.

She could feel Susan shaking with sobs beside her. A tear slipped down her own cheek in sympathy. She had to focus on the shaft of sunlight beaming through a stained glass window for the rest of the service, to tune out the vicar and the heartache. A picture of Amy sprang into her mind. Her face. Her curly blonde hair. Amy, squealing with joy in the sunshine, as she finally rode her small tricycle alone.

The service ended and everyone began filing out. The church fell silent and peaceful. Jess got up and went over to the candles. She lit three. One for Jack, one for Amy, and one for Ellen Chambers. Then she went back and sat down again next to Susan, who hadn't moved.

Susan slipped her arm in hers and laid her head on her shoulder. They sat in quiet companionship until a creaking noise made Jess look round.

Tom Sangster got up and walked out of the door.

Patting Susan's hand, she stood up and followed Tom outside. She saw him break away from the crowd and walk further into the graveyard. She hurried after him, footsteps crunching on dead leaves as she walked along the path in the sunlight. The voices from the congregation were fading now.

She saw him ahead, standing beside a grave. It seemed like an intrusion, but she walked over and stood next to him. "Who's Lily?" she asked, looking down at the gravestone.

"My first murder case," he said. "She was just 15 when we found her down by the river. I'll never get the sight of her out of my head." He took a deep breath. "I come here from time to time to remind myself why I stay in the Police Service." He glanced at Jess. "I guess our ghosts are always around us."

Jess bowed her head.

"I'm sorry about your daughter and husband. The High Commissioner told me what happened to them."

She nodded. "I never got the chance to properly thank you, Tom. If you hadn't arrived when you did, Susan and I would have died on that yacht."

He shuffled his feet.

"I'm still not sure how you found us."

"A lucky break," he said. "You see, by then, I was pretty sure John Langhurst was behind all this."

"How did you know?"

"The lab sent me those blown up photos from Ellen's camera card. There, bang in the middle of all the crowds in Beijing, were John Langhurst and Chen Xiamen shaking hands. Ellen had caught them red-handed."

"I see."

"By then, we had the diary too. I'd found it in the cupboard under the bathroom sink in Susan's house, just like you said. But we had no idea where Roberts had taken you both." He glanced at her. "Or if you were still alive."

Jess nodded.

"We'd checked Roberts' house of course. But when the neighbours said he was hardly ever there, we started thinking he had another place. Then came the breakthrough. Roberts was known by the working girls in the area. One in particular had a narrow escape. She told us Roberts had taken her to a motel in the Valley a couple of times. While she was there, she saw clothes and other possessions that made her think he was staying there."

"Ah."

"I was in the vicinity when that information came through. So I went to the motel. I couldn't believe my luck when John Langhurst drove up and knocked on a room door. And who should answer, but Roberts himself. I crept over and watched through the window. I heard them arguing. Langhurst was refusing to give Roberts the money he'd promised him until he had the diary."

"I see."

"So I waited for one of them to leave, in the hope they would lead me to you. Roberts set off alone first. I went to follow him, as I was certain he'd be the one holding you, if you were still alive." He glanced at her apologetically again. "But then Langhurst got into his car and followed Roberts down the street. I noticed him hanging back a little, as if he didn't want Roberts to see him. I wondered what the hell was going on. So, I followed some way behind them both. And that's how I found you."

Jess nodded. "Have they found Roberts's body yet?"

Sangster shook his head. "He'll be feeding the sharks in the South Pacific Ocean by now."

She sighed. "He followed me in his grey jeep from the moment I arrived at Brisbane airport."

Sangster nodded. "He'd been at The Palms looking for the diary. He didn't find it in Ellen's room, and he knew we didn't have it. He must have assumed you knew about the corruption and affair." He glanced at her. "As did I, by the way, since it was your Government who told *us*."

"Except I didn't."

"No, but Roberts didn't know that. He knew you were flying up to Brisbane. I guess he thought from the start *you* would lead him to the diary." He paused "And he was right, wasn't he?"

She sighed. But there was one loose end still playing on her mind. "So who *was* Roberts, Tom?"

"Ah, well that's quite a story." Sangster shook his head as if he couldn't quite believe it himself. "His real name was James Lynch. He was born on a farm in the Northern Territories. It's a tragic story really that turned into a nightmare." He glanced at her. "He killed his drunken, abusive father when he was only 12 years old."

"*Really?*"

Sangster nodded. "He came home from school one day and found his mother lying dead on the kitchen floor. She'd been beaten to death by his father in a drunken rampage. The boy went into the bedroom where his father was sleeping it off, and stabbed him in the heart with his own hunting knife. The boy had picked a desert rose on his way home from school, his mother's favourite flower.

He put it in her hand and just sat with her body, until neighbours found them a couple of days later."

Jess stared at him. "*He* was allowed to join the police?"

"It's not that straightforward." Sangster took a deep breath. "You see, young James spent the next few years in an orphanage. There, he met Derek Roberts, a boy of the same age. The two of them were inseparable. When they were old enough to leave care, they went off together. Months later, they were both involved in a motorbike accident. One died, the other survived. The death register says James Lynch was killed, but it was Derek who died. You see, after the crash, James adopted Derek's identity. I guess he realised his future would be easier in Derek's skin, rather than his own."

"How the hell did he get away with that?"

Sangster looked at her. "Is it so unbelievable? No one cares about these kids in institutions. The two boys had no family or friends, just each other. They had access to each other's personal effects and documents. Anyway, the next trace of Derek Roberts was when he enrolled in technical college in Perth, Western Australia. Who would suspect he wasn't who he said he was?"

"Yes." She sighed. "I can see that. So how did you find out?"

"A lady in the orphanage where the two boys grew up saw the news bulletin and a photo of Roberts. She rang up and told us we'd got it wrong, and that the killer was James Lynch."

Jess couldn't help but feel sad for that little boy, but not for the lethal killer he'd turned into.

There was a pause.

"Tom."

He turned to her.

"I feel you deserve a full explanation from our side too. But please keep it to yourself."

His eyes lit up. "Are you going to tell me Ellen Chambers was working for MI6 all along?"

Jess lowered her voice even though they were alone in the open air. "I doubt we'll ever know that for sure. But Ellen did know their Station Manager in Beijing. They'd been close friends since studying Mandarin together at university. They often met up for dinner in Beijing, when Ellen was visiting. She was a mine of information with her background and business links." Jess paused. "He of course knew all about the rumours that someone inside Western Energy was working for Chen Xiamen and taking bribes; and that Ellen had been identified as the culprit. Of course, he didn't believe a word of it; and told her everything, including about the offshore bank accounts."

"So *he* tipped Ellen off that she was being set up; *not* Harris."

"*Exactly!*"

Sangster let that information sink in. "Was her relationship with Langhurst genuinely affectionate?" he asked. "Or was she cosying up to him for intelligence reasons?"

Jess shrugged. "We're never going to know that either, Tom. Anyway, Ellen set about finding out who *was* responsible. Imagine her shock when it turned out to be John Langhurst himself, and that he'd set her up to take the blame."

"So *that's* how it unfolded?"

Jess nodded. "Ellen rang Langhurst and gave him an ultimatum. He had 48 hours to go to the police and confess everything, or she'd tell them herself. Trying to stall her, he persuaded her to meet him at The Palms on Sunday night to talk. What a terrible twist of fate that turned out to be."

Sangster nodded and they fell silent again.

"Tom." She looked at him. "I can't stop thinking about the way I just watched Roberts drown in front of my eyes, without a flicker of regret."

"He *had* been trying to kill you."

"*And* John Langhurst. I deliberately tried to push him over the side to drown him, before you shot him. All I could think about was what he'd done to Ellen, to all of them."

"He would have done the same to you."

She nodded. "He was clever and manipulative. There was nothing to implicate him in all these murders. Without that diary, there would have been no trace of any money to him, only to Ellen. He'd got Roberts to do his dirty work, and set him up to take the blame. And once Roberts was dead, well, Langhurst may actually have got away with it." She shivered. "He was deadly serious when he said he'd be Prime Minister one day. Just think!"

He nodded.

"I would have shot him myself if I'd had the gun," she said. "So what kind of a person does that make me?"

"Someone I'd like to have watching my back on the streets." He smiled, and held out a large manila envelope awkwardly. "I'm not sure if this is the right time to give you this."

Surprised, Jess took the envelope and opened it. She gasped as she pulled out a sketch. It was *her* Amy.

"I did it from the photo we found in your briefcase in Susan's house. I hope you like it."

Jess stared at the drawing. "It's lovely," she said, choking back tears. "You've captured her pretty face and spirit so well."

"You've been through a lot, Jess."

She nodded. "You know, Tom, sometimes I feel as if I'm *touched* by death." She looked over and saw his eyes glisten. "How do you deal with it?"

"I just take it one day at a time. One case at a time."

As the sun ducked behind a cloud, a sudden breeze whipped her hair across her face. "There's still no sign of Chen," she said. "He made it to Hong Kong, you know?"

"He'll be back in mainland China, somewhere. They'll get him."

"I wish I had your faith," she said, wryly.

Sangster gave her a rueful smile this time. "And none of this has affected the gas deal."

"No. Richard Price rang to say he couldn't attend Ellen's funeral because he had to stay in Canberra for the official signing ceremony. He and those specs are in sole charge now, you know."

They both laughed.

His mobile rang, and he checked the caller ID. "I have to take this." He stepped a few paces away for privacy as he answered.

Jess watched his eyes flash as he listened to the caller.

He turned back to her. "I'm sorry, I have to go. But if you want to talk again, or anything else crops up, give me a call." He pulled a business card out of his breast pocket. "Any time."

She took the card. "Thanks, Tom, for everything."

He nodded and hurried off without a word of goodbye.

She watched him stride down the path. But when he reached the corner, he stopped and turned.

Their eyes met in the last glow of sunlight and he raised his hand in a kind of salute, before disappearing round the corner.

Alone now, Jess sat down on a wooden seat under an old eucalyptus tree. She closed her eyes and saw Jack and Amy walking along, hand in hand. For the first time, she could hear their chatter and their laughter.

She opened her eyes, kissed the drawing of Amy and hugged it close to her. She watched the sunlight filter through the swaying branches of the gnarled gum tree, and listened to its dry leaves rattling in the breeze. For the first time in two years, in this beautiful country she had come to love, a feeling of peace settled over her.

★ ★ ★ **COMING SOON** ★ ★ ★

DEADLY DECEIT
Chapter One

Bay of Cap-Haitien
North Coast of Haiti

The sloop slipped out of the bay on the strong swell in the dead of night. The sea was already rough. Too rough.

Nobody spoke. But in the dark, she could feel their fear. Soft crying and moaning echoed all around. And retching. Bile rose in her throat as the smell of vomit filled her nostrils, making her want to heave.

A soft whimper made her gaze down at her baby, squirming in her arms. She pulled the shawl around him and started softly singing...

Dodo titit
Si ou pa dodo
Krab la va manje ou ...

She could feel pins and needles creeping into her toes. She uncrossed her legs and stamped her feet. She wanted to stand up. Move about. But she couldn't. They were squashed together in the bowel of the small boat. Eighty women and children. Maybe more.

At least she was sitting under the hatchway. She took deep breaths of fresh air squeezing through the cracks. The wind rattled around the edges of its ill-fitting wooden cover, as if trying to find the weakest spot to wrench it off and carry it away.

She had watched the men in the village building the sloop by hand from old planks of wood; and the women stitching together bits of fabric and nylon to make the sails. It was a rough vessel. Just like the one her 'papa' used to fish from; until the sea had taken him, and brought her family nothing but grief.

She closed her eyes, trying to picture him. Big, round face, with smooth skin made even darker by working in the sun. And cropped, curly brown hair, with dark eyes that lit up when he saw her. He'd tell her stories of the sea whenever he came home. She had loved that. Loved him.

She jolted as the sloop shuddered. It was travelling upwind into the waves, so she expected a rough crossing. She respected the sea, and knew its ways. But even below deck, she could feel the swell getting higher. We should go back, and wait for better weather. But she knew they couldn't. The police might catch them, and scupper the boat. Then they would lose all their money. It had taken Pierre years of hard work to save up for their passage. He had gone ahead first. Now he'd sent for her and the son he'd never seen.

They had to go on.

Everything will be all right when we reach Pierre, she told herself over and over. She pulled an envelope out of her pocket, drew out a photo and kissed it in the dark.

The baby moaned again. Was he sick or hungry? She offered her breast, but he refused to latch on. Perhaps he was sensing her fear? "You're going to meet your Papa soon, child. Very soon," she whispered, as she finished the lullaby...

Sleep little one
If you don't sleep
The crab will eat you …

When the baby was asleep, she pulled the shawl tight around him, and tied the ends in a knot around her waist to bind them even closer together. Never to be parted. Singing the lullaby again, more to comfort herself than the child, her mind returned to happier times; to her wedding in the village. The excitement, the joy, the love. Replaying it over and over in her head, she drifted off.

Her head rolled onto her chest, and she tipped over sideways into the lap of the woman next to her. She sat up straight with confusion. Where was she? Reality sunk in as she felt the sloop rolling up and down, side to side, on the rising waves; and heard the wind still howling through the sails and rigging.

But now, she could hear men shouting to each other on deck. The rickety vessel's wooden frame creaked and moaned, as if protesting about being out on the ocean on such a stormy night. Was it light yet? They seemed to have been travelling for hours.

When you see light in the sky, you'll be here, with me. That's what Pierre had written. But it was still pitch black below deck. She wriggled her toes and rubbed her feet again.

The shouting became louder, more urgent. Her heart started pounding. She could hear many footsteps running around on deck. She listened intently…

Land! That's what they're shouting. *Land!*

She felt a surge of happiness.

Suddenly, she was catapulted forward as the old vessel crashed into something. It stood still for a moment as if dazed by the blow.

"*The reef!*" Voices screamed on deck.

She heard a loud crack, and felt the vessel roll and tip over to one side. Piercing cries rang out above as the men were plunged into the sea. Below deck, women and children started tumbling on top of each other, screaming in panic. Suddenly, a wall of water rushed through the cracked hull, sweeping her and the baby out the hatch, and into the sea.

The cold. The shock...

Water rushed into her mouth and lungs. She coughed and spluttered as she felt herself being dragged under by the weight of her long skirt. With one arm, she gripped the baby to her body like a vice. With the other she scrabbled through the water, kicking furiously. Disorientated in the dark, she didn't know whether she was swimming to the bottom of the ocean or the top.

Finally, surfacing, she took big gasps of air, half-breathing, half-sobbing with terror. *My baby!* She turned onto her back to float and get him out of the water.

Light in the sky! She could see light breaking in the sky.

The waves seemed smaller now, calmer. Were they inside the reef? Voices all around her screamed and shouted for help.

"*Requins!*"

Sharks? Hysterical, she cried out as something brushed past her. But it was just a plank of wood floating by. She reached out and grabbed it. Struggling, she pulled her baby out of the shawl and laid it on its back on the plank. Then, she pulled off her skirt, and kicked it away.

A man swam past, heading for shore. "*Help me,*" she cried. "*Please, my baby!*"

He didn't even look her way.

Holding the baby on the wood in front of her, she kicked and pushed her way towards shore. It looked so far

328

away. She kept steady, pushing and kicking. Pushing and kicking. She could hardly breathe with the exhaustion, but she had to keep going. Pushing and kicking.

"Nearly there, child," she whispered, more for her own sake than his. The baby didn't move or cry. It was as if he sensed his mother was fighting for their lives.

Her toes brushed something. She froze, terrified.

But it wasn't a shark. She put one foot down gingerly on the soft seabed, then the other. Gasping, she realised she was standing on wobbly, exhausted legs, shoulder high in water. Sobbing with relief, she picked her baby up from the plank of wood and waded towards shore.

Staggering and scrambling out of the waves, she flopped down onto soft sand. Lying on her back, lungs ready to burst, she couldn't move. Her heart felt it would explode with the exertion and shock.

Someone was beside her now. Hands were pulling at her. Her baby started crying. She clutched him tight. But the hands wouldn't let go. "No," she screamed, struggling to sit up. A strong blow to the back of her head sent pain searing through her body. Exhausted, her head spun. Then another blow. And another.

Losing consciousness, she could hear her baby screaming as he was wrenched from her arms.